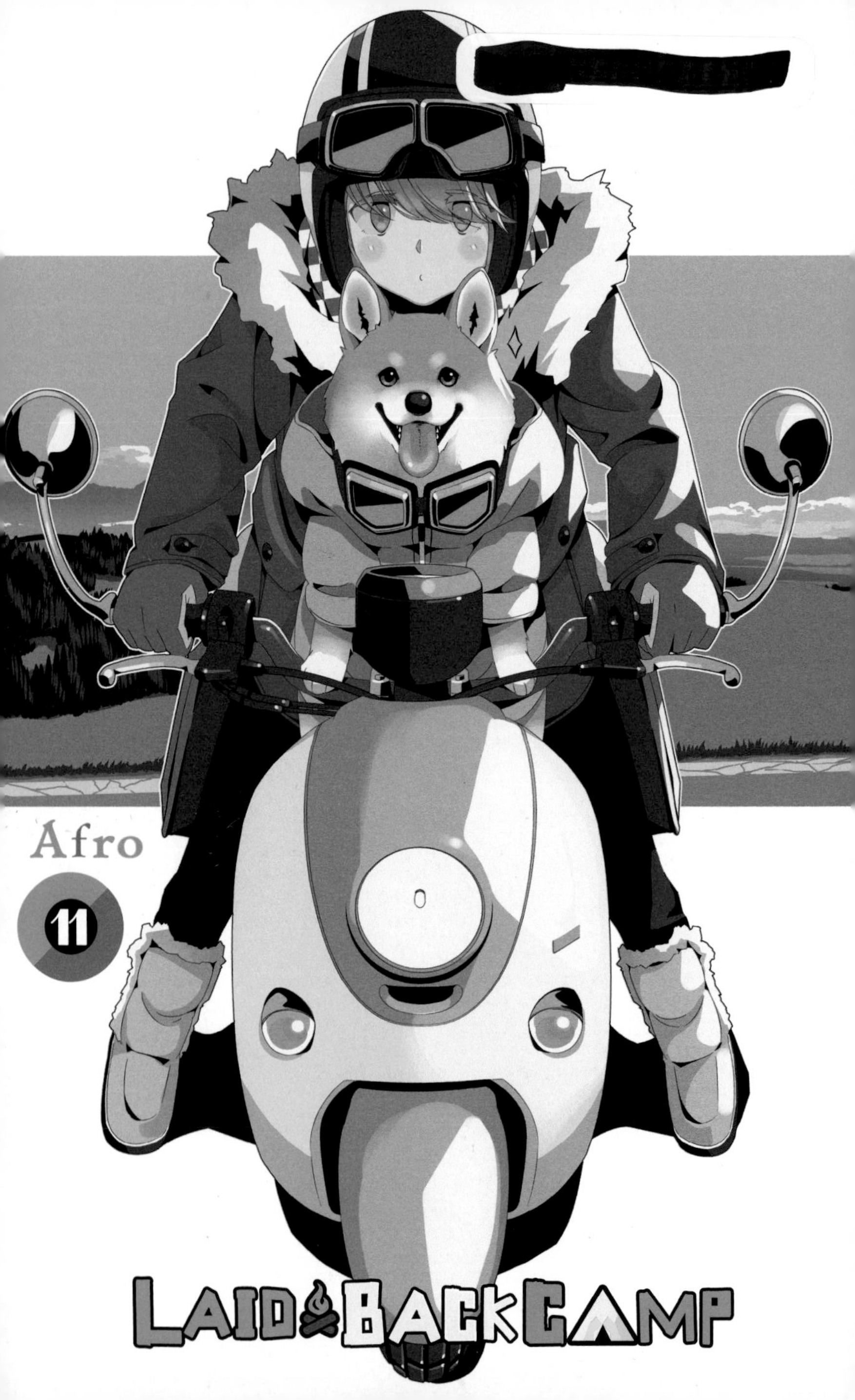
Afro
11
LAID BACK CAMP

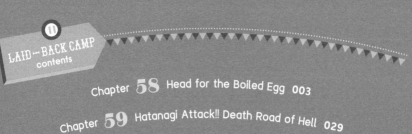

LAID-BACK CAMP
contents

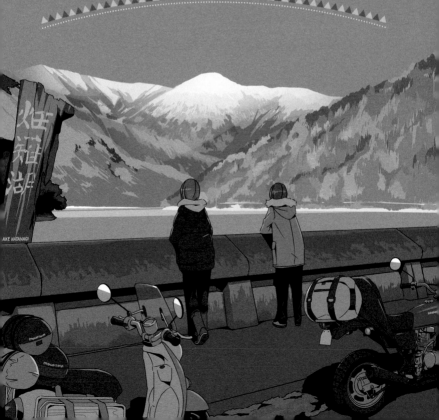

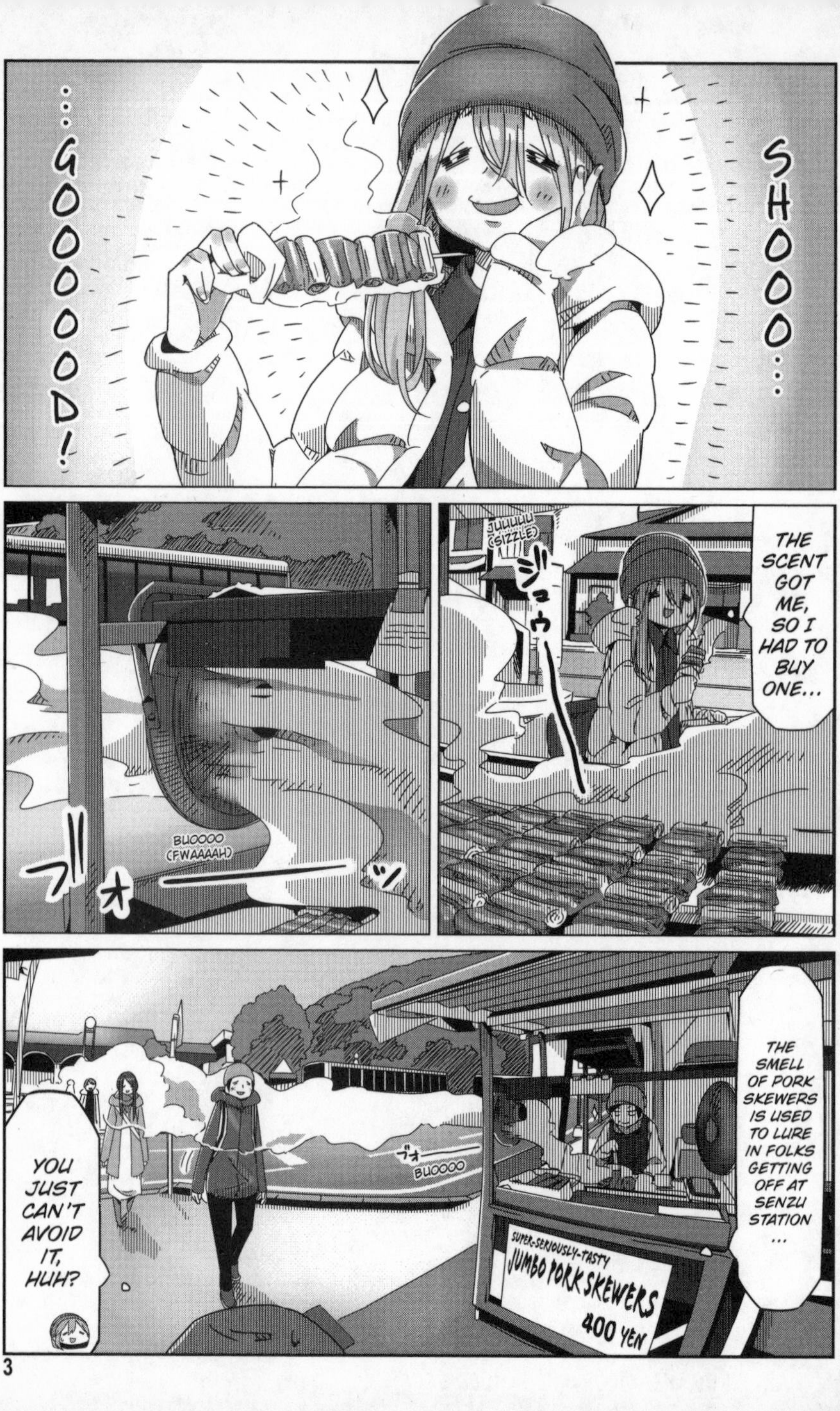
SHOOOO...
...GOOOOOOD!
THE SCENT GOT ME, SO I HAD TO BUY ONE...
JUUUUU (SIZZLE)
BUOOOO (FWAAAAH)
THE SMELL OF PORK SKEWERS IS USED TO LURE IN FOLKS GETTING OFF AT SENZU STATION...
SUPER-SERIOUSLY-TASTY
JUMBO PORK SKEWERS
400 YEN
BUOOOO
YOU JUST CAN'T AVOID IT, HUH?

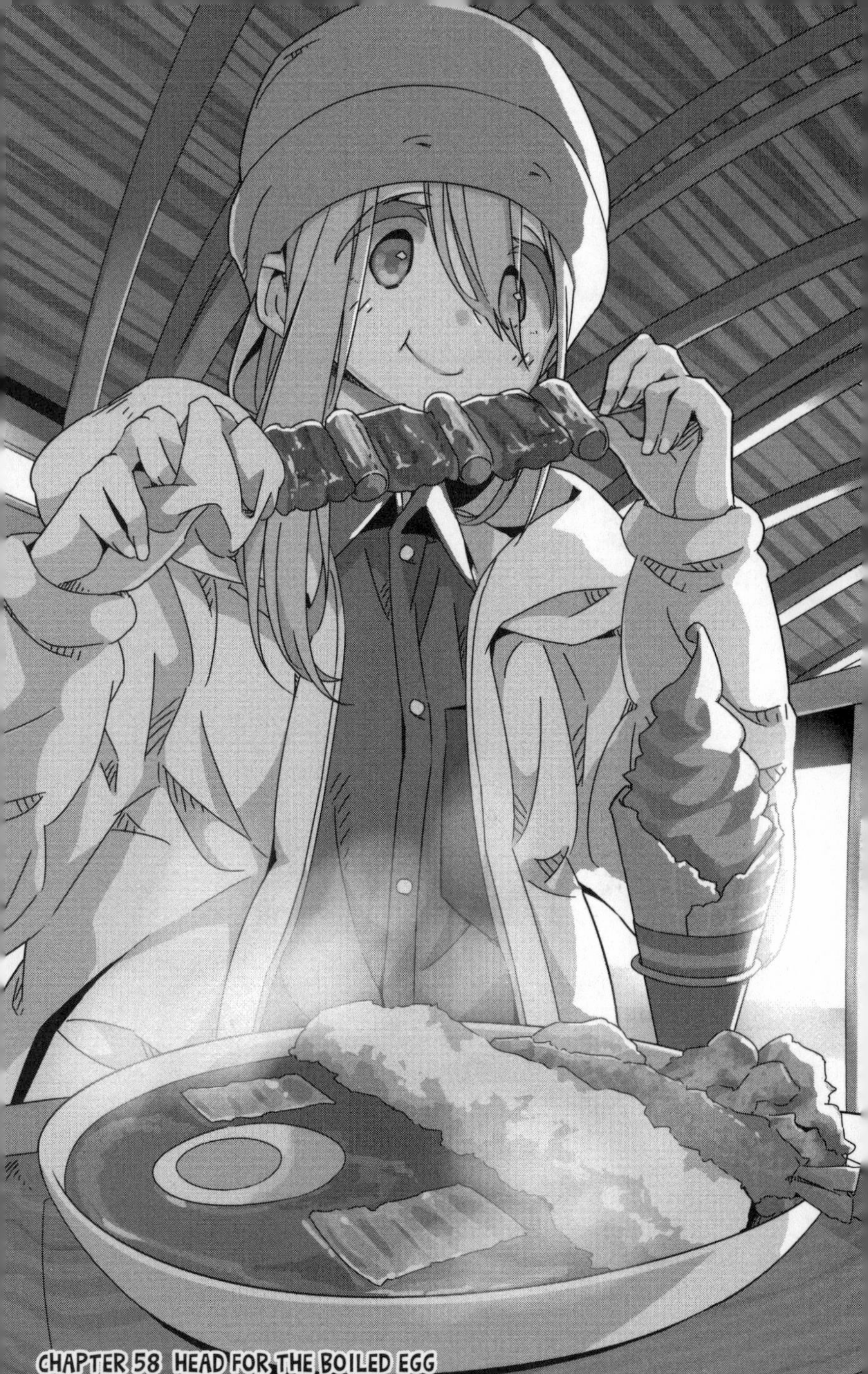

CHAPTER 58 HEAD FOR THE BOILED EGG

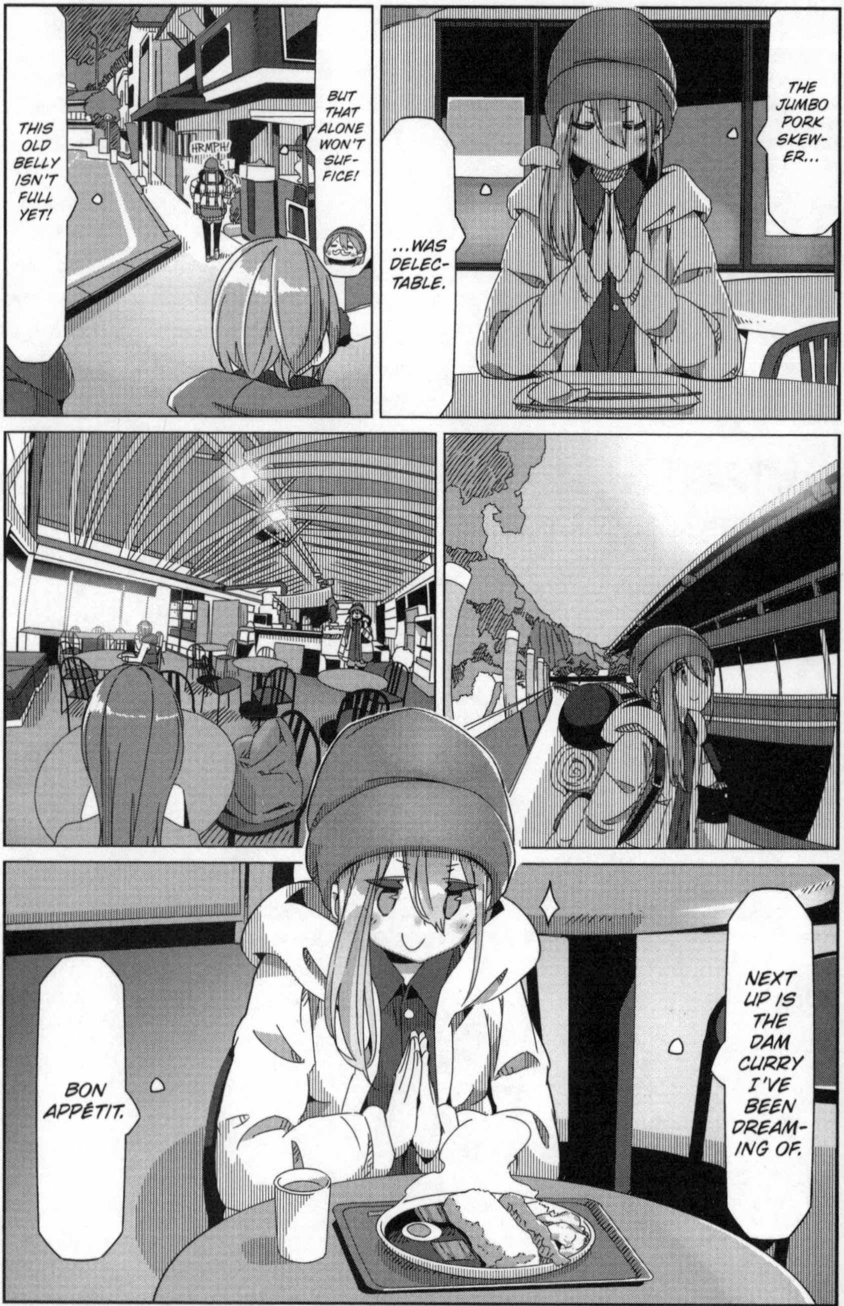
THE JUMBO PORK SKEWER...
...WAS DELECTABLE.
BUT THAT ALONE WON'T SUFFICE!
HRMPH!
THIS OLD BELLY ISN'T FULL YET!
NEXT UP IS THE DAM CURRY I'VE BEEN DREAMING OF.
BON APPÉTIT.

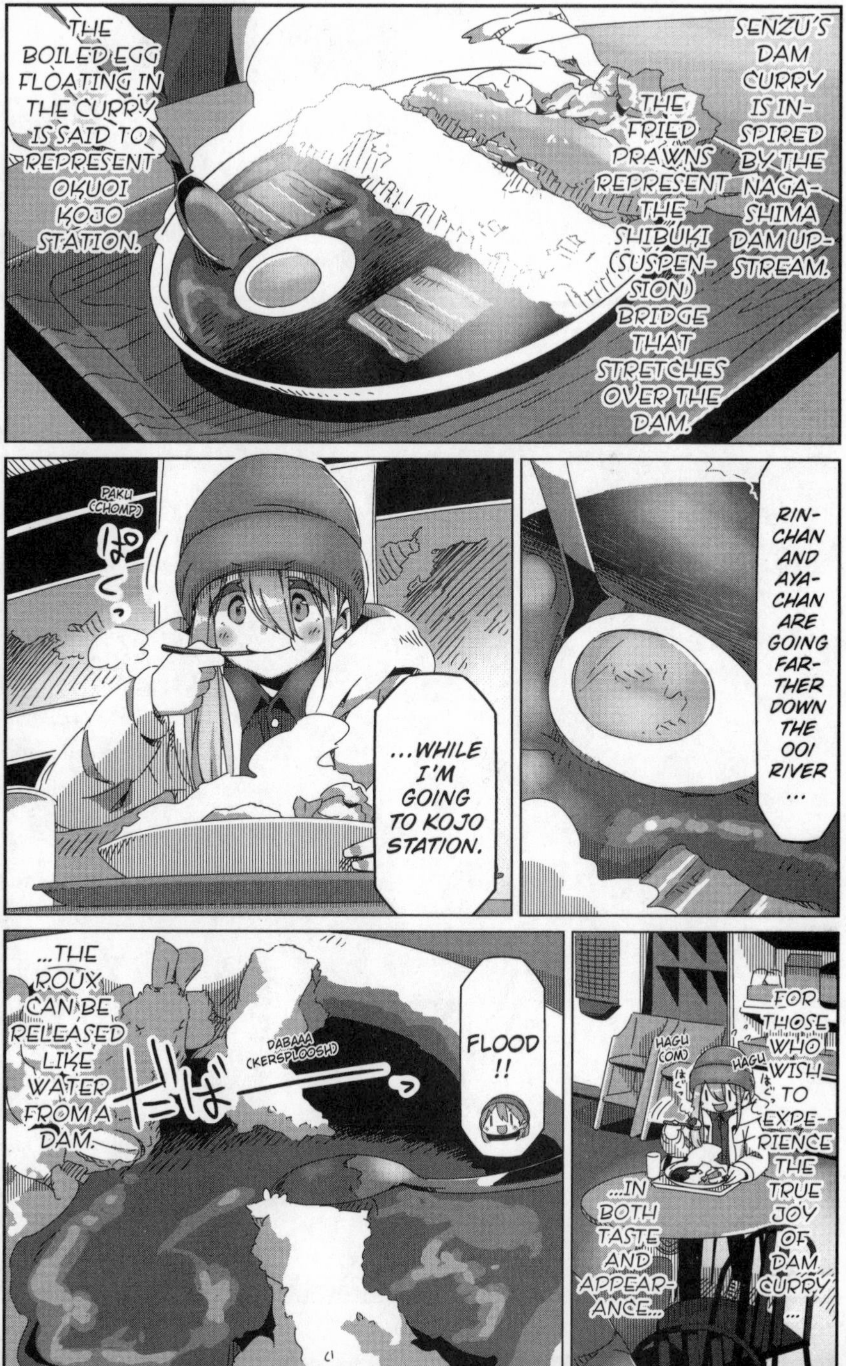
SENZU'S DAM CURRY IS INSPIRED BY THE NAGASHIMA DAM UPSTREAM.
THE FRIED PRAWNS REPRESENT THE SHIBUKI (SUSPENSION) BRIDGE THAT STRETCHES OVER THE DAM.
THE BOILED EGG FLOATING IN THE CURRY IS SAID TO REPRESENT OKUOI KOJO STATION.
RIN-CHAN AND AYA-CHAN ARE GOING FARTHER DOWN THE OOI RIVER...
PAKU (CHOMP)
ぱくっ
...WHILE I'M GOING TO KOJO STATION.
FOR THOSE WHO WISH TO EXPERIENCE THE TRUE JOY OF DAM CURRY...
HAGU
はぐ
HAGU (OM)
はぐっ
...IN BOTH TASTE AND APPEARANCE...
FLOOD!!
DABAAA (KERSPLOOSH)
だば――っ
...THE ROUX CAN BE RELEASED LIKE WATER FROM A DAM.

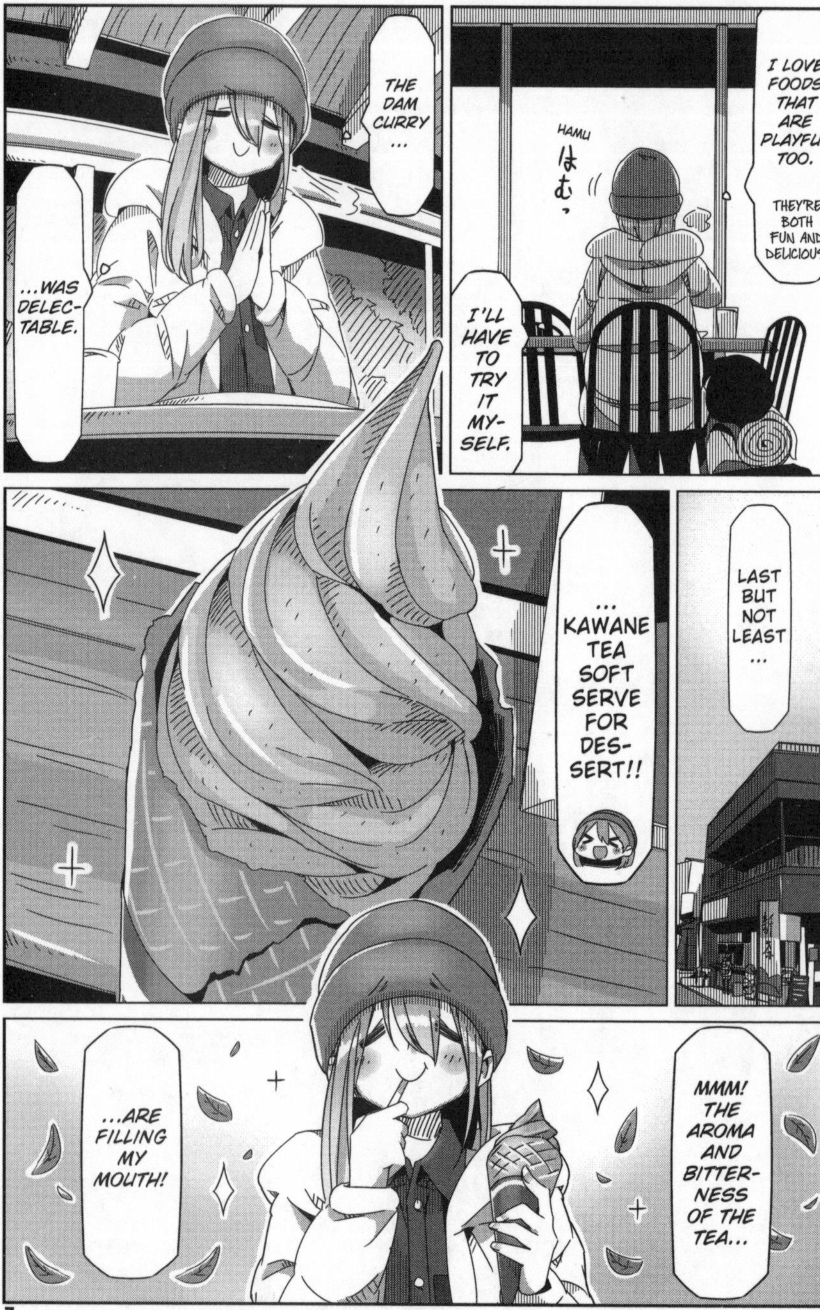
I LOVE FOODS THAT ARE PLAYFUL TOO.
THEY'RE BOTH FUN AND DELICIOUS.
HAMU
はむっ
I'LL HAVE TO TRY IT MYSELF.
THE DAM CURRY...
...WAS DELECTABLE.
LAST BUT NOT LEAST...
...KAWANE TEA SOFT SERVE FOR DESSERT!!
MMM! THE AROMA AND BITTERNESS OF THE TEA...
...ARE FILLING MY MOUTH!

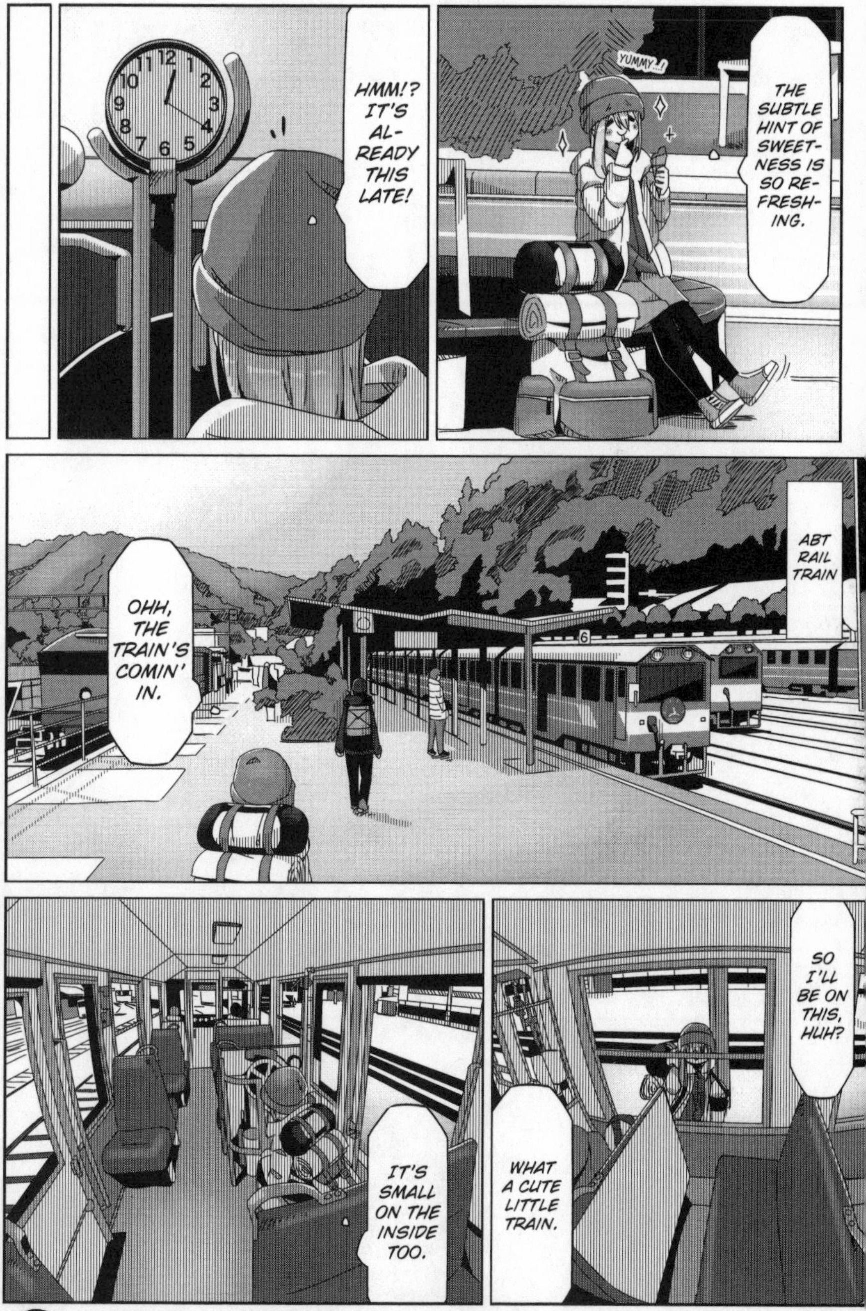
THE SUBTLE HINT OF SWEETNESS IS SO REFRESHING.
YUMMY...!
HMM!? IT'S ALREADY THIS LATE!
ABT RAIL TRAIN
OHH, THE TRAIN'S COMIN' IN.
SO I'LL BE ON THIS, HUH?
WHAT A CUTE LITTLE TRAIN.
IT'S SMALL ON THE INSIDE TOO.

STRICTLY SPEAKING, IT'S NOT JUST ANY TRAIN BUT A DIESEL TRAIN. ONE SEGMENT CAN BE CONNECTED TO A CONVENTIONAL ELECTRIC-POWERED TRAIN.

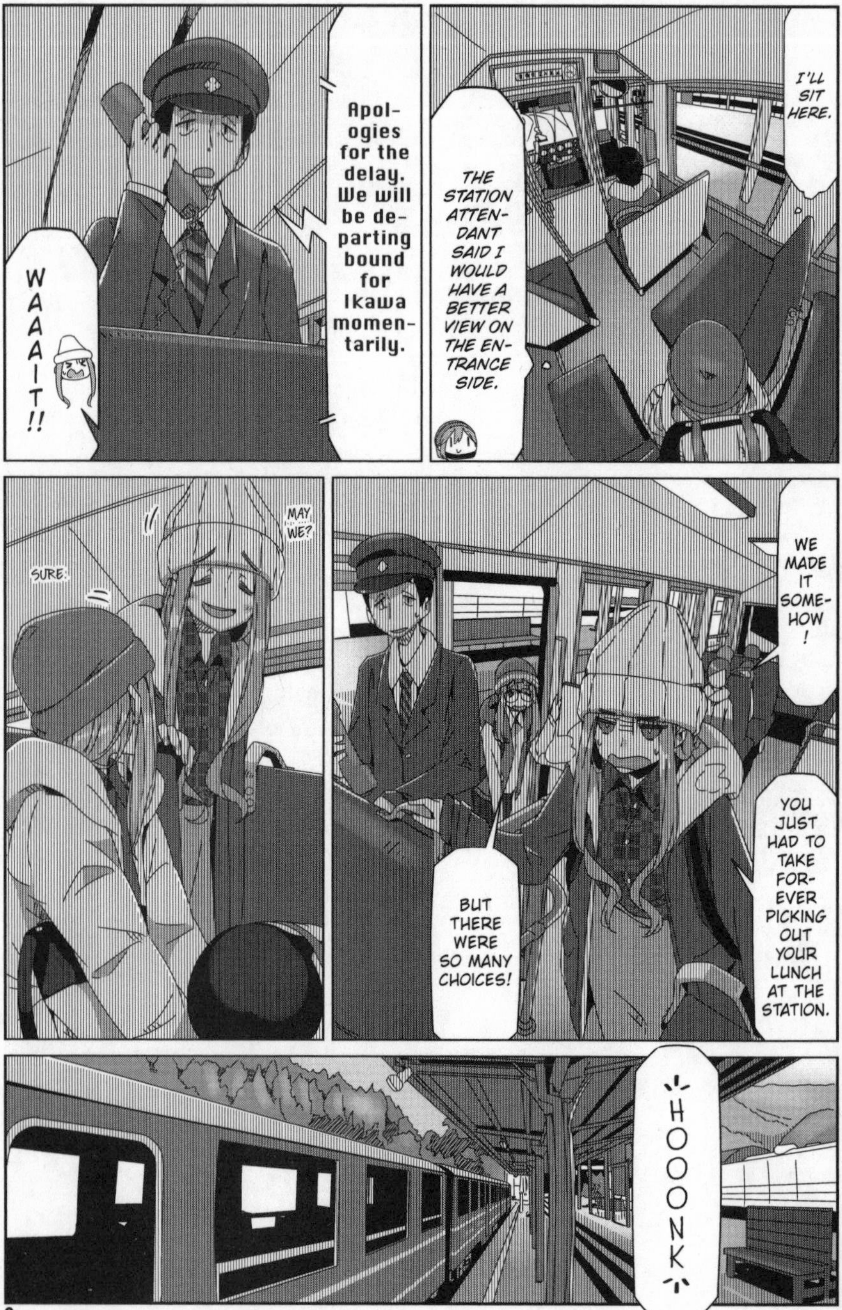
I'LL SIT HERE.
THE STATION ATTENDANT SAID I WOULD HAVE A BETTER VIEW ON THE ENTRANCE SIDE.
Apologies for the delay. We will be departing bound for Ikawa momentarily.
WAAAIT!!
WE MADE IT SOMEHOW!
YOU JUST HAD TO TAKE FOREVER PICKING OUT YOUR LUNCH AT THE STATION.
BUT THERE WERE SO MANY CHOICES!
MAY WE?
SURE.
HOOONK

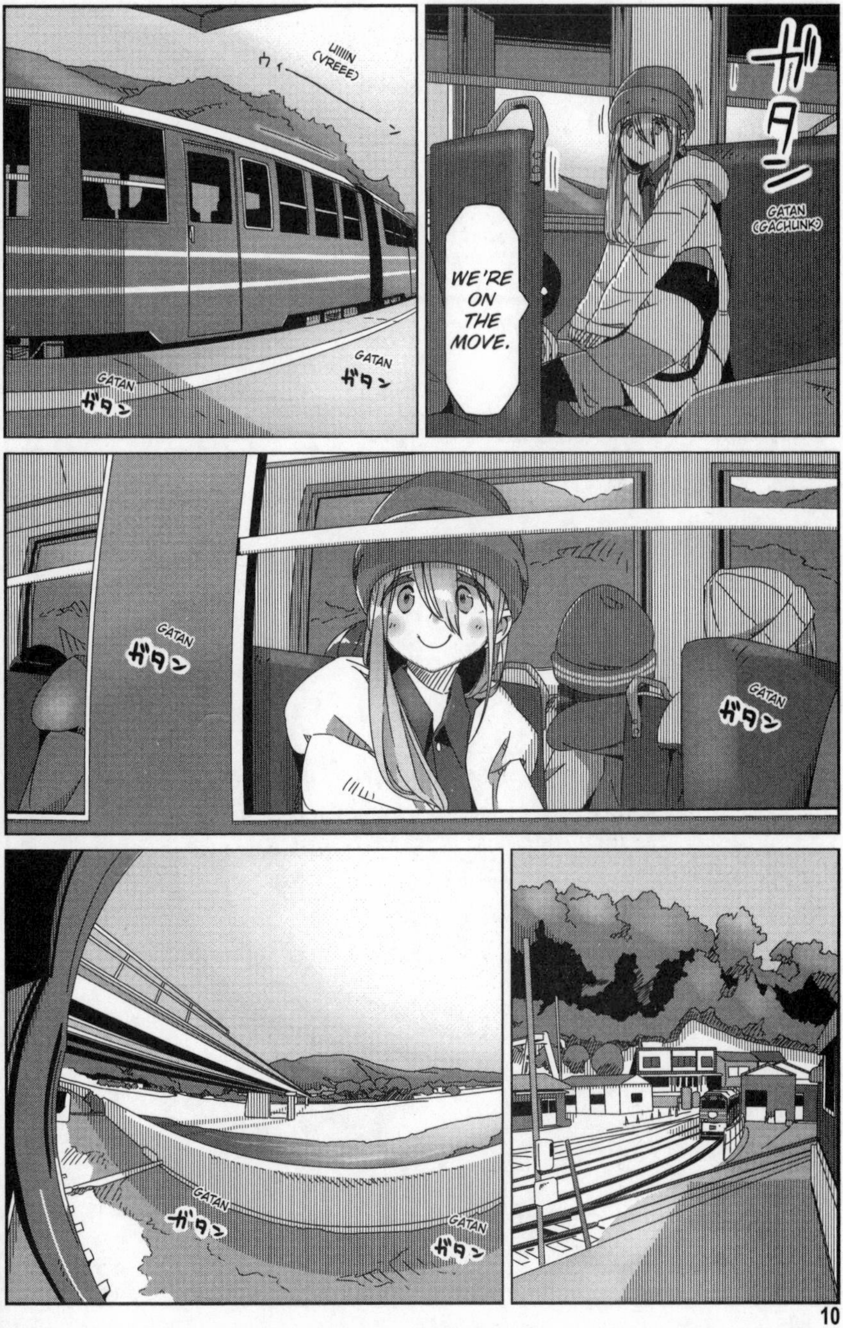
ガタン
GATAN (GACHUNK)
WE'RE ON THE MOVE.
ウィー
UIIIIN (VREEE)
GATAN ガタン
GATAN ガタン
GATAN ガタン
GATAN ガタン
GATAN ガタン
GATAN ガタン

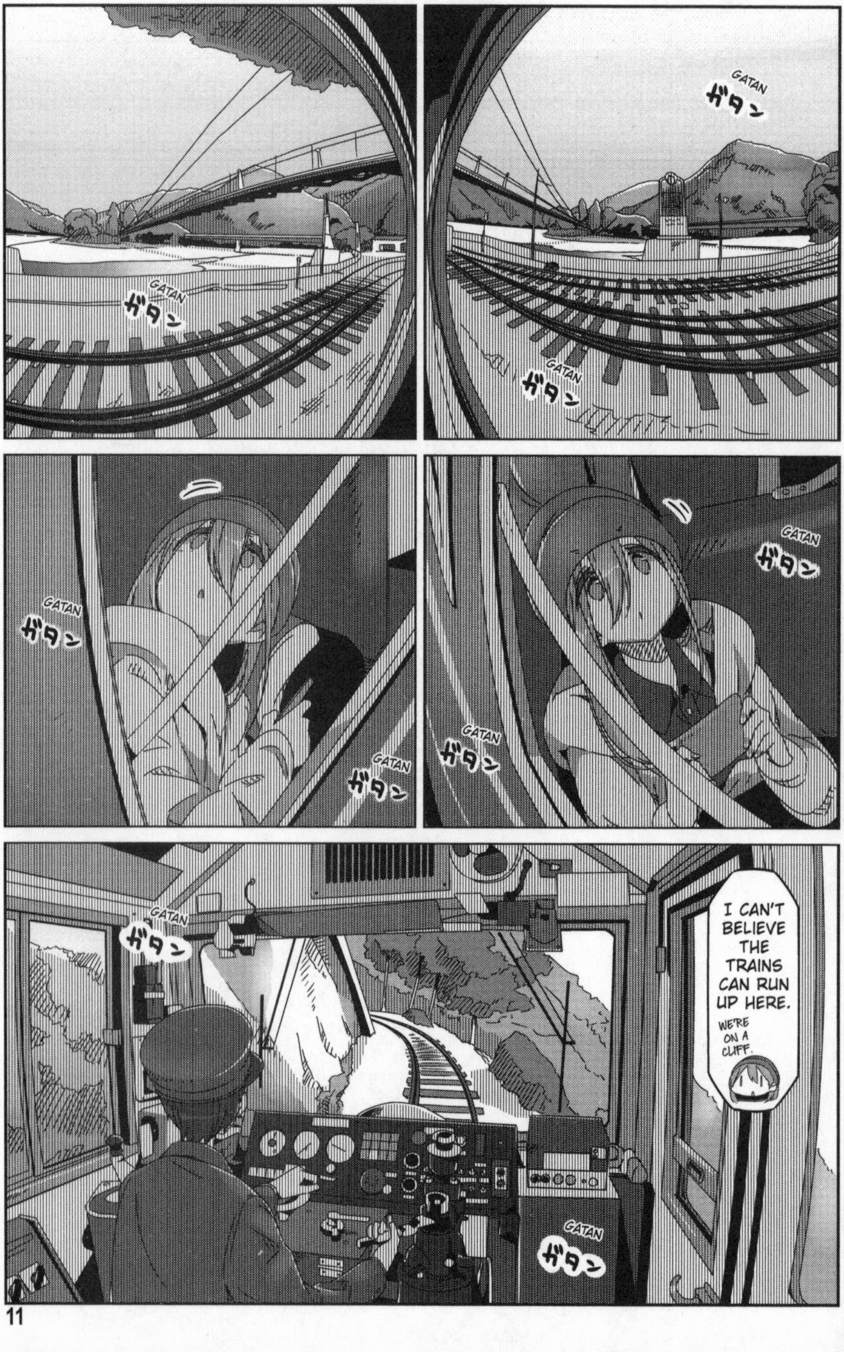
GATAN ガタン
GATAN ガタン
GATAN ガタン
GATAN ガタン
GATAN ガタン
GATAN ガタン
GATAN ガタン
I CAN'T BELIEVE THE TRAINS CAN RUN UP HERE.
WE'RE ON A CLIFF.
GATAN ガタン
GATAN ガタン

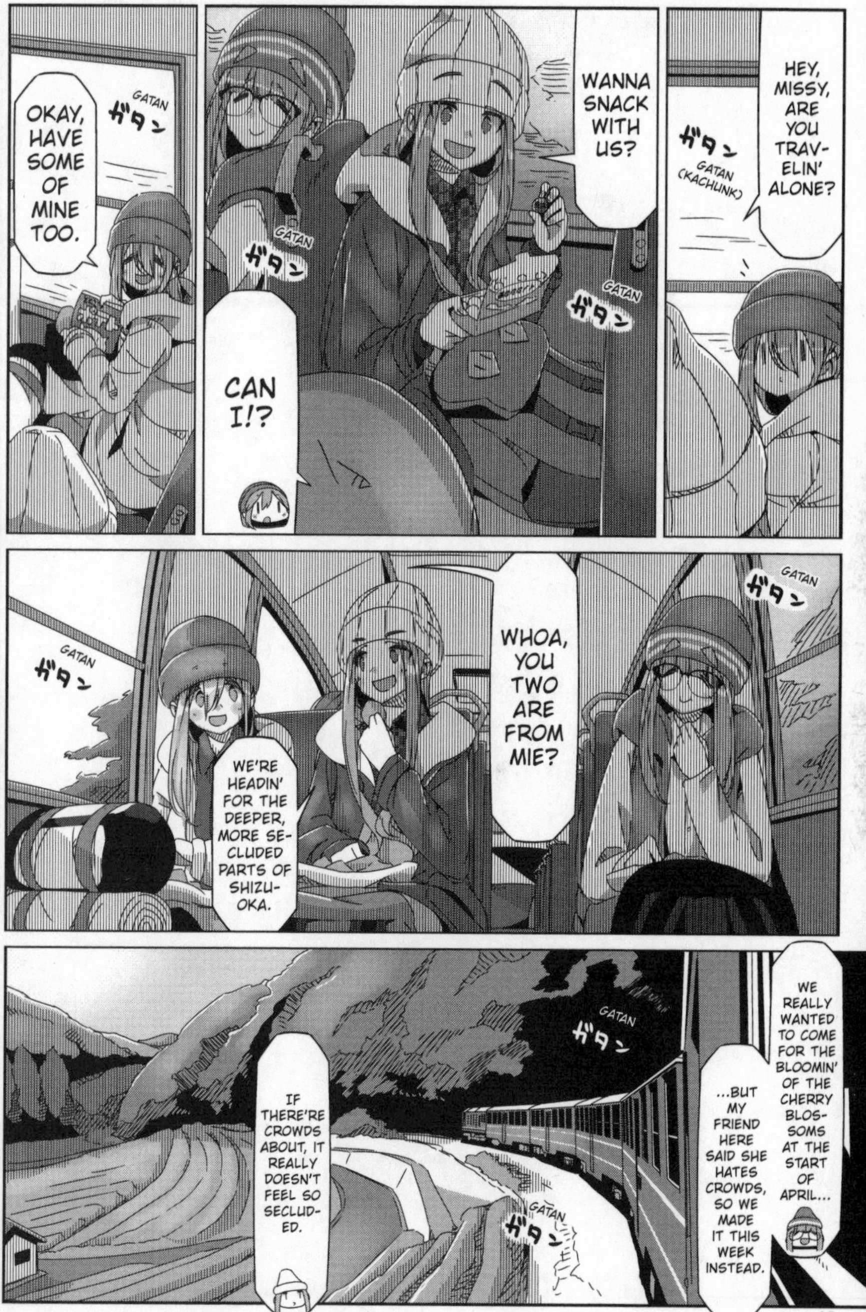
HEY, MISSY, ARE YOU TRAVELIN' ALONE?
ガタン
GATAN (KACHUNK)
WANNA SNACK WITH US?
GATAN
ガタン
GATAN
ガタン
CAN I!?
GATAN
ガタン
OKAY, HAVE SOME OF MINE TOO.
GATAN
ガタン
WHOA, YOU TWO ARE FROM MIE?
WE'RE HEADIN' FOR THE DEEPER, MORE SECLUDED PARTS OF SHIZUOKA.
GATAN
ガタン
WE REALLY WANTED TO COME FOR THE BLOOMIN' OF THE CHERRY BLOSSOMS AT THE START OF APRIL...
...BUT MY FRIEND HERE SAID SHE HATES CROWDS, SO WE MADE IT THIS WEEK INSTEAD.
GATAN
ガタン
GATAN
ガタン
IF THERE'RE CROWDS ABOUT, IT REALLY DOESN'T FEEL SO SECLUDED.

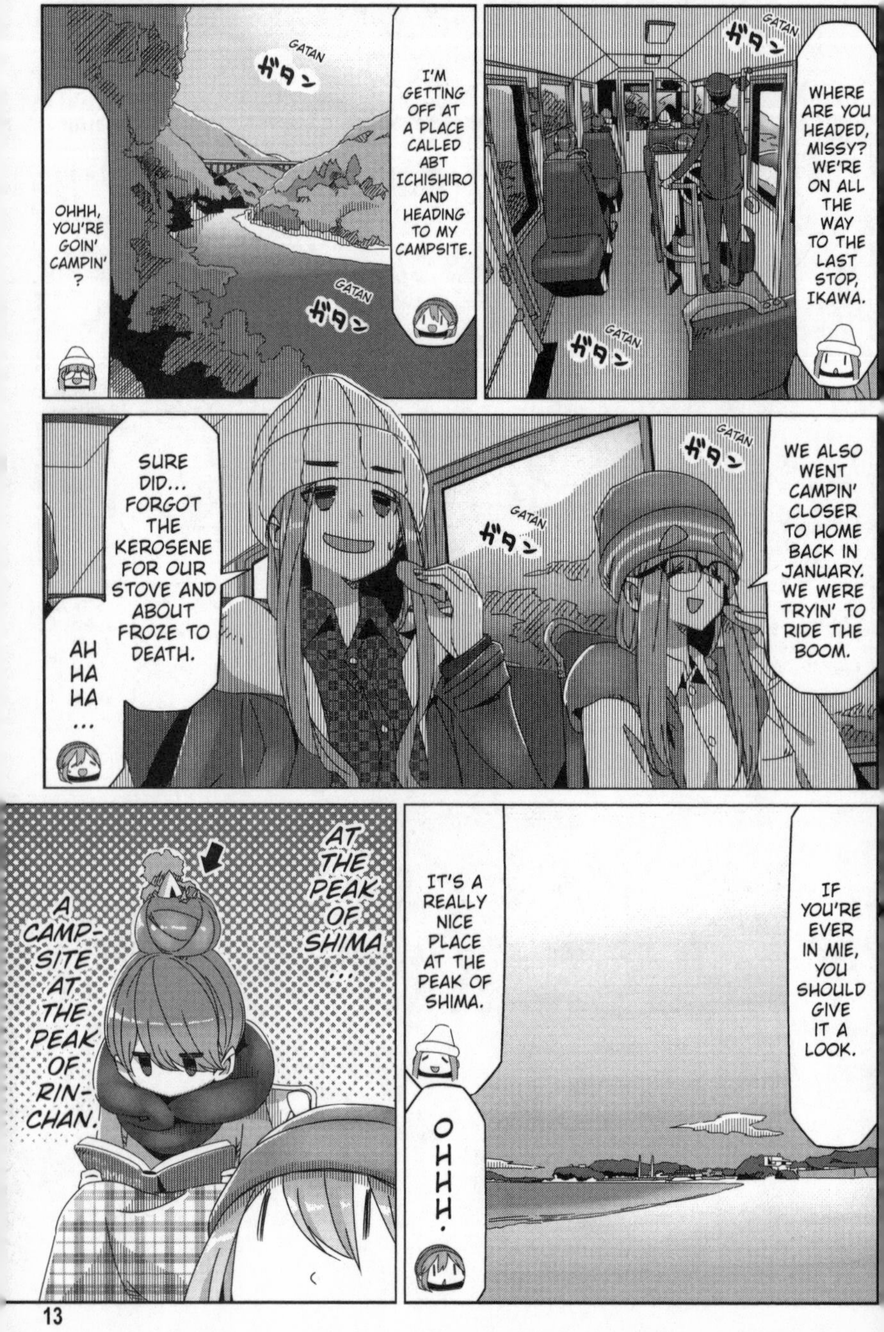
GATAN ガタン
WHERE ARE YOU HEADED, MISSY? WE'RE ON ALL THE WAY TO THE LAST STOP, IKAWA.
GATAN ガタン
GATAN ガタン
I'M GETTING OFF AT A PLACE CALLED ABT ICHISHIRO AND HEADING TO MY CAMPSITE.
OHHH, YOU'RE GOIN' CAMPIN'?
GATAN ガタン
GATAN ガタン
WE ALSO WENT CAMPIN' CLOSER TO HOME BACK IN JANUARY. WE WERE TRYIN' TO RIDE THE BOOM.
GATAN ガタン
SURE DID... FORGOT THE KEROSENE FOR OUR STOVE AND ABOUT FROZE TO DEATH.
AH HA HA...
IF YOU'RE EVER IN MIE, YOU SHOULD GIVE IT A LOOK.
IT'S A REALLY NICE PLACE AT THE PEAK OF SHIMA.
OHHH.
AT THE PEAK OF SHIMA...
A CAMPSITE AT THE PEAK OF RIN-CHAN.

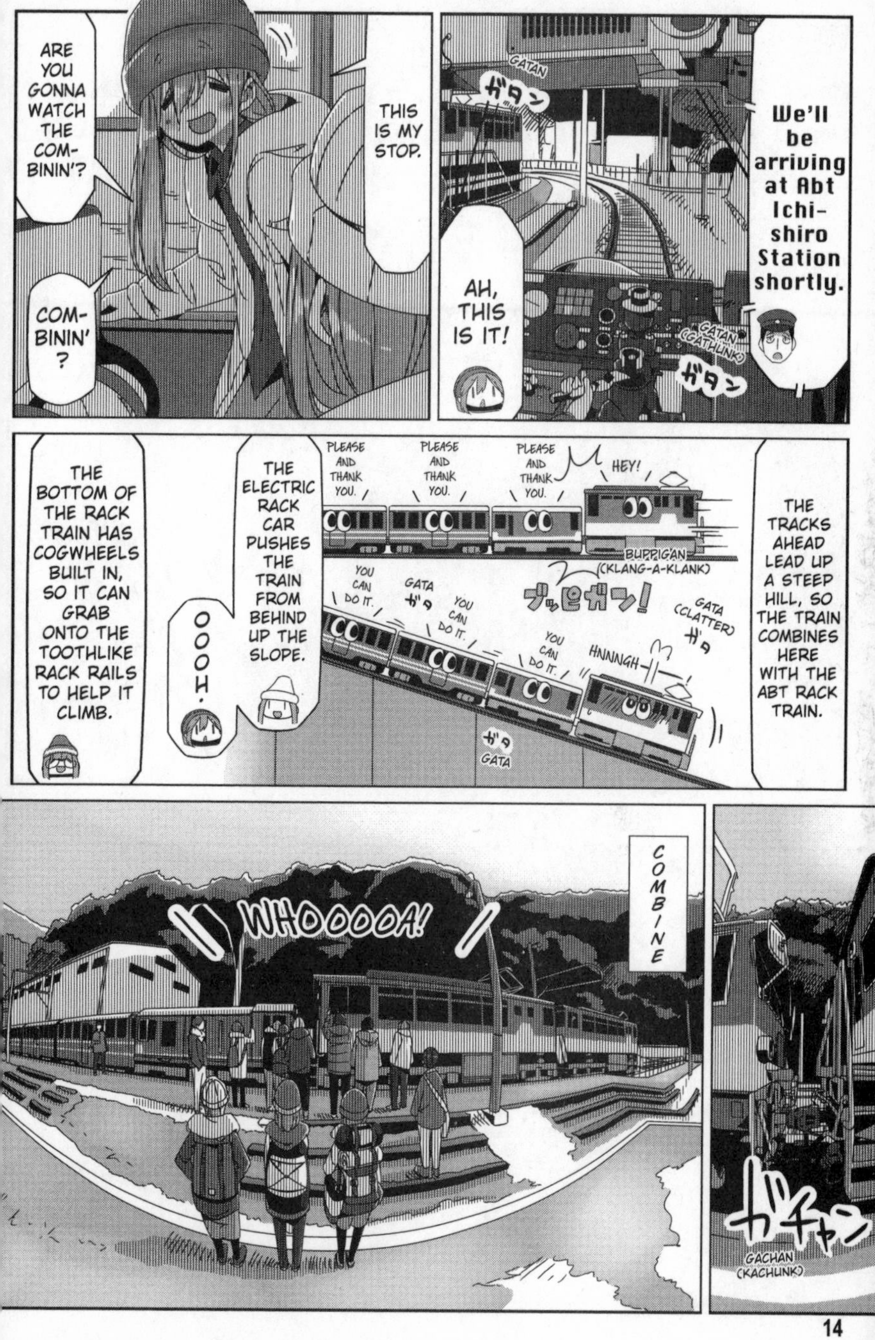
We'll be arriving at Abt Ichi-shiro Station shortly.
GATAN
ガタン
AH, THIS IS IT!
GATAN (GATHLUNK)
ガタン
THIS IS MY STOP.
ARE YOU GONNA WATCH THE COMBININ'?
COMBININ'?
THE TRACKS AHEAD LEAD UP A STEEP HILL, SO THE TRAIN COMBINES HERE WITH THE ABT RACK TRAIN.
HEY!
PLEASE AND THANK YOU.
PLEASE AND THANK YOU.
PLEASE AND THANK YOU.
BUPPIGAN (KLANG-A-KLANK)
ブッピガン!
GATA (CLATTER)
ガタ
HNNNGH
YOU CAN DO IT.
YOU CAN DO IT.
GATA
ガタ
YOU CAN DO IT.
ガタ
GATA
THE ELECTRIC RACK CAR PUSHES THE TRAIN FROM BEHIND UP THE SLOPE.
OOOH.
THE BOTTOM OF THE RACK TRAIN HAS COGWHEELS BUILT IN, SO IT CAN GRAB ONTO THE TOOTHLIKE RACK RAILS TO HELP IT CLIMB.
ガチャン
GACHAN (KACHUNK)
COMBINE
WHOOOOA!

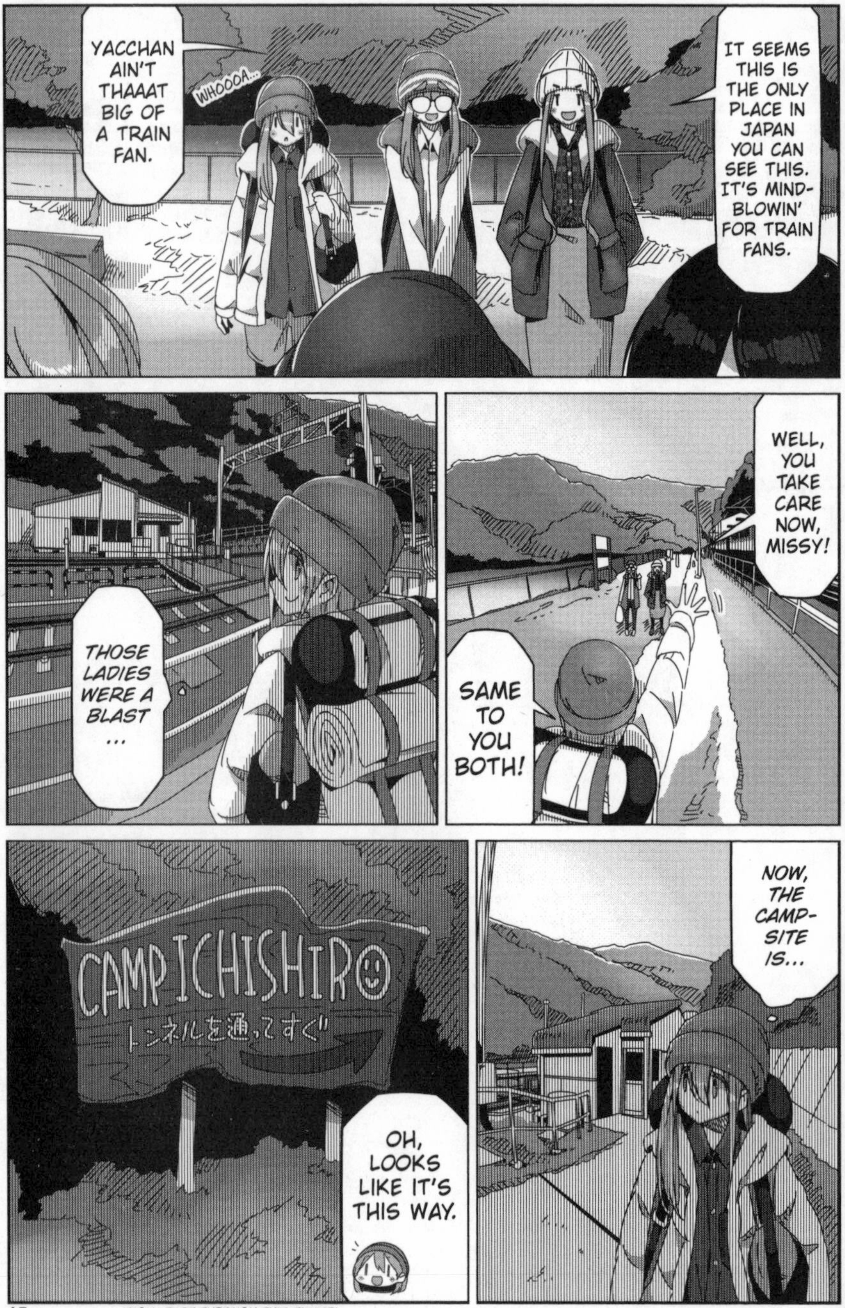
IT SEEMS THIS IS THE ONLY PLACE IN JAPAN YOU CAN SEE THIS. IT'S MIND-BLOWIN' FOR TRAIN FANS.
YACCHAN AIN'T THAAAT BIG OF A TRAIN FAN.
WHOOOA...
WELL, YOU TAKE CARE NOW, MISSY!
SAME TO YOU BOTH!
THOSE LADIES WERE A BLAST ...
NOW, THE CAMP-SITE IS...
CAMP ICHISHIRO
トンネルを通ってすぐ
OH, LOOKS LIKE IT'S THIS WAY.

SIGN: JUST THROUGH THIS TUNNEL

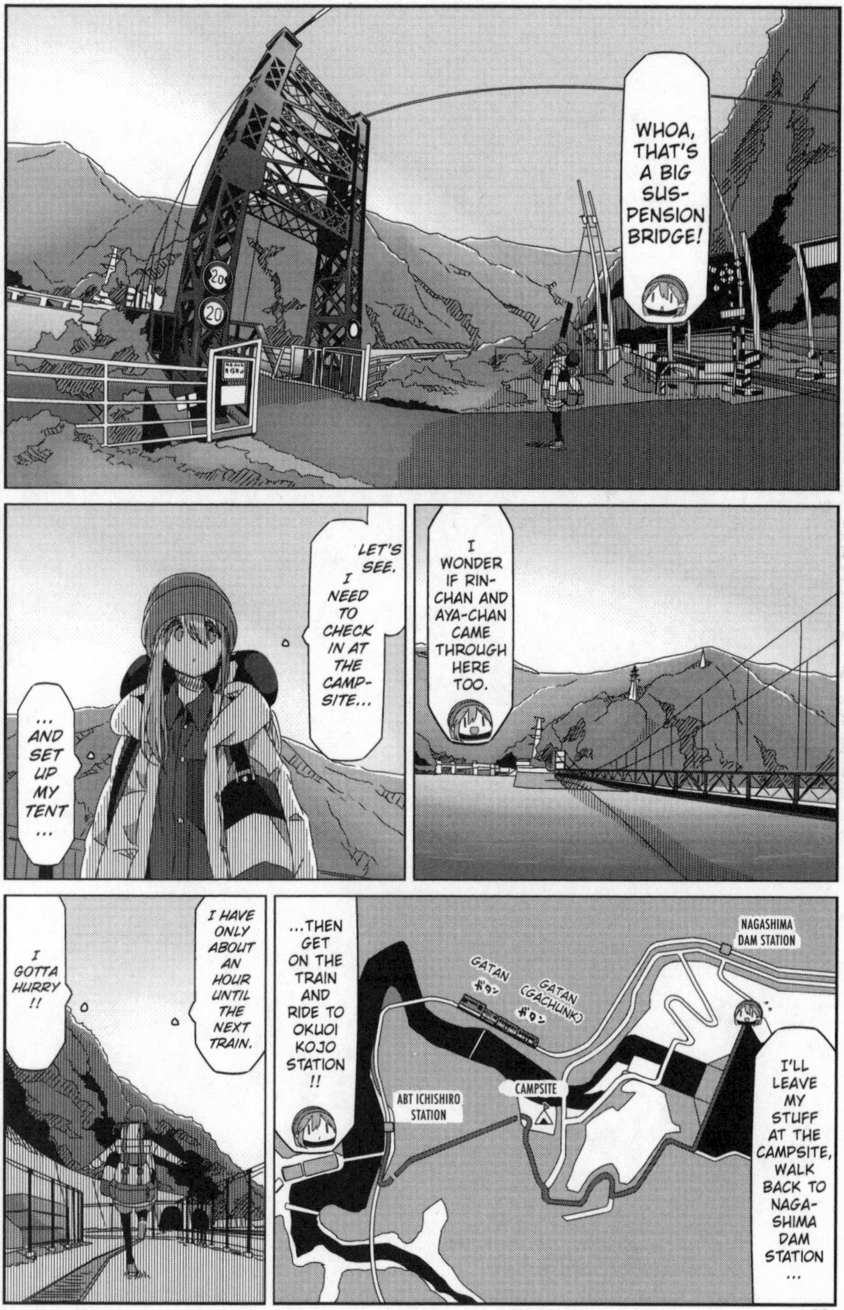
WHOA, THAT'S A BIG SUS-PENSION BRIDGE!
I WONDER IF RIN-CHAN AND AYA-CHAN CAME THROUGH HERE TOO.
LET'S SEE. I NEED TO CHECK IN AT THE CAMP-SITE...
...AND SET UP MY TENT...
NAGASHIMA DAM STATION
I'LL LEAVE MY STUFF AT THE CAMPSITE, WALK BACK TO NAGA-SHIMA DAM STATION...
GATAN
GATAN (GACHUNK)
CAMPSITE
ABT ICHISHIRO STATION
...THEN GET ON THE TRAIN AND RIDE TO OKUOI KOJO STATION!!
I HAVE ONLY ABOUT AN HOUR UNTIL THE NEXT TRAIN.
I GOTTA HURRY!!

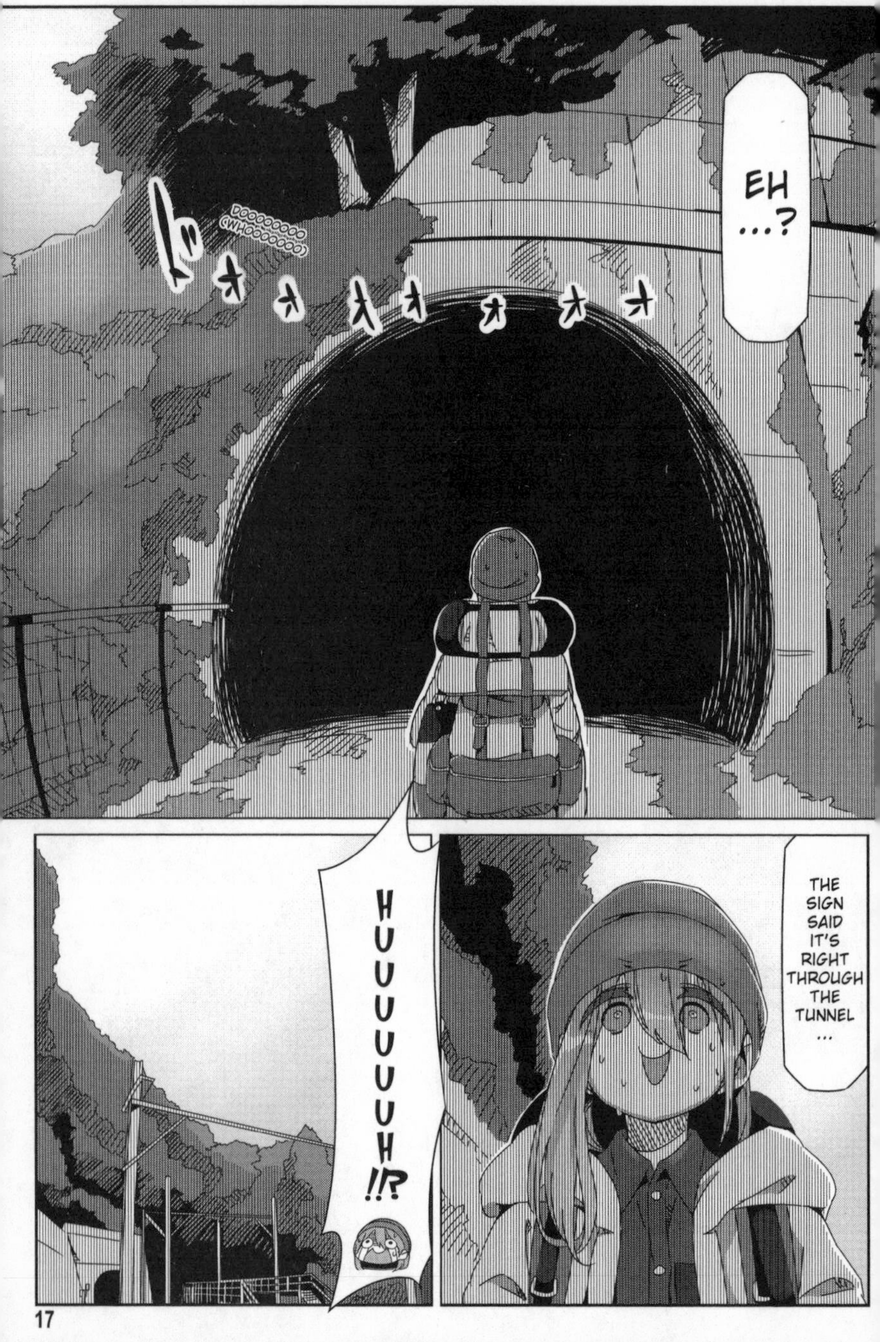
EH ...?
DOOOOOOOO (WHOOOOOOO)
THE SIGN SAID IT'S RIGHT THROUGH THE TUNNEL ...
HUUUUUUUUH!!?

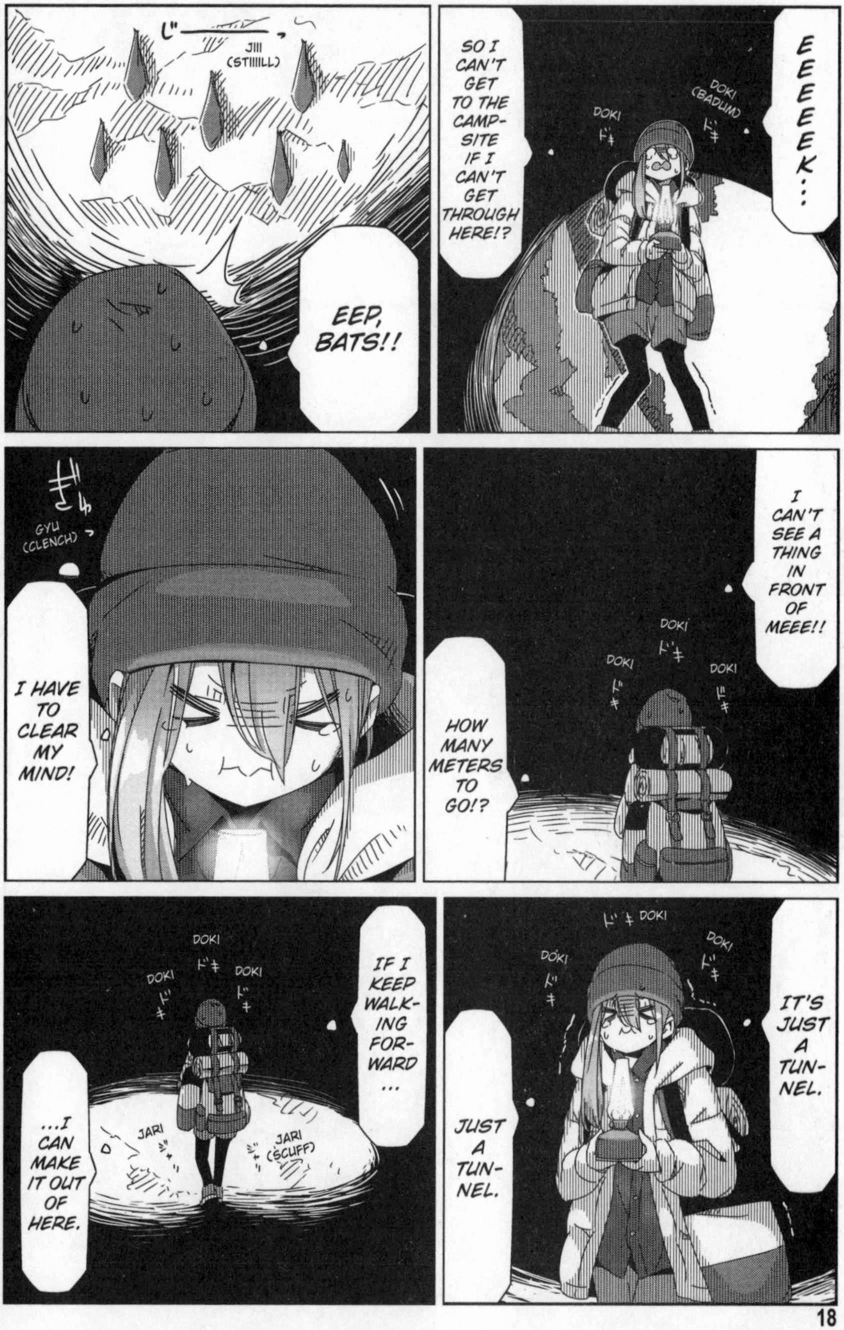
EEEEEK...
DOKI (BADUM)
DOKI
SO I CAN'T GET TO THE CAMPSITE IF I CAN'T GET THROUGH HERE!?
JIII (STIIIILL)
EEP, BATS!!
I CAN'T SEE A THING IN FRONT OF MEEE!!
DOKI
DOKI
DOKI
HOW MANY METERS TO GO!?
GYU (CLENCH)
I HAVE TO CLEAR MY MIND!
DOKI
DOKI
DOKI
IT'S JUST A TUNNEL.
JUST A TUNNEL.
DOKI
DOKI
DOKI
IF I KEEP WALKING FORWARD...
JARI
JARI (SCUFF)
...I CAN MAKE IT OUT OF HERE.

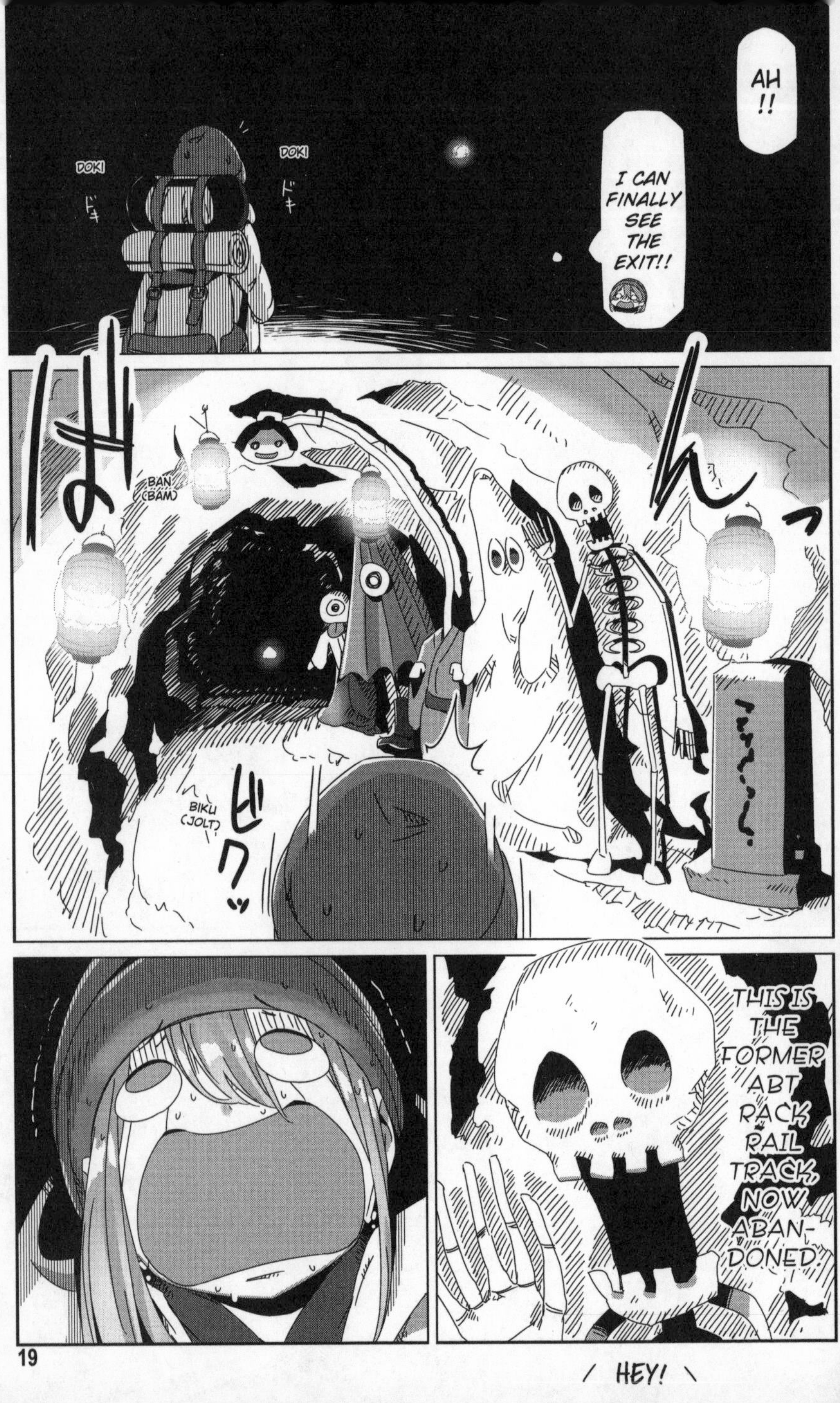
AH!!
I CAN FINALLY SEE THE EXIT!!
DOKI
DOKI
BAN (BAM)
BIKU (JOLT)
THIS IS THE FORMER ABT RACK RAIL TRACK, NOW ABAN-DONED.
HEY!

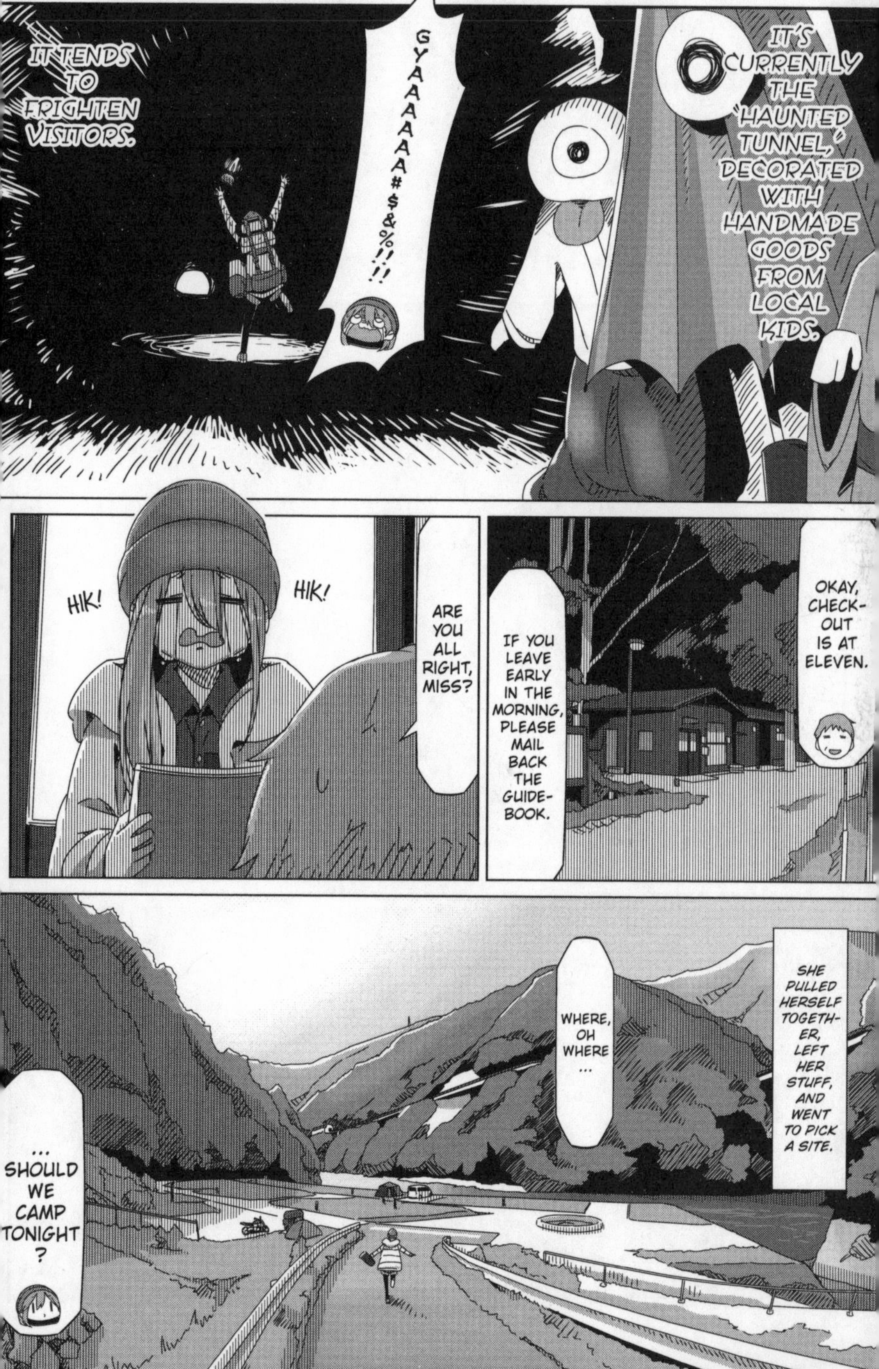
IT'S CURRENTLY THE 'HAUNTED TUNNEL,' DECORATED WITH HANDMADE GOODS FROM LOCAL KIDS.
GYAAAAAAA#$&%!!!!
IT TENDS TO FRIGHTEN VISITORS.
OKAY, CHECK-OUT IS AT ELEVEN.
IF YOU LEAVE EARLY IN THE MORNING, PLEASE MAIL BACK THE GUIDE-BOOK.
ARE YOU ALL RIGHT, MISS?
HIK!
HIK!
SHE PULLED HERSELF TOGETH-ER, LEFT HER STUFF, AND WENT TO PICK A SITE.
WHERE, OH WHERE ...
... SHOULD WE CAMP TONIGHT ?

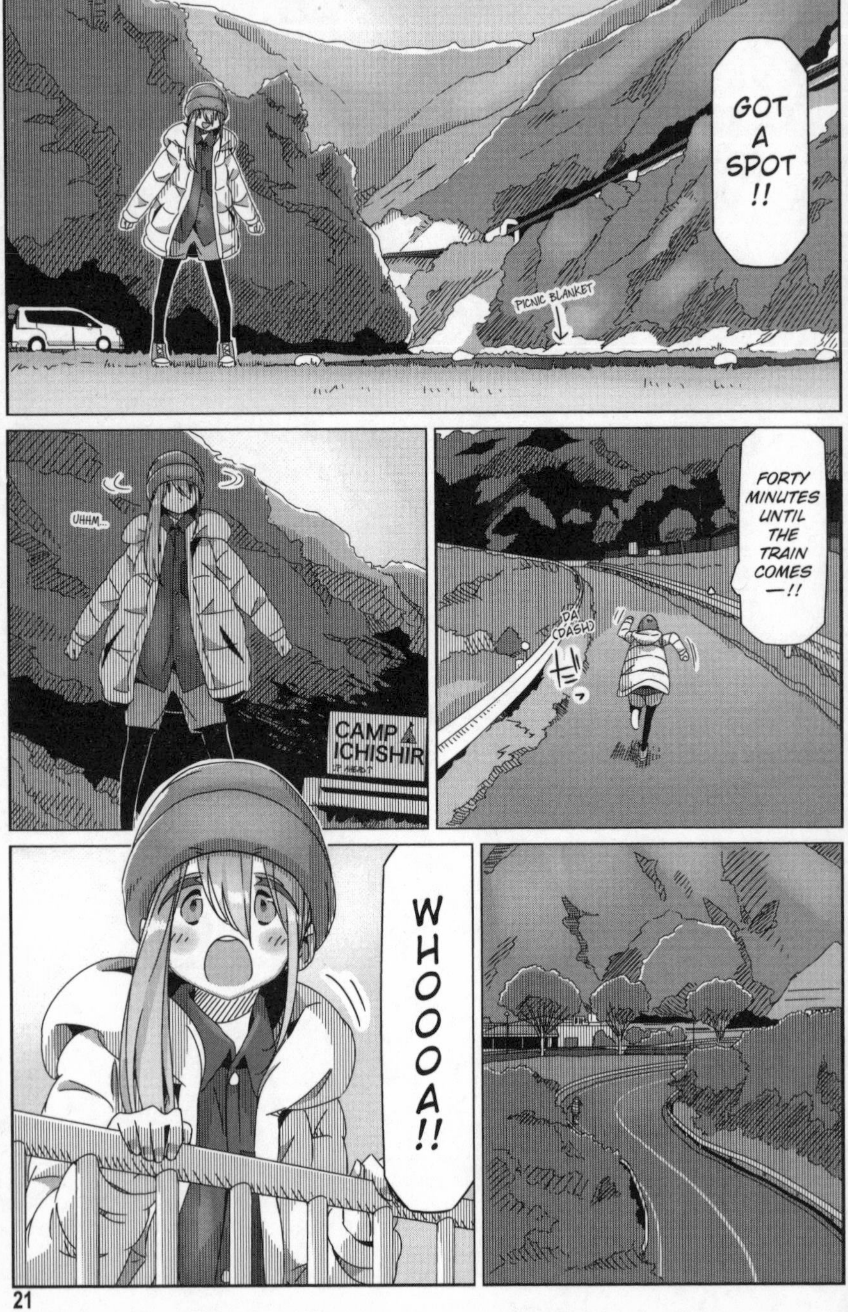
GOT A SPOT !!
PICNIC BLANKET
FORTY MINUTES UNTIL THE TRAIN COMES —!!
DA (DASH)
UHHM...
CAMP ICHISHIR
WHOOOOA!!

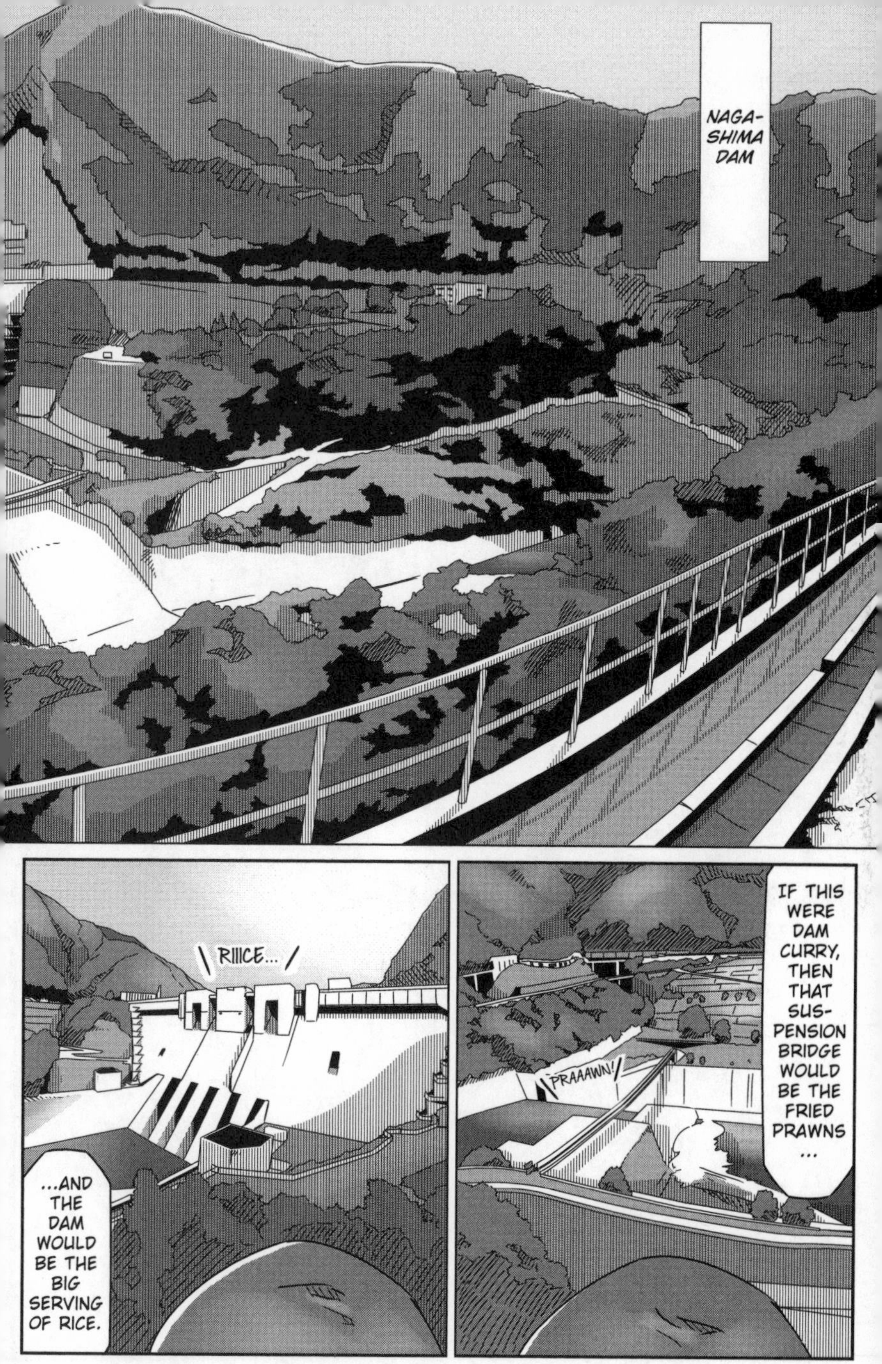
NAGA-SHIMA DAM
IF THIS WERE DAM CURRY, THEN THAT SUS-PENSION BRIDGE WOULD BE THE FRIED PRAWNS...
PRAAAWN!
RIIICE...
...AND THE DAM WOULD BE THE BIG SERVING OF RICE.

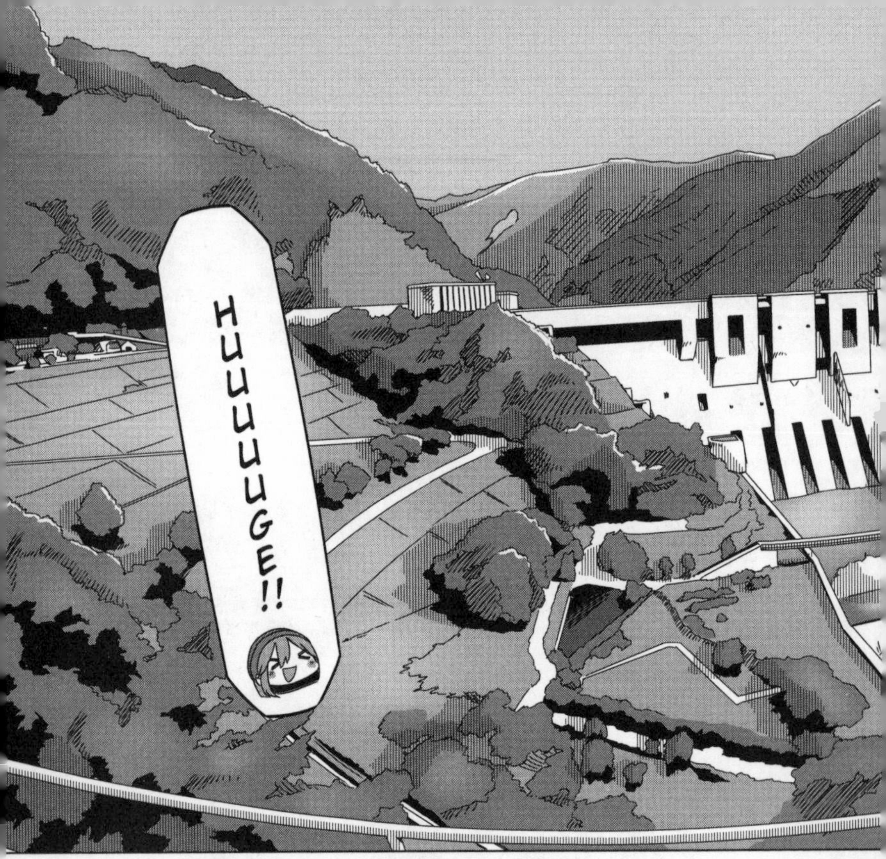
HUUUUUGE!!

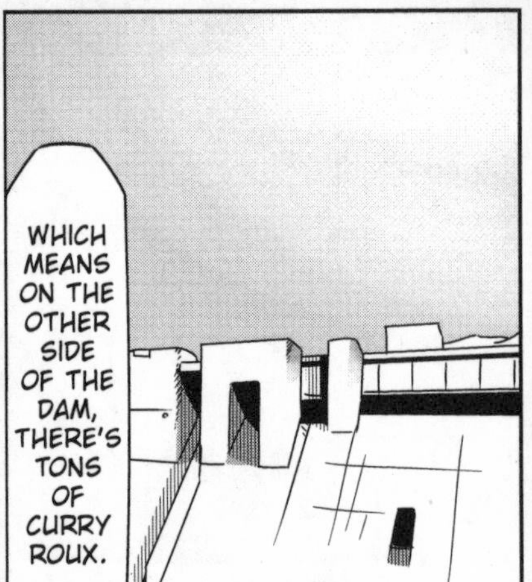
WHICH MEANS ON THE OTHER SIDE OF THE DAM, THERE'S TONS OF CURRY ROUX.

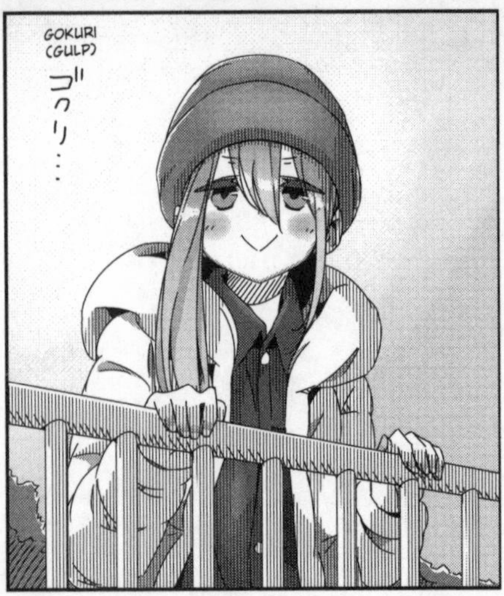
GOKURI (GULP)
ゴクリ…

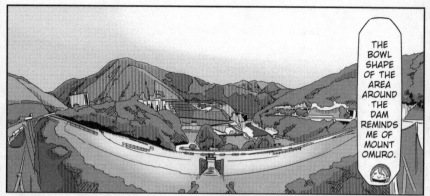

THE BOWL SHAPE OF THE AREA AROUND THE DAM REMINDS ME OF MOUNT OMURO.

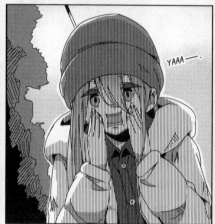

YAAA——.

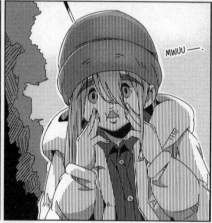

MWUU——.

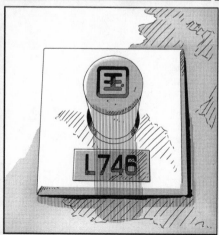

L746

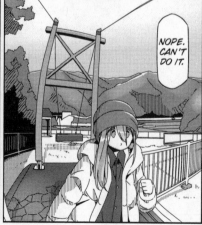

NOPE. CAN'T DO IT.

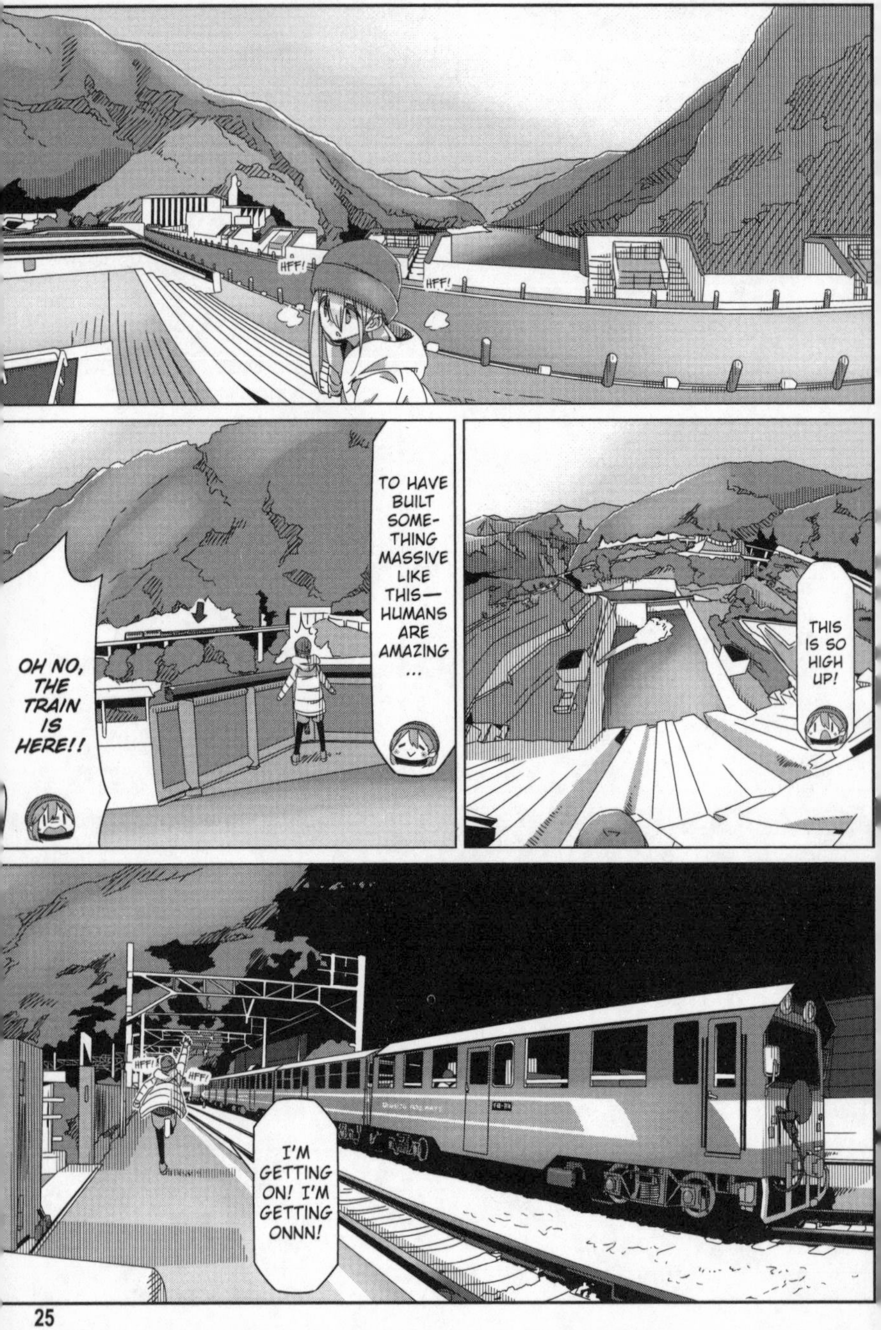
HFF!
HFF!
THIS IS SO HIGH UP!
TO HAVE BUILT SOMETHING MASSIVE LIKE THIS—HUMANS ARE AMAZING...
OH NO, THE TRAIN IS HERE!!
HFF!
HFF!
I'M GETTING ON! I'M GETTING ONNN!

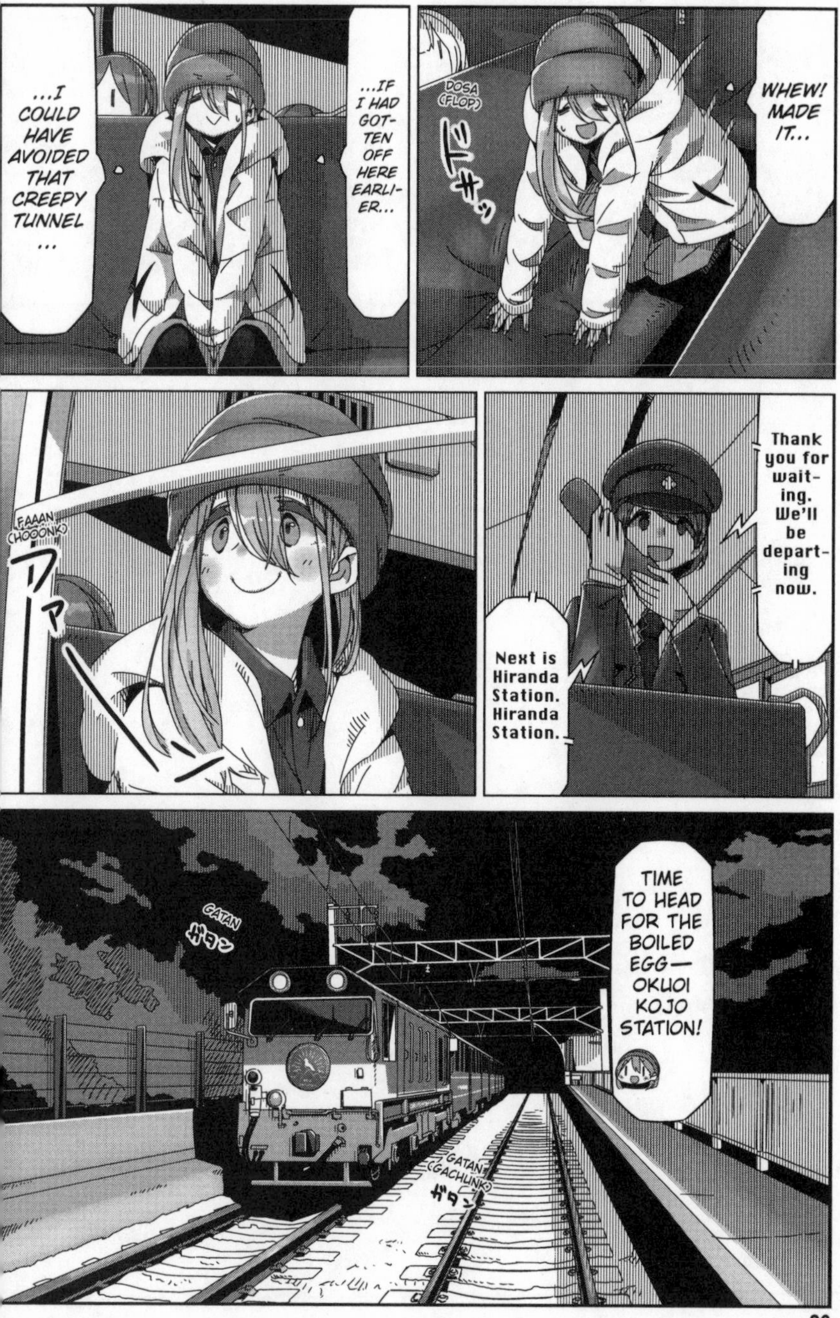
WHEW! MADE IT...
DOSA (FLOP)
...IF I HAD GOT-TEN OFF HERE EARLI-ER...
...I COULD HAVE AVOIDED THAT CREEPY TUNNEL...
Thank you for wait-ing. We'll be depart-ing now.
Next is Hiranda Station. Hiranda Station.
FAAAN (HOOONK)
GATAN
TIME TO HEAD FOR THE BOILED EGG—OKUOI KOJO STATION!
GATAN (GACHUNK)

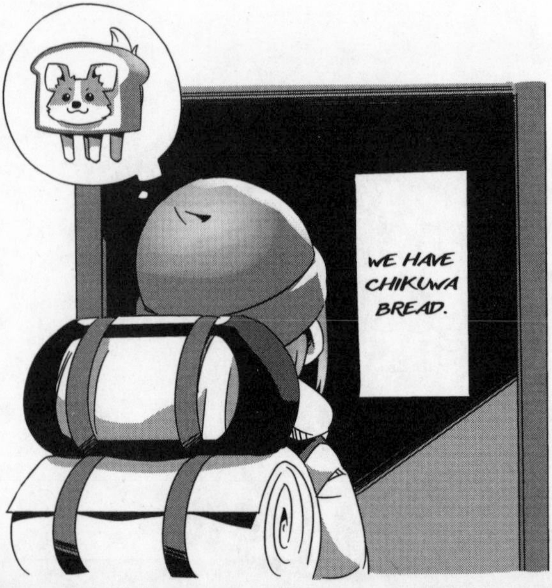
WE HAVE CHIKUWA BREAD.

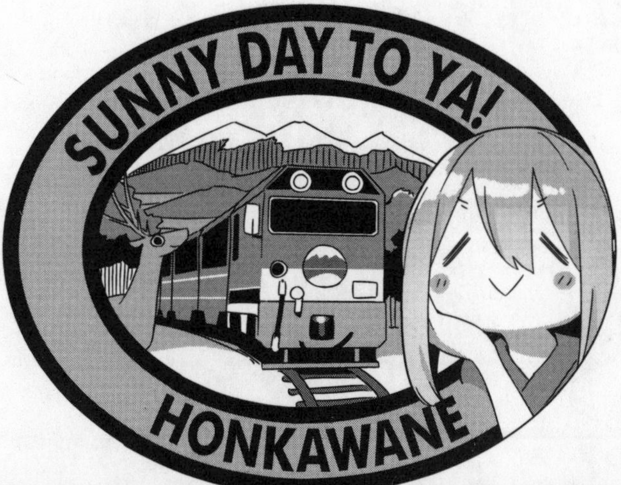
SUNNY DAY TO YA!
HONKAWANE

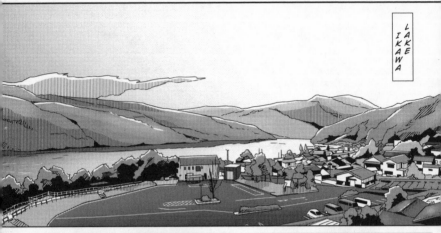

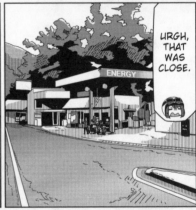

URGH, THAT WAS CLOSE.

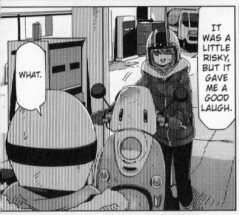

WHAT.

IT WAS A LITTLE RISKY, BUT IT GAVE ME A GOOD LAUGH.

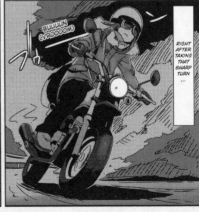

RIGHT AFTER TAKING THAT SHARP TURN...

BULULULU (VROOOOM)

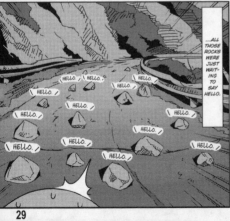

...ALL THOSE ROCKS WERE JUST WAITING TO SAY HELLO.

HELLO.

HELLO.

HELLO.

HELLO.

HELLO.

HELLO.

HELLO.

HELLO.

HELLO.

HELLO.

HELLO.

HELLO.

HELLO.

29

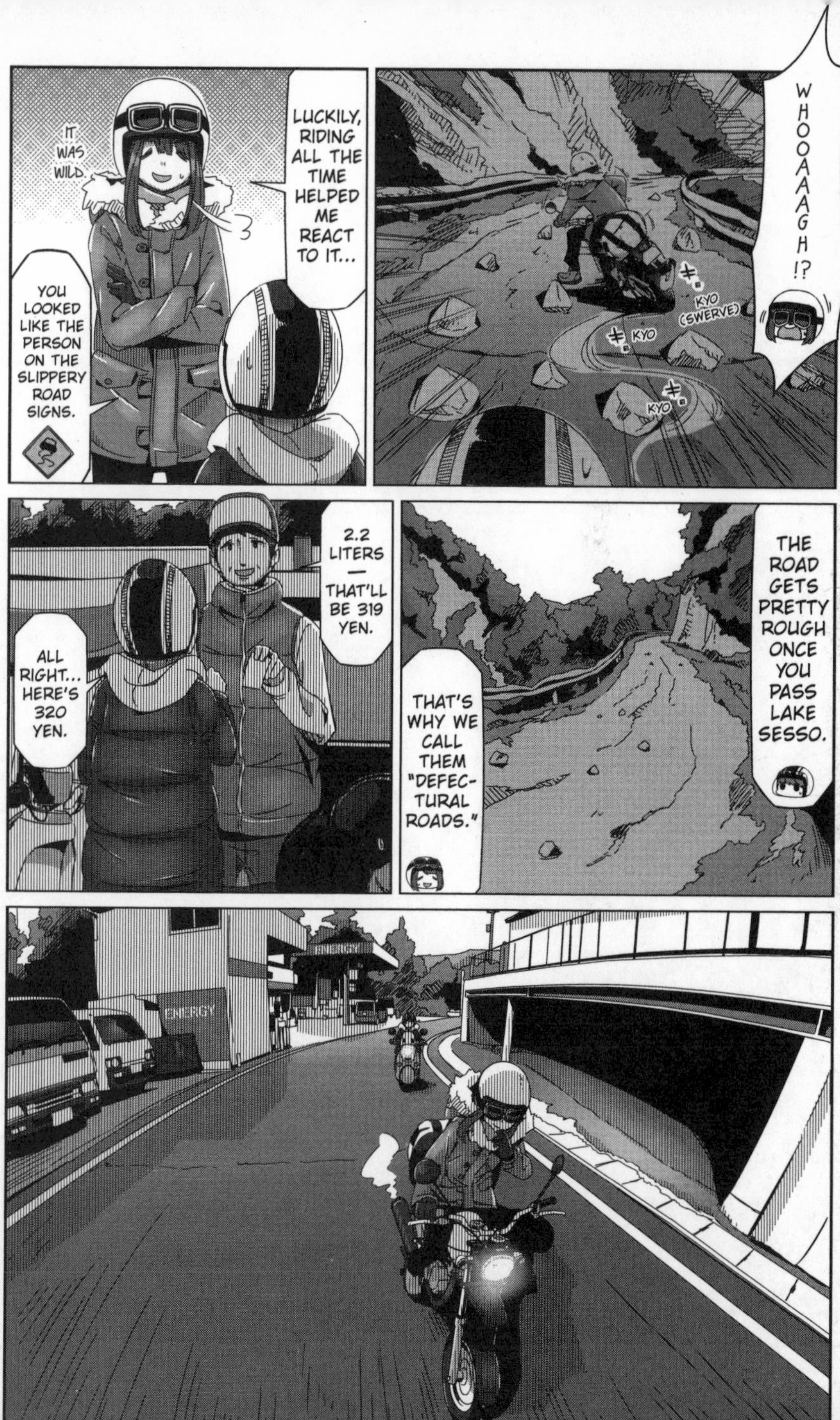
WHOOAAAAGH!?
KYO (SWERVE)
KYO
KYO
LUCKILY, RIDING ALL THE TIME HELPED ME REACT TO IT...
IT WAS WILD.
YOU LOOKED LIKE THE PERSON ON THE SLIPPERY ROAD SIGNS.
THE ROAD GETS PRETTY ROUGH ONCE YOU PASS LAKE SESSO.
THAT'S WHY WE CALL THEM "DEFECTURAL ROADS."
2.2 LITERS—THAT'LL BE 319 YEN.
ALL RIGHT... HERE'S 320 YEN.
ENERGY
ENERGY

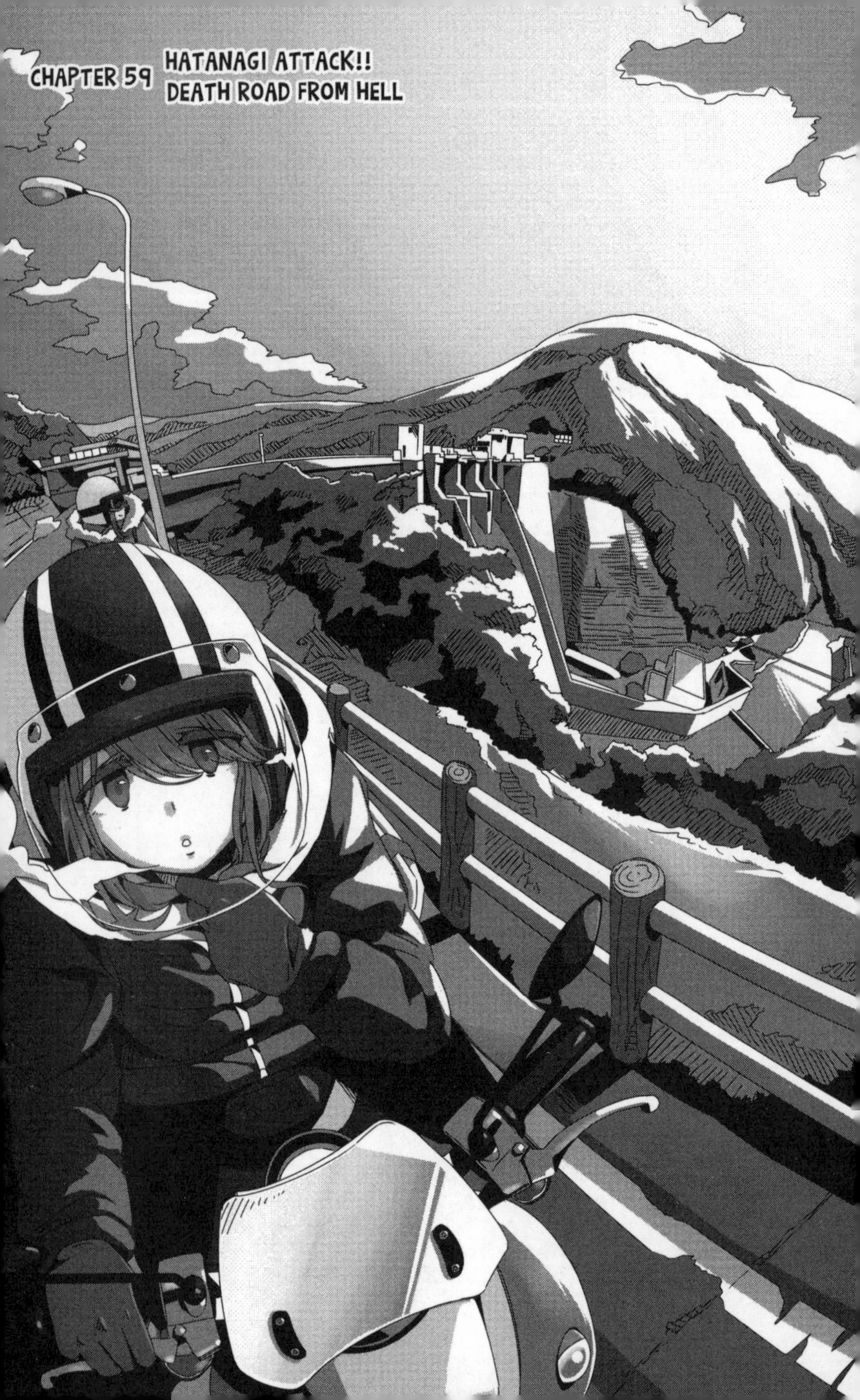
CHAPTER 59
HATANAGI ATTACK!!
DEATH ROAD FROM HELL

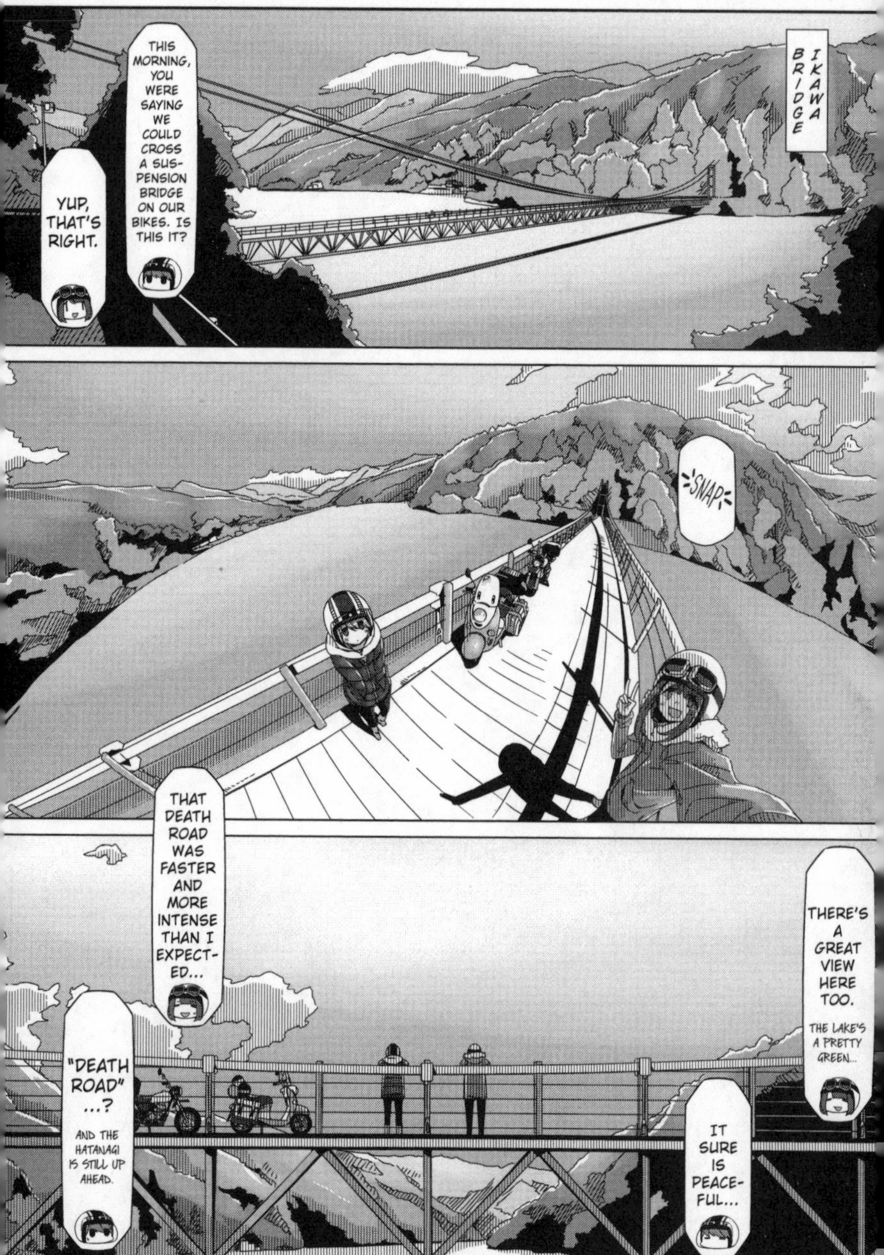
IKAWA BRIDGE
THIS MORNING, YOU WERE SAYING WE COULD CROSS A SUS-PENSION BRIDGE ON OUR BIKES. IS THIS IT?
YUP, THAT'S RIGHT.
SNAP
THERE'S A GREAT VIEW HERE TOO.
THE LAKE'S A PRETTY GREEN...
IT SURE IS PEACE-FUL...
THAT DEATH ROAD WAS FASTER AND MORE INTENSE THAN I EXPECT-ED...
"DEATH ROAD" ...?
AND THE HATANAGI IS STILL UP AHEAD.

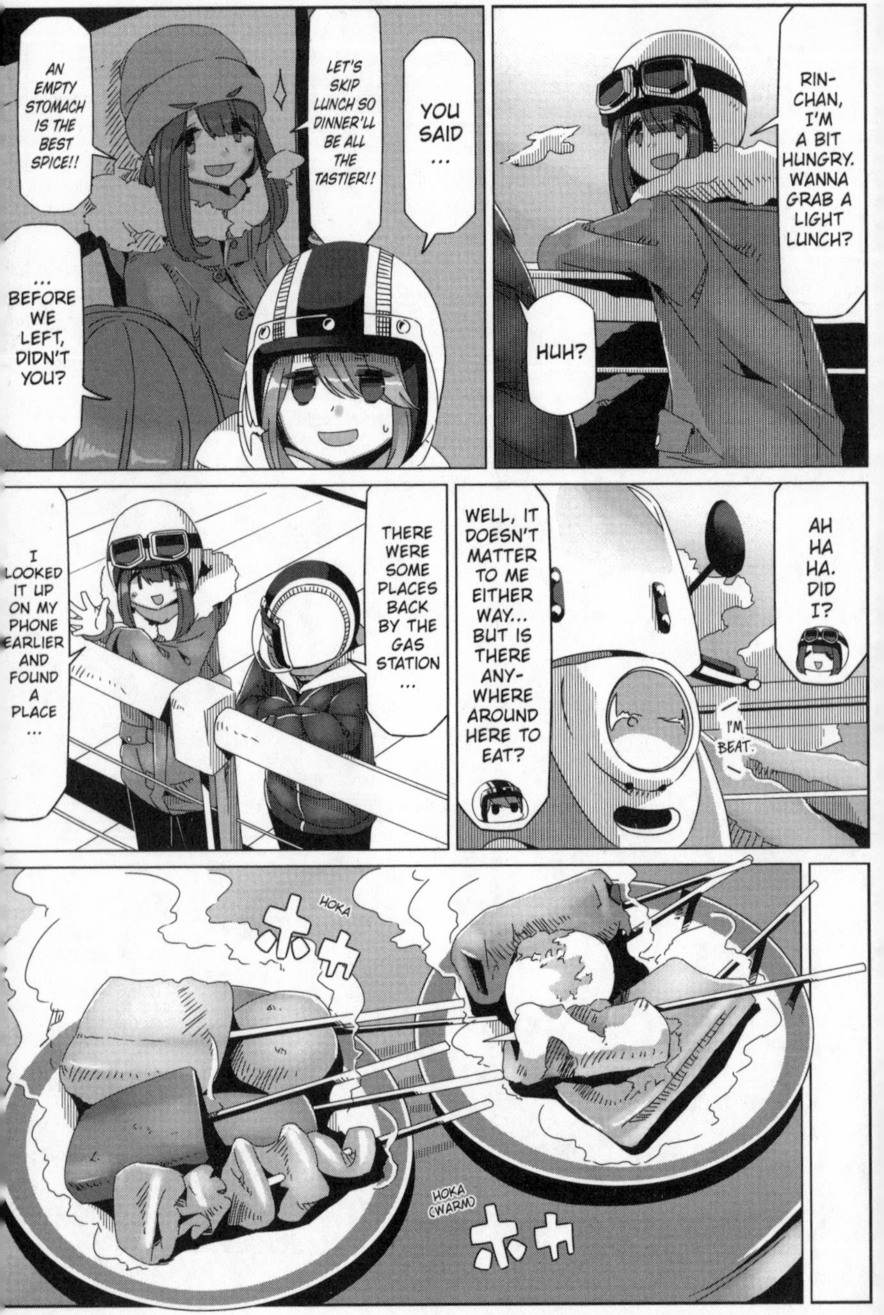
RIN-CHAN, I'M A BIT HUNGRY. WANNA GRAB A LIGHT LUNCH?
HUH?
YOU SAID ...
LET'S SKIP LUNCH SO DINNER'LL BE ALL THE TASTIER!!
AN EMPTY STOMACH IS THE BEST SPICE!!
... BEFORE WE LEFT, DIDN'T YOU?
AH HA HA. DID I?
I'M BEAT.
WELL, IT DOESN'T MATTER TO ME EITHER WAY... BUT IS THERE ANYWHERE AROUND HERE TO EAT?
THERE WERE SOME PLACES BACK BY THE GAS STATION ...
I LOOKED IT UP ON MY PHONE EARLIER AND FOUND A PLACE ...
HOKA
ホカ
HOKA (WARM)
ホカ

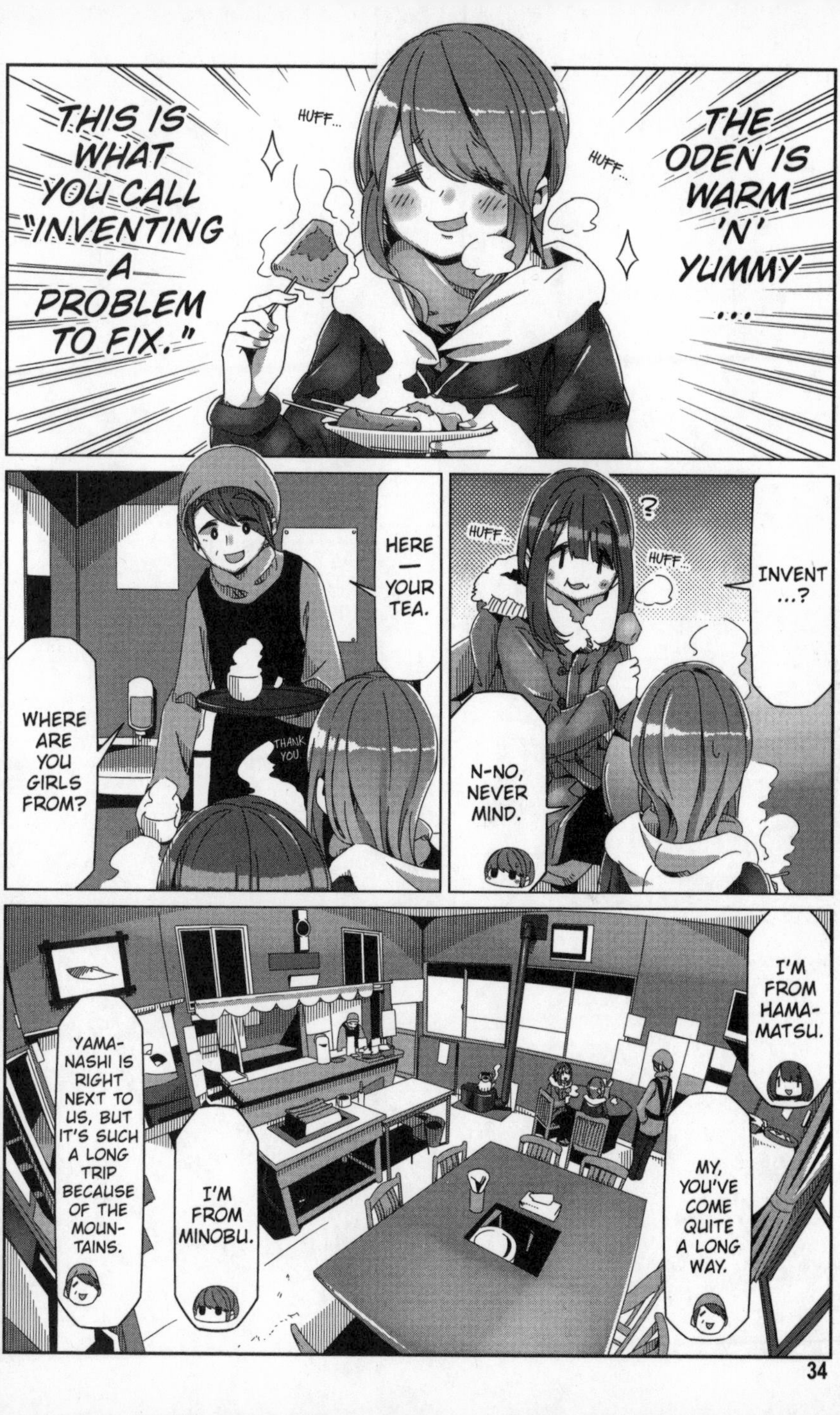
THE ODEN IS WARM 'N' YUMMY...
HUFF...
HUFF...
THIS IS WHAT YOU CALL "INVENTING A PROBLEM TO FIX."
INVENT...?
HUFF...
HUFF...
N-NO, NEVER MIND.
HERE—YOUR TEA.
THANK YOU.
WHERE ARE YOU GIRLS FROM?
I'M FROM HAMA-MATSU.
MY, YOU'VE COME QUITE A LONG WAY.
I'M FROM MINOBU.
YAMA-NASHI IS RIGHT NEXT TO US, BUT IT'S SUCH A LONG TRIP BECAUSE OF THE MOUN-TAINS.

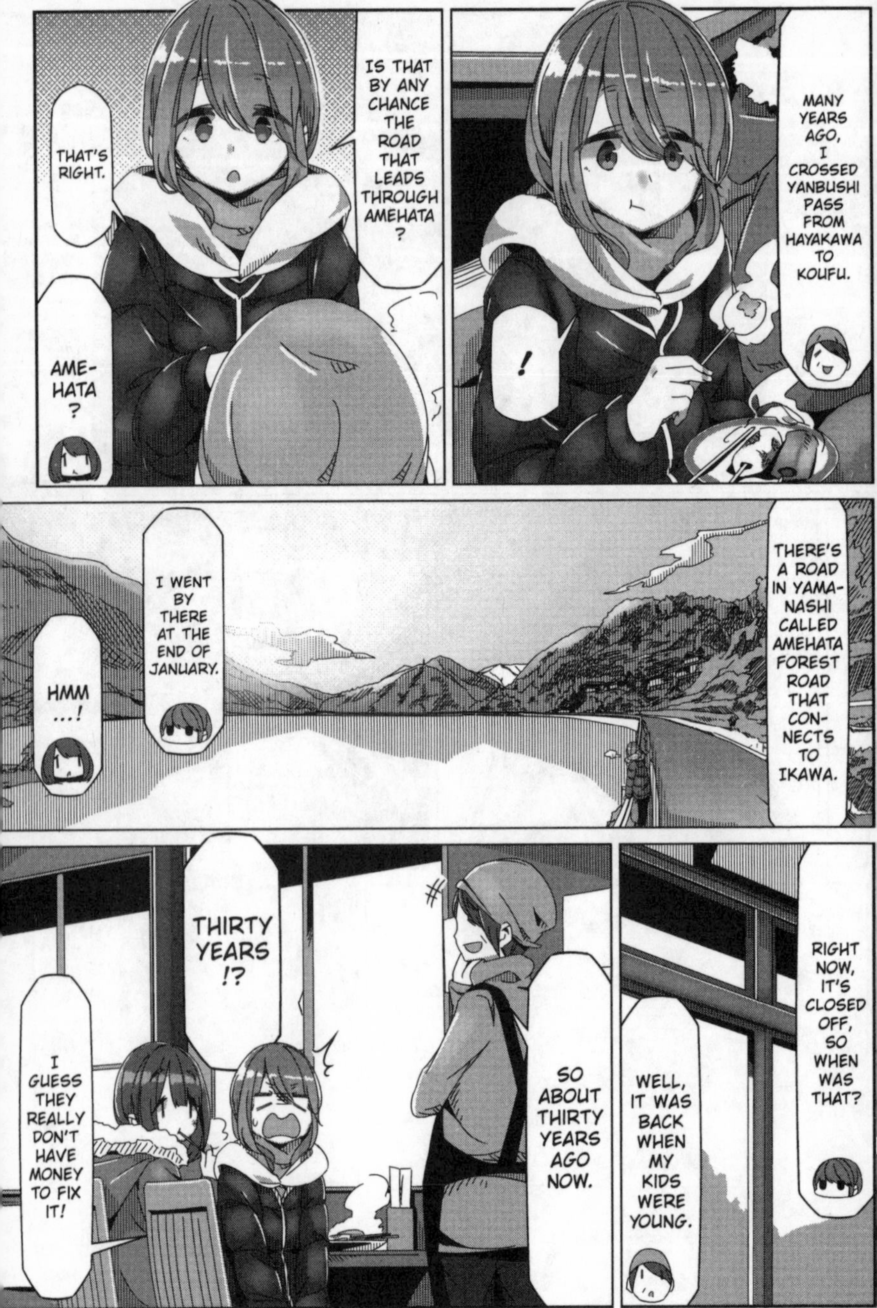
MANY YEARS AGO, I CROSSED YANBUSHI PASS FROM HAYAKAWA TO KOUFU.
!
IS THAT BY ANY CHANCE THE ROAD THAT LEADS THROUGH AMEHATA?
THAT'S RIGHT.
AME-HATA?
THERE'S A ROAD IN YAMA-NASHI CALLED AMEHATA FOREST ROAD THAT CON-NECTS TO IKAWA.
I WENT BY THERE AT THE END OF JANUARY.
HMM...!
RIGHT NOW, IT'S CLOSED OFF, SO WHEN WAS THAT?
WELL, IT WAS BACK WHEN MY KIDS WERE YOUNG.
SO ABOUT THIRTY YEARS AGO NOW.
THIRTY YEARS!?
I GUESS THEY REALLY DON'T HAVE MONEY TO FIX IT!

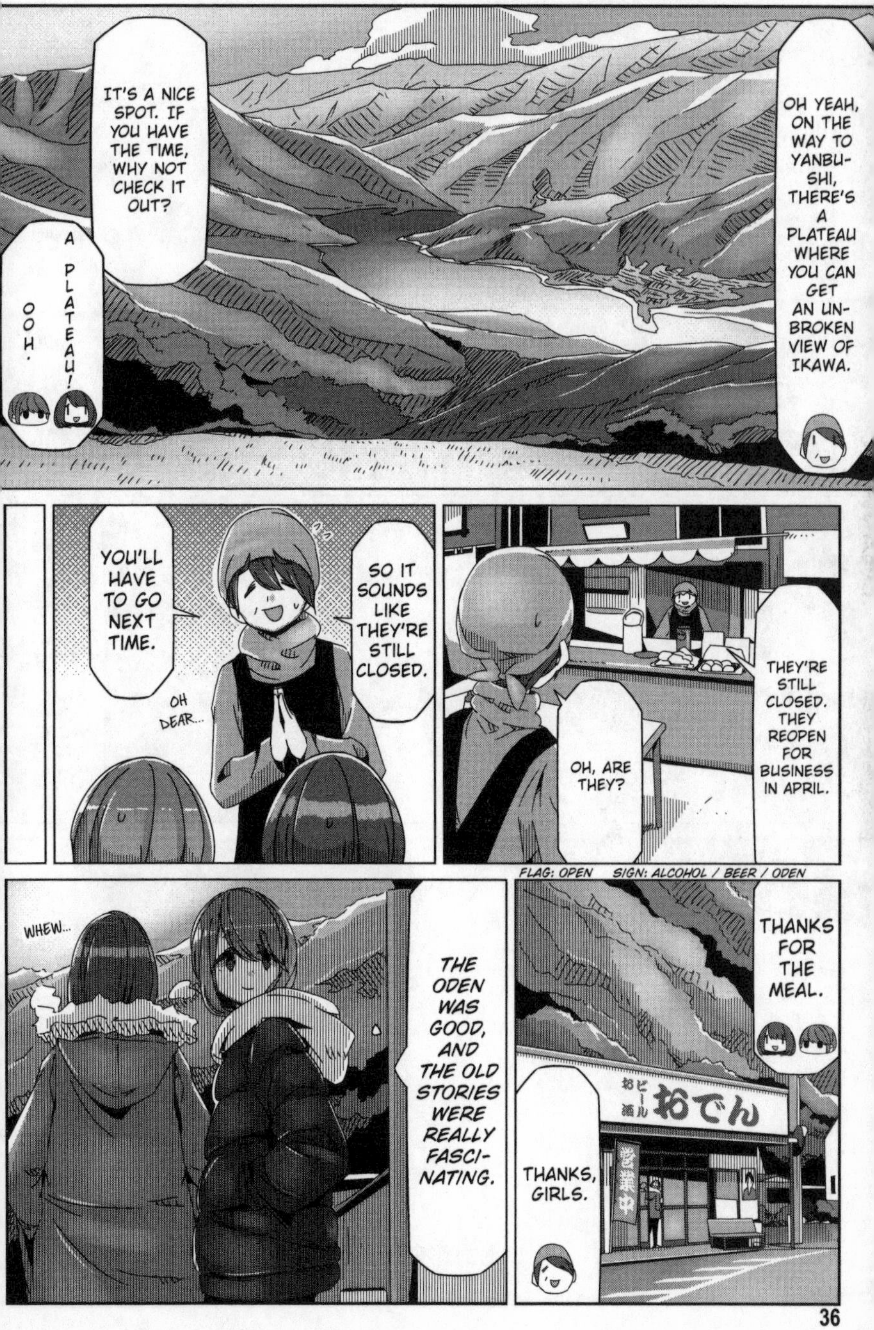
OH YEAH, ON THE WAY TO YANBU-SHI, THERE'S A PLATEAU WHERE YOU CAN GET AN UN-BROKEN VIEW OF IKAWA.
IT'S A NICE SPOT. IF YOU HAVE THE TIME, WHY NOT CHECK IT OUT?
A PLATEAU!
OOH.
THEY'RE STILL CLOSED. THEY REOPEN FOR BUSINESS IN APRIL.
OH, ARE THEY?
SO IT SOUNDS LIKE THEY'RE STILL CLOSED.
YOU'LL HAVE TO GO NEXT TIME.
OH DEAR...
THANKS FOR THE MEAL.
THANKS, GIRLS.
おでん
THE ODEN WAS GOOD, AND THE OLD STORIES WERE REALLY FASCI-NATING.
WHEW...
FLAG: OPEN SIGN: ALCOHOL / BEER / ODEN

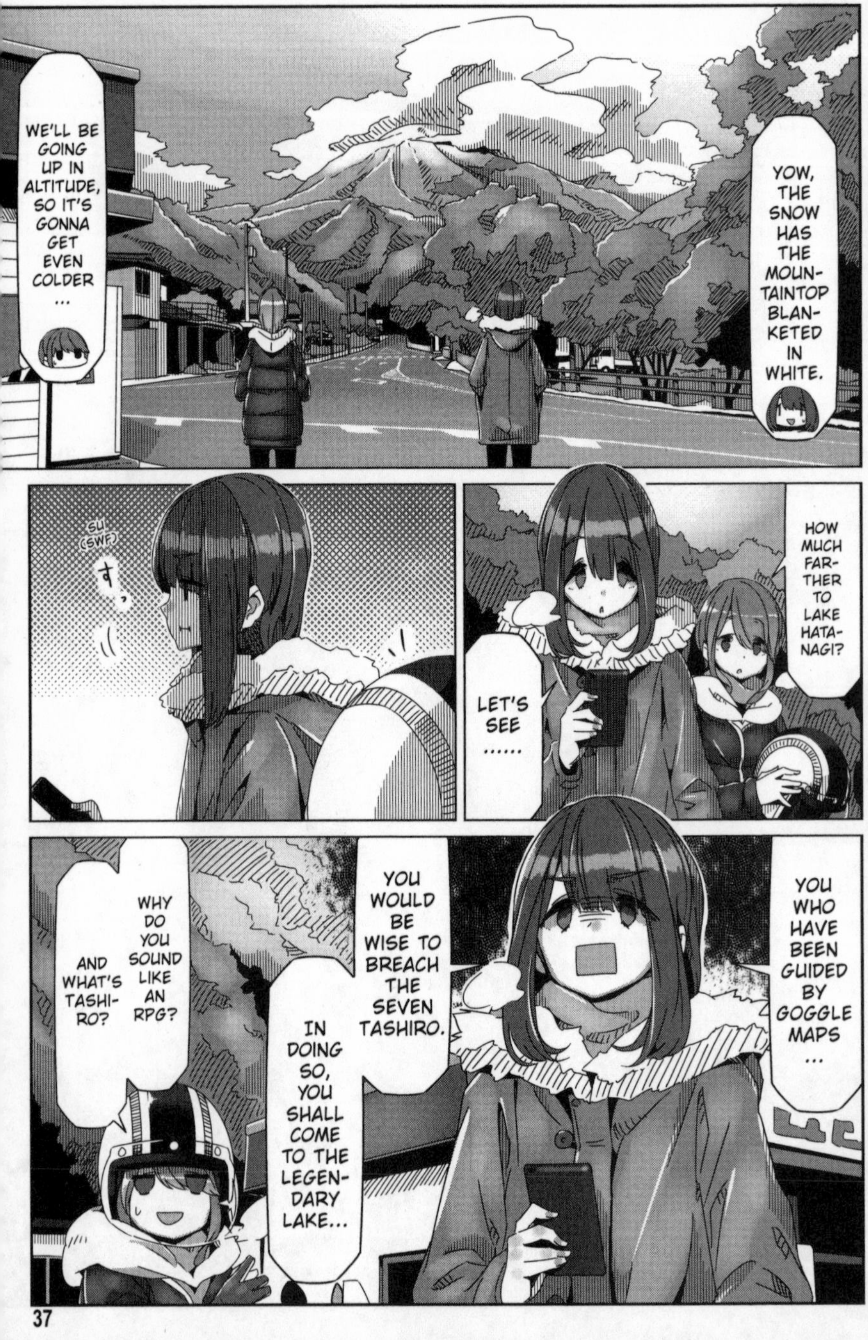
YOW, THE SNOW HAS THE MOUNTAINTOP BLANKETED IN WHITE.
WE'LL BE GOING UP IN ALTITUDE, SO IT'S GONNA GET EVEN COLDER ...
HOW MUCH FARTHER TO LAKE HATANAGI?
LET'S SEE ......
SU (SWF)
す
YOU WHO HAVE BEEN GUIDED BY GOGGLE MAPS ...
YOU WOULD BE WISE TO BREACH THE SEVEN TASHIRO.
IN DOING SO, YOU SHALL COME TO THE LEGENDARY LAKE...
WHY DO YOU SOUND LIKE AN RPG?
AND WHAT'S TASHIRO?

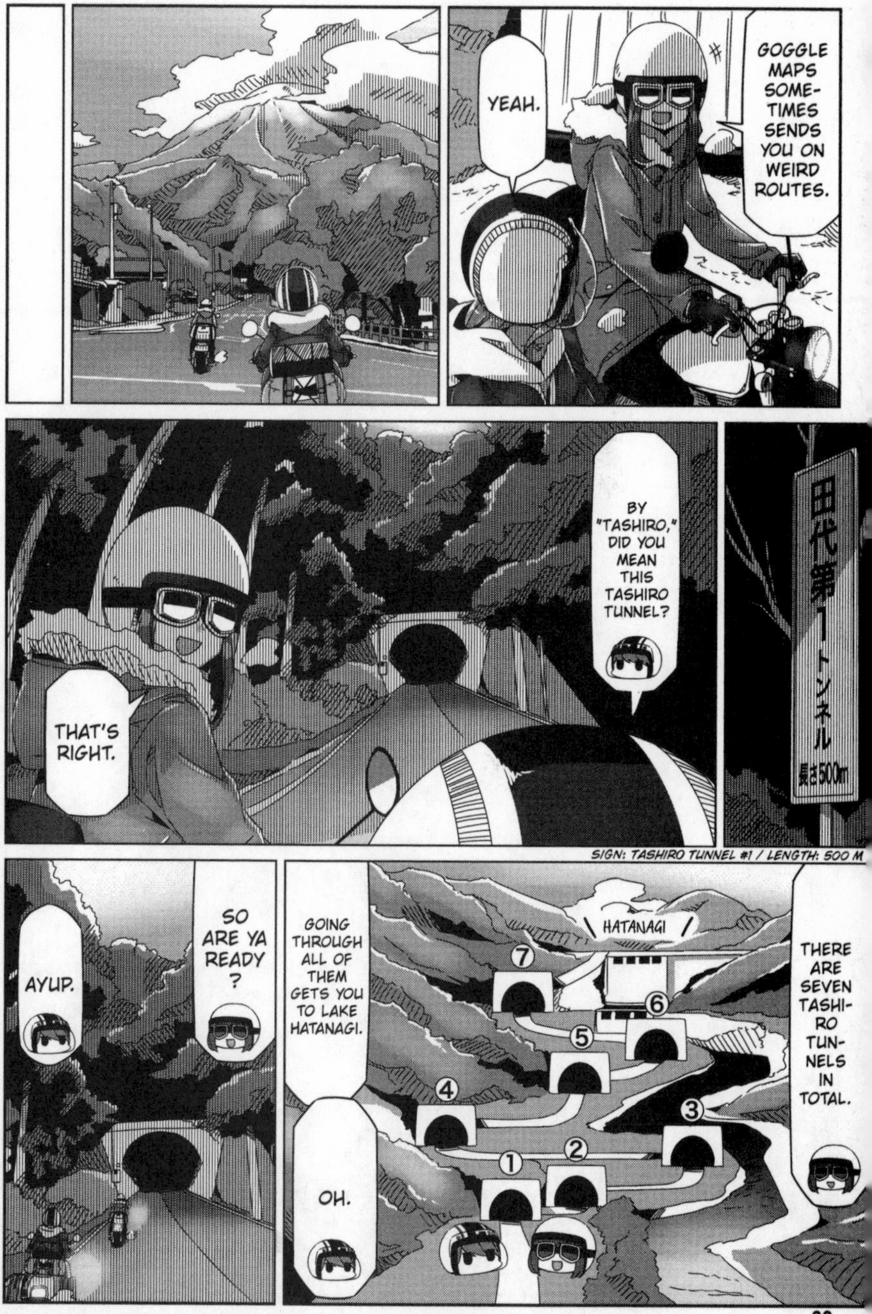
GOGGLE MAPS SOMETIMES SENDS YOU ON WEIRD ROUTES.
YEAH.
田代第1トンネル
長さ500m
BY "TASHIRO," DID YOU MEAN THIS TASHIRO TUNNEL?
THAT'S RIGHT.
SIGN: TASHIRO TUNNEL #1 / LENGTH: 500 M
THERE ARE SEVEN TASHIRO TUNNELS IN TOTAL.
HATANAGI
GOING THROUGH ALL OF THEM GETS YOU TO LAKE HATANAGI.
OH.
SO ARE YA READY?
AYUP.

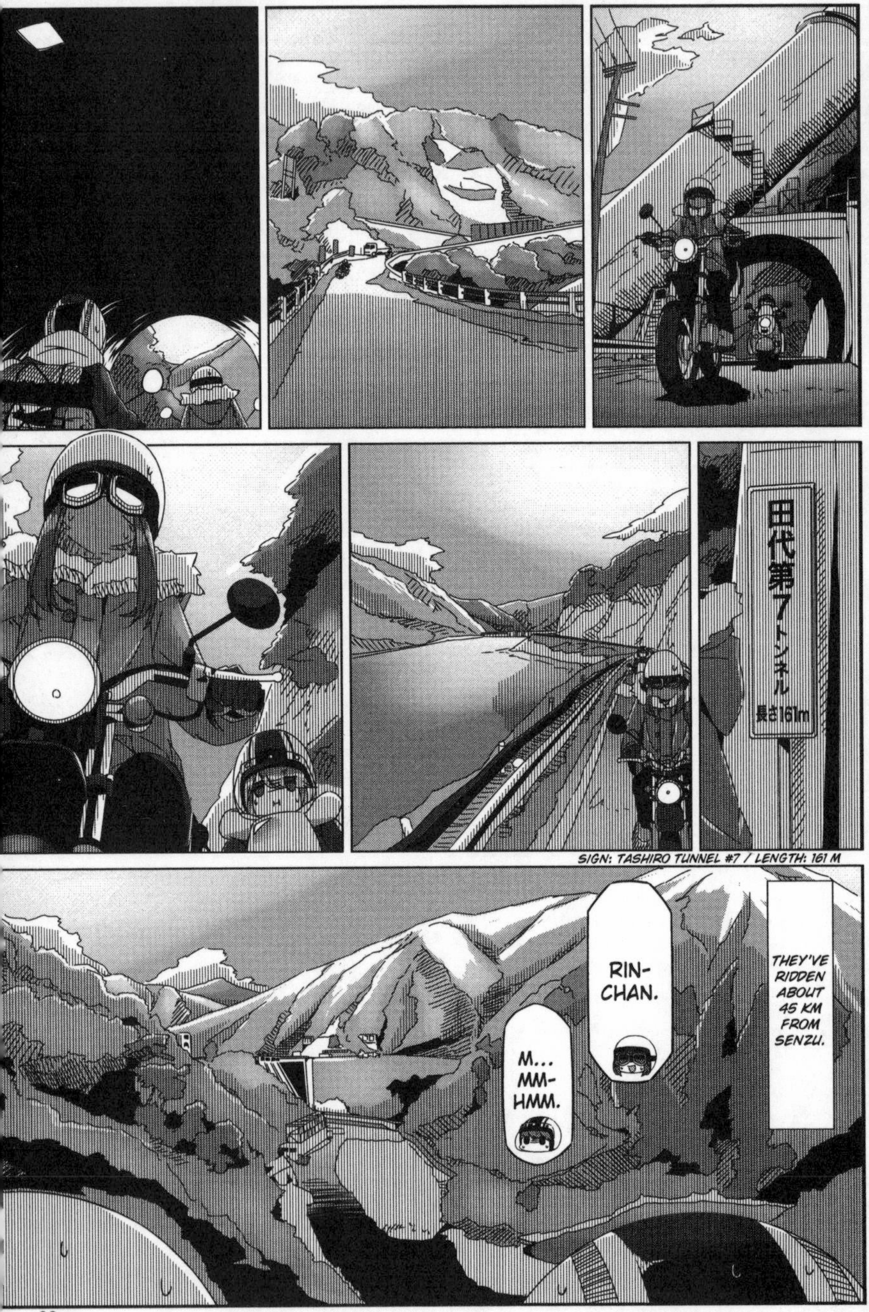
田代第7トンネル
長さ161m
SIGN: TASHIRO TUNNEL #7 / LENGTH: 161 M
THEY'VE RIDDEN ABOUT 45 KM FROM SENZU.
RIN-CHAN.
M... MM-HMM.

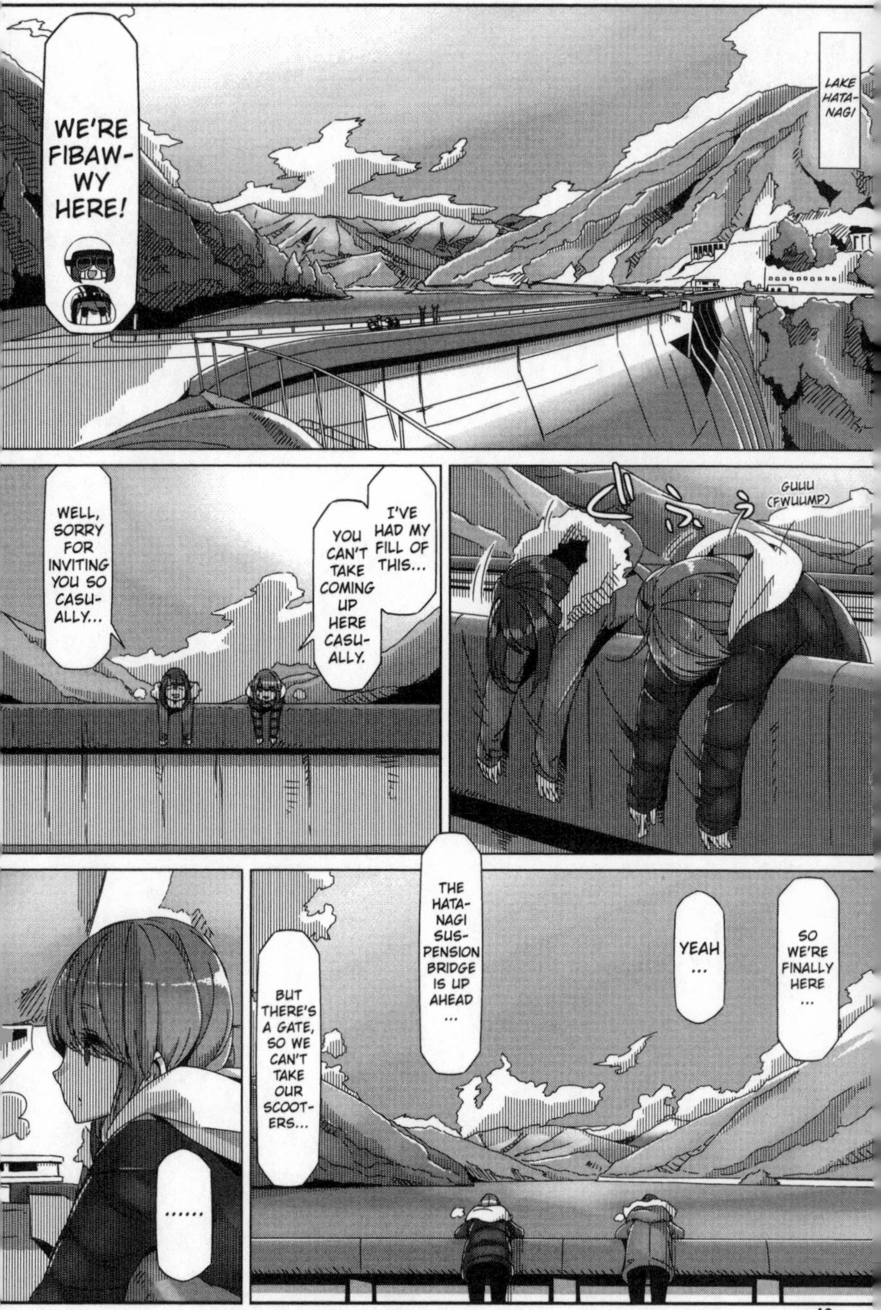
LAKE HATANAGI
WE'RE FIBAWWY HERE!
GUUU (FWUUMP)
I'VE HAD MY FILL OF THIS...
YOU CAN'T TAKE COMING UP HERE CASUALLY.
WELL, SORRY FOR INVITING YOU SO CASUALLY...
SO WE'RE FINALLY HERE...
YEAH...
THE HATANAGI SUSPENSION BRIDGE IS UP AHEAD...
BUT THERE'S A GATE, SO WE CAN'T TAKE OUR SCOOTERS...
......

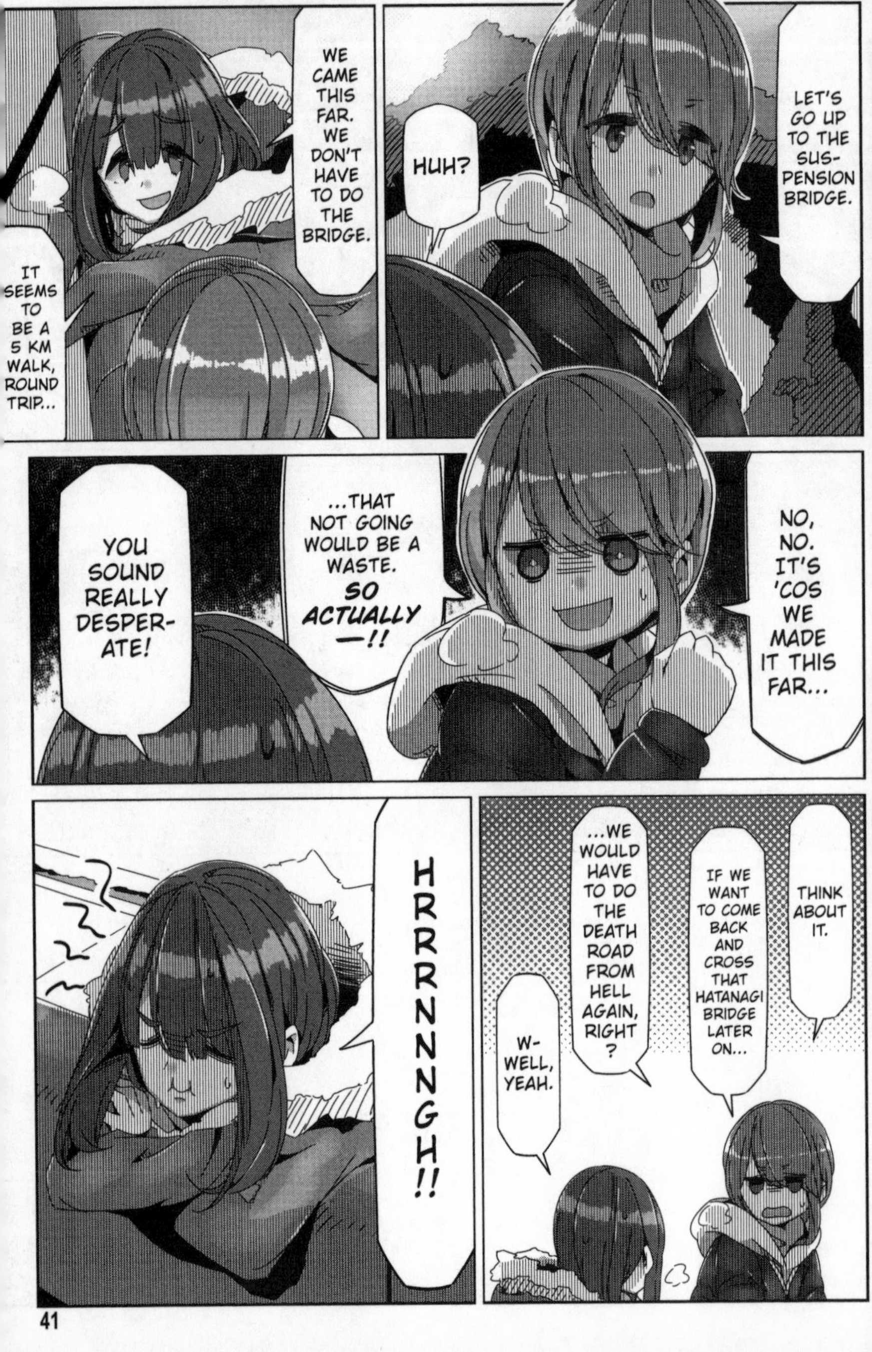
LET'S GO UP TO THE SUSPENSION BRIDGE.
HUH?
WE CAME THIS FAR. WE DON'T HAVE TO DO THE BRIDGE.
IT SEEMS TO BE A 5 KM WALK, ROUND TRIP...
NO, NO. IT'S 'COS WE MADE IT THIS FAR...
...THAT NOT GOING WOULD BE A WASTE. SO ACTUALLY—!!
YOU SOUND REALLY DESPERATE!
THINK ABOUT IT.
IF WE WANT TO COME BACK AND CROSS THAT HATANAGI BRIDGE LATER ON...
...WE WOULD HAVE TO DO THE DEATH ROAD FROM HELL AGAIN, RIGHT?
W-WELL, YEAH.
HRRRNNNGH!!

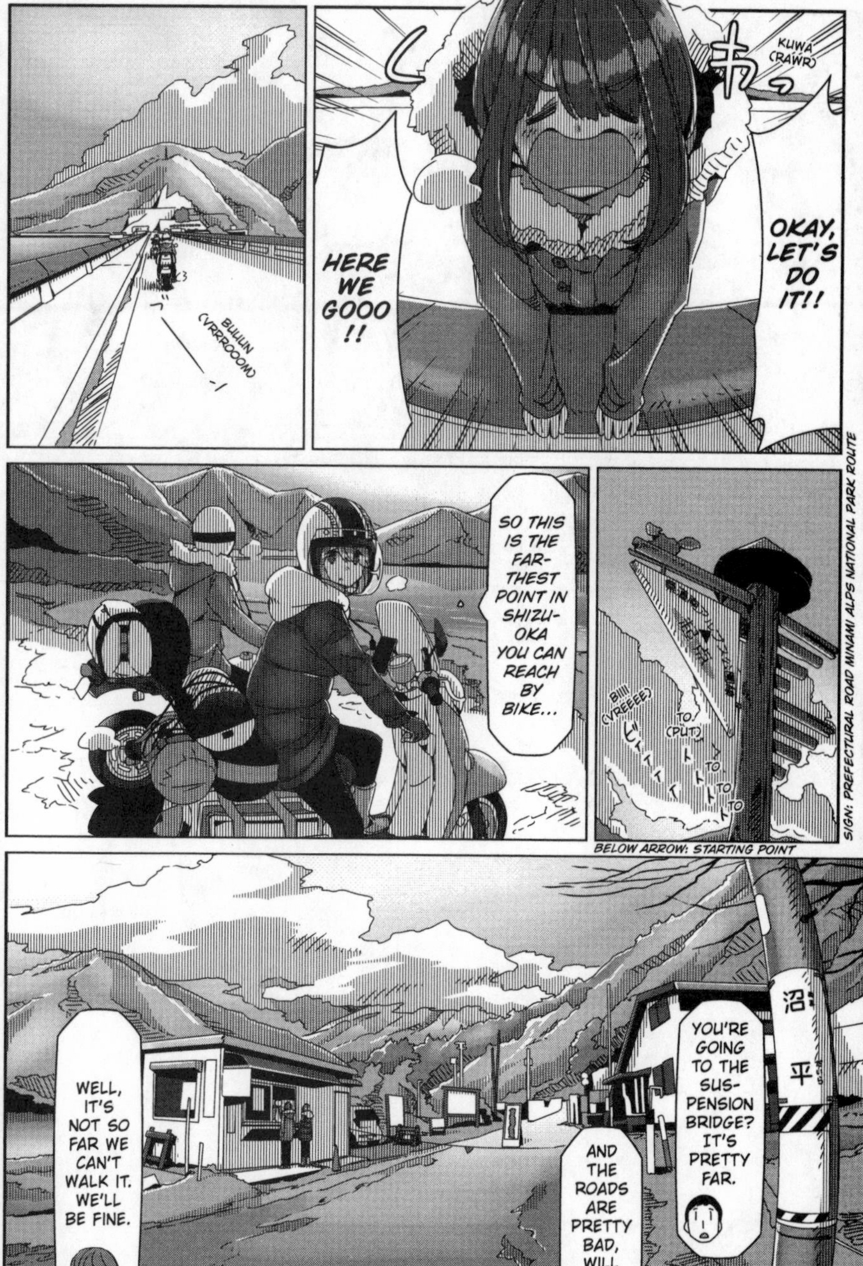
KUWA (RAWR)
OKAY, LET'S DO IT!!
HERE WE GOOO!!
BULUN (VRRROOOM)
SIGN: PREFECTURAL ROAD MINAMI ALPS NATIONAL PARK ROUTE
BELOW ARROW: STARTING POINT
BIIII (VREEEE)
TO (PUT) TO TO TO
SO THIS IS THE FAR-THEST POINT IN SHIZU-OKA YOU CAN REACH BY BIKE...
沼平
YOU'RE GOING TO THE SUS-PENSION BRIDGE? IT'S PRETTY FAR.
AND THE ROADS ARE PRETTY BAD, WILL YOU BE OKAY?
WELL, IT'S NOT SO FAR WE CAN'T WALK IT. WE'LL BE FINE.
SIGN: NUMADAIRA

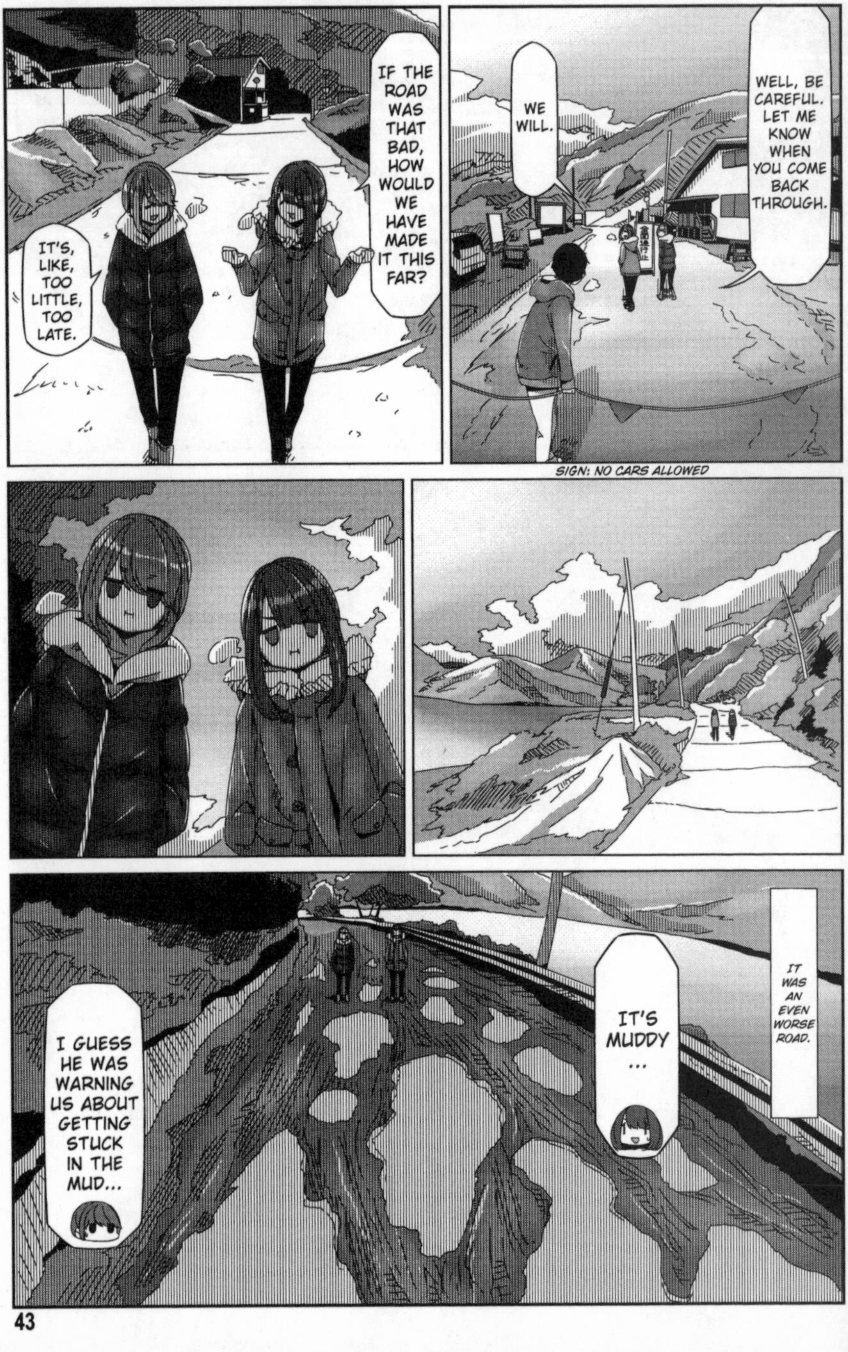
WELL, BE CAREFUL. LET ME KNOW WHEN YOU COME BACK THROUGH.
WE WILL.
SIGN: NO CARS ALLOWED
IF THE ROAD WAS THAT BAD, HOW WOULD WE HAVE MADE IT THIS FAR?
IT'S, LIKE, TOO LITTLE, TOO LATE.
IT WAS AN EVEN WORSE ROAD.
IT'S MUDDY...
I GUESS HE WAS WARNING US ABOUT GETTING STUCK IN THE MUD...

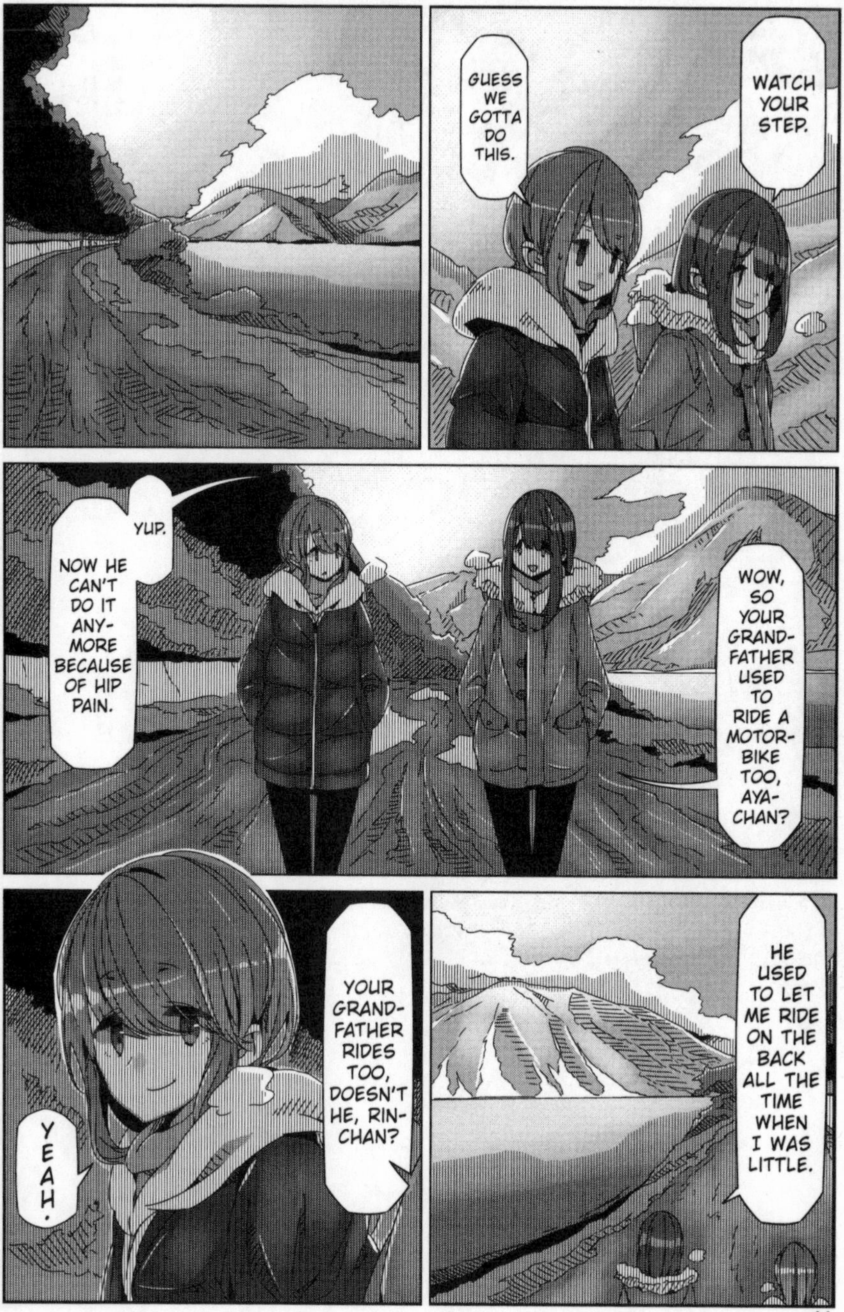
WATCH YOUR STEP.
GUESS WE GOTTA DO THIS.
WOW, SO YOUR GRANDFATHER USED TO RIDE A MOTORBIKE TOO, AYA-CHAN?
YUP.
NOW HE CAN'T DO IT ANYMORE BECAUSE OF HIP PAIN.
HE USED TO LET ME RIDE ON THE BACK ALL THE TIME WHEN I WAS LITTLE.
YOUR GRANDFATHER RIDES TOO, DOESN'T HE, RIN-CHAN?
YEAH.

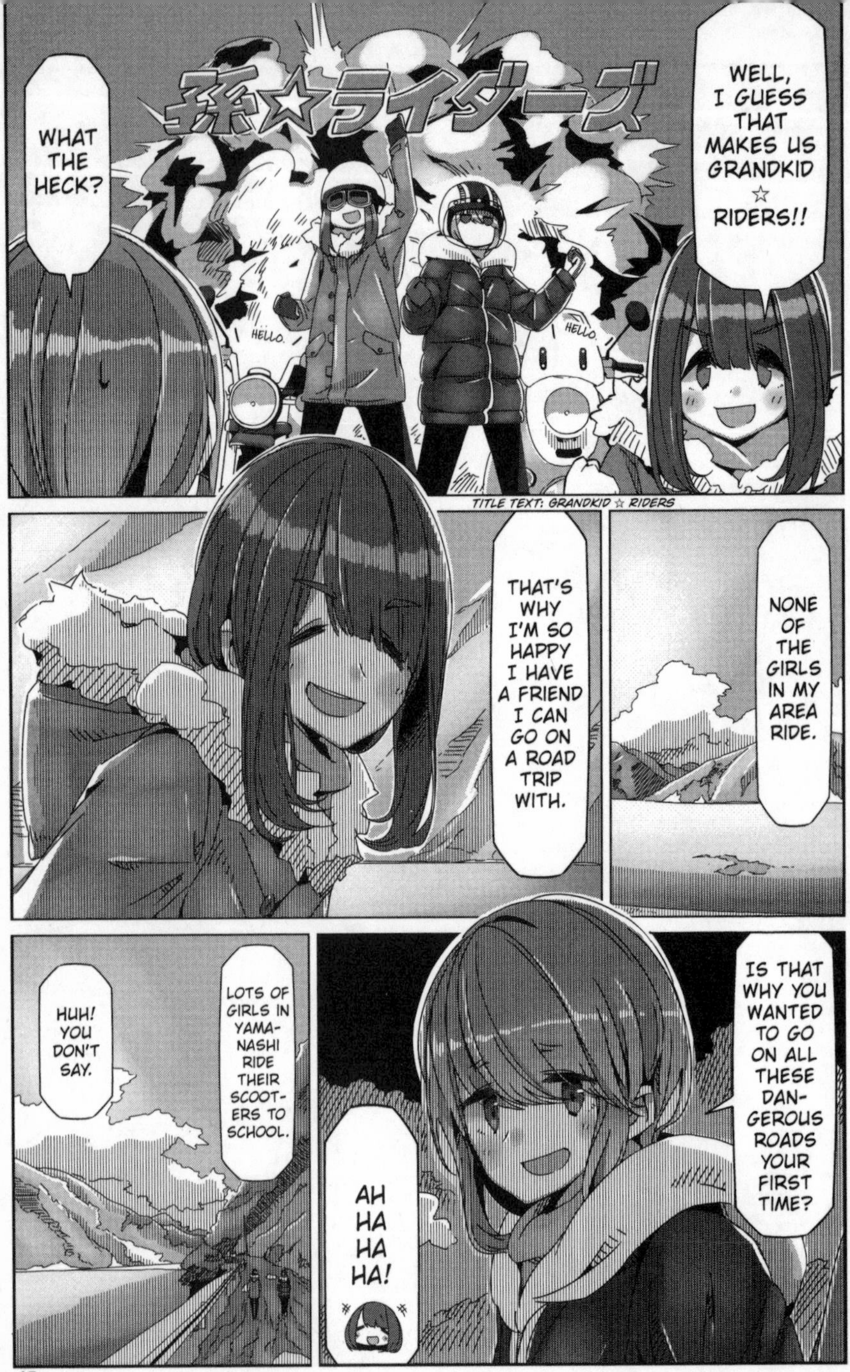
WELL, I GUESS THAT MAKES US GRANDKID ☆ RIDERS!!
孫☆ライダーズ
HELLO.
HELLO.
WHAT THE HECK?
TITLE TEXT: GRANDKID ☆ RIDERS
NONE OF THE GIRLS IN MY AREA RIDE.
THAT'S WHY I'M SO HAPPY I HAVE A FRIEND I CAN GO ON A ROAD TRIP WITH.
IS THAT WHY YOU WANTED TO GO ON ALL THESE DAN-GEROUS ROADS YOUR FIRST TIME?
AH HA HA HA!
LOTS OF GIRLS IN YAMA-NASHI RIDE THEIR SCOOT-ERS TO SCHOOL.
HUH! YOU DON'T SAY.

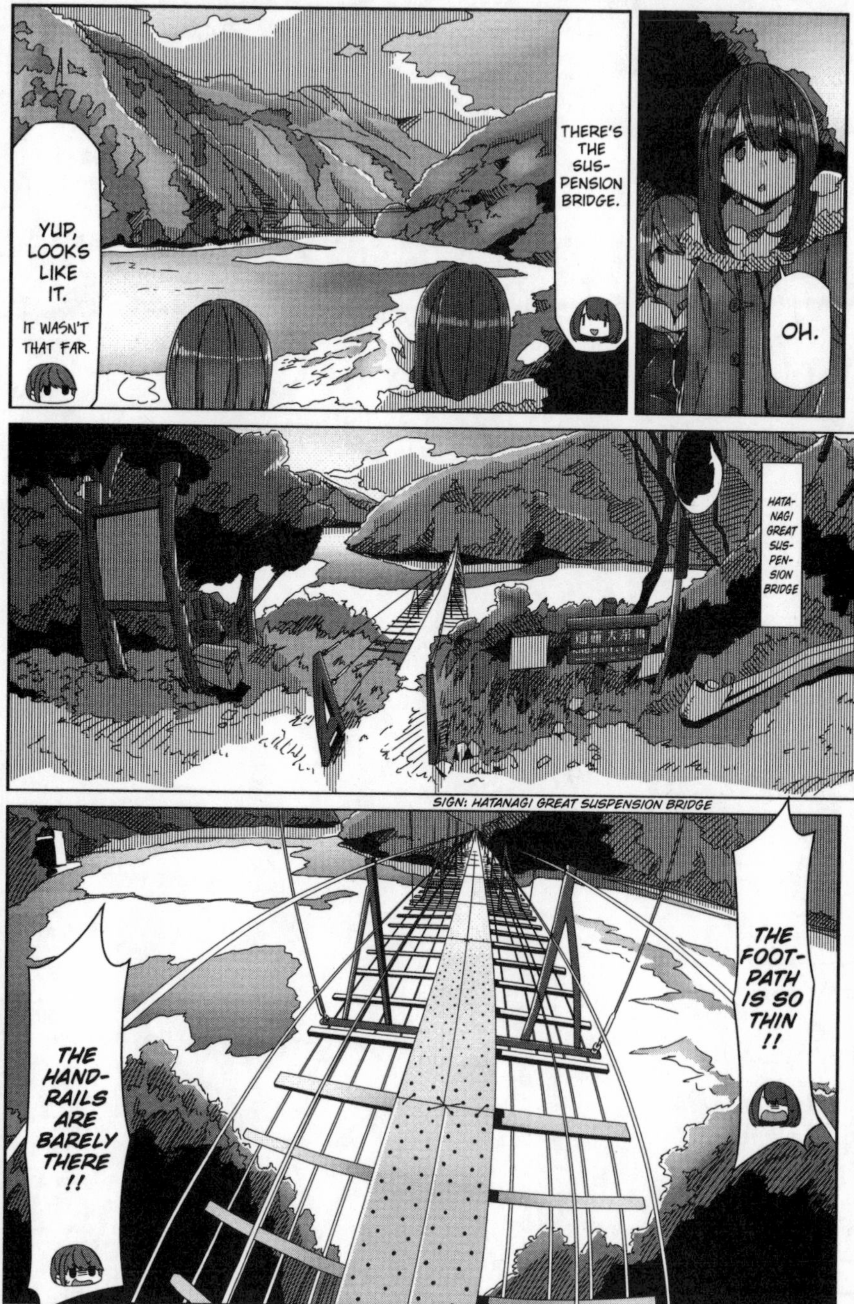
OH.
THERE'S THE SUS-PENSION BRIDGE.
YUP, LOOKS LIKE IT.
IT WASN'T THAT FAR.
HATA-NAGI GREAT SUS-PEN-SION BRIDGE
SIGN: HATANAGI GREAT SUSPENSION BRIDGE
THE FOOT-PATH IS SO THIN!!
THE HAND-RAILS ARE BARELY THERE!!

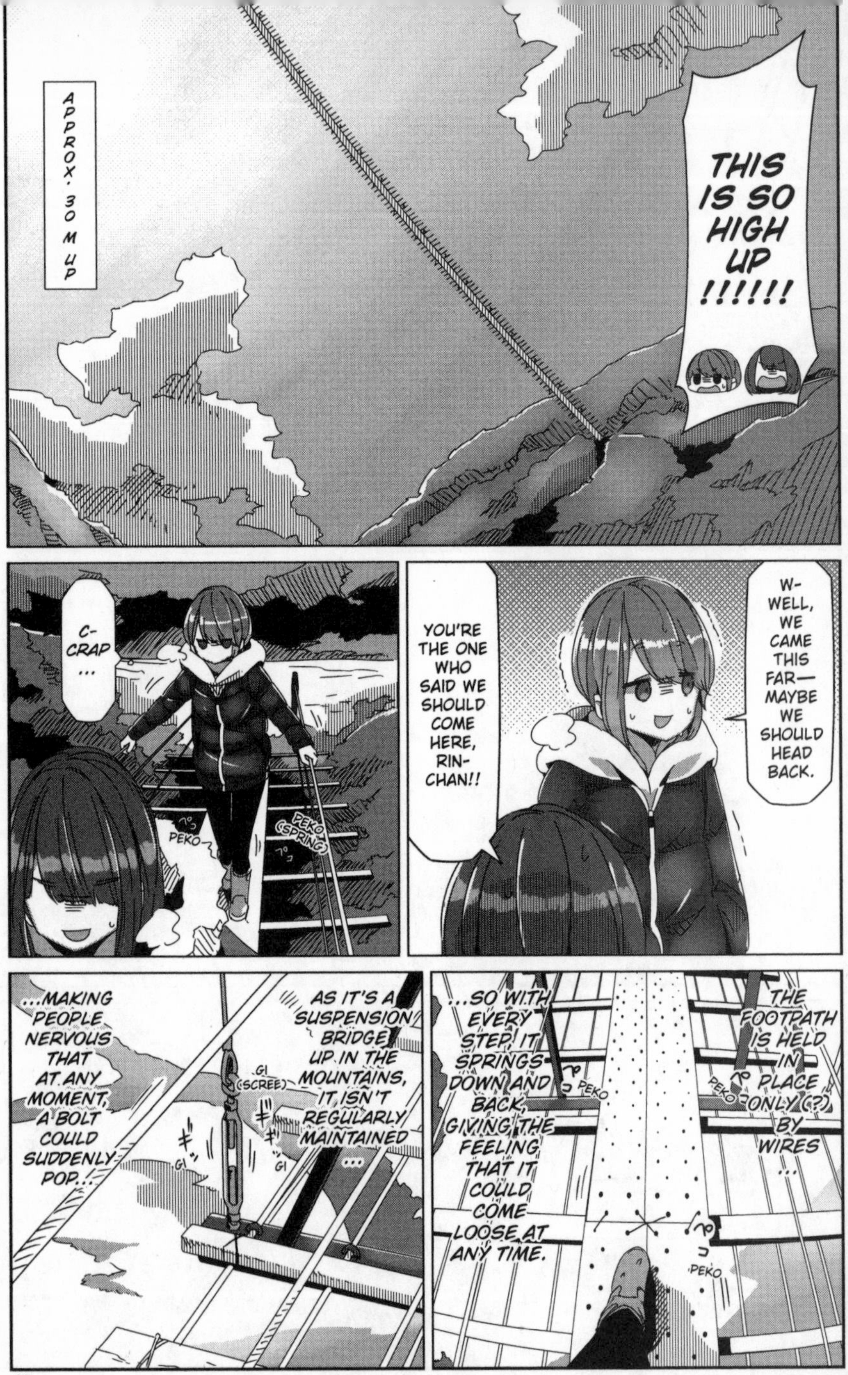
THIS IS SO HIGH UP!!!!!!
APPROX. 30 M UP
W-WELL, WE CAME THIS FAR—MAYBE WE SHOULD HEAD BACK.
YOU'RE THE ONE WHO SAID WE SHOULD COME HERE, RIN-CHAN!!
C-CRAP...
PEKO (SPRING)
PEKO
THE FOOTPATH IS HELD IN PLACE ONLY (?) BY WIRES...
PEKO
...SO WITH EVERY STEP, IT SPRINGS DOWN AND BACK, GIVING THE FEELING THAT IT COULD COME LOOSE AT ANY TIME.
PEKO
PEKO
AS IT'S A SUSPENSION BRIDGE UP IN THE MOUNTAINS, IT ISN'T REGULARLY MAINTAINED...
GI (SCREE)
GI
GI
...MAKING PEOPLE NERVOUS THAT AT ANY MOMENT, A BOLT COULD SUDDENLY POP...!

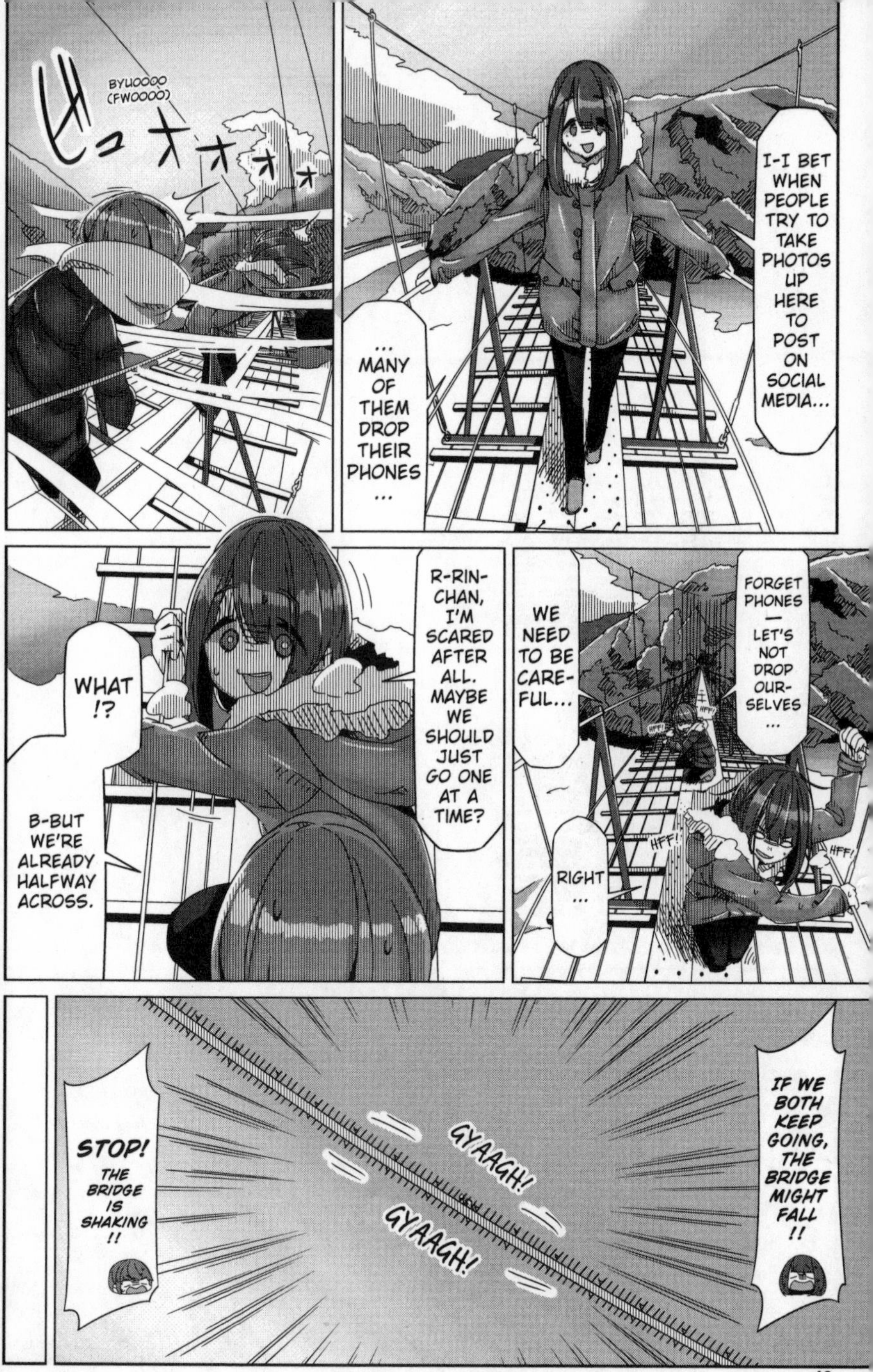
I-I BET WHEN PEOPLE TRY TO TAKE PHOTOS UP HERE TO POST ON SOCIAL MEDIA...
...MANY OF THEM DROP THEIR PHONES...
BYUOOOO (FWOOOO)
FORGET PHONES—LET'S NOT DROP OURSELVES...
WE NEED TO BE CAREFUL...
RIGHT...
HFF!
HFF!
HFF!
HFF!
R-RIN-CHAN, I'M SCARED AFTER ALL. MAYBE WE SHOULD JUST GO ONE AT A TIME?
WHAT!?
B-BUT WE'RE ALREADY HALFWAY ACROSS.
IF WE BOTH KEEP GOING, THE BRIDGE MIGHT FALL!!
GYAAGH!
GYAAGH!
STOP! THE BRIDGE IS SHAKING!!

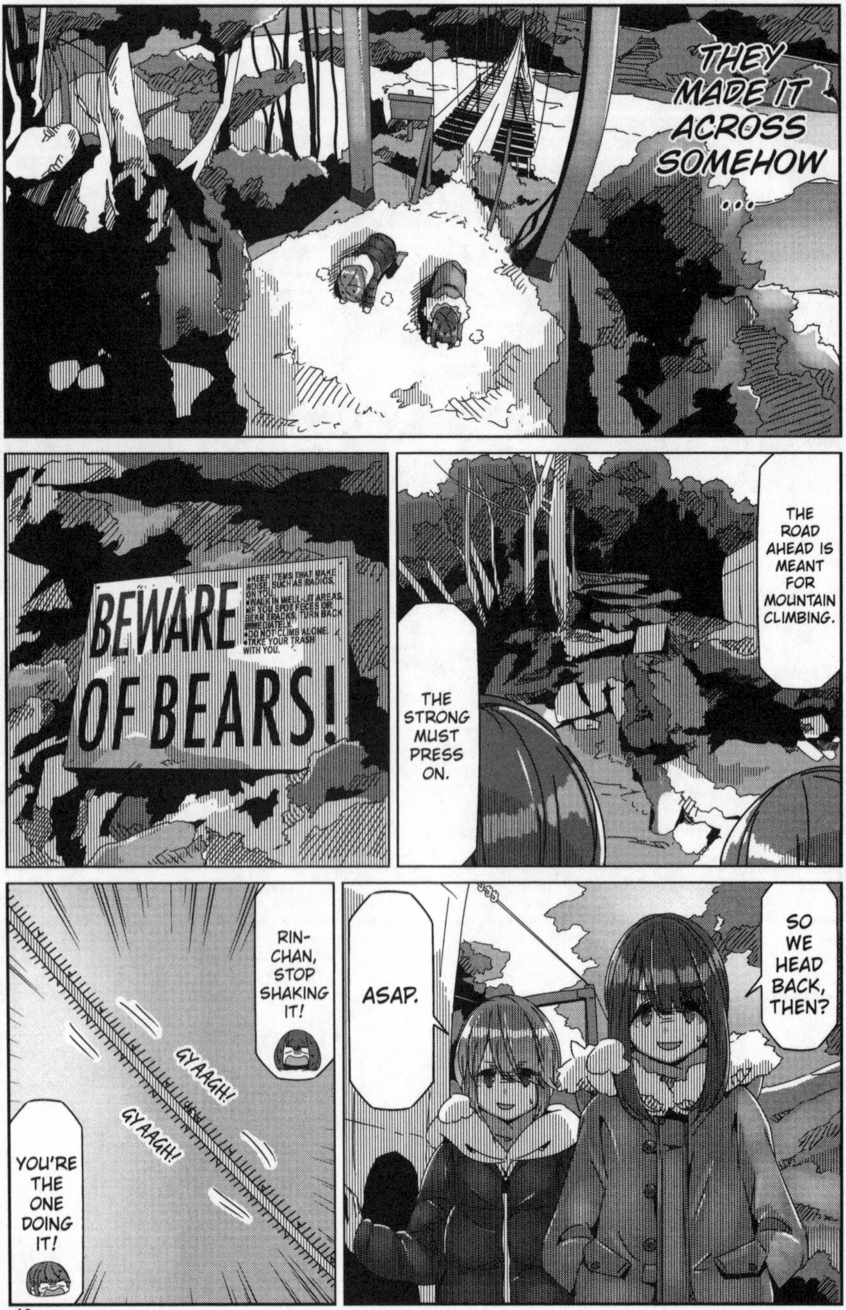
THEY MADE IT ACROSS SOMEHOW...
THE ROAD AHEAD IS MEANT FOR MOUNTAIN CLIMBING.
THE STRONG MUST PRESS ON.
BEWARE OF BEARS!
●KEEP ITEMS THAT MAKE NOISE, SUCH AS RADIOS, ON YOU.
●WALK IN WELL-LIT AREAS.
●IF YOU SPOT FECES OR BEAR TRACKS, TURN BACK IMMEDIATELY.
●DO NOT CLIMB ALONE.
●TAKE YOUR TRASH WITH YOU.
SO WE HEAD BACK, THEN?
ASAP.
RIN-CHAN, STOP SHAKING IT!
GYAAGH!
GYAAGH!
YOU'RE THE ONE DOING IT!

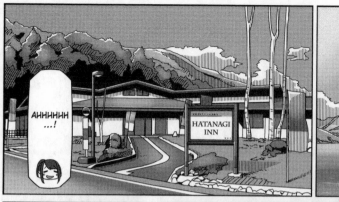

AHHHHHH...!

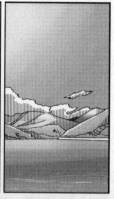

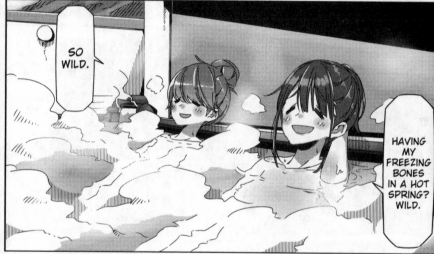

SO WILD.

HAVING MY FREEZING BONES IN A HOT SPRING? WILD.

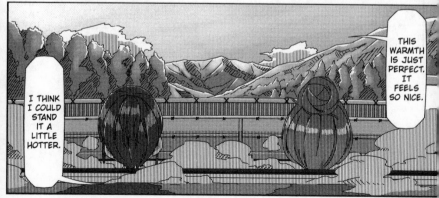

THIS WARMTH IS JUST PERFECT. IT FEELS SO NICE.

I THINK I COULD STAND IT A LITTLE HOTTER.

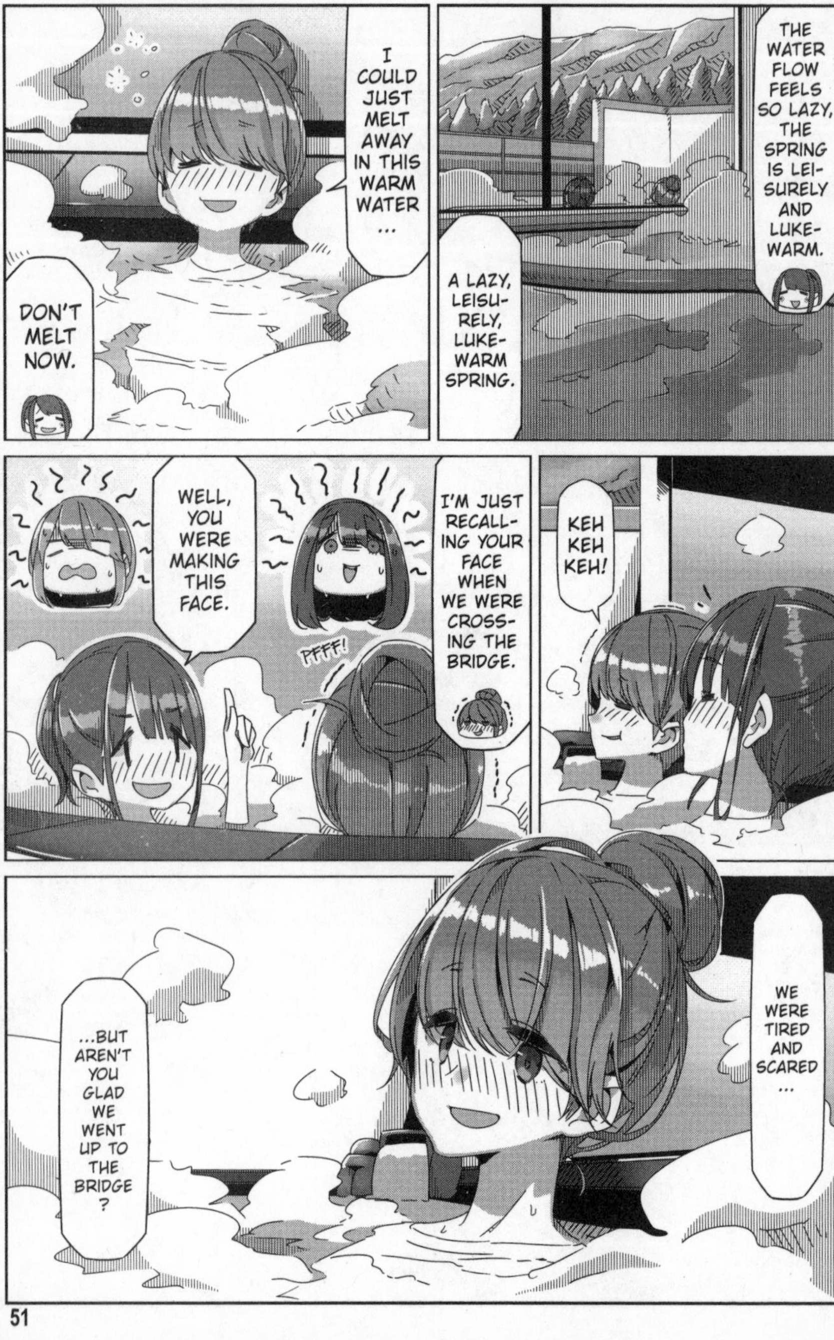
THE WATER FLOW FEELS SO LAZY, THE SPRING IS LEISURELY AND LUKEWARM.
A LAZY, LEISURELY, LUKEWARM SPRING.
I COULD JUST MELT AWAY IN THIS WARM WATER...
DON'T MELT NOW.
KEH KEH KEH!
I'M JUST RECALLING YOUR FACE WHEN WE WERE CROSSING THE BRIDGE.
PFFF!
WELL, YOU WERE MAKING THIS FACE.
WE WERE TIRED AND SCARED...
...BUT AREN'T YOU GLAD WE WENT UP TO THE BRIDGE?

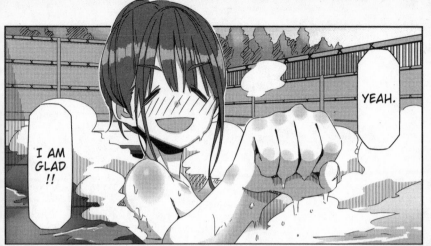

YEAH.
I AM GLAD!!
AHHHH ———!
GOING BACK IS GONNA BE A PAIN!!
34 KM UNTIL THE CAMP-SITE

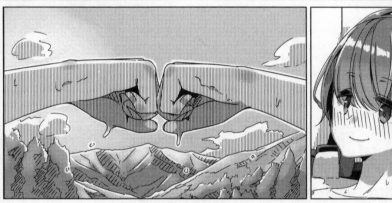

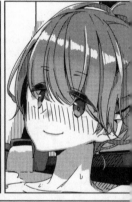

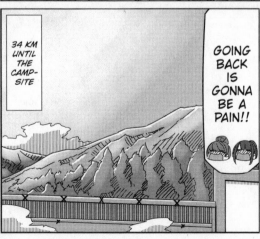

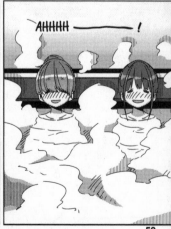

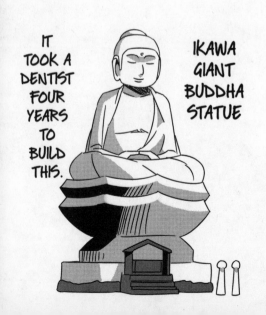

IKAWA GIANT BUDDHA STATUE
IT TOOK A DENTIST FOUR YEARS TO BUILD THIS.

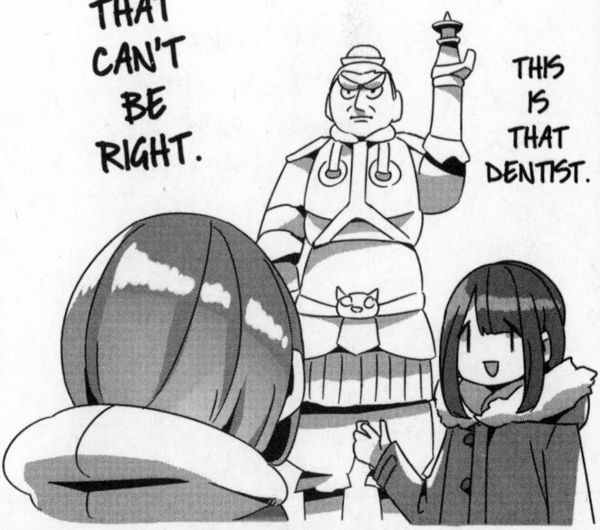
THIS IS THAT DENTIST.
THAT CAN'T BE RIGHT.

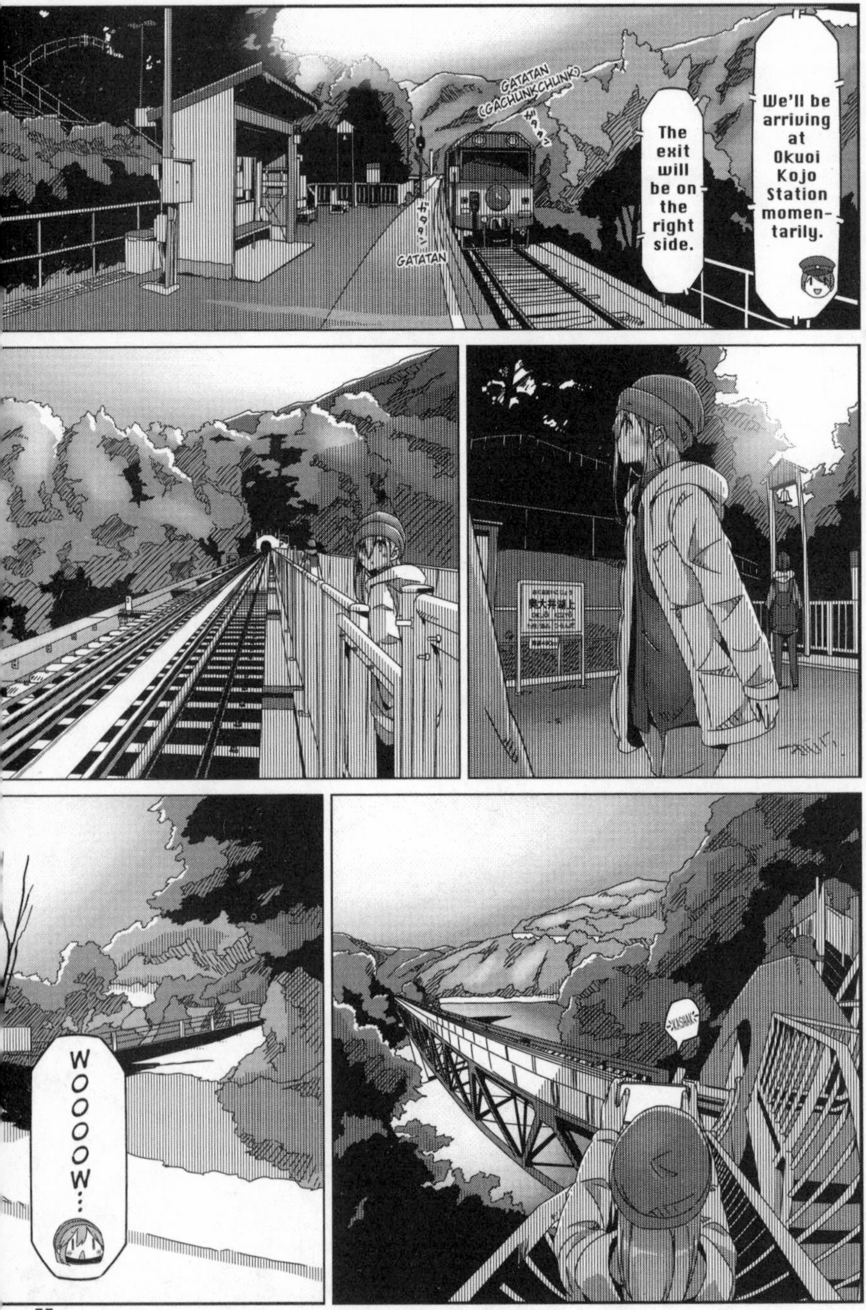
We'll be arriving at Okuoi Kojo Station momentarily.
The exit will be on the right side.
GATATAN (GACHUNKCHUNK)
GATATAN
KASHAK
WOOOOOW...

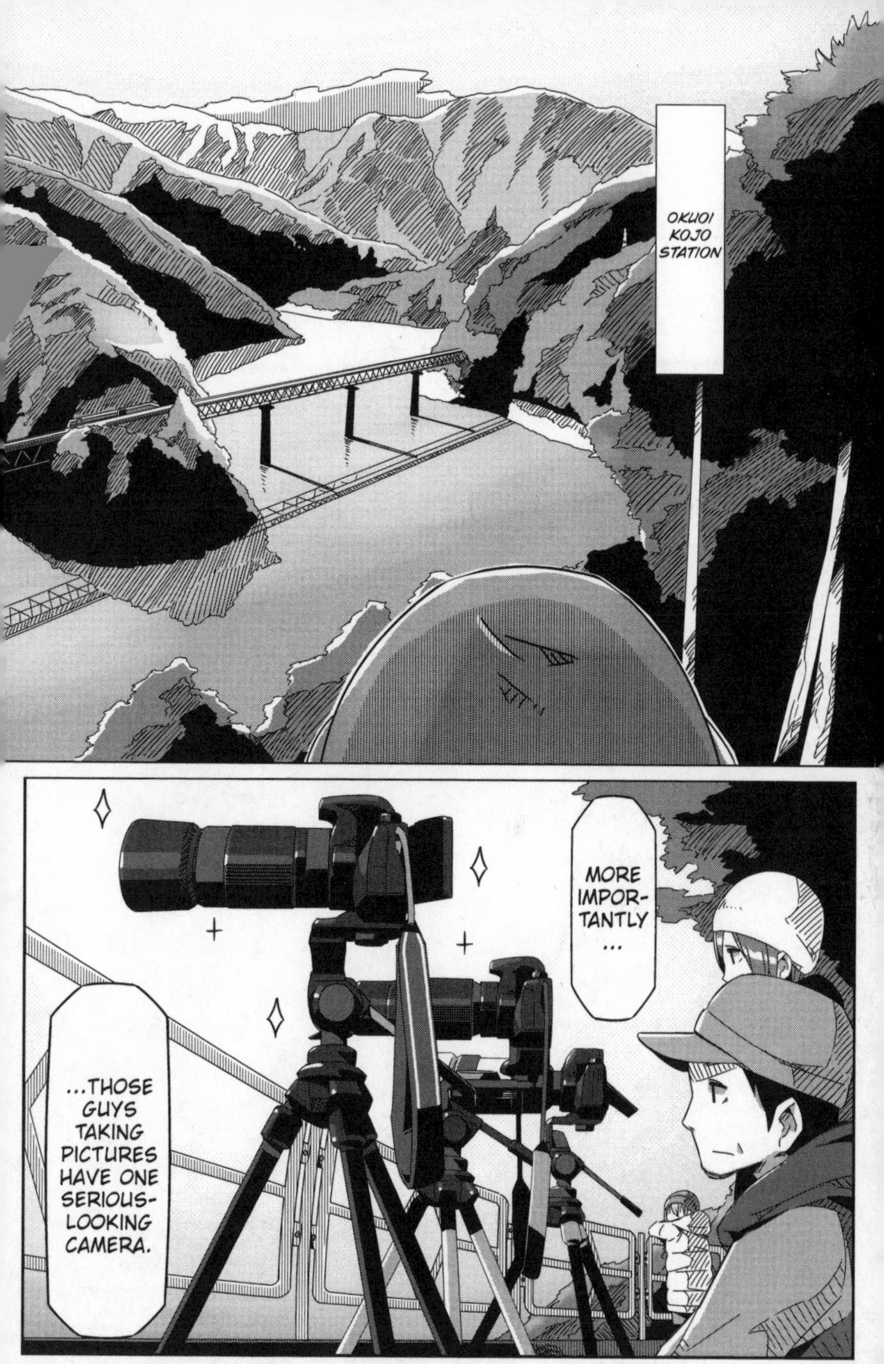
OKUOI KOJO STATION
MORE IMPORTANTLY ...
...THOSE GUYS TAKING PICTURES HAVE ONE SERIOUS-LOOKING CAMERA.

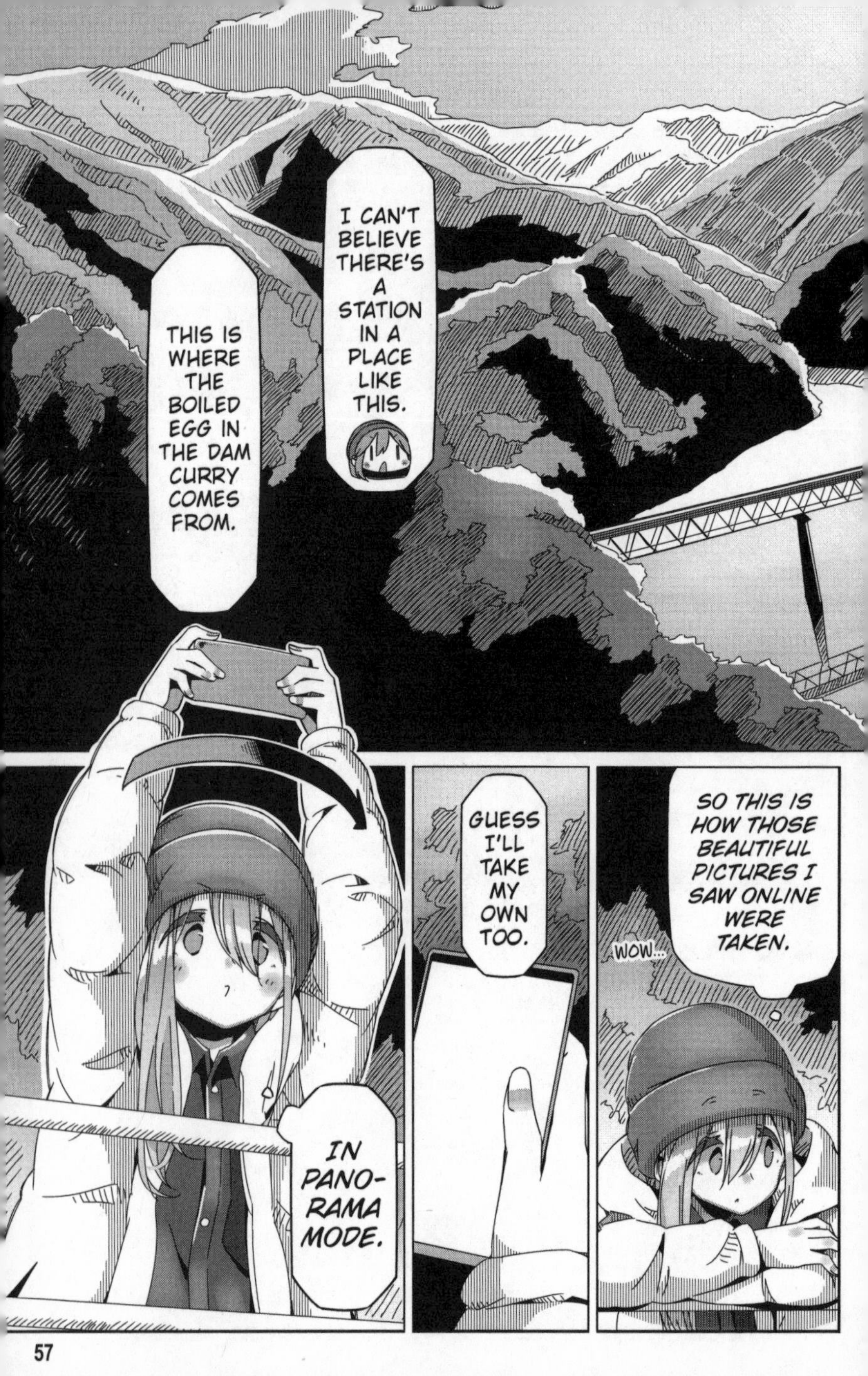
I CAN'T BELIEVE THERE'S A STATION IN A PLACE LIKE THIS.
THIS IS WHERE THE BOILED EGG IN THE DAM CURRY COMES FROM.
SO THIS IS HOW THOSE BEAUTIFUL PICTURES I SAW ONLINE WERE TAKEN.
WOW...
GUESS I'LL TAKE MY OWN TOO.
IN PANO-RAMA MODE.

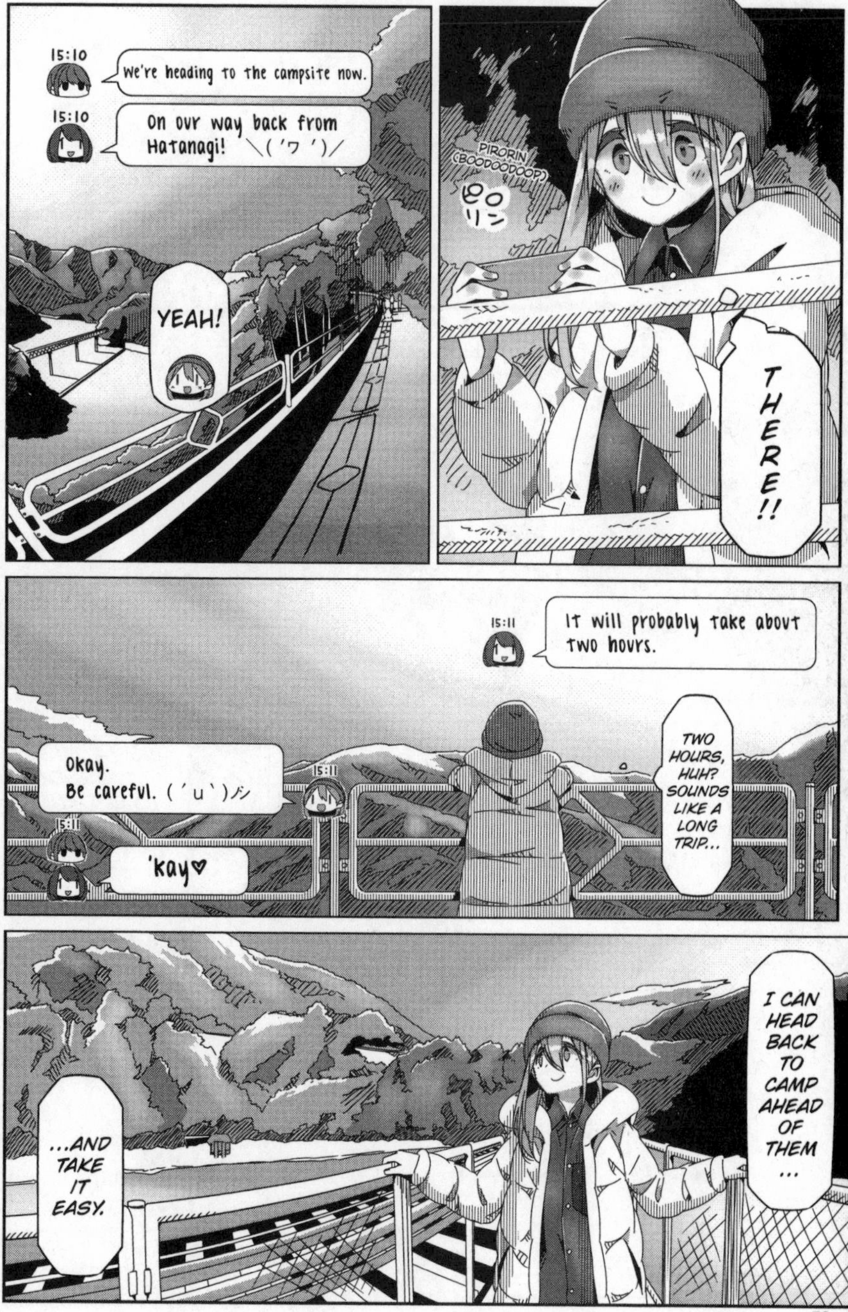
PIRORIN (BOODOODOOP)
ピロリン
THERE!!
15:10
We're heading to the campsite now.
15:10
On our way back from Hatanagi! \(’ワ’)/
YEAH!
15:11
It will probably take about two hours.
TWO HOURS, HUH? SOUNDS LIKE A LONG TRIP...
15:11
Okay. Be careful. (’u`)ノシ
15:11
'kay♡
I CAN HEAD BACK TO CAMP AHEAD OF THEM...
...AND TAKE IT EASY.

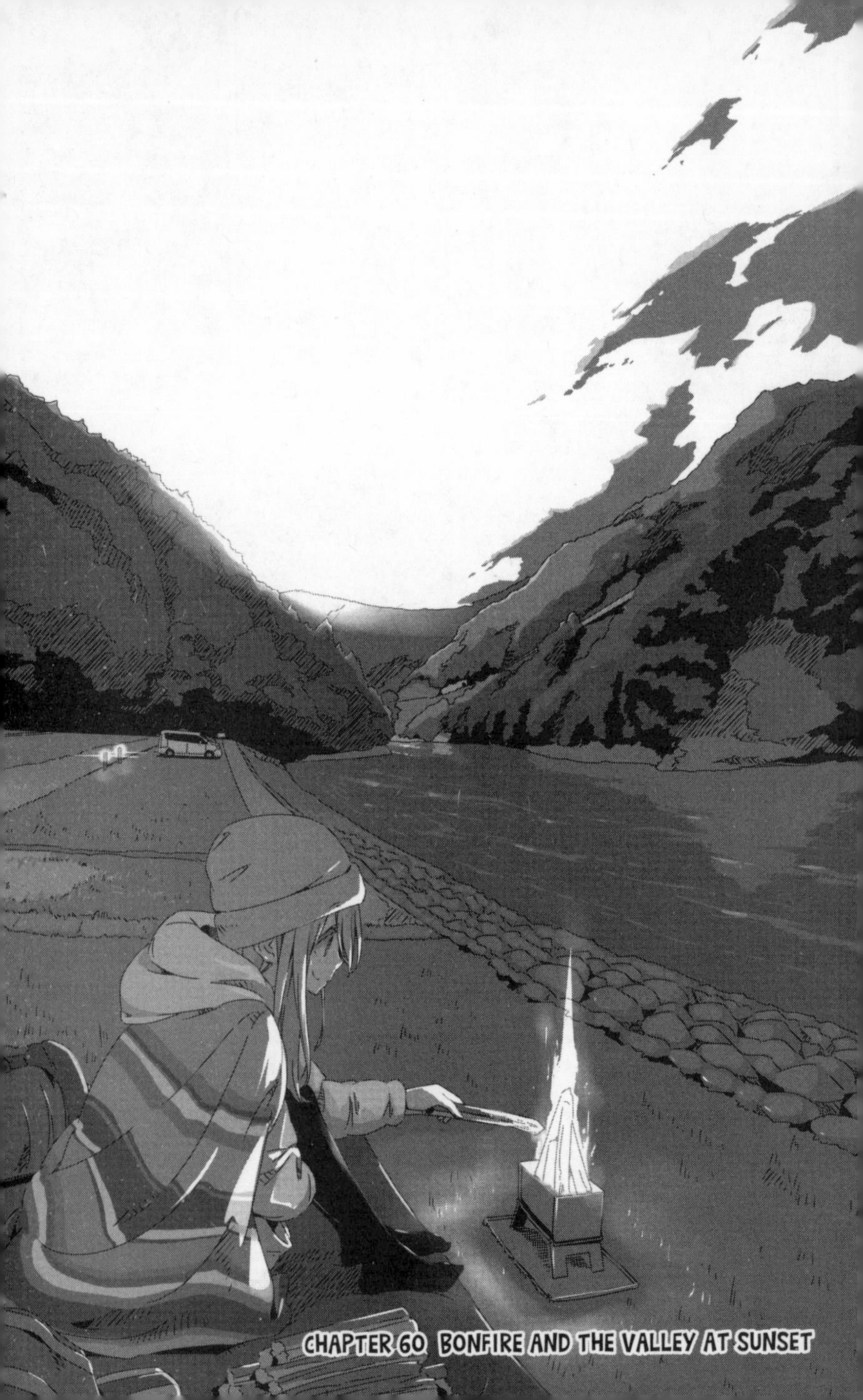
CHAPTER 60 BONFIRE AND THE VALLEY AT SUNSET

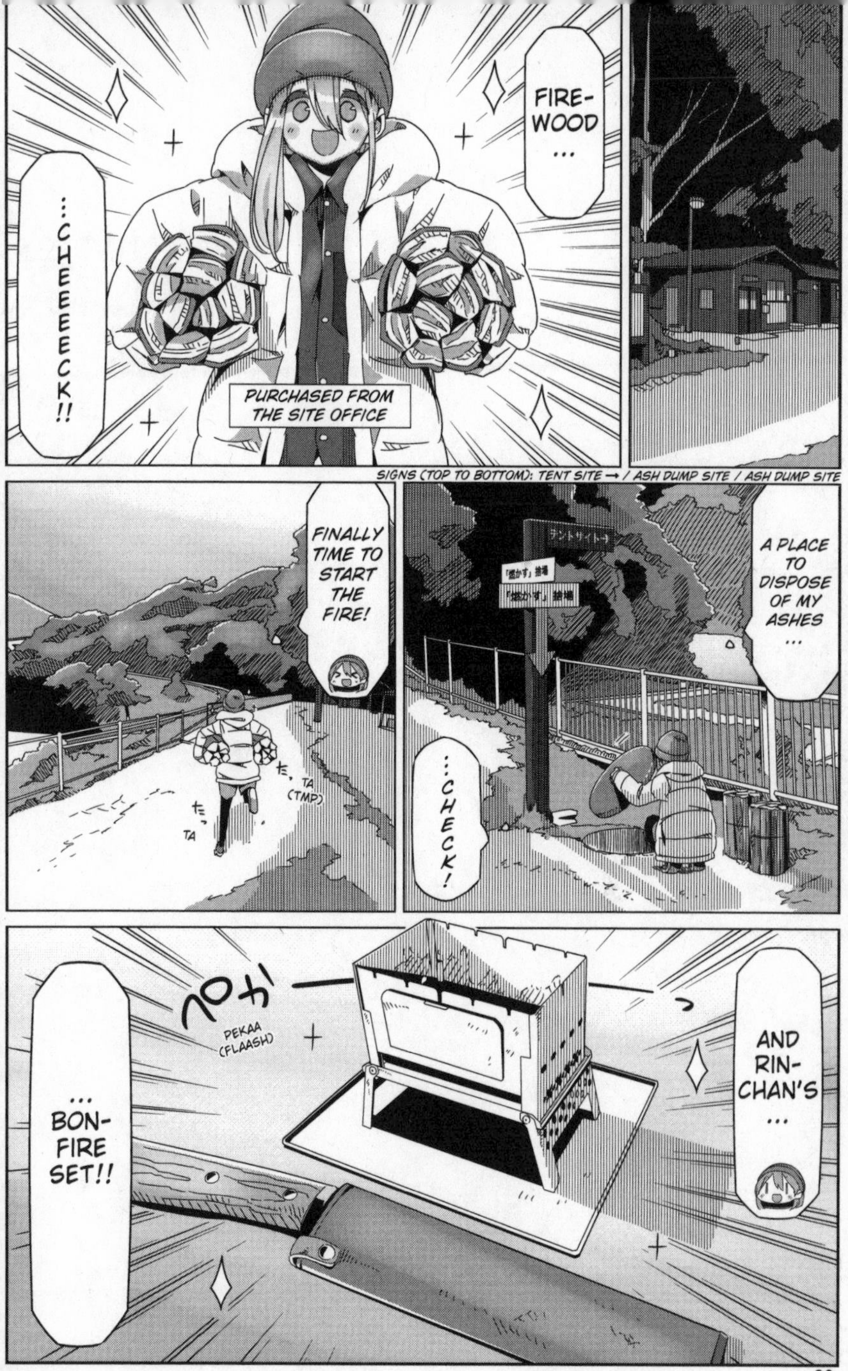
FIRE-WOOD ...
...CHEEEEECK!!
PURCHASED FROM THE SITE OFFICE
SIGNS (TOP TO BOTTOM): TENT SITE → / ASH DUMP SITE / ASH DUMP SITE
A PLACE TO DISPOSE OF MY ASHES ...
...CHECK!
FINALLY TIME TO START THE FIRE!
TA (TMP)
TA
AND RIN-CHAN'S ...
PEKAA (FLAASH)
... BON-FIRE SET!!

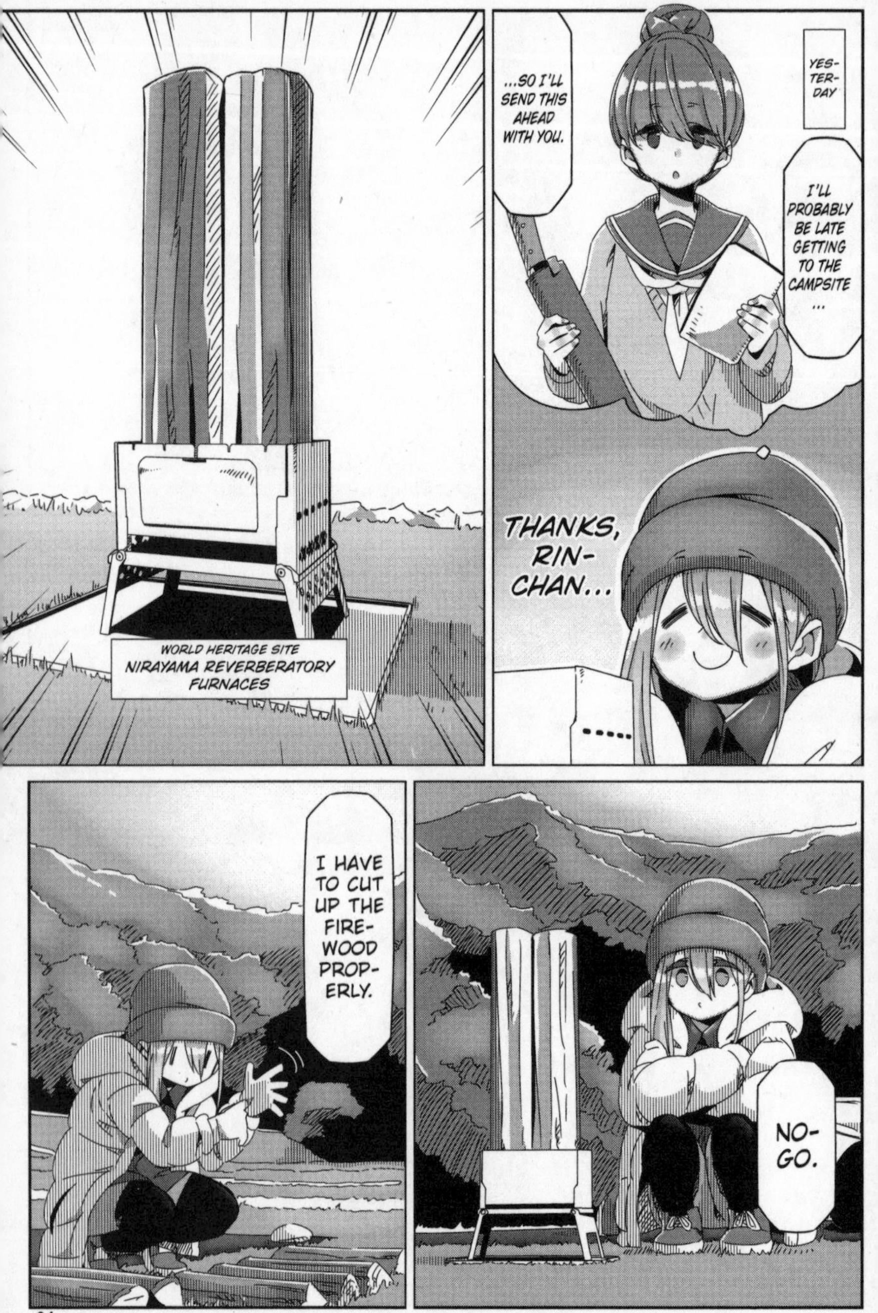
YESTERDAY
I'LL PROBABLY BE LATE GETTING TO THE CAMPSITE...
...SO I'LL SEND THIS AHEAD WITH YOU.
THANKS, RIN-CHAN...
WORLD HERITAGE SITE
NIRAYAMA REVERBERATORY FURNACES
NO-GO.
I HAVE TO CUT UP THE FIREWOOD PROPERLY.

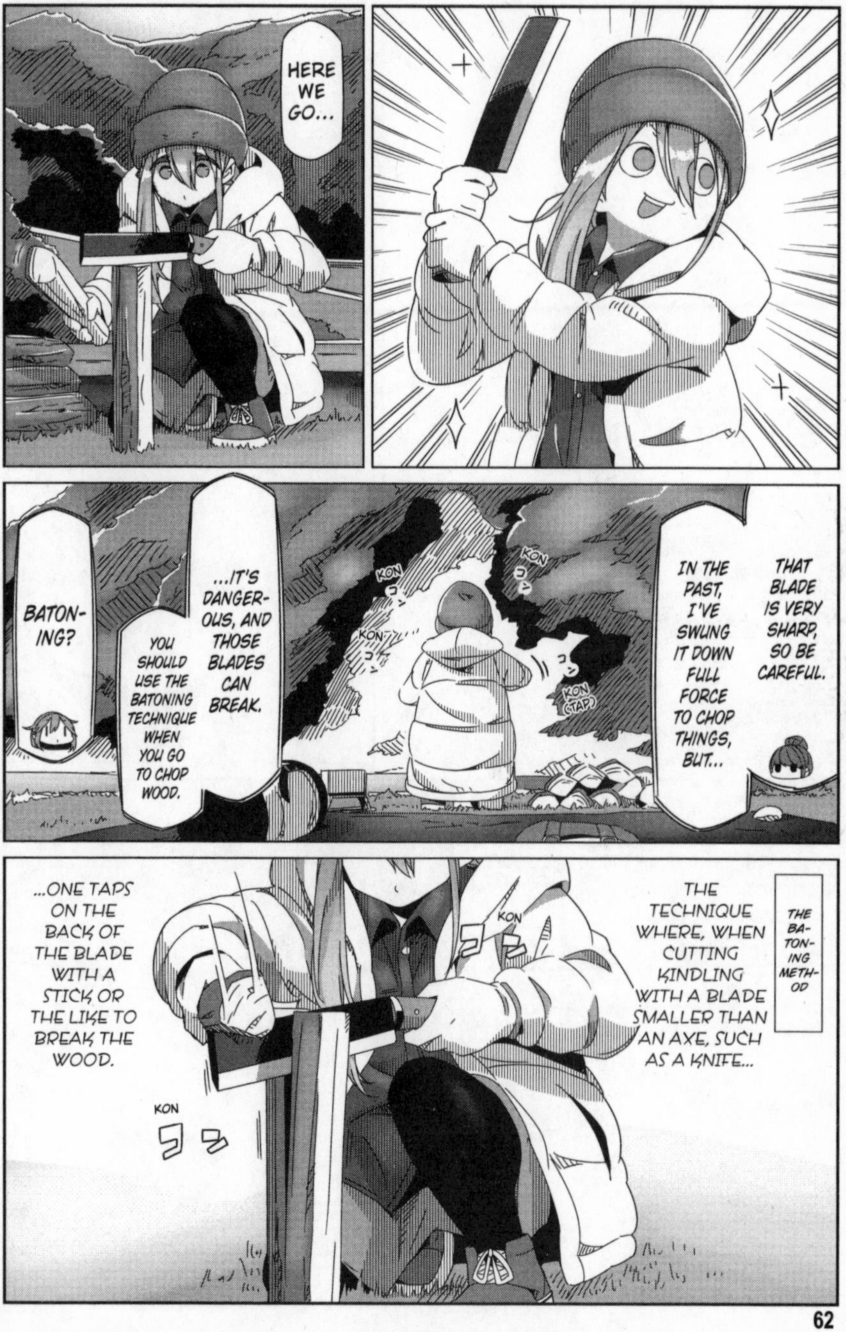
HERE WE GO...
THAT BLADE IS VERY SHARP, SO BE CAREFUL.
IN THE PAST, I'VE SWUNG IT DOWN FULL FORCE TO CHOP THINGS, BUT...
KON
KON (TAP)
KON
KON
...IT'S DANGEROUS, AND THOSE BLADES CAN BREAK.
YOU SHOULD USE THE BATONING TECHNIQUE WHEN YOU GO TO CHOP WOOD.
BATONING?
THE BATONING METHOD
THE TECHNIQUE WHERE, WHEN CUTTING KINDLING WITH A BLADE SMALLER THAN AN AXE, SUCH AS A KNIFE...
KON
...ONE TAPS ON THE BACK OF THE BLADE WITH A STICK OR THE LIKE TO BREAK THE WOOD.
KON

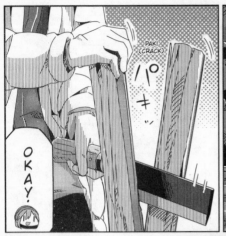

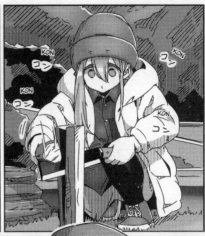

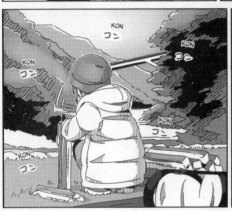

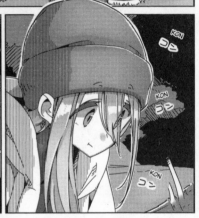

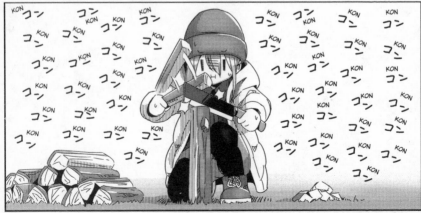

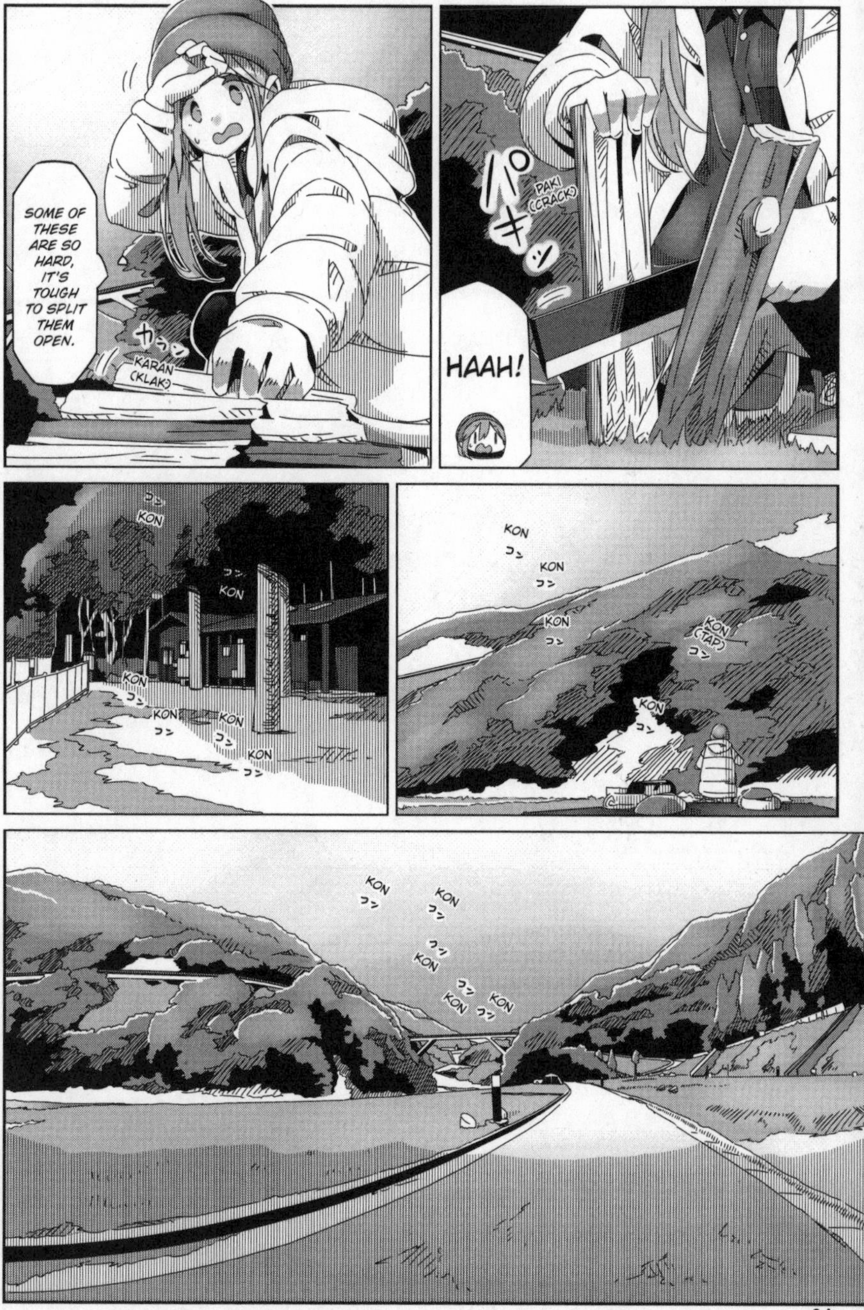
PAKI (CRACK)
HAAH!
SOME OF THESE ARE SO HARD, IT'S TOUGH TO SPLIT THEM OPEN.
KARAN (KLAK)
KON
KON
KON
KON (TAP)
KON
KON
KON
KON
KON
KON
KON
KON
KON
KON
KON
KON

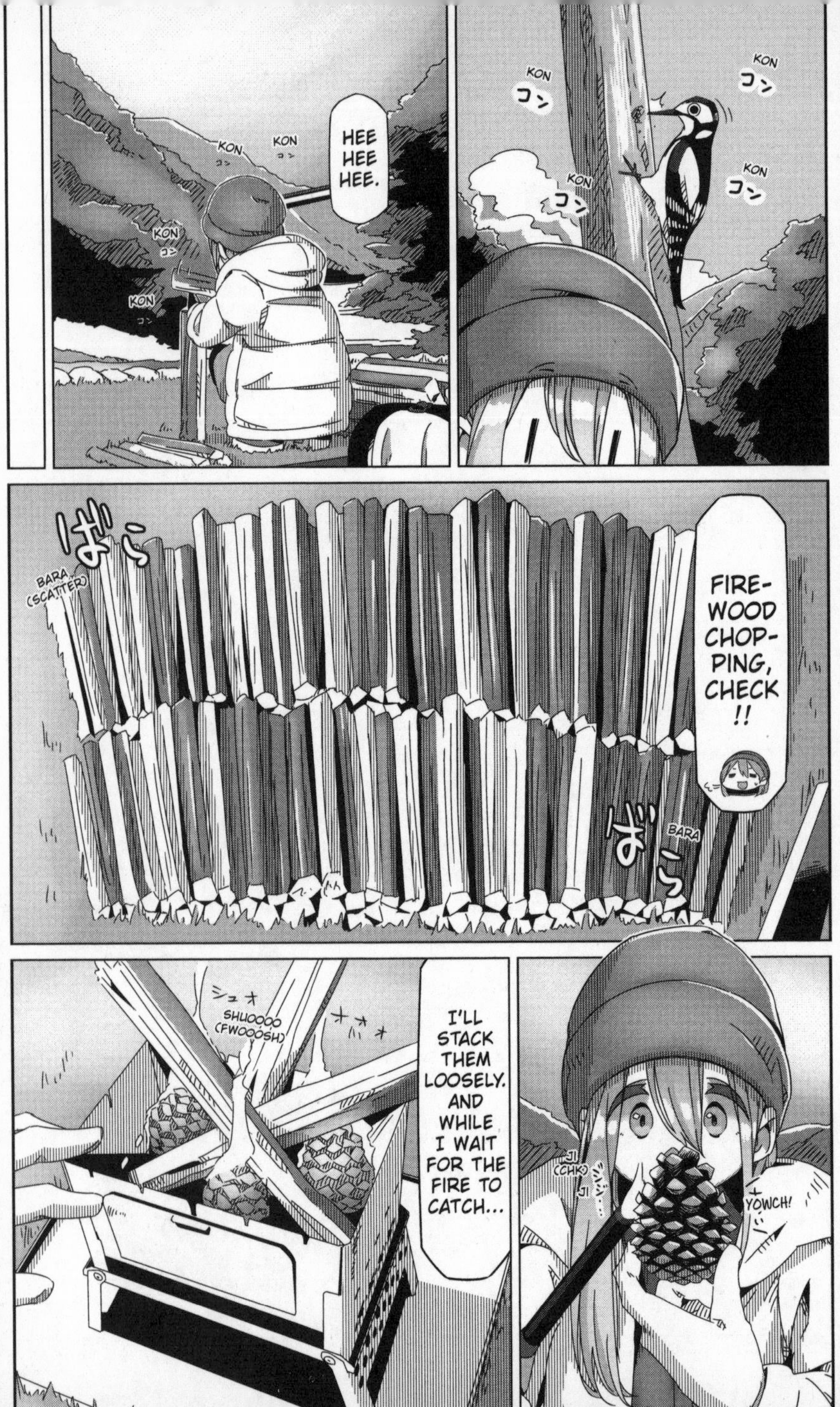

KON
コン
KON
コン
KON
コン
HEE HEE HEE.
KON
コン
KON
コン
KON
コン
KON
コン
FIRE-WOOD CHOP-PING, CHECK!!
ばら
BARA (SCATTER)
ばら
BARA
YOWCH!
JI (CHK) JI
I'LL STACK THEM LOOSELY. AND WHILE I WAIT FOR THE FIRE TO CATCH...
シュオ
SHUOOOO (FWOOOSH)

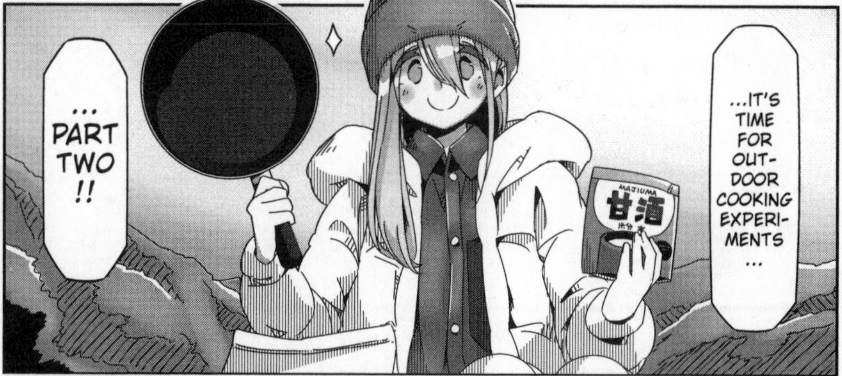
...IT'S TIME FOR OUTDOOR COOKING EXPERIMENTS...
MAJIUMA
甘酒
...PART TWO!!

PACKAGE: MAJIUMA AMAZAKE POWDER

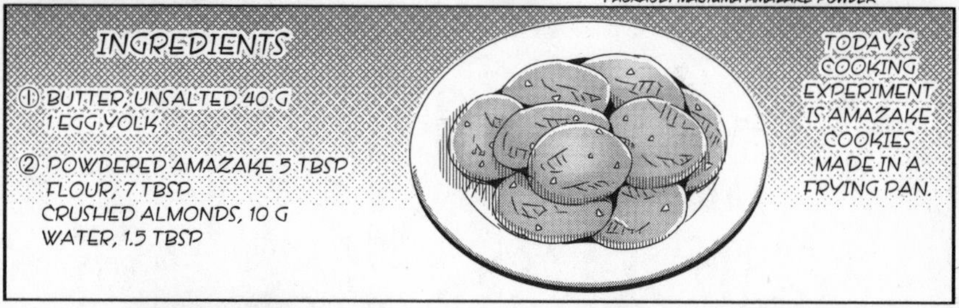
TODAY'S COOKING EXPERIMENT IS AMAZAKE COOKIES MADE IN A FRYING PAN.
INGREDIENTS
① BUTTER, UNSALTED 40 G
1 EGG YOLK
② POWDERED AMAZAKE 5 TBSP
FLOUR, 7 TBSP
CRUSHED ALMONDS, 10 G
WATER, 1.5 TBSP

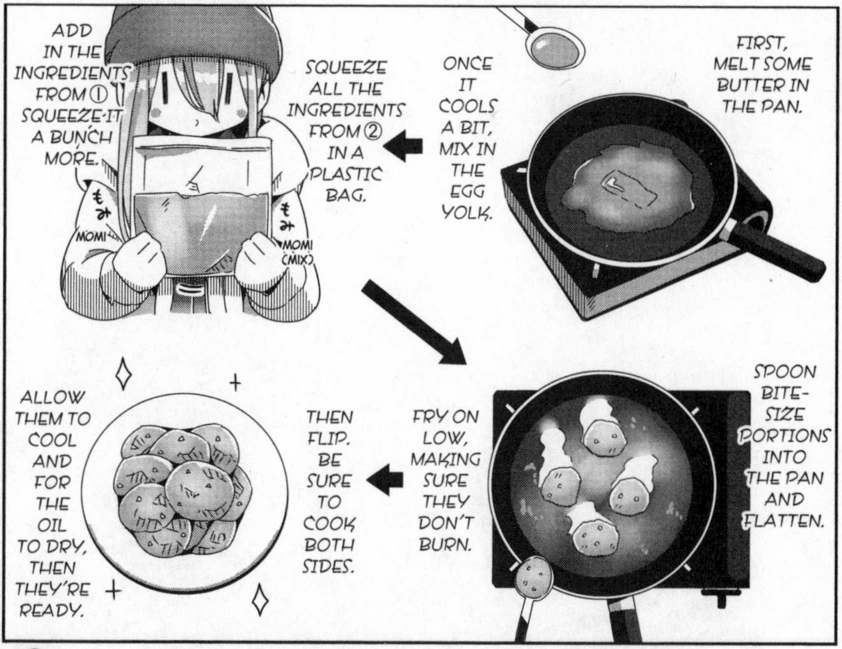
FIRST, MELT SOME BUTTER IN THE PAN.
ONCE IT COOLS A BIT, MIX IN THE EGG YOLK.
SQUEEZE ALL THE INGREDIENTS FROM ② IN A PLASTIC BAG.
ADD IN THE INGREDIENTS FROM ① SQUEEZE IT A BUNCH MORE.
もみ
MOMI (MIX)
もみ
MOMI
SPOON BITE-SIZE PORTIONS INTO THE PAN AND FLATTEN.
FRY ON LOW, MAKING SURE THEY DON'T BURN.
THEN FLIP. BE SURE TO COOK BOTH SIDES.
ALLOW THEM TO COOL AND FOR THE OIL TO DRY, THEN THEY'RE READY.

SINCE I DIDN'T USE THE EGG WHITES, I'LL FRY THEM UP, ADD SALT, AND EAT THEM SEPARATELY.

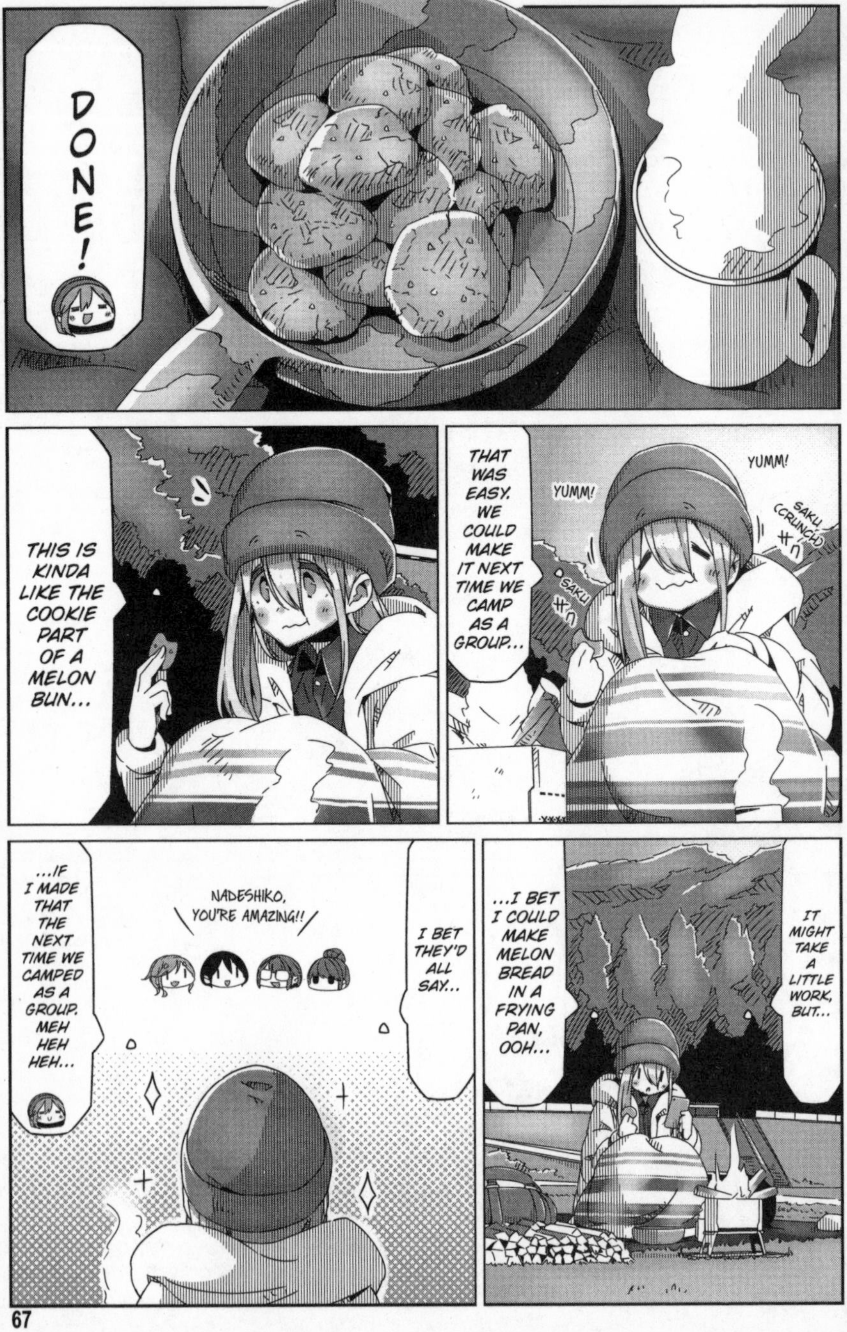

DONE!
YUMM!
SAKU (CRUNCH)
サク
YUMM!
SAKU
サク
THAT WAS EASY. WE COULD MAKE IT NEXT TIME WE CAMP AS A GROUP...
THIS IS KINDA LIKE THE COOKIE PART OF A MELON BUN...
IT MIGHT TAKE A LITTLE WORK, BUT...
...I BET I COULD MAKE MELON BREAD IN A FRYING PAN, OOH...
I BET THEY'D ALL SAY...
NADESHIKO, YOU'RE AMAZING!!
...IF I MADE THAT THE NEXT TIME WE CAMPED AS A GROUP. MEH HEH HEH...

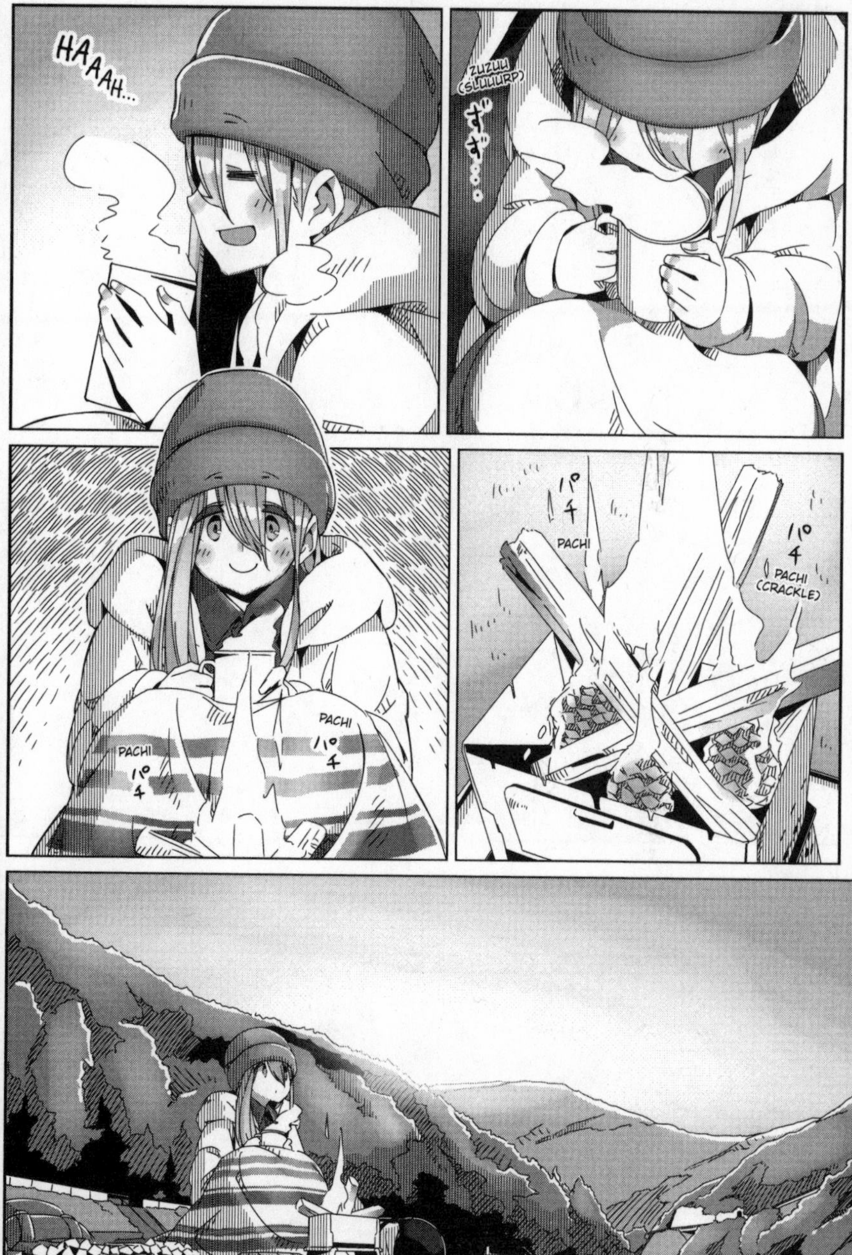
ZUZUU (SLUUURP)
ずず…。
HAAAH...
パチ
PACHI (CRACKLE)
パチ
PACHI
PACHI
パチ
PACHI
パチ

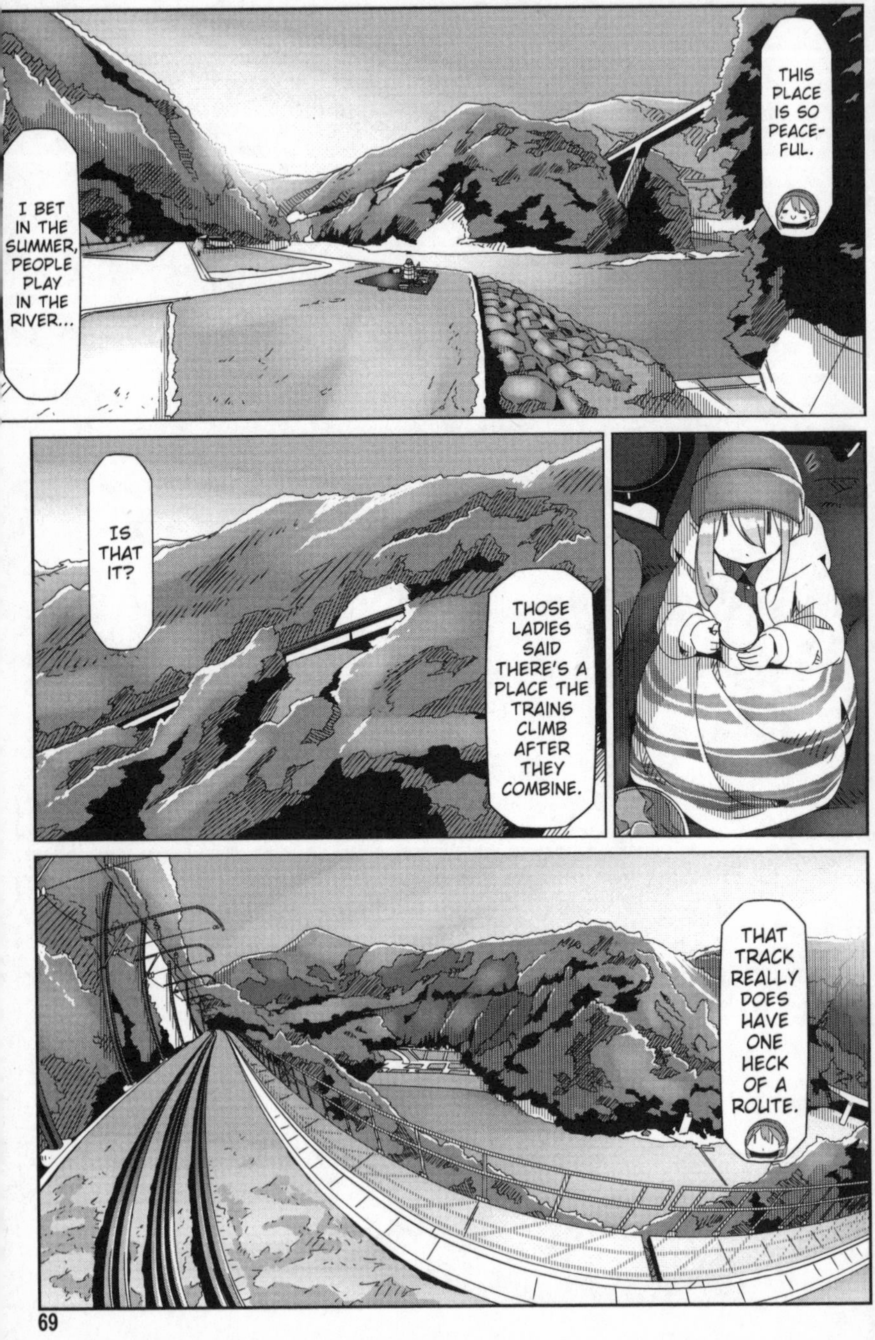
THIS PLACE IS SO PEACE-FUL.
I BET IN THE SUMMER, PEOPLE PLAY IN THE RIVER...
THOSE LADIES SAID THERE'S A PLACE THE TRAINS CLIMB AFTER THEY COMBINE.
IS THAT IT?
THAT TRACK REALLY DOES HAVE ONE HECK OF A ROUTE.

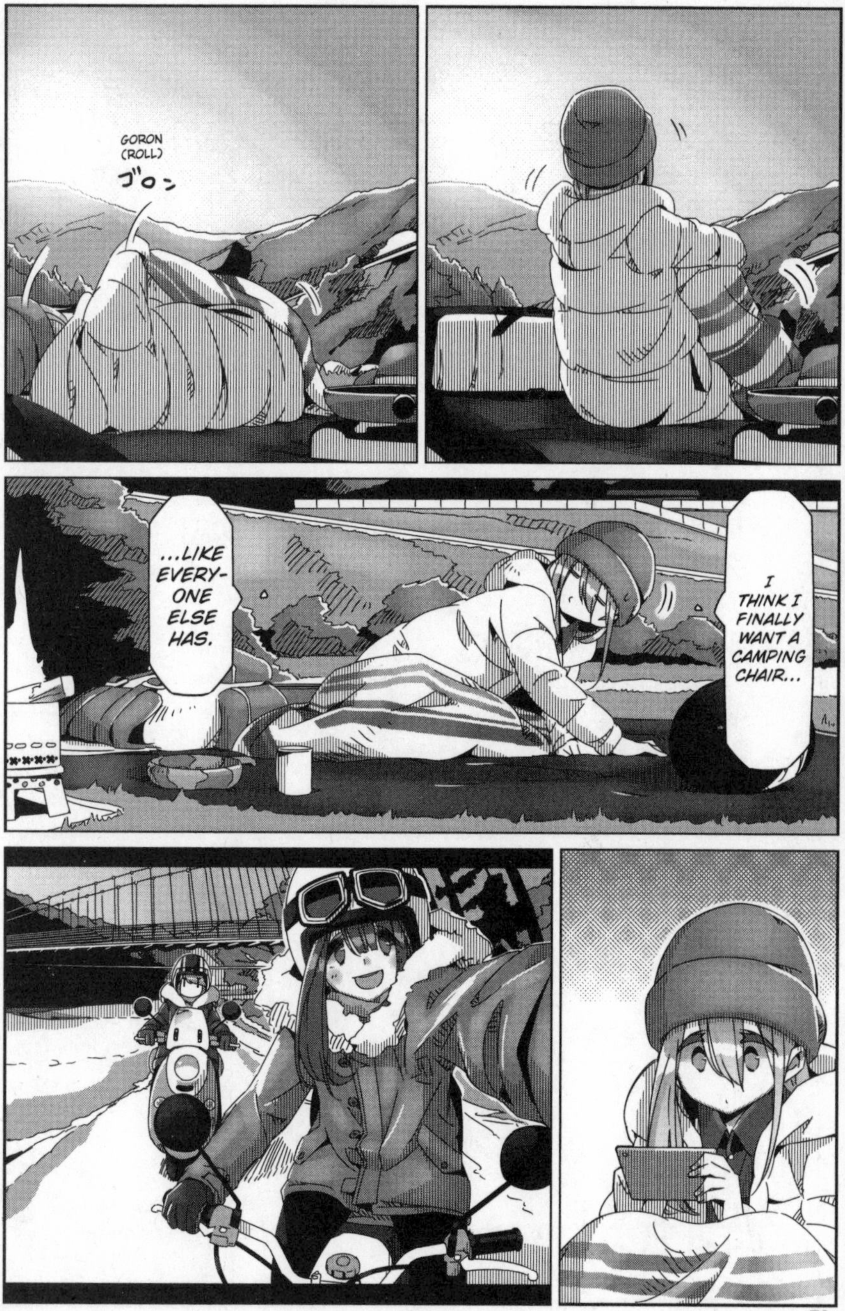
GORON (ROLL)
ゴロン
I THINK I FINALLY WANT A CAMPING CHAIR...
...LIKE EVERY-ONE ELSE HAS.

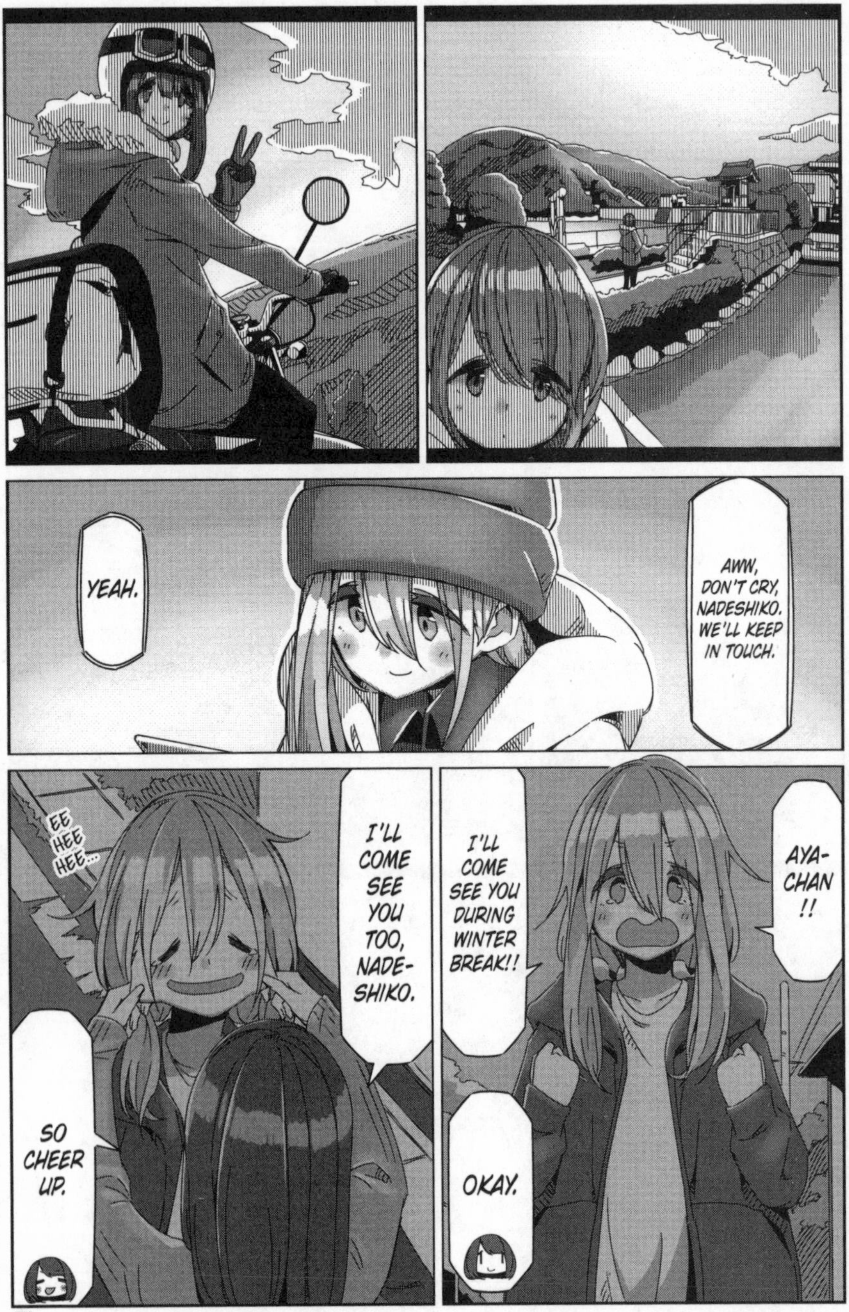
AWW, DON'T CRY, NADESHIKO. WE'LL KEEP IN TOUCH.
YEAH.
AYA-CHAN!!
I'LL COME SEE YOU DURING WINTER BREAK!!
OKAY.
I'LL COME SEE YOU TOO, NADE-SHIKO.
EE HEE HEE...
SO CHEER UP.

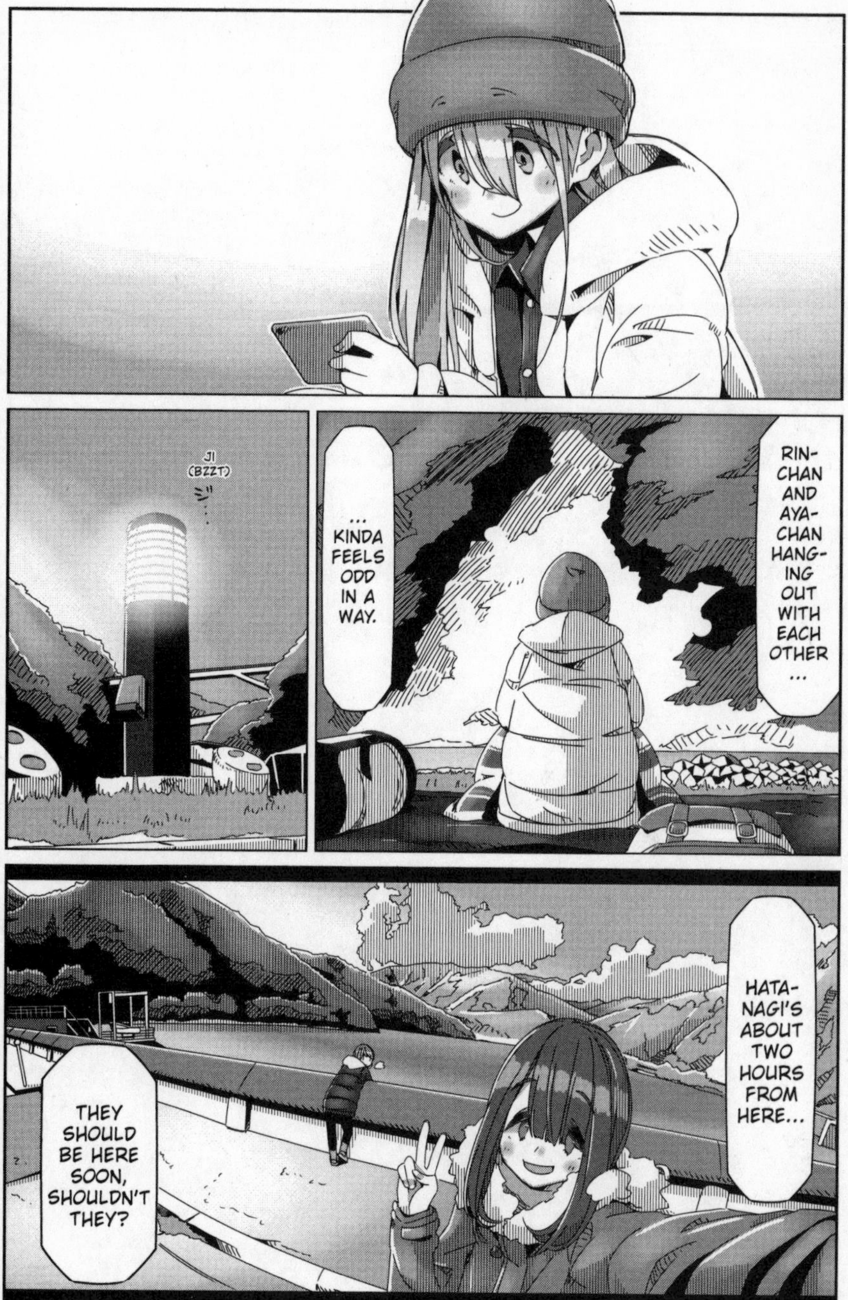
RIN-CHAN AND AYA-CHAN HANG-ING OUT WITH EACH OTHER...
...KINDA FEELS ODD IN A WAY.
JI (BZZT)
HATA-NAGI'S ABOUT TWO HOURS FROM HERE...
THEY SHOULD BE HERE SOON, SHOULDN'T THEY?

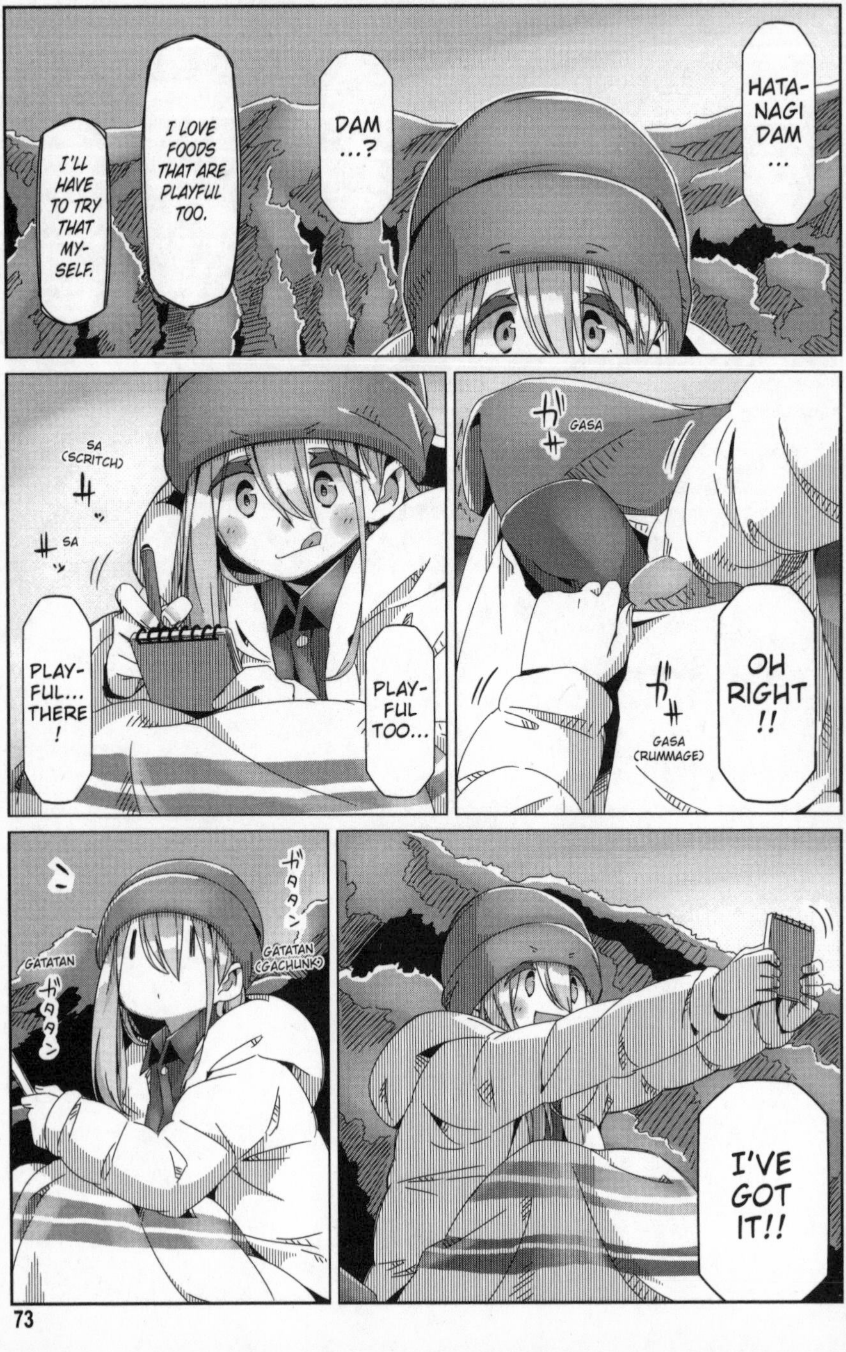
HATA-NAGI DAM...
DAM...?
I LOVE FOODS THAT ARE PLAYFUL TOO.
I'LL HAVE TO TRY THAT MY-SELF.
GASA
OH RIGHT!!
GASA (RUMMAGE)
SA (SCRITCH)
SA
PLAY-FUL TOO...
PLAY-FUL... THERE!
I'VE GOT IT!!
GATATAN (GACHUNK)
GATATAN

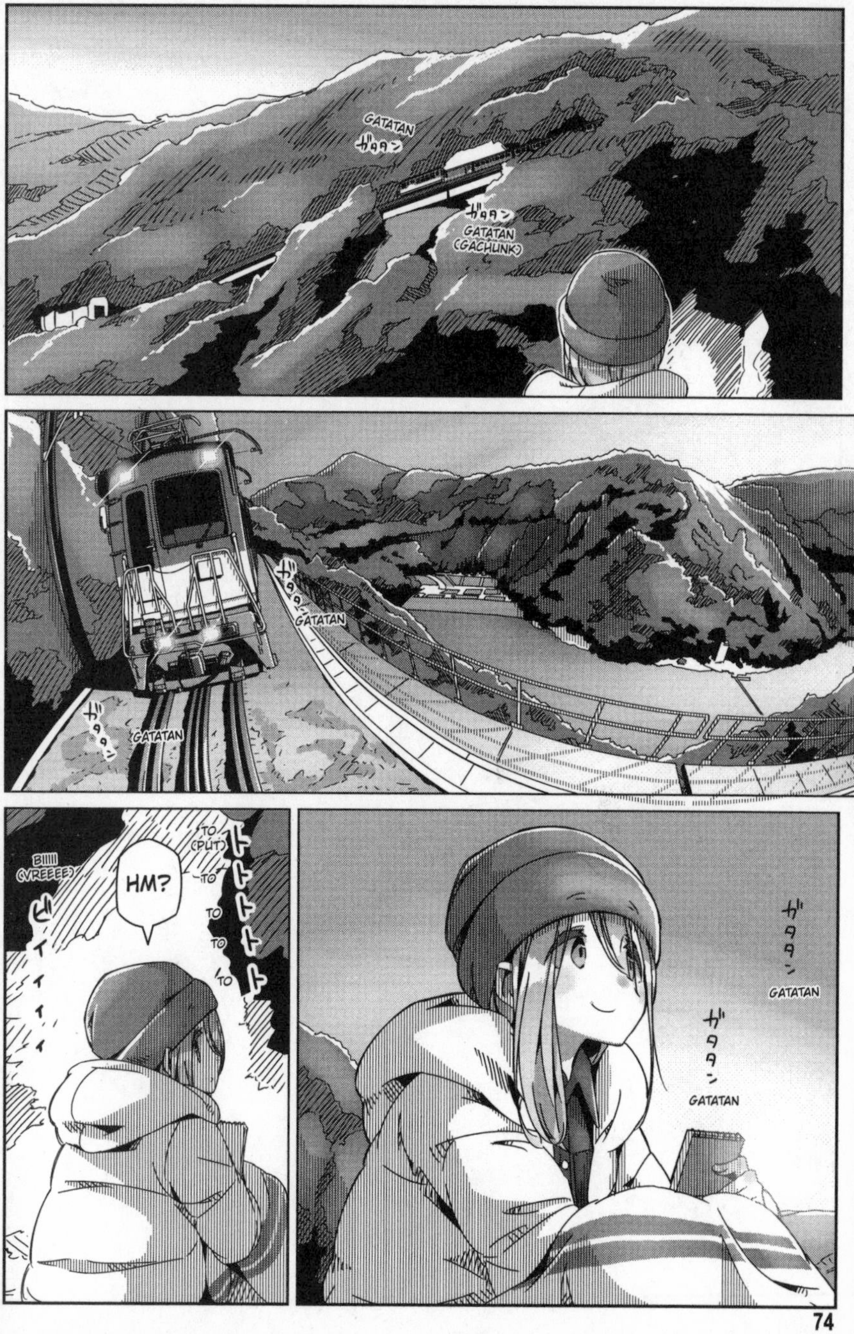
GATATAN
ガタタン
ガタタン
GATATAN
(GACHUNK)
ガタタン
GATATAN
ガタタン
GATATAN
ガタタン
GATATAN
ガタタン
GATATAN
トトトトト
TO
(PUT)
TO
TO
TO
TO
HM?
ビイイイイ
BIIIII
(VREEEE)

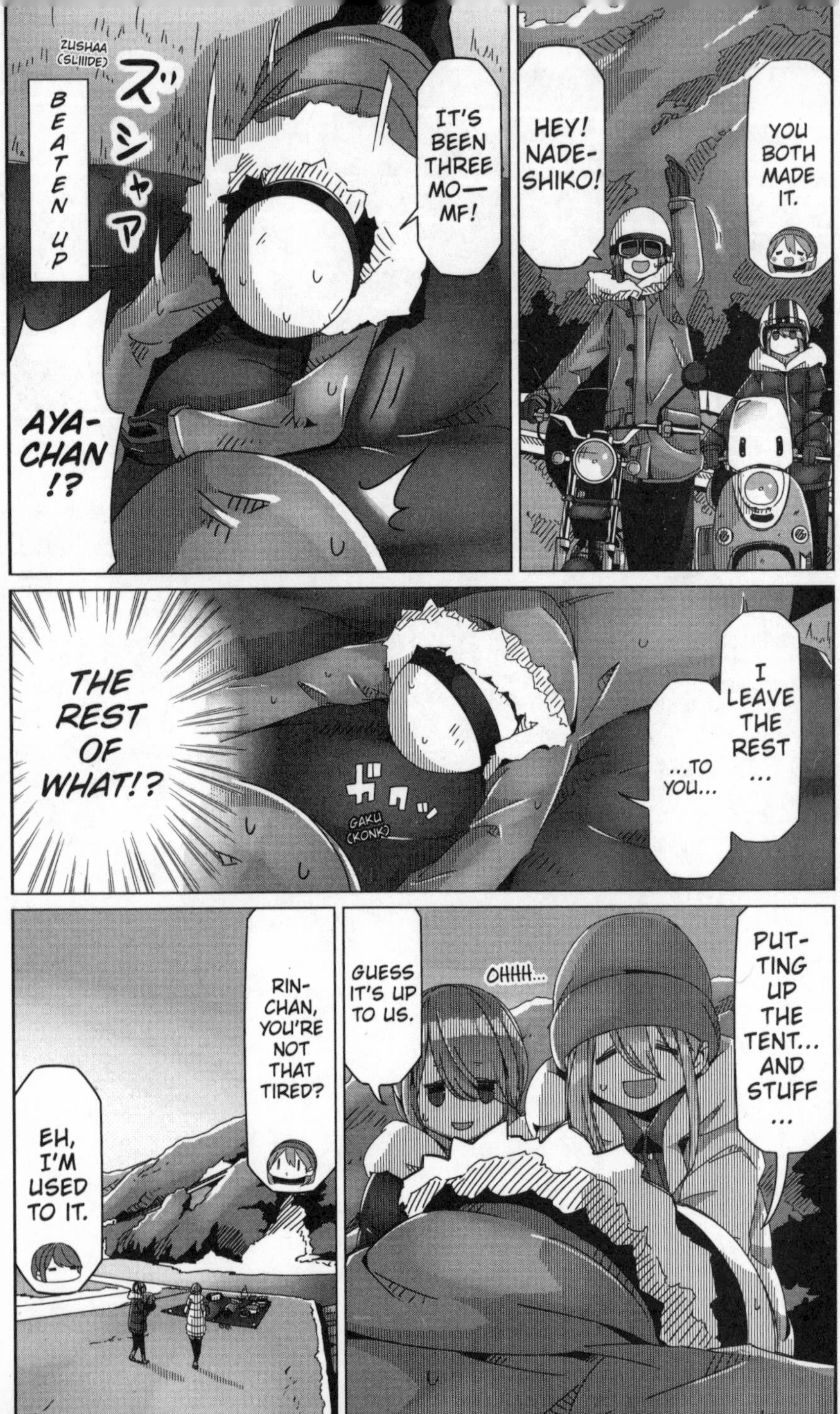
YOU BOTH MADE IT.
HEY! NADE-SHIKO!
IT'S BEEN THREE MO— MF!
ZUSHAA (SLIIIDE)
ズシャア
BEATEN UP
AYA-CHAN!?
I LEAVE THE REST...
...TO YOU...
THE REST OF WHAT!?
ガクッ
GAKU (KONK)
PUT-TING UP THE TENT... AND STUFF...
OHHH...
GUESS IT'S UP TO US.
RIN-CHAN, YOU'RE NOT THAT TIRED?
EH, I'M USED TO IT.

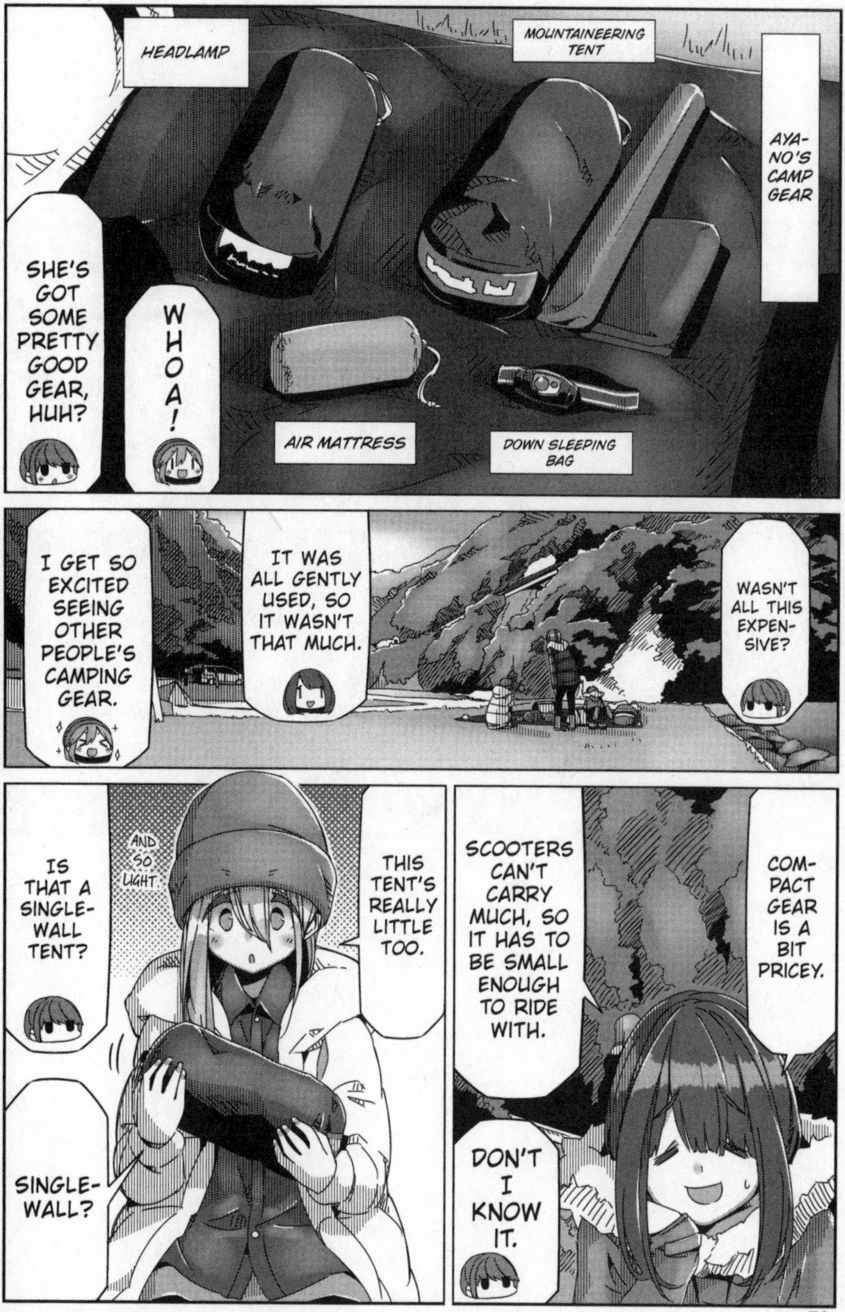
AYANO'S CAMP GEAR
MOUNTAINEERING TENT
HEADLAMP
DOWN SLEEPING BAG
AIR MATTRESS
WHOA!
SHE'S GOT SOME PRETTY GOOD GEAR, HUH?
WASN'T ALL THIS EXPENSIVE?
IT WAS ALL GENTLY USED, SO IT WASN'T THAT MUCH.
I GET SO EXCITED SEEING OTHER PEOPLE'S CAMPING GEAR.
COMPACT GEAR IS A BIT PRICEY.
SCOOTERS CAN'T CARRY MUCH, SO IT HAS TO BE SMALL ENOUGH TO RIDE WITH.
DON'T I KNOW IT.
THIS TENT'S REALLY LITTLE TOO.
AND SO LIGHT
IS THAT A SINGLE-WALL TENT?
SINGLE-WALL?

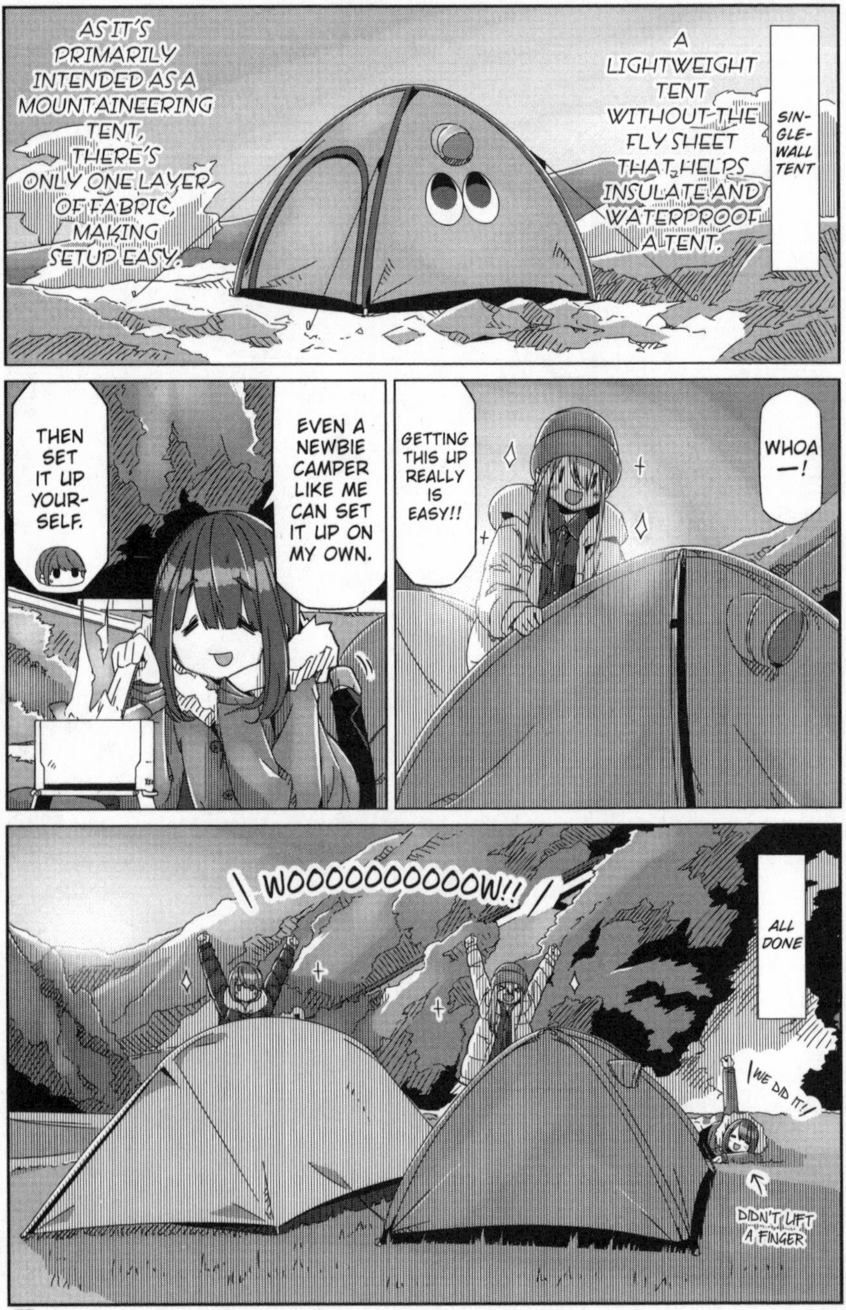
SINGLE-WALL TENT
A LIGHTWEIGHT TENT WITHOUT THE FLY SHEET THAT HELPS INSULATE AND WATERPROOF A TENT.
AS IT'S PRIMARILY INTENDED AS A MOUNTAINEERING TENT, THERE'S ONLY ONE LAYER OF FABRIC, MAKING SETUP EASY.
WHOA—!
GETTING THIS UP REALLY IS EASY!!
EVEN A NEWBIE CAMPER LIKE ME CAN SET IT UP ON MY OWN.
THEN SET IT UP YOURSELF.
ALL DONE
WOOOOOOOOOOW!!
WE DID IT!
DIDN'T LIFT A FINGER

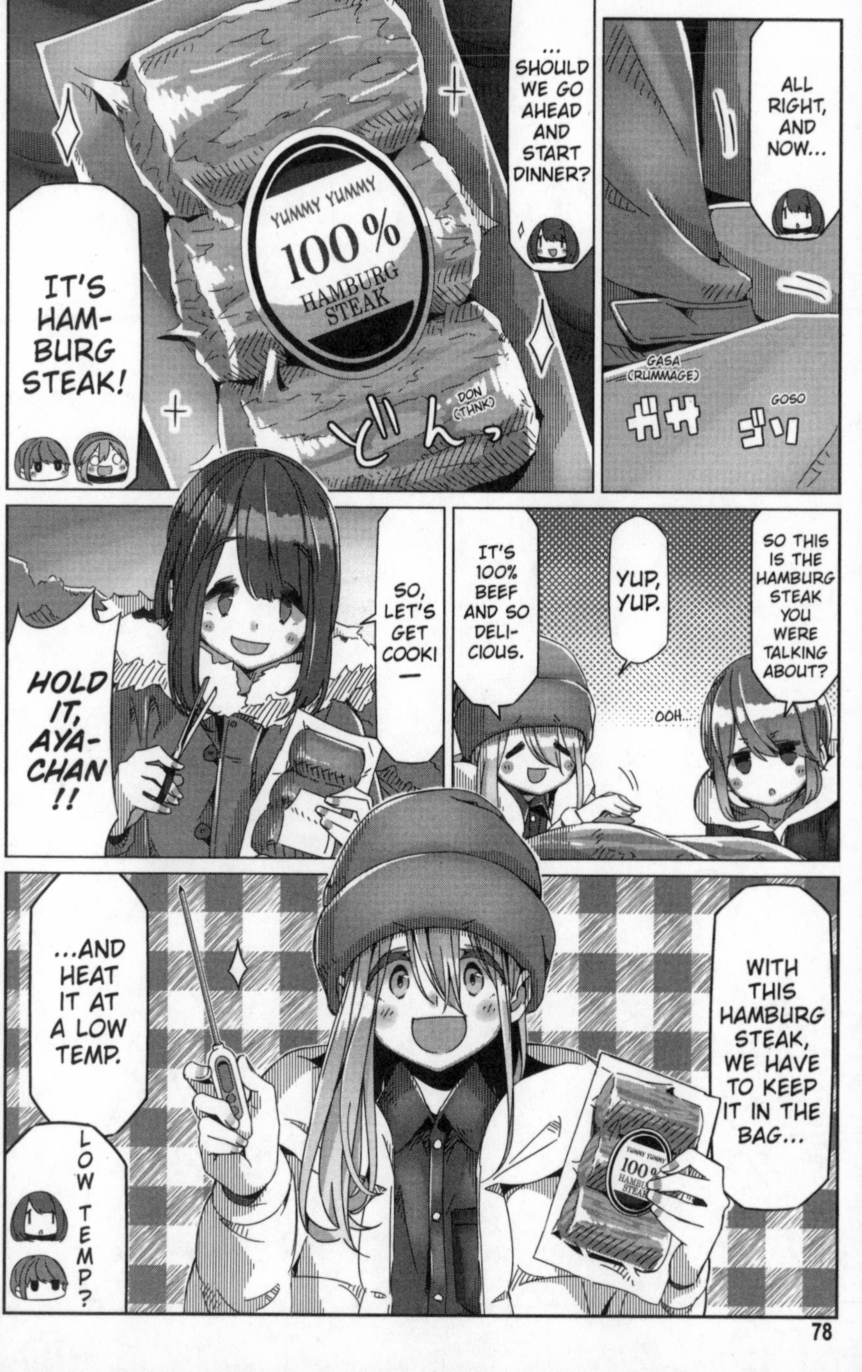
ALL RIGHT, AND NOW...
GASA (RUMMAGE)
GOSO
...SHOULD WE GO AHEAD AND START DINNER?
YUMMY YUMMY 100% HAMBURG STEAK
DON (THNK)
IT'S HAM-BURG STEAK!
SO THIS IS THE HAMBURG STEAK YOU WERE TALKING ABOUT?
YUP, YUP.
IT'S 100% BEEF AND SO DELI-CIOUS.
OOH...
SO, LET'S GET COOKI—
HOLD IT, AYA-CHAN!!
WITH THIS HAMBURG STEAK, WE HAVE TO KEEP IT IN THE BAG...
...AND HEAT IT AT A LOW TEMP.
LOW TEMP?

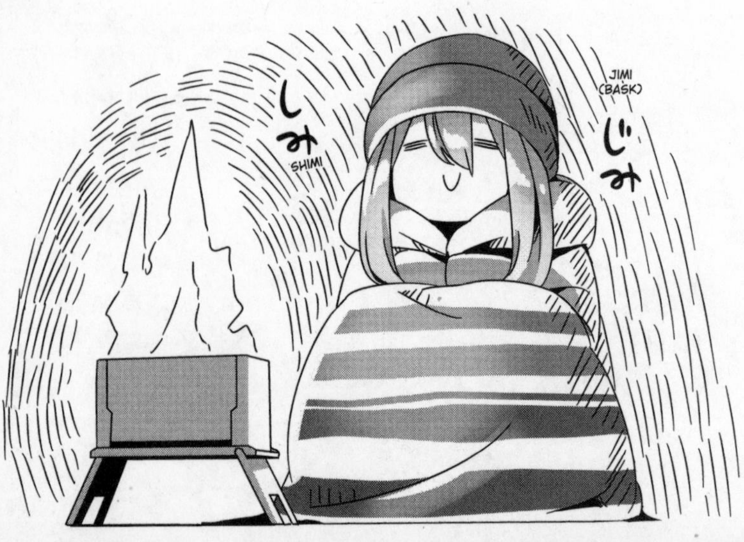
JIMI (BASK)
じみ
しみ
SHIMI

LOOK—THE SLEEPING-BAG BUG MAKES HER WAY BACK TO HER NEST.
YOU'RE RIGHT.

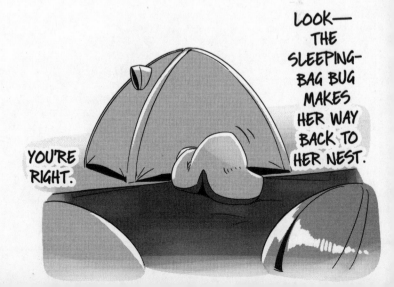

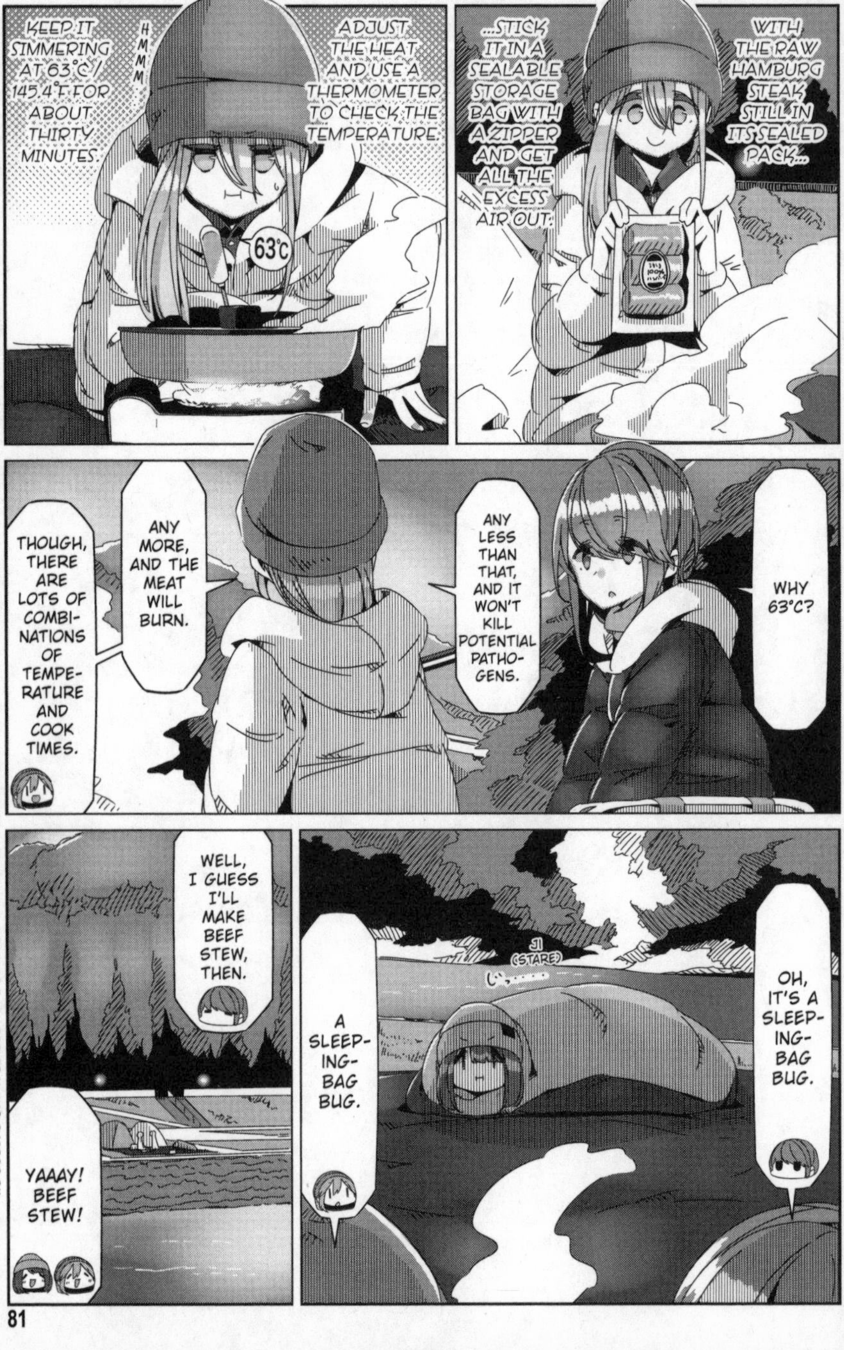
WITH THE RAW HAMBURG STEAK STILL IN ITS SEALED PACK...
...STICK IT IN A SEALABLE STORAGE BAG WITH A ZIPPER AND GET ALL THE EXCESS AIR OUT.
ADJUST THE HEAT AND USE A THERMOMETER TO CHECK THE TEMPERATURE.
HMMM.
63°C
KEEP IT SIMMERING AT 63°C/145.4°F FOR ABOUT THIRTY MINUTES.
WHY 63°C?
ANY LESS THAN THAT, AND IT WON'T KILL POTENTIAL PATHOGENS.
ANY MORE, AND THE MEAT WILL BURN.
THOUGH, THERE ARE LOTS OF COMBINATIONS OF TEMPERATURE AND COOK TIMES.
OH, IT'S A SLEEPING-BAG BUG.
JI (STARE)
A SLEEPING-BAG BUG.
WELL, I GUESS I'LL MAKE BEEF STEW, THEN.
YAAAY! BEEF STEW!

*TO PREVENT THE BAG FROM COMING INTO CONTACT WITH THE PAN AND MELTING, PLACE SOMETHING HEAT-SAFE AT THE BOTTOM, SUCH AS A CIRCULAR RACK FOR DRAINING EXCESS OIL.

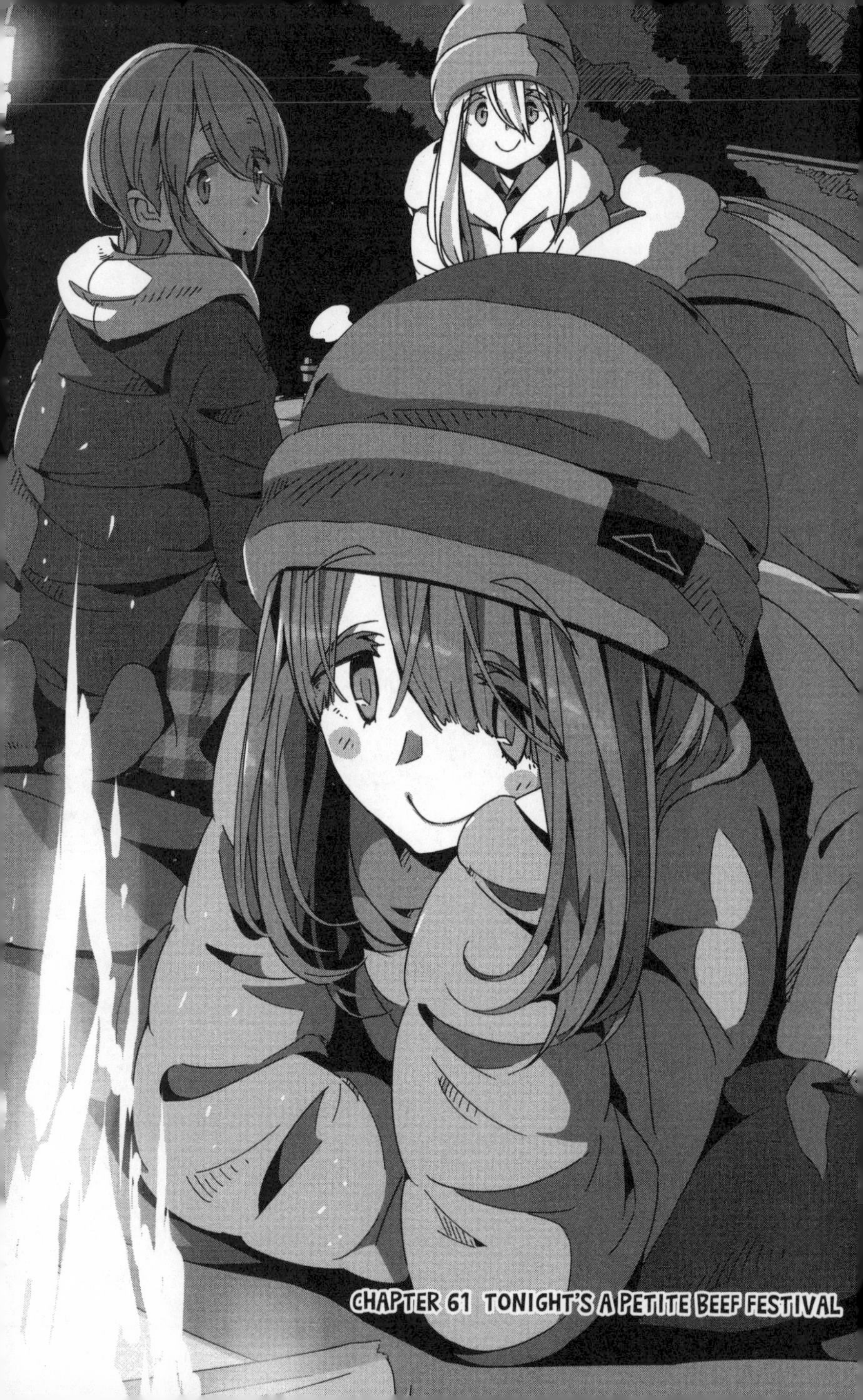
CHAPTER 61 TONIGHT'S A PETITE BEEF FESTIVAL

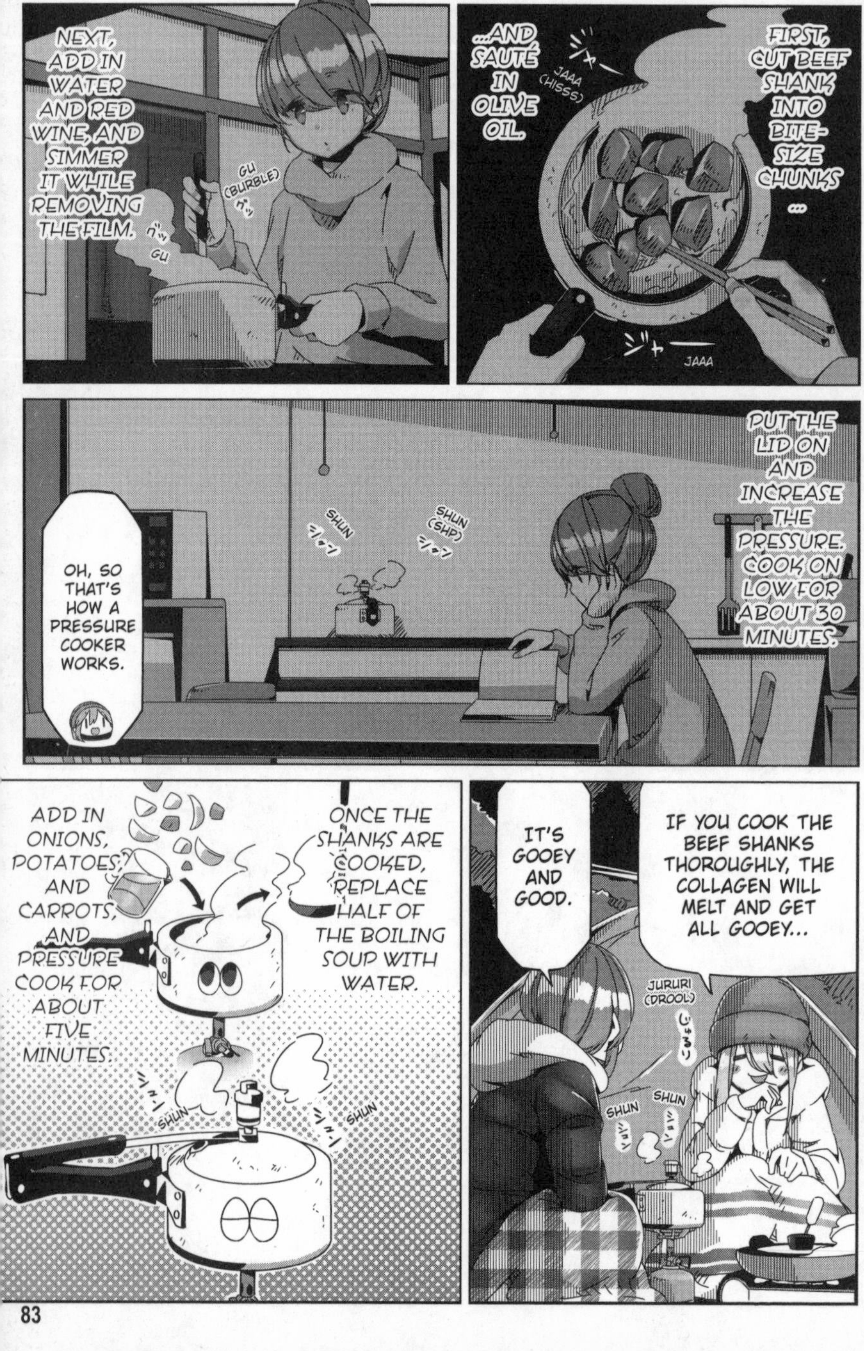
FIRST, CUT BEEF SHANK INTO BITE-SIZE CHUNKS ...
JAAA (HISSS)
...AND SAUTÉ IN OLIVE OIL.
JAAA
NEXT, ADD IN WATER AND RED WINE, AND SIMMER IT WHILE REMOVING THE FILM.
GU (BURBLE)
GU
PUT THE LID ON AND INCREASE THE PRESSURE. COOK ON LOW FOR ABOUT 30 MINUTES.
SHUN (SHP)
SHUN
OH, SO THAT'S HOW A PRESSURE COOKER WORKS.
IF YOU COOK THE BEEF SHANKS THOROUGHLY, THE COLLAGEN WILL MELT AND GET ALL GOOEY...
IT'S GOOEY AND GOOD.
JURURI (DROOL)
SHUN
SHUN
ONCE THE SHANKS ARE COOKED, REPLACE HALF OF THE BOILING SOUP WITH WATER.
ADD IN ONIONS, POTATOES, AND CARROTS, AND PRESSURE COOK FOR ABOUT FIVE MINUTES.
SHUN
SHUN

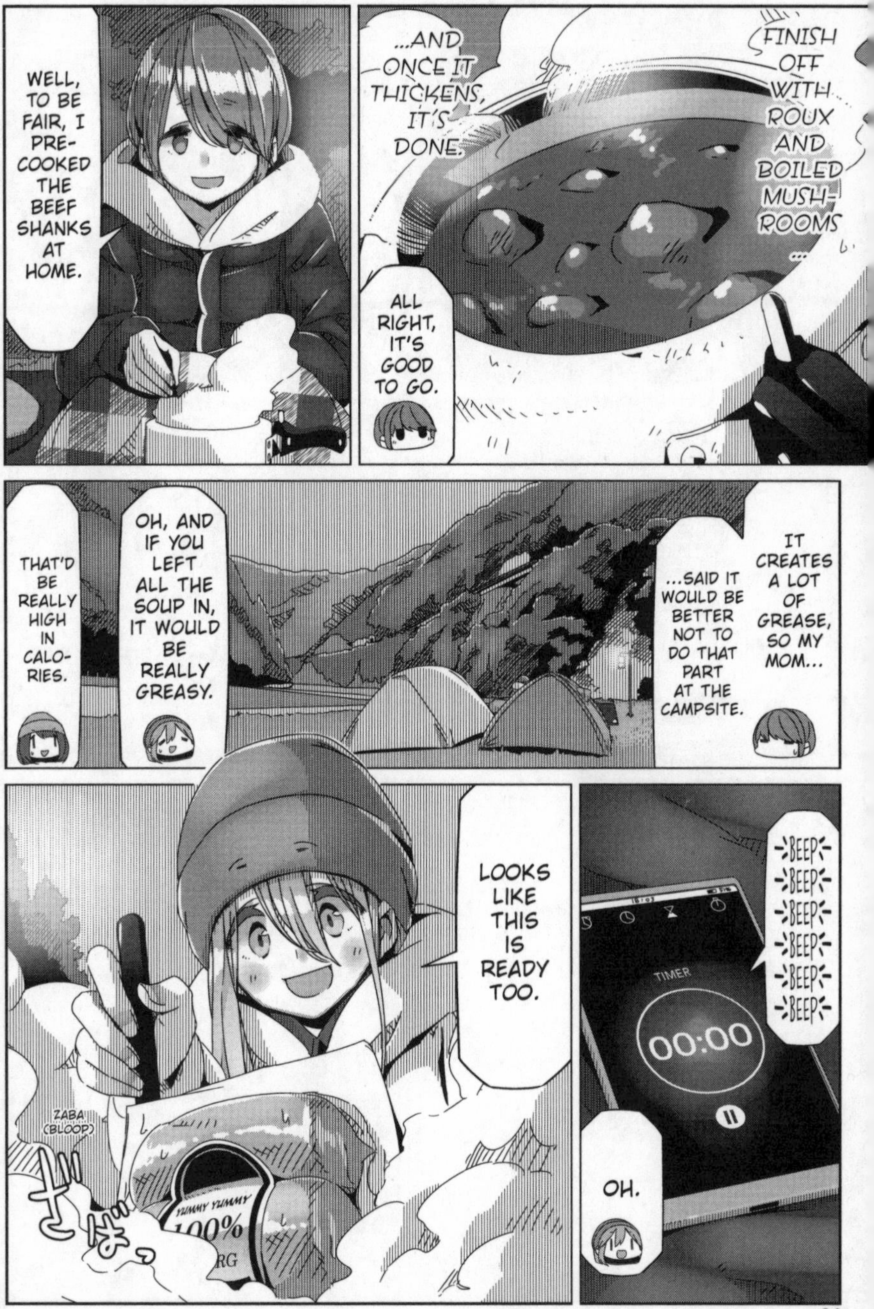
FINISH OFF WITH ROUX AND BOILED MUSHROOMS...
...AND ONCE IT THICKENS, IT'S DONE.
ALL RIGHT, IT'S GOOD TO GO.
WELL, TO BE FAIR, I PRE-COOKED THE BEEF SHANKS AT HOME.
IT CREATES A LOT OF GREASE, SO MY MOM...
...SAID IT WOULD BE BETTER NOT TO DO THAT PART AT THE CAMPSITE.
OH, AND IF YOU LEFT ALL THE SOUP IN, IT WOULD BE REALLY GREASY.
THAT'D BE REALLY HIGH IN CALORIES.
BEEP BEEP BEEP BEEP BEEP BEEP
TIMER
00:00
OH.
LOOKS LIKE THIS IS READY TOO.
ZABA (BLOOP)
YUMMY YUMMY
100%

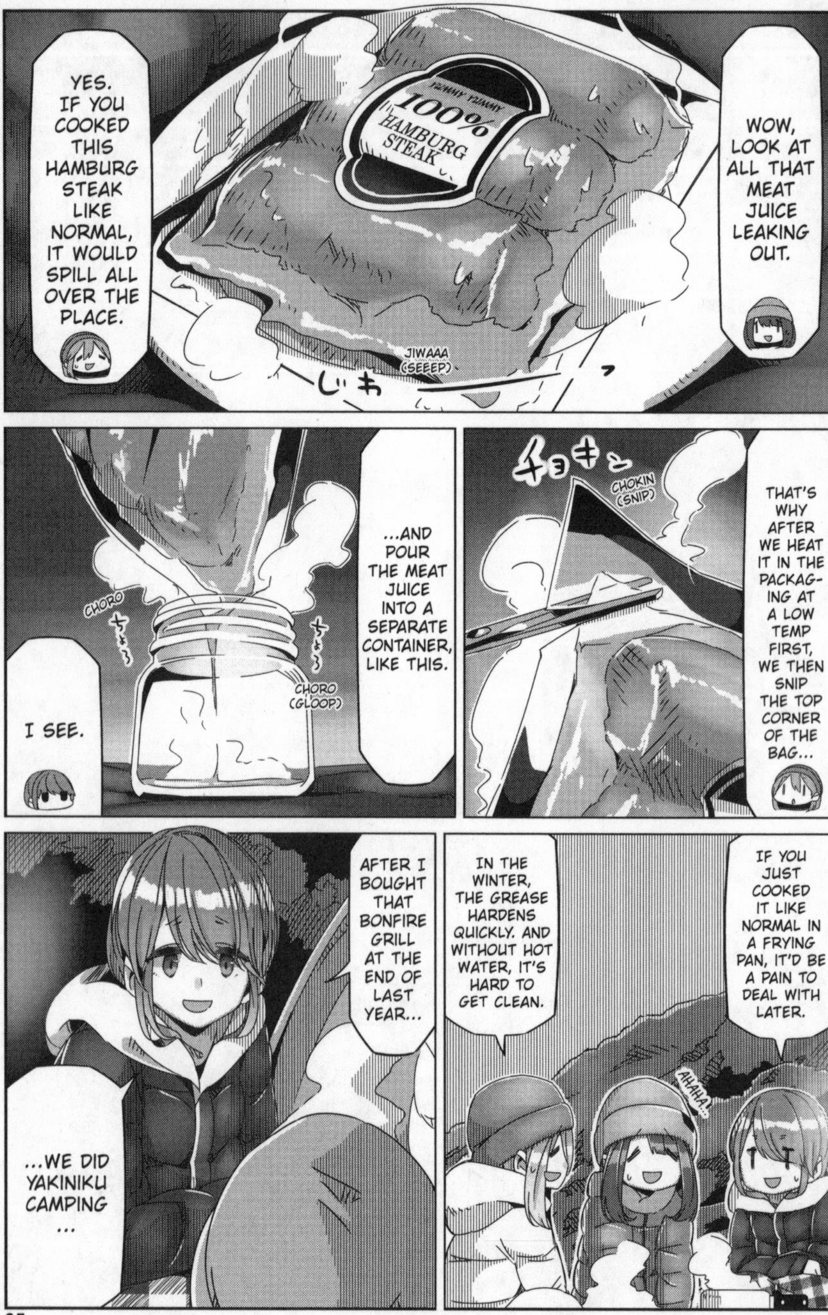
100% HAMBURG STEAK
WOW, LOOK AT ALL THAT MEAT JUICE LEAKING OUT.
YES. IF YOU COOKED THIS HAMBURG STEAK LIKE NORMAL, IT WOULD SPILL ALL OVER THE PLACE.
じわ
JIWAAA (SEEEP)
チョキン
CHOKIN (SNIP)
THAT'S WHY AFTER WE HEAT IT IN THE PACKAGING AT A LOW TEMP FIRST, WE THEN SNIP THE TOP CORNER OF THE BAG...
...AND POUR THE MEAT JUICE INTO A SEPARATE CONTAINER, LIKE THIS.
ちょろ
CHORO (GLOOP)
ちょろ
CHORO
I SEE.
IF YOU JUST COOKED IT LIKE NORMAL IN A FRYING PAN, IT'D BE A PAIN TO DEAL WITH LATER.
IN THE WINTER, THE GREASE HARDENS QUICKLY. AND WITHOUT HOT WATER, IT'S HARD TO GET CLEAN.
AHAHA...
AFTER I BOUGHT THAT BONFIRE GRILL AT THE END OF LAST YEAR...
...WE DID YAKINIKU CAMPING...

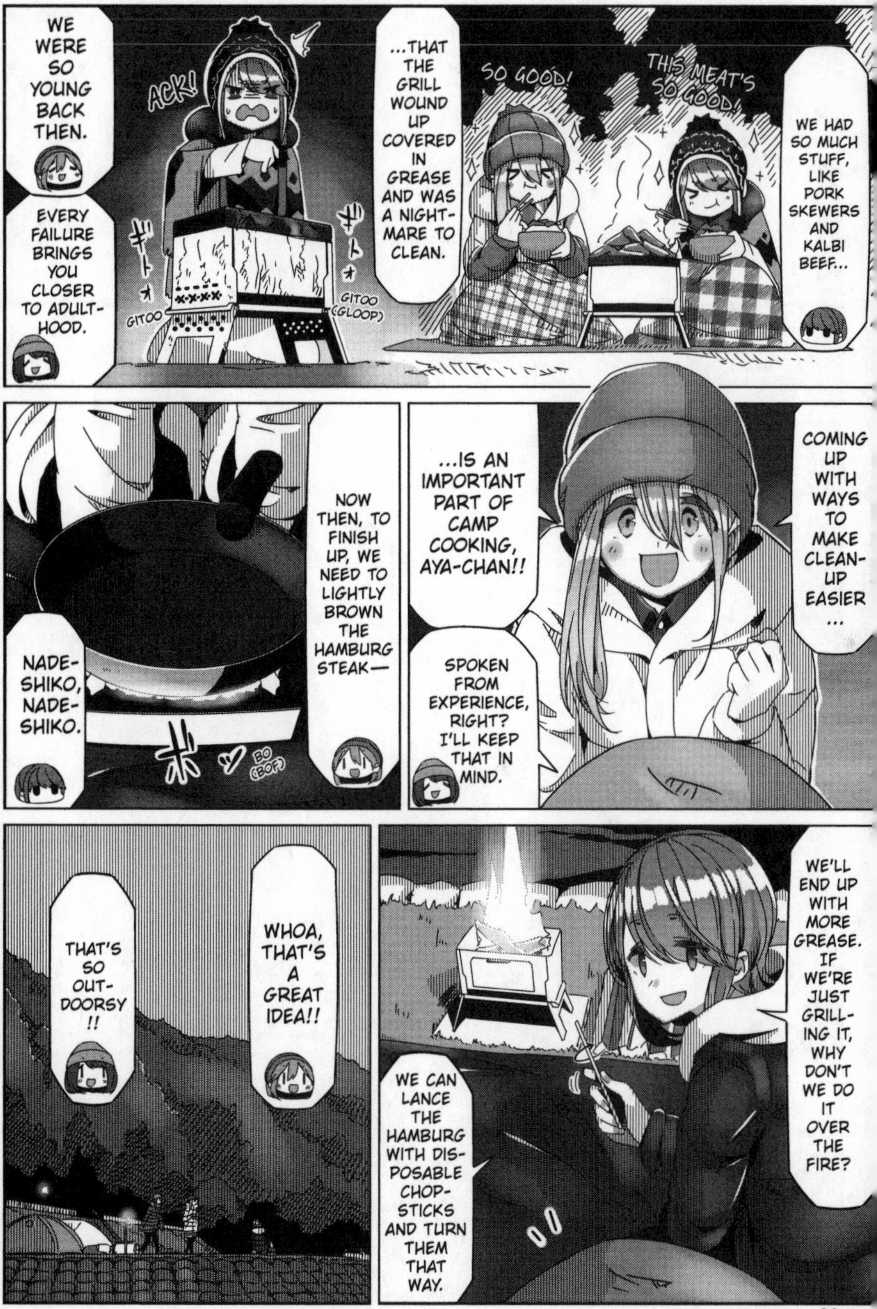
WE HAD SO MUCH STUFF, LIKE PORK SKEWERS AND KALBI BEEF...
THIS MEAT'S SO GOOD!
SO GOOD!
...THAT THE GRILL WOUND UP COVERED IN GREASE AND WAS A NIGHTMARE TO CLEAN.
ACK!
GITOO (GLOOP)
GITOO
WE WERE SO YOUNG BACK THEN.
EVERY FAILURE BRINGS YOU CLOSER TO ADULTHOOD.
COMING UP WITH WAYS TO MAKE CLEAN-UP EASIER...
...IS AN IMPORTANT PART OF CAMP COOKING, AYA-CHAN!!
SPOKEN FROM EXPERIENCE, RIGHT? I'LL KEEP THAT IN MIND.
NOW THEN, TO FINISH UP, WE NEED TO LIGHTLY BROWN THE HAMBURG STEAK—
BO (BOF)
NADE-SHIKO, NADE-SHIKO.
WE'LL END UP WITH MORE GREASE. IF WE'RE JUST GRILLING IT, WHY DON'T WE DO IT OVER THE FIRE?
WE CAN LANCE THE HAMBURG WITH DISPOSABLE CHOPSTICKS AND TURN THEM THAT WAY.
WHOA, THAT'S A GREAT IDEA!!
THAT'S SO OUTDOORSY!!

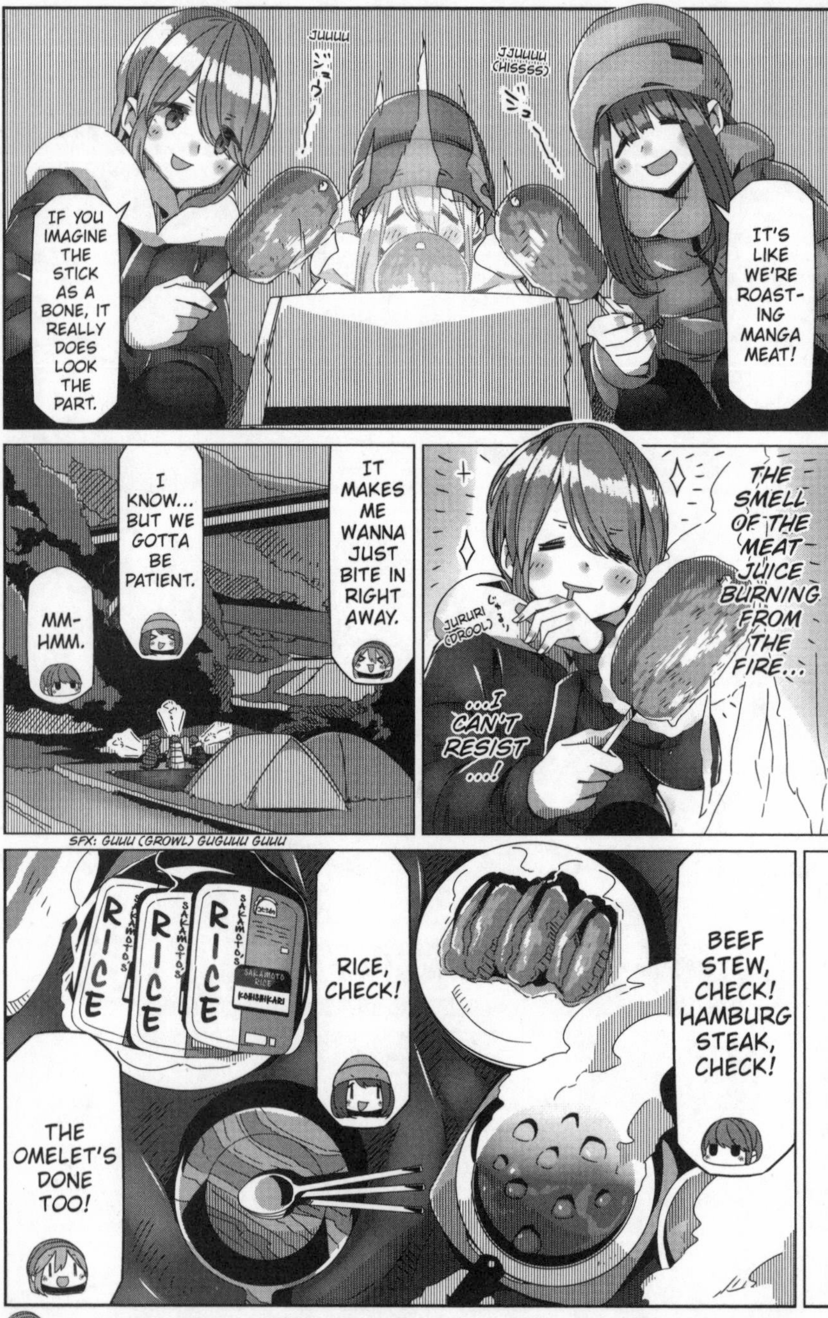
JUUUU
JJUUUU (HISSSS)
IT'S LIKE WE'RE ROASTING MANGA MEAT!
IF YOU IMAGINE THE STICK AS A BONE, IT REALLY DOES LOOK THE PART.
THE SMELL OF THE MEAT JUICE BURNING FROM THE FIRE...
JURURI (DROOL)
...I CAN'T RESIST...!
IT MAKES ME WANNA JUST BITE IN RIGHT AWAY.
I KNOW... BUT WE GOTTA BE PATIENT.
MM-HMM.
SFX: GUUU (GROWL) GUGUUU GUUU
BEEF STEW, CHECK! HAMBURG STEAK, CHECK!
RICE, CHECK!
SAKAMOTO'S RICE
SAKAMOTO'S RICE
SAKAMOTO'S RICE
THE OMELET'S DONE TOO!

IT'S DANGEROUS TO SERVE HAMBURG STEAK RARE, SO CUT IT OPEN AND MAKE SURE IT'S COOKED FIRST.

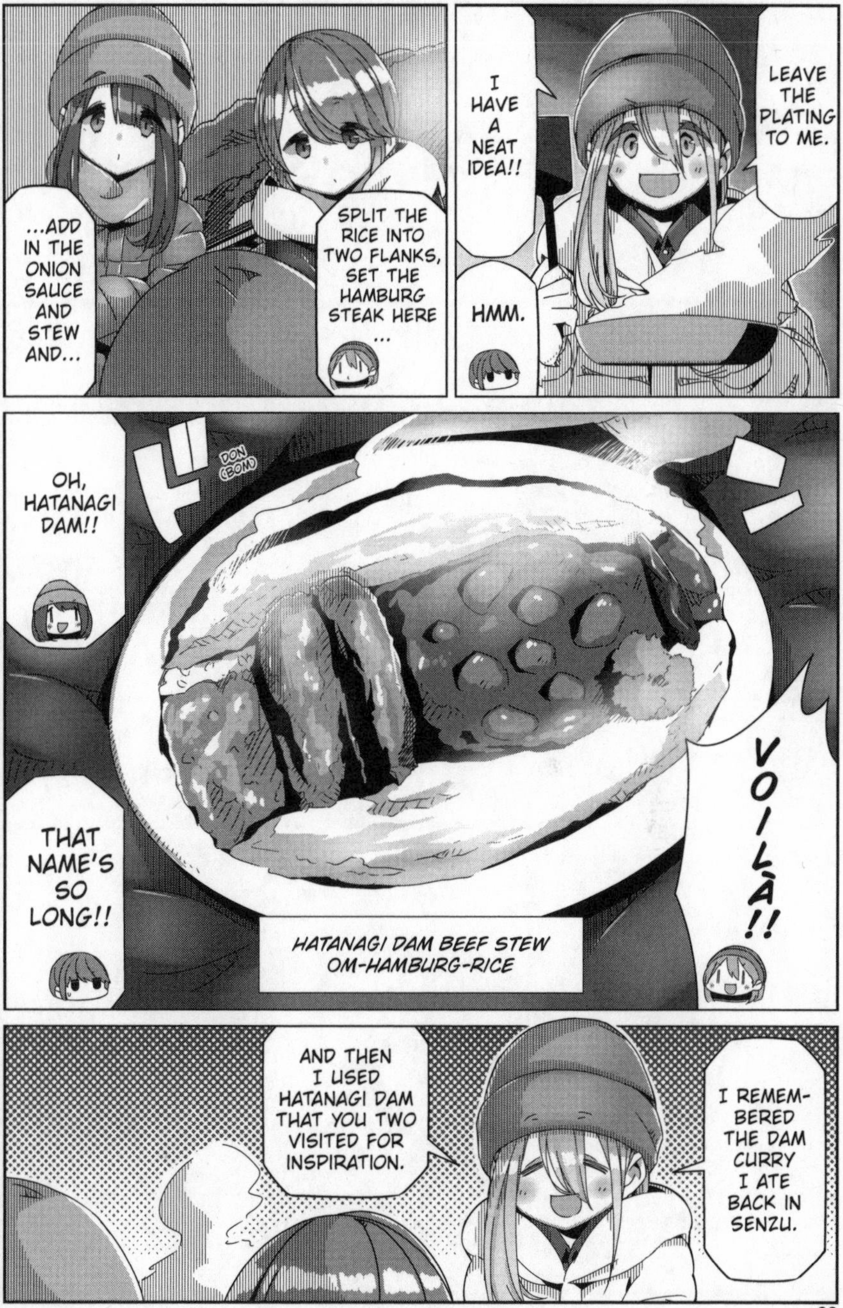
LEAVE THE PLATING TO ME.
I HAVE A NEAT IDEA!!
HMM.
SPLIT THE RICE INTO TWO FLANKS, SET THE HAMBURG STEAK HERE ...
...ADD IN THE ONION SAUCE AND STEW AND...
ドーン
DON (BOM)
VOILÀ!!
OH, HATANAGI DAM!!
HATANAGI DAM BEEF STEW OM-HAMBURG-RICE
THAT NAME'S SO LONG!!
I REMEMBERED THE DAM CURRY I ATE BACK IN SENZU.
AND THEN I USED HATANAGI DAM THAT YOU TWO VISITED FOR INSPIRATION.

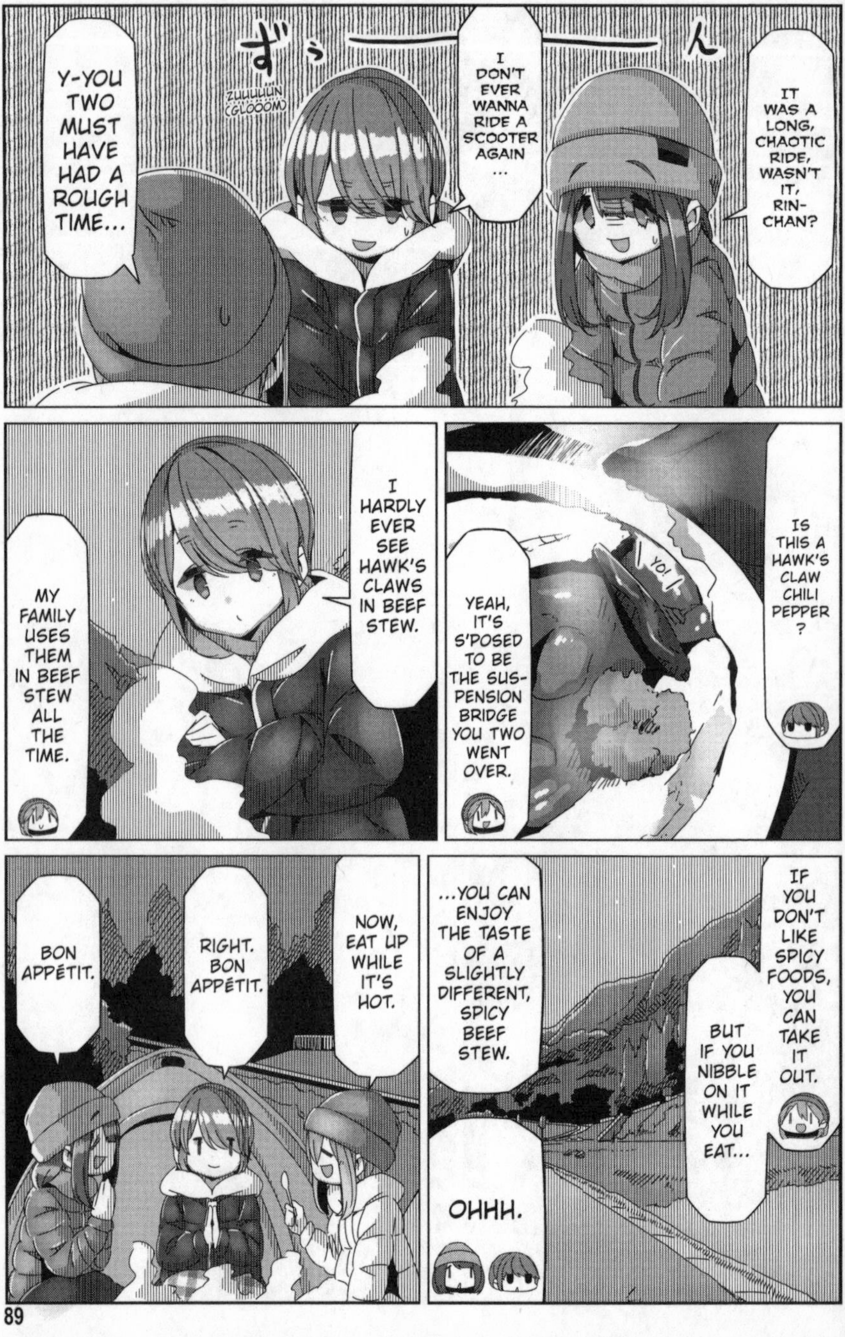
IT WAS A LONG, CHAOTIC RIDE, WASN'T IT, RIN-CHAN?
ずぅーーーーん
ZUUUUUUN (GLOOOM)
I DON'T EVER WANNA RIDE A SCOOTER AGAIN ...
Y-YOU TWO MUST HAVE HAD A ROUGH TIME...
IS THIS A HAWK'S CLAW CHILI PEPPER?
YO!
YEAH, IT'S S'POSED TO BE THE SUSPENSION BRIDGE YOU TWO WENT OVER.
I HARDLY EVER SEE HAWK'S CLAWS IN BEEF STEW.
MY FAMILY USES THEM IN BEEF STEW ALL THE TIME.
IF YOU DON'T LIKE SPICY FOODS, YOU CAN TAKE IT OUT.
BUT IF YOU NIBBLE ON IT WHILE YOU EAT...
...YOU CAN ENJOY THE TASTE OF A SLIGHTLY DIFFERENT, SPICY BEEF STEW.
OHHH.
NOW, EAT UP WHILE IT'S HOT.
RIGHT. BON APPÉTIT.
BON APPÉTIT.

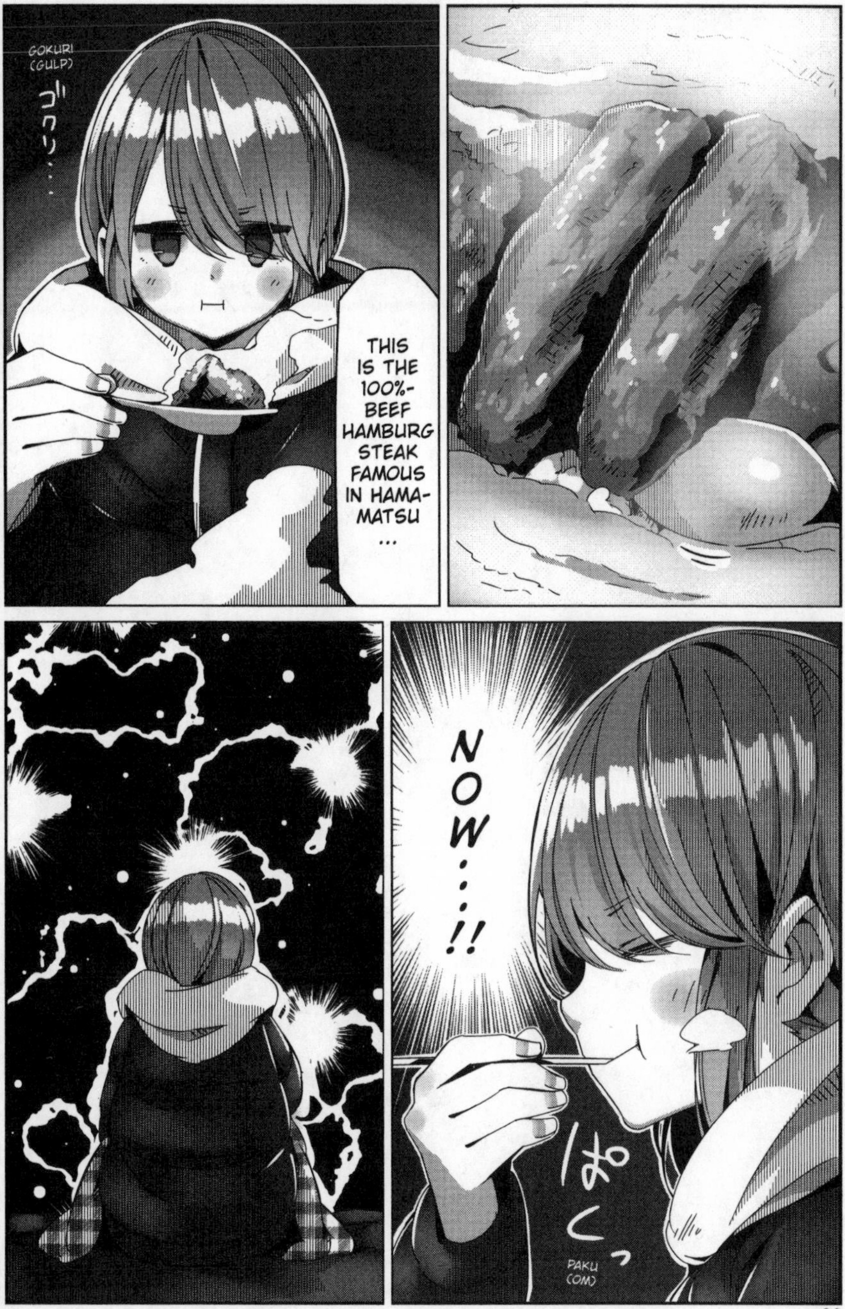
THIS IS THE 100%-BEEF HAMBURG STEAK FAMOUS IN HAMAMATSU ...
ゴクリ・・・
GOKURI (GULP)
NOW...!!
ぱくっ
PAKU (OM)

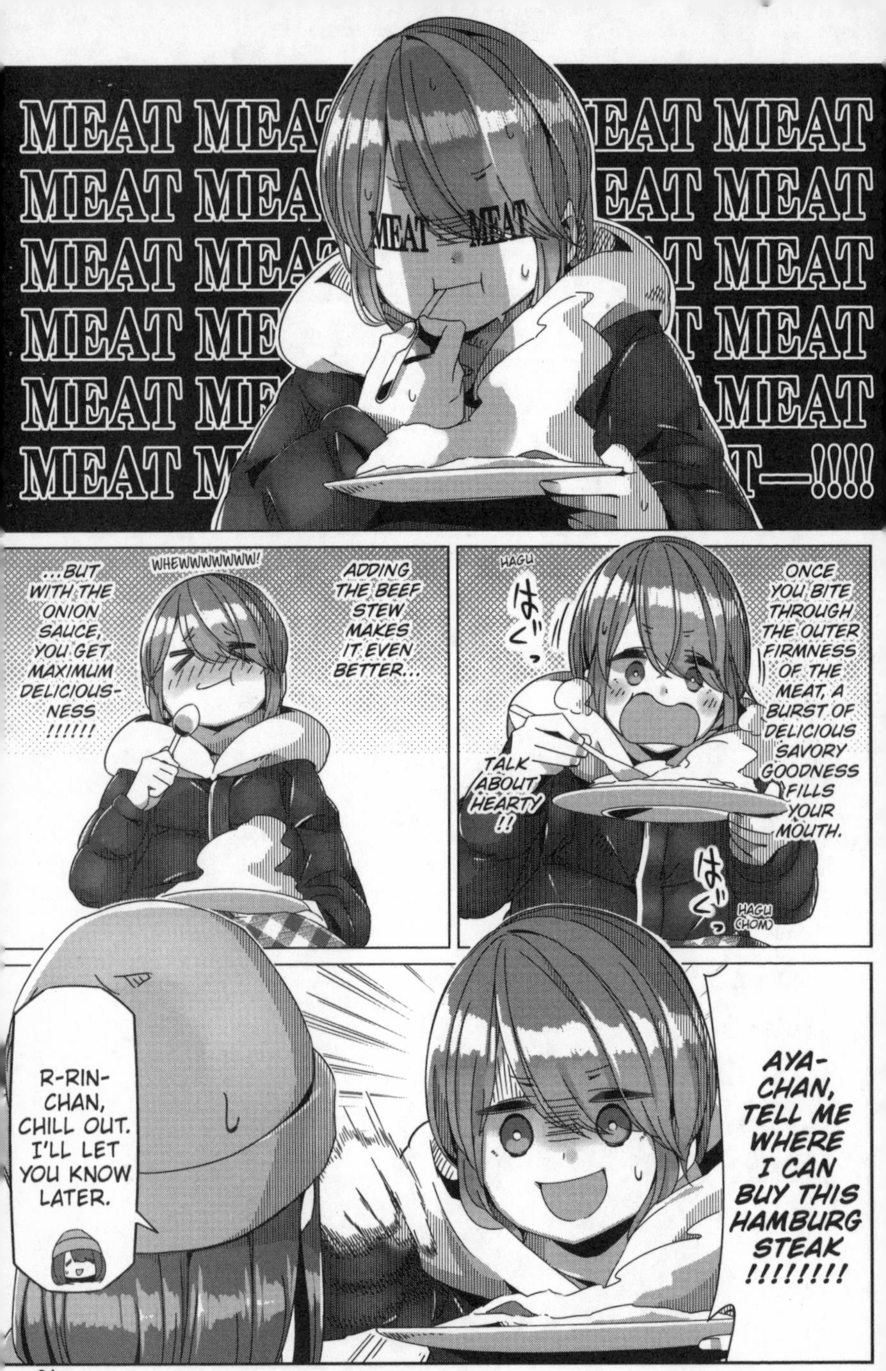

MEAT MEAT MEAT MEAT
MEAT MEAT MEAT MEAT
MEAT MEAT
MEAT MEAT MEAT MEAT
MEAT MEAT MEAT MEAT
MEAT MEAT MEAT MEAT
MEAT MEAT—!!!!
HAGU
ONCE YOU BITE THROUGH THE OUTER FIRMNESS OF THE MEAT, A BURST OF DELICIOUS SAVORY GOODNESS FILLS YOUR MOUTH.
TALK ABOUT HEARTY!!
HAGU (CHOM)
ADDING THE BEEF STEW MAKES IT EVEN BETTER...
WHEWWWWWWWW!
...BUT WITH THE ONION SAUCE, YOU GET MAXIMUM DELICIOUS-NESS!!!!!!
AYA-CHAN, TELL ME WHERE I CAN BUY THIS HAMBURG STEAK!!!!!!!!
R-RIN-CHAN, CHILL OUT. I'LL LET YOU KNOW LATER.

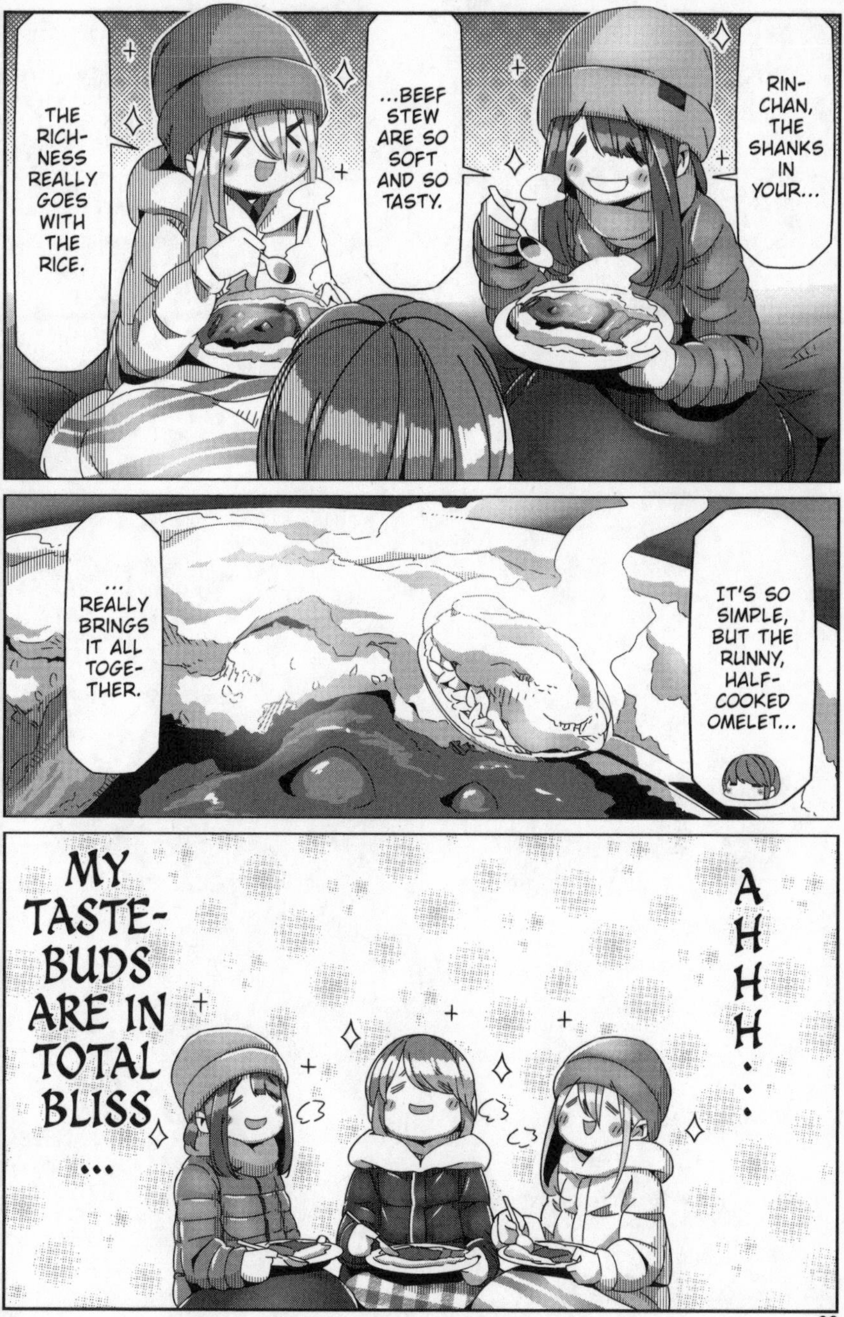
RIN-CHAN, THE SHANKS IN YOUR...
...BEEF STEW ARE SO SOFT AND SO TASTY.
THE RICHNESS REALLY GOES WITH THE RICE.
IT'S SO SIMPLE, BUT THE RUNNY, HALF-COOKED OMELET...
...REALLY BRINGS IT ALL TOGETHER.
AHHH...
MY TASTEBUDS ARE IN TOTAL BLISS...

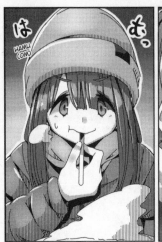

HAMI
(OM)

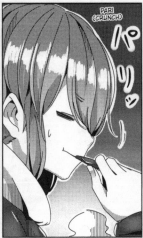

PARI
(CRUNCH)

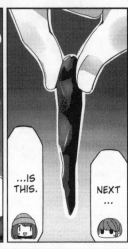

...IS THIS.

NEXT...

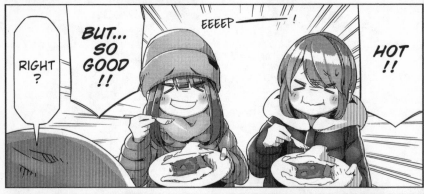

RIGHT?

BUT... SO GOOD!!

EEEEP————!

HOT!!

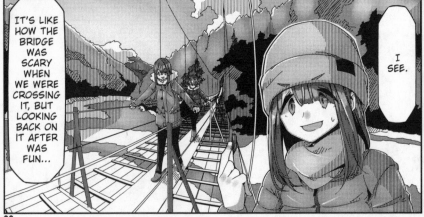

IT'S LIKE HOW THE BRIDGE WAS SCARY WHEN WE WERE CROSSING IT, BUT LOOKING BACK ON IT AFTER WAS FUN...

I SEE.

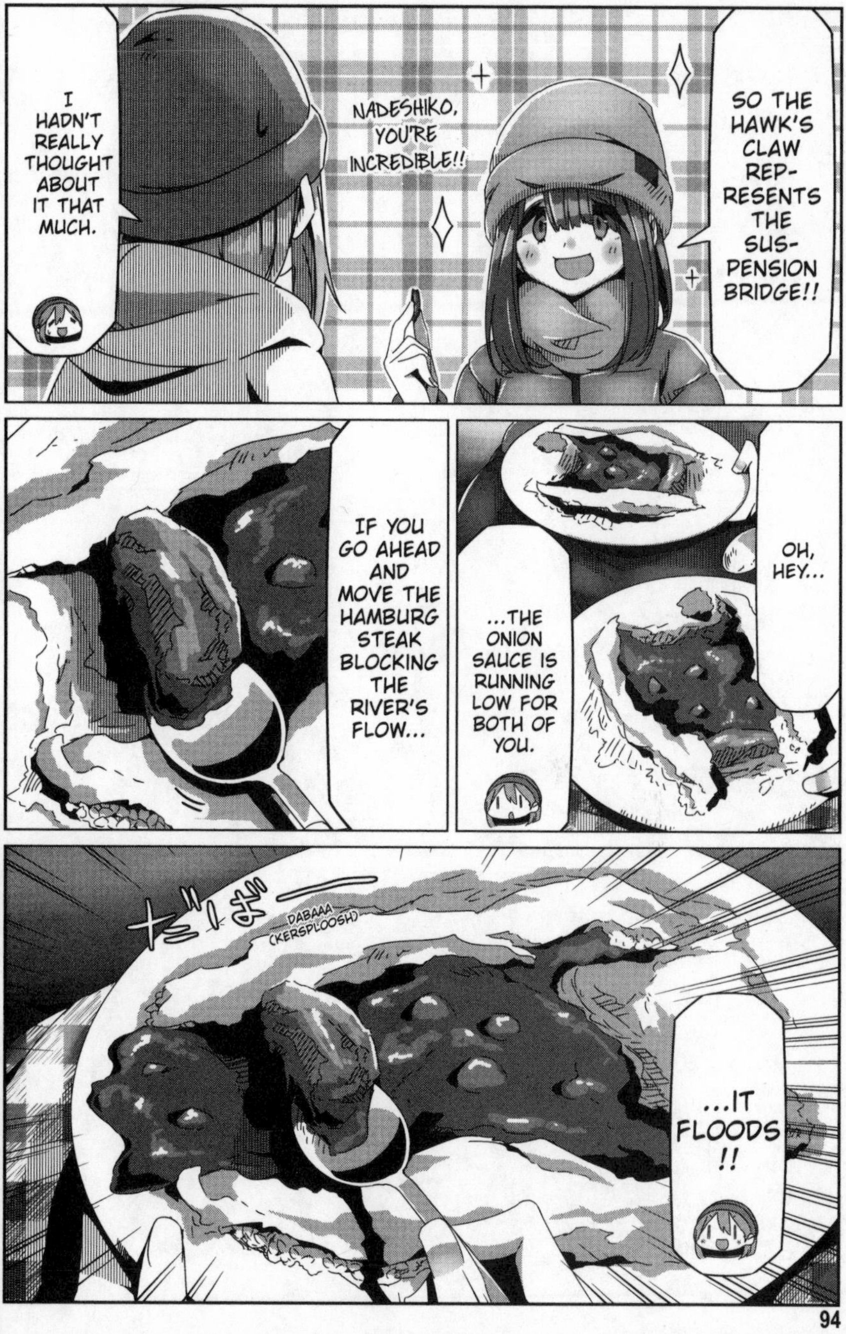
SO THE HAWK'S CLAW REPRESENTS THE SUSPENSION BRIDGE!!
NADESHIKO, YOU'RE INCREDIBLE!!
I HADN'T REALLY THOUGHT ABOUT IT THAT MUCH.
OH, HEY...
...THE ONION SAUCE IS RUNNING LOW FOR BOTH OF YOU.
IF YOU GO AHEAD AND MOVE THE HAMBURG STEAK BLOCKING THE RIVER'S FLOW...
DABAAA (KERSPLOOSH)
...IT FLOODS!!

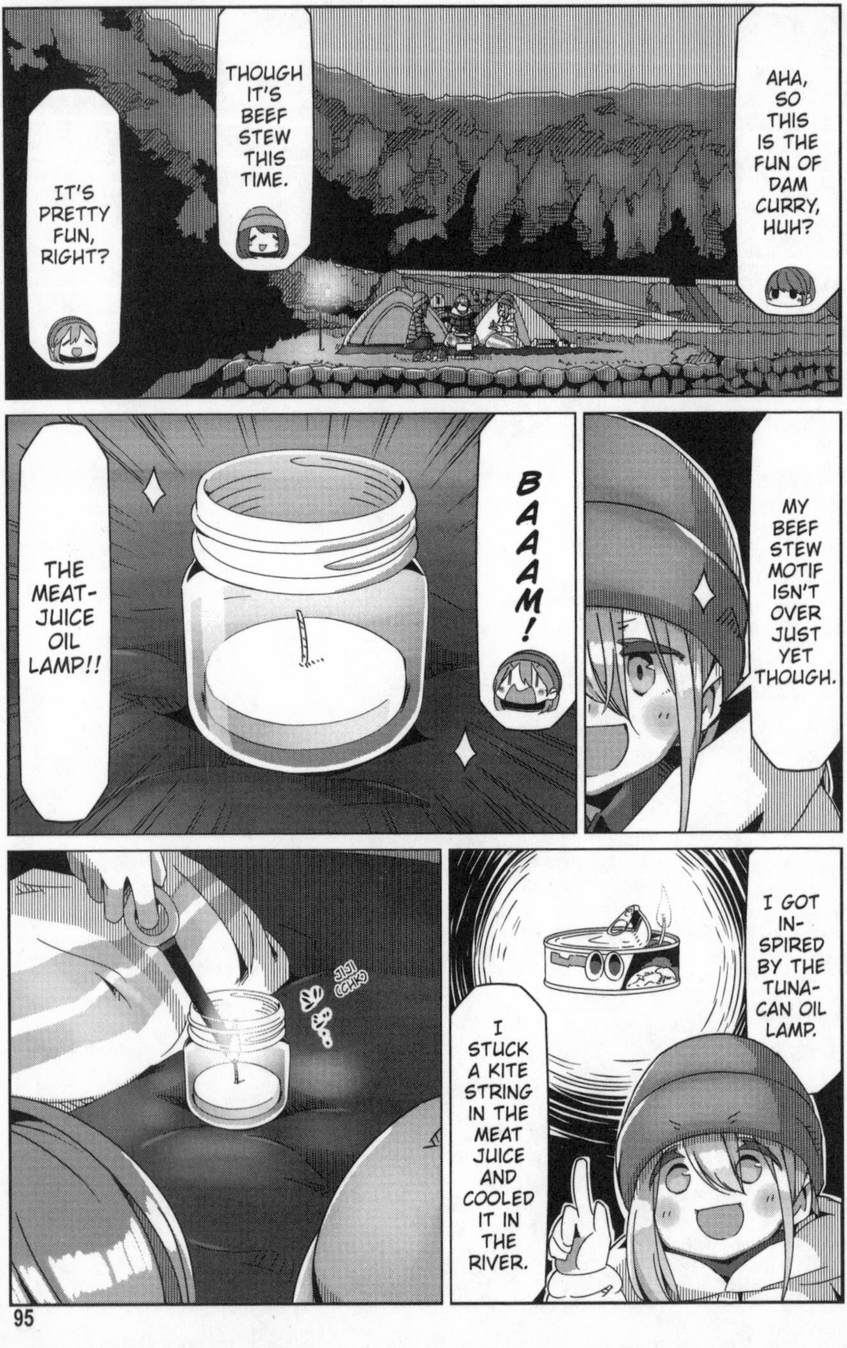
AHA, SO THIS IS THE FUN OF DAM CURRY, HUH?
THOUGH IT'S BEEF STEW THIS TIME.
IT'S PRETTY FUN, RIGHT?
MY BEEF STEW MOTIF ISN'T OVER JUST YET THOUGH.
BAAAAM!
THE MEAT-JUICE OIL LAMP!!
I GOT IN-SPIRED BY THE TUNA-CAN OIL LAMP.
I STUCK A KITE STRING IN THE MEAT JUICE AND COOLED IT IN THE RIVER.
JI JI (CHK)

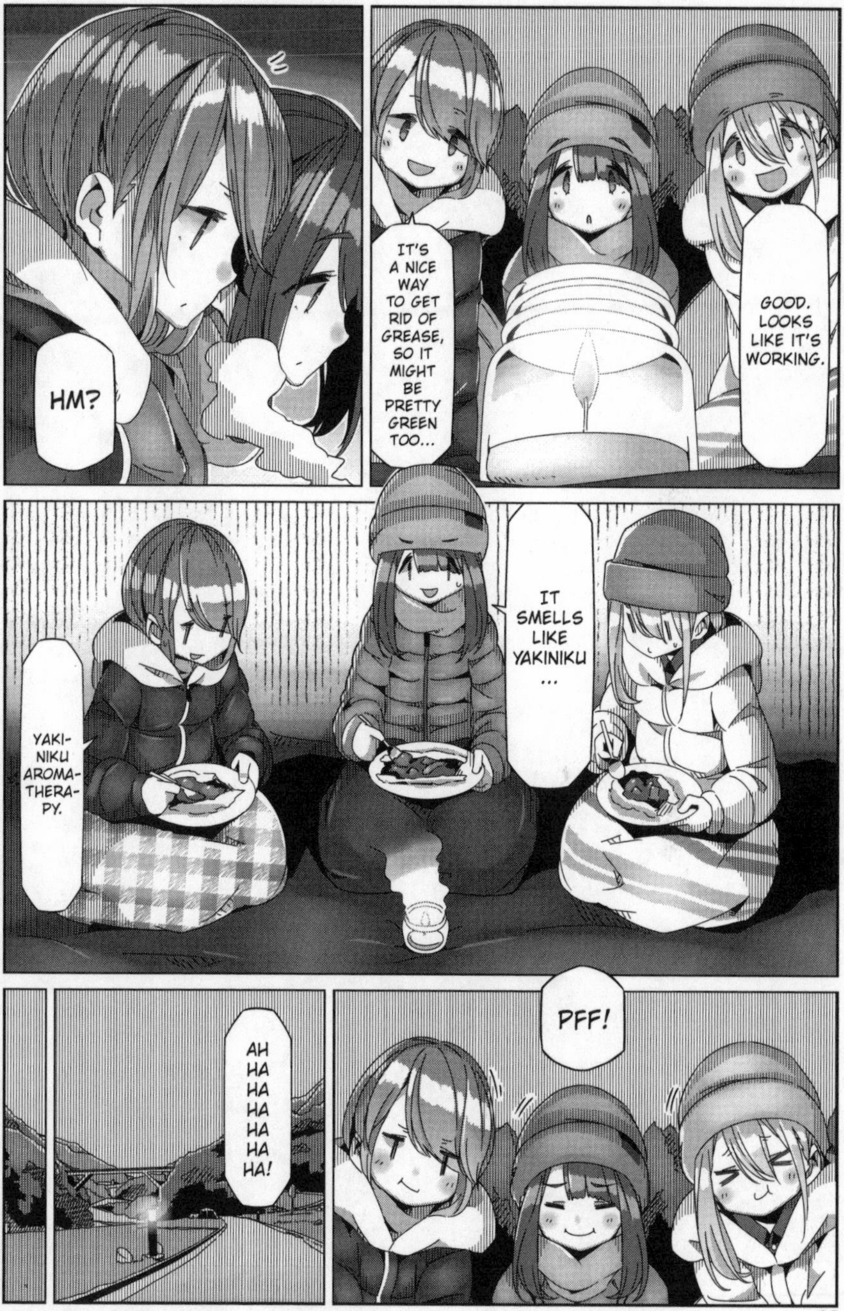
GOOD. LOOKS LIKE IT'S WORKING.
IT'S A NICE WAY TO GET RID OF GREASE, SO IT MIGHT BE PRETTY GREEN TOO...
HM?
IT SMELLS LIKE YAKINIKU...
YAKI-NIKU AROMA-THERA-PY.
PFF!
AH HA HA HA HA HA HA!

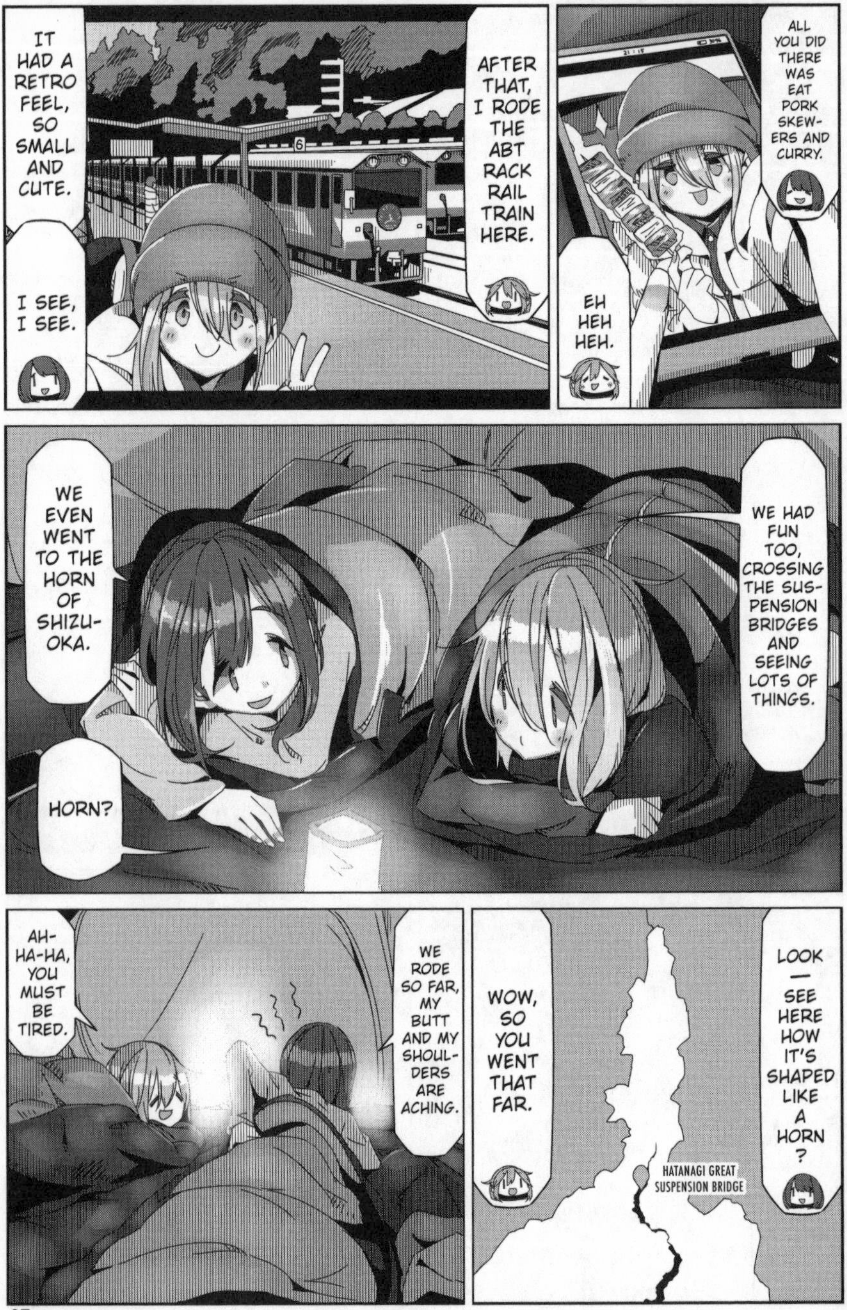
ALL YOU DID THERE WAS EAT PORK SKEWERS AND CURRY.
EH HEH HEH.
AFTER THAT, I RODE THE ABT RACK RAIL TRAIN HERE.
IT HAD A RETRO FEEL, SO SMALL AND CUTE.
I SEE, I SEE.
WE HAD FUN TOO, CROSSING THE SUSPENSION BRIDGES AND SEEING LOTS OF THINGS.
WE EVEN WENT TO THE HORN OF SHIZUOKA.
HORN?
LOOK—SEE HERE HOW IT'S SHAPED LIKE A HORN?
WOW, SO YOU WENT THAT FAR.
HATANAGI GREAT SUSPENSION BRIDGE
WE RODE SO FAR, MY BUTT AND MY SHOULDERS ARE ACHING.
AH-HA-HA, YOU MUST BE TIRED.

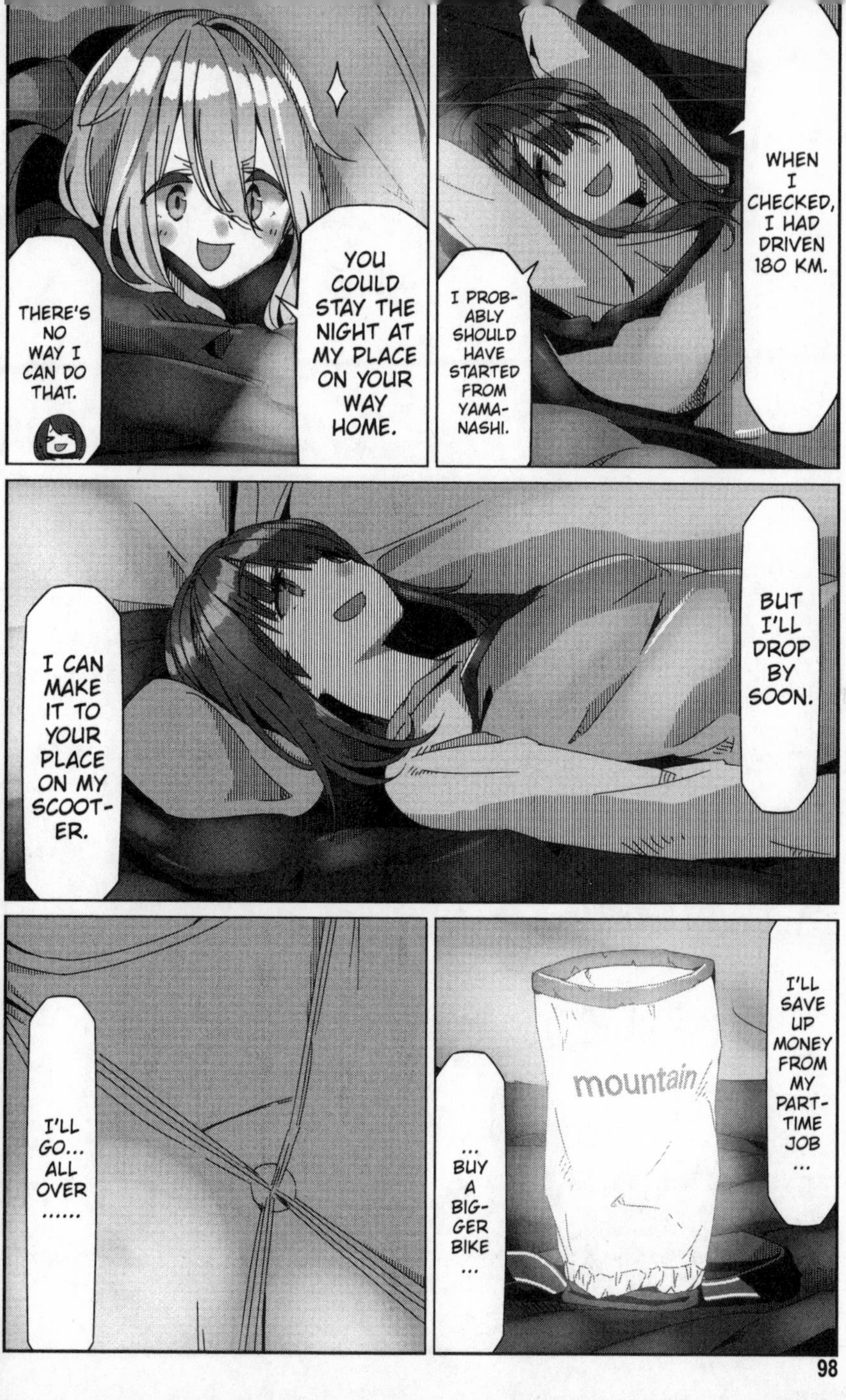
WHEN I CHECKED, I HAD DRIVEN 180 KM.
I PROBABLY SHOULD HAVE STARTED FROM YAMANASHI.
YOU COULD STAY THE NIGHT AT MY PLACE ON YOUR WAY HOME.
THERE'S NO WAY I CAN DO THAT.
BUT I'LL DROP BY SOON.
I CAN MAKE IT TO YOUR PLACE ON MY SCOOTER.
I'LL SAVE UP MONEY FROM MY PART-TIME JOB ...
mountain
... BUY A BIGGER BIKE ...
I'LL GO... ALL OVER ......

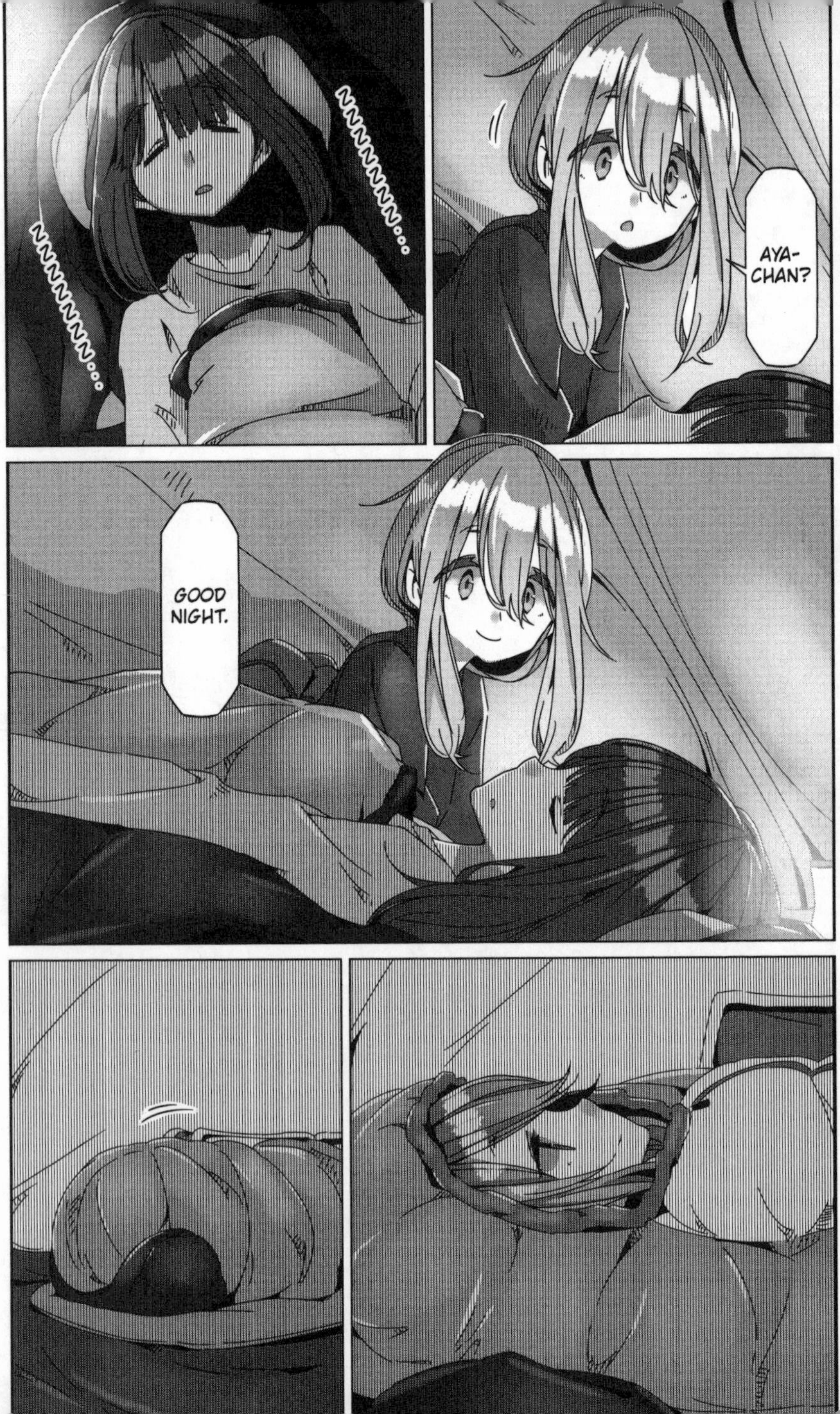
AYA-CHAN?
NNNNNNNN...
NNNNNNNN...
GOOD NIGHT.

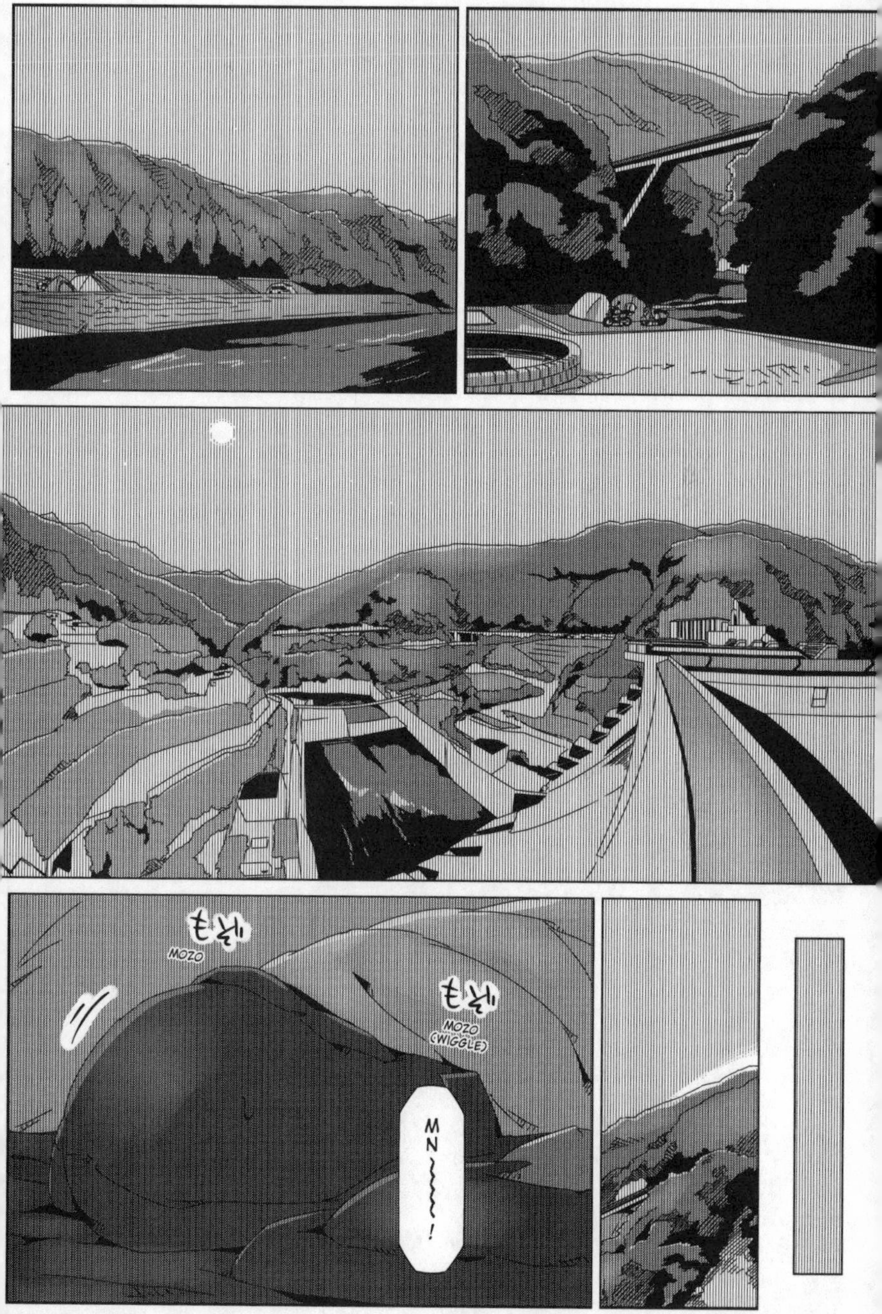
もぞ
MOZO
もぞ
MOZO (WIGGLE)
MN~~~!

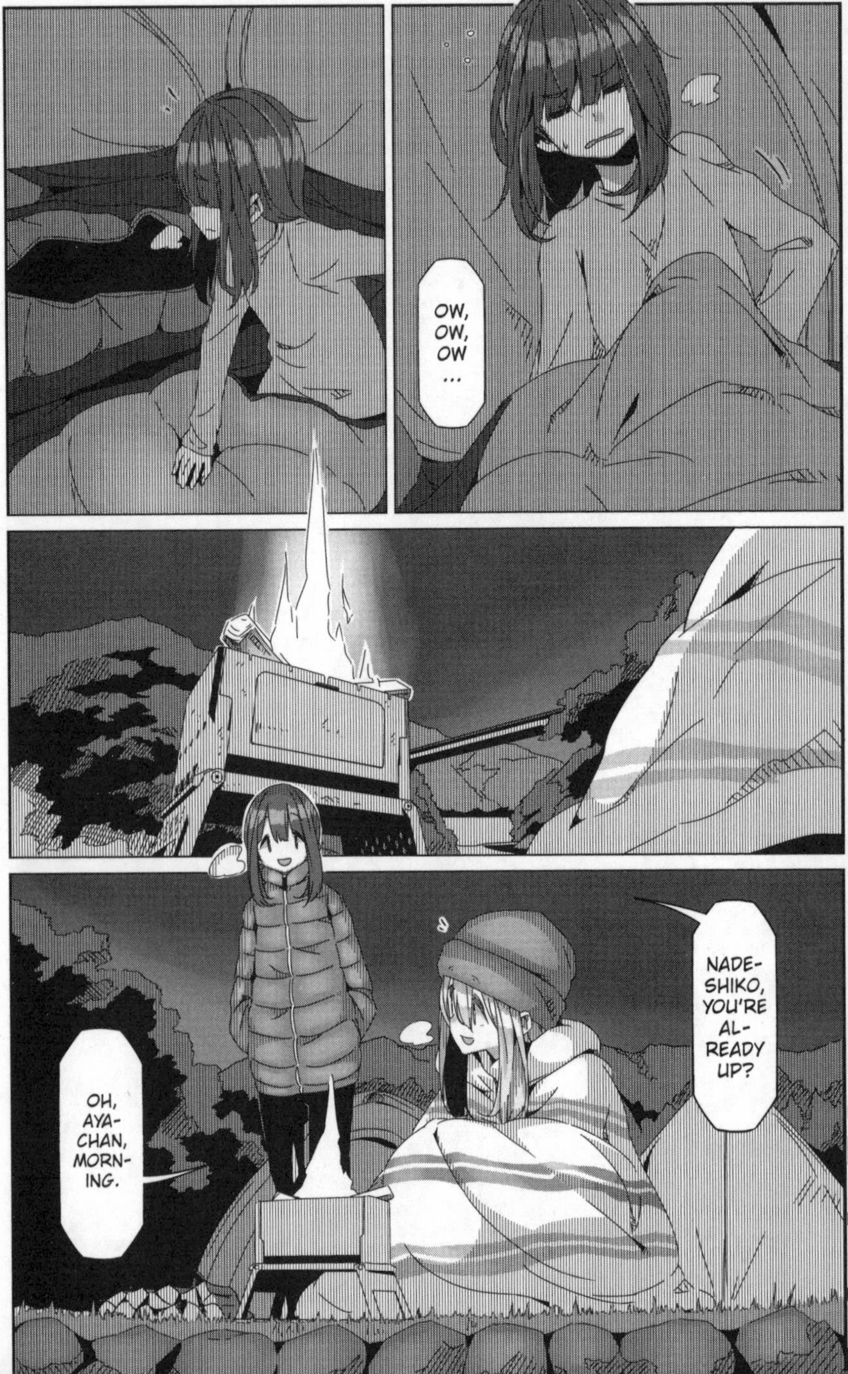
OW, OW, OW ...
NADE-SHIKO, YOU'RE AL-READY UP?
OH, AYA-CHAN, MORNING.

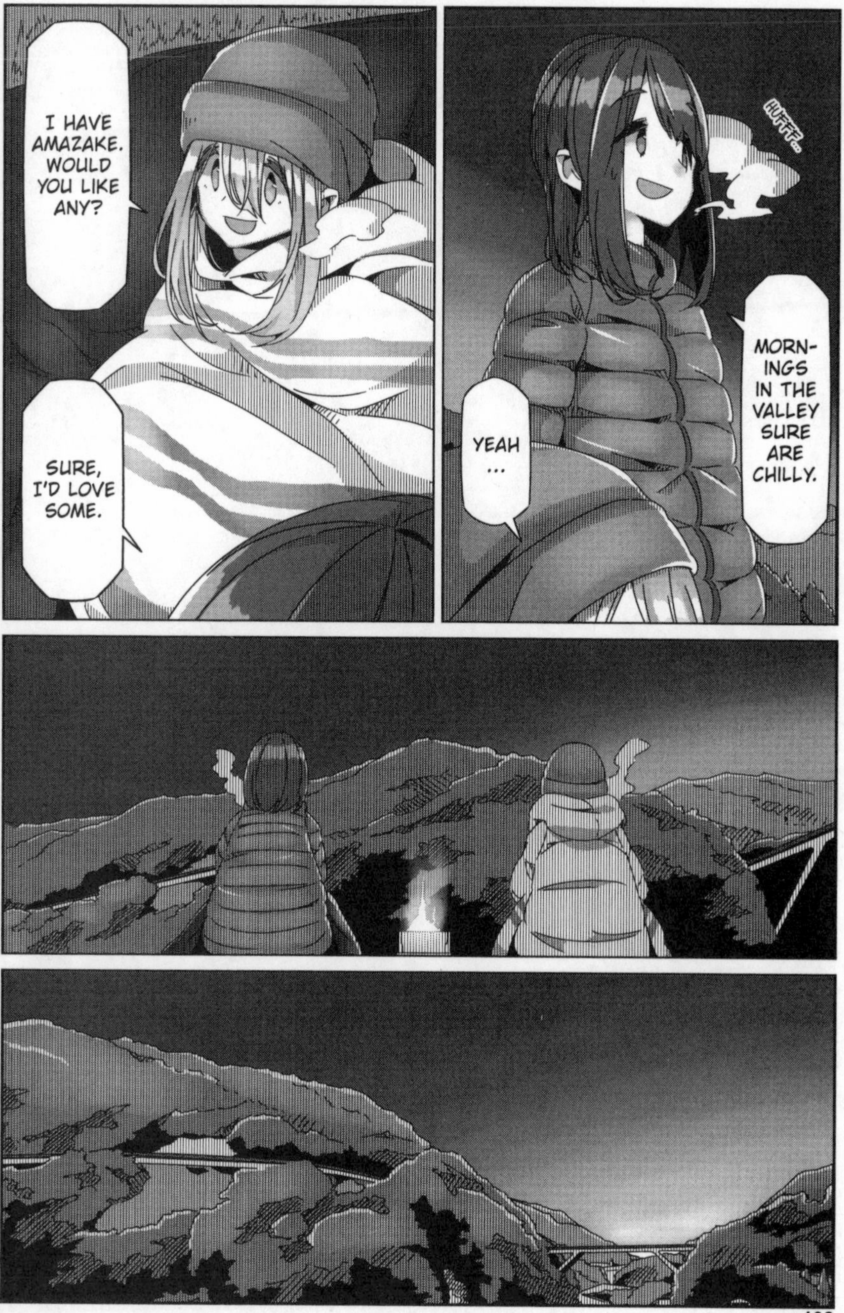
HUFFF...
MORN-INGS IN THE VALLEY SURE ARE CHILLY.
YEAH...
I HAVE AMAZAKE. WOULD YOU LIKE ANY?
SURE, I'D LOVE SOME.

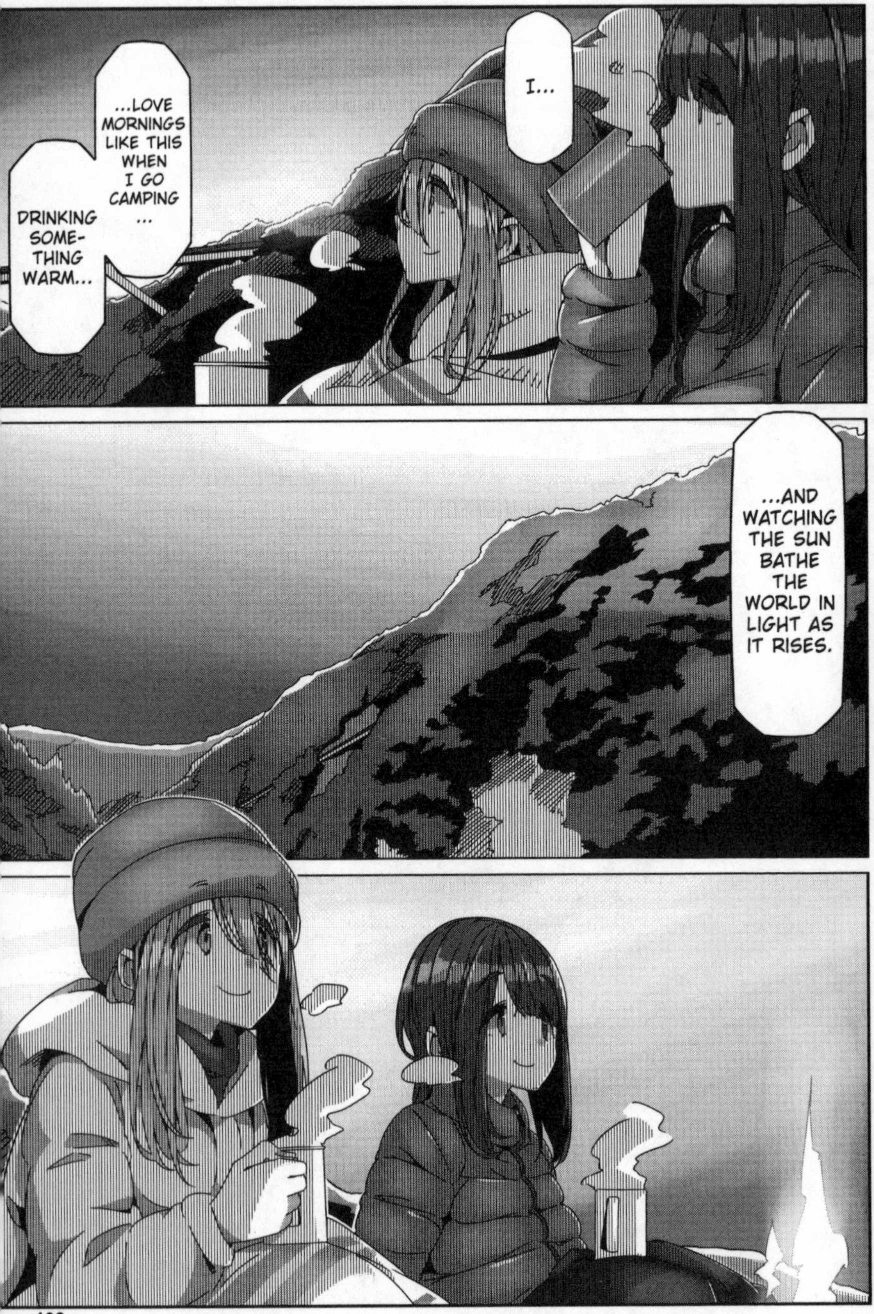
I...
...LOVE MORNINGS LIKE THIS WHEN I GO CAMPING ...
DRINKING SOME-THING WARM...
...AND WATCHING THE SUN BATHE THE WORLD IN LIGHT AS IT RISES.

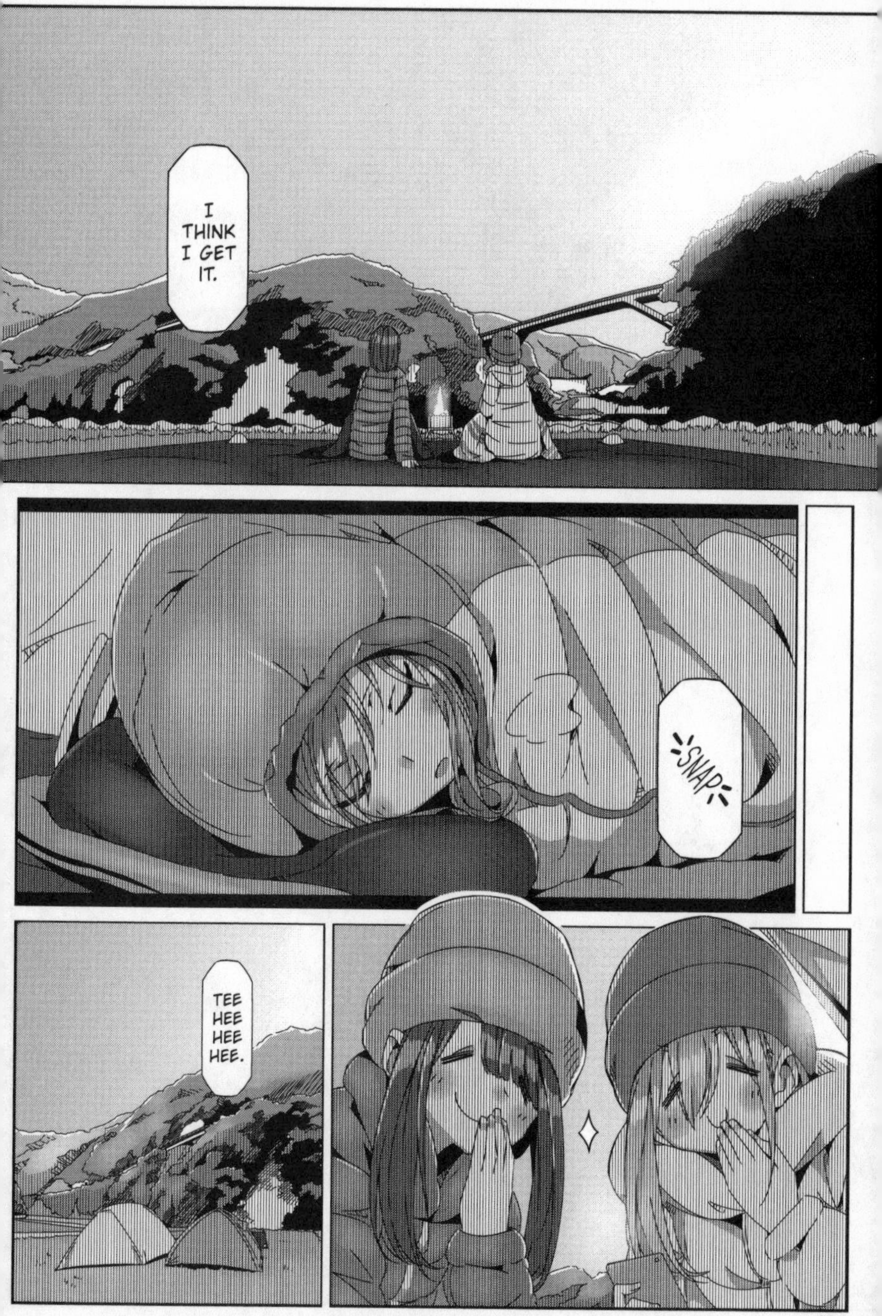
I THINK I GET IT.
SNAP
TEE HEE HEE HEE.

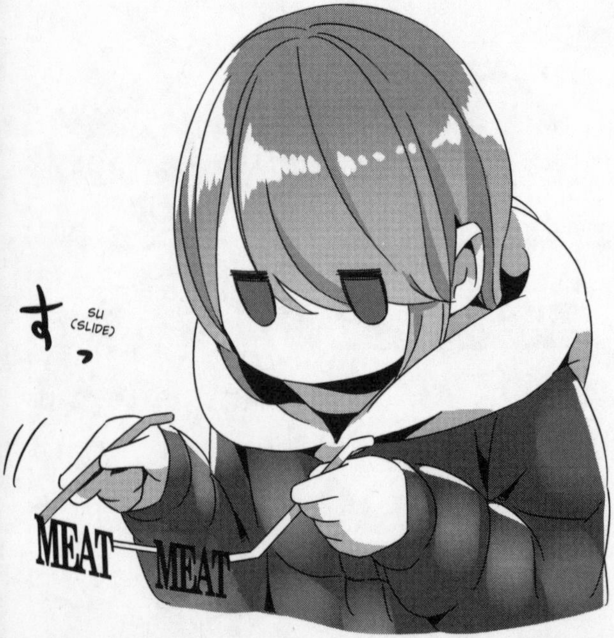
す っ
SU (SLIDE)
MEAT
MEAT

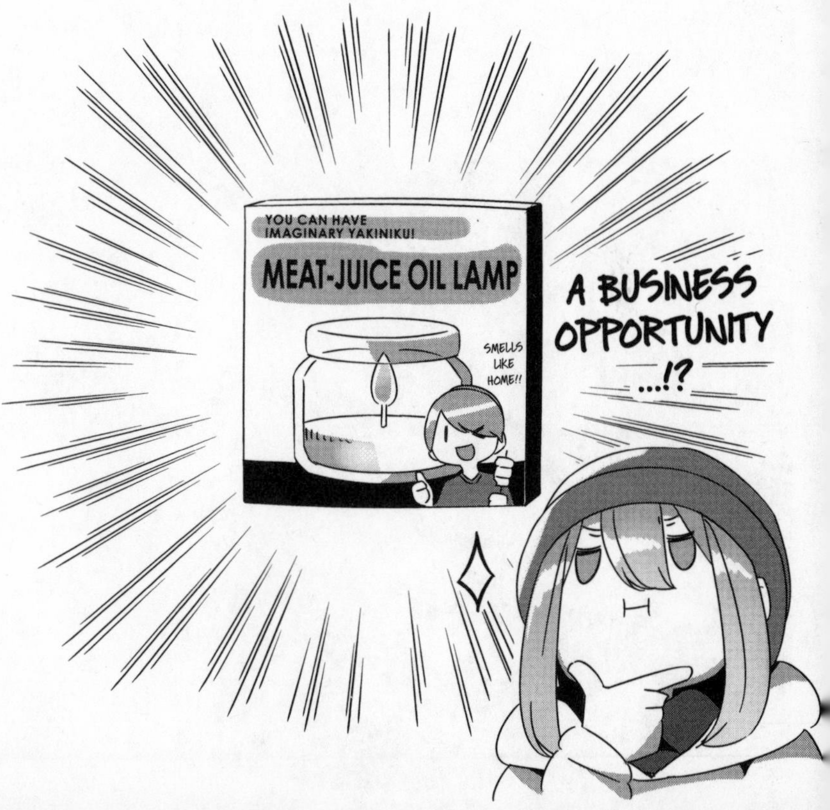
YOU CAN HAVE IMAGINARY YAKINIKU!
MEAT-JUICE OIL LAMP
SMELLS LIKE HOME!!
A BUSINESS OPPORTUNITY ...!?

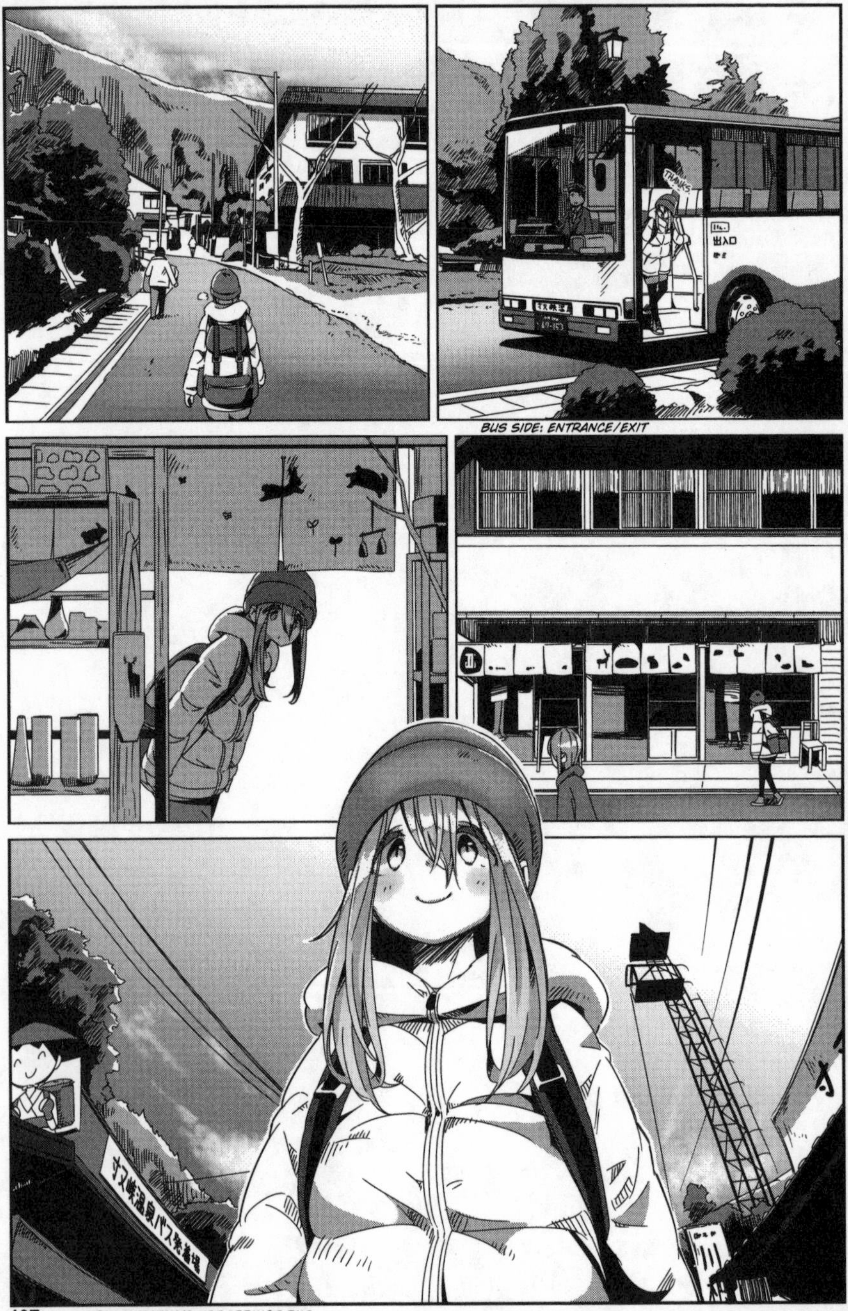
THANKS
出入口
BUS SIDE: ENTRANCE/EXIT

SIGN: SUMATAKYO HOT SPRINGS BUS

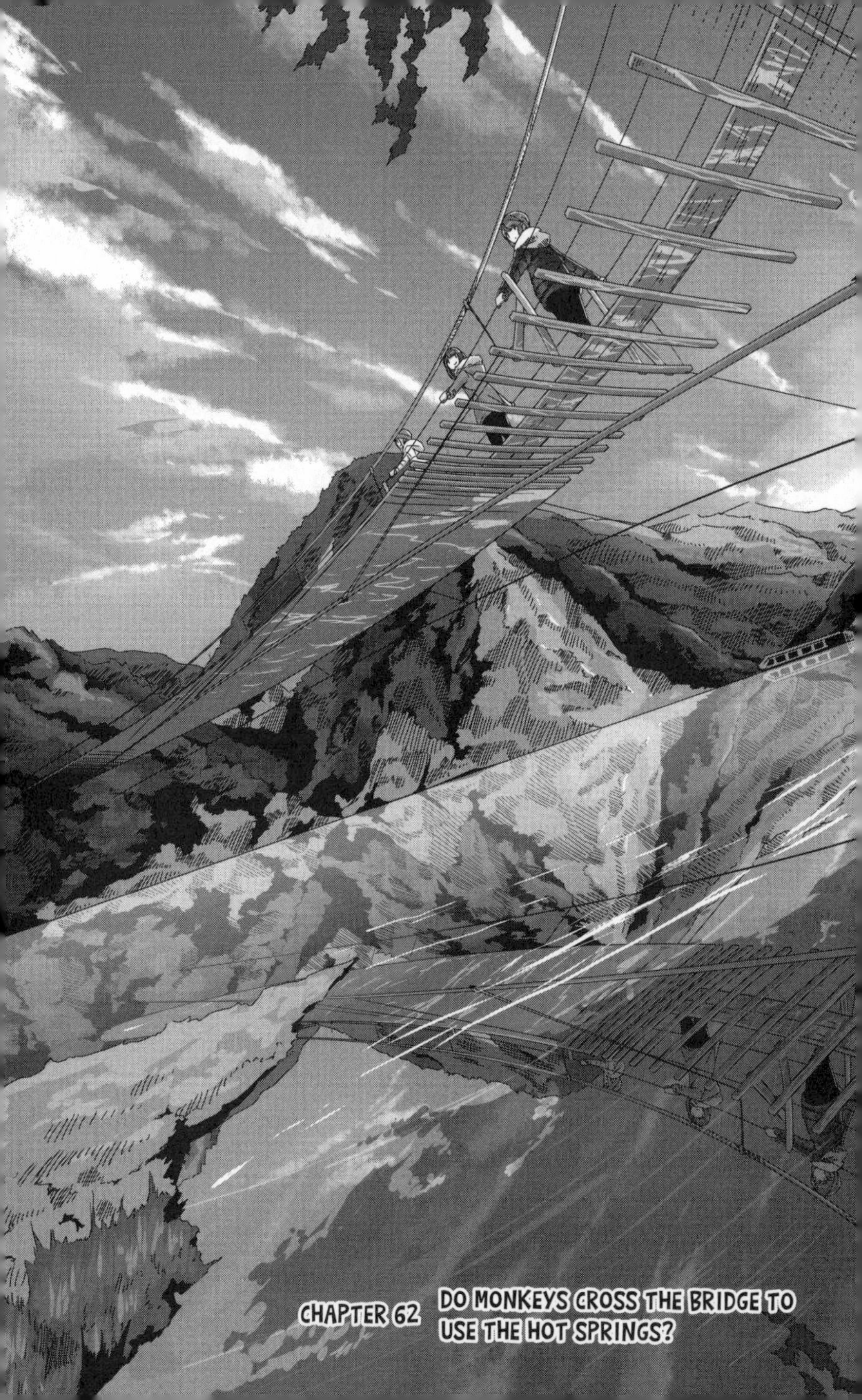
CHAPTER 62
DO MONKEYS CROSS THE BRIDGE TO USE THE HOT SPRINGS?

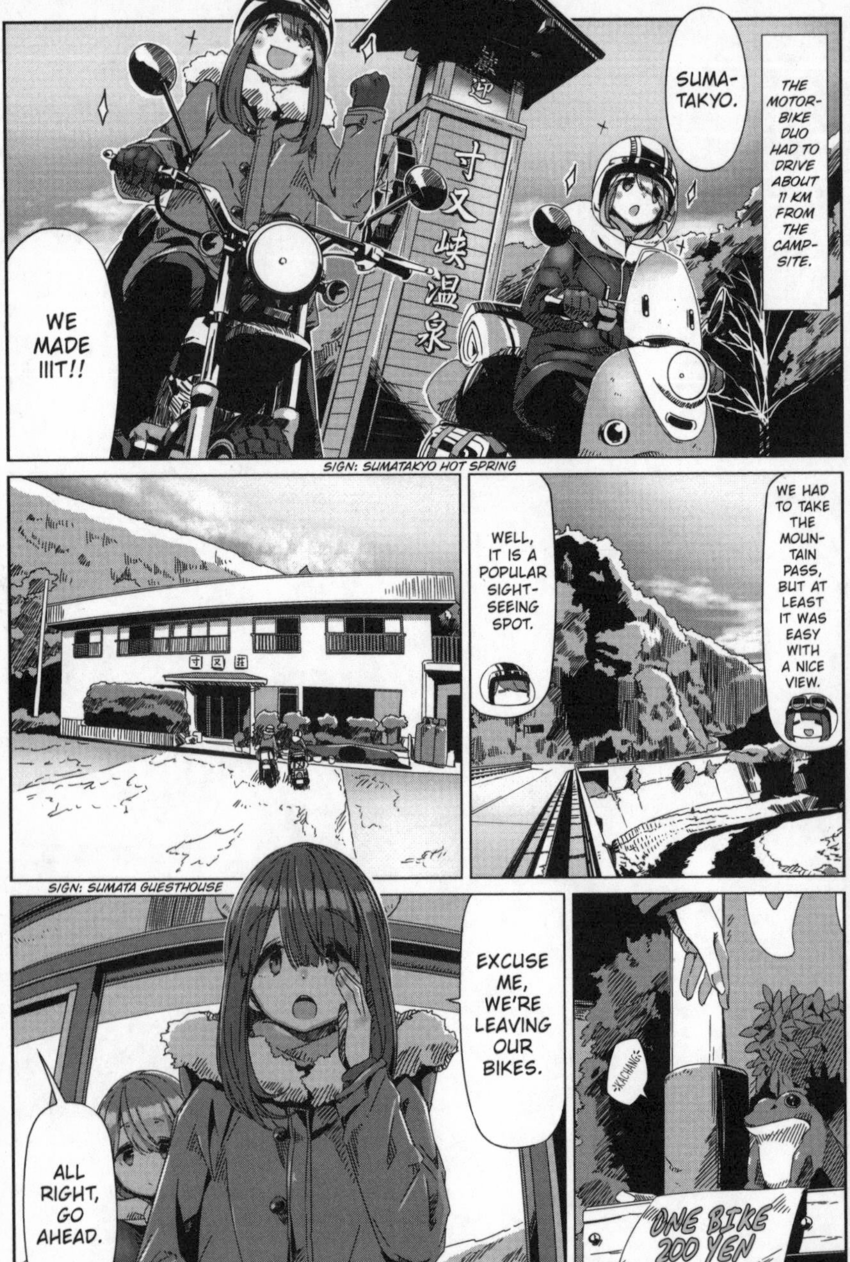
THE MOTOR-BIKE DUO HAD TO DRIVE ABOUT 11 KM FROM THE CAMP-SITE.
SUMA-TAKYO.
寸又峡温泉
WE MADE IIIT!!
SIGN: SUMATAKYO HOT SPRING
WE HAD TO TAKE THE MOUNTAIN PASS, BUT AT LEAST IT WAS EASY WITH A NICE VIEW.
WELL, IT IS A POPULAR SIGHT-SEEING SPOT.
寸又荘
SIGN: SUMATA GUESTHOUSE
KACHANG
ONE BIKE 200 YEN
EXCUSE ME, WE'RE LEAVING OUR BIKES.
ALL RIGHT, GO AHEAD.

SIGN: SUMATAKYO HOT SPRING

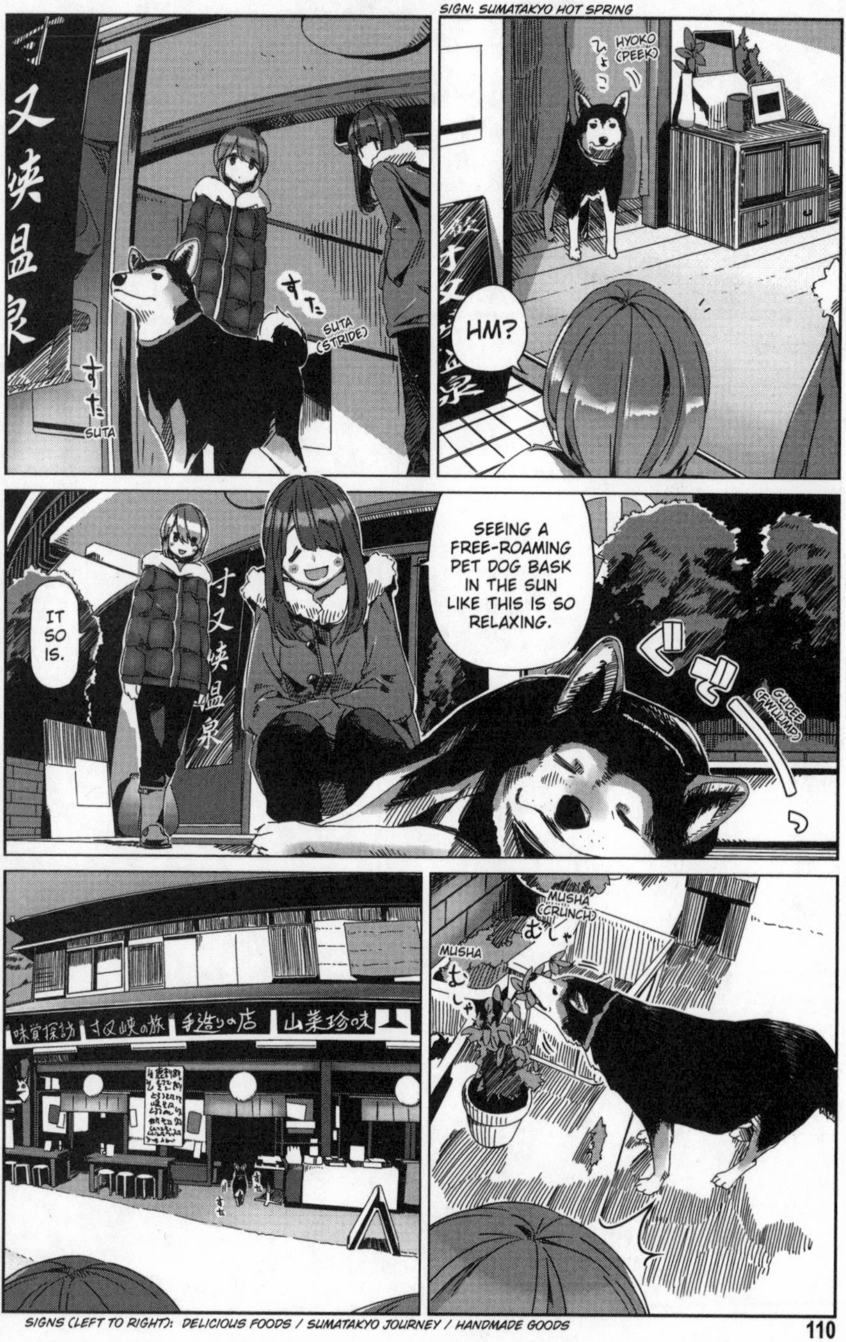

ひょこ
HYOKO (PEEK)
寸又峡温泉
HM?
寸又峡温泉
すた
SUTA (STRIDE)
すた
SUTA
SEEING A FREE-ROAMING PET DOG BASK IN THE SUN LIKE THIS IS SO RELAXING.
GUDEE (FWUMP)
寸又峡温泉
IT SO IS.
むしゃ
MUSHA (CRUNCH)
むしゃ
MUSHA
味覚探訪
寸又峡の旅
手造りの店
山菜珍味

SIGNS (LEFT TO RIGHT): DELICIOUS FOODS / SUMATAKYO JOURNEY / HANDMADE GOODS

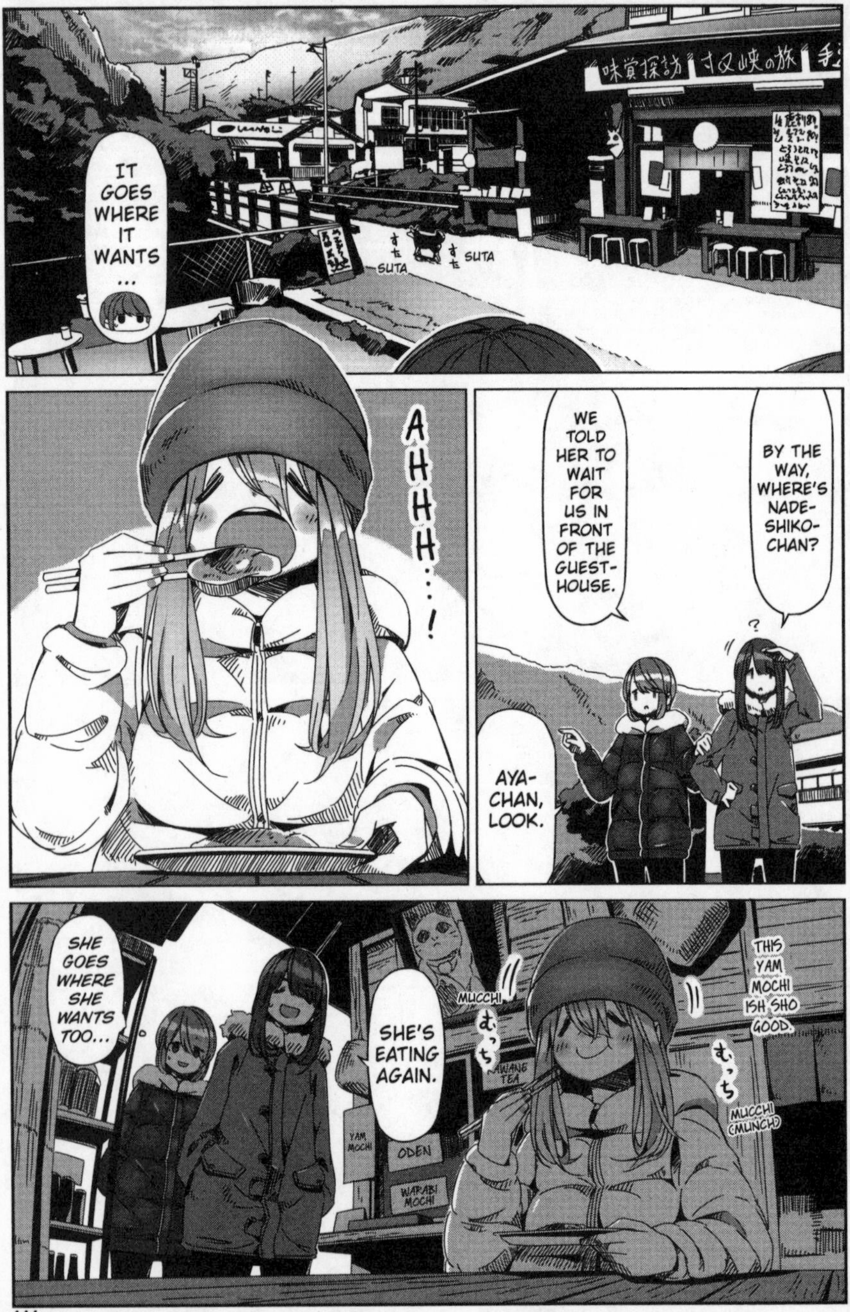
味覚探訪 寸又峡の旅
IT GOES WHERE IT WANTS...
すた SUTA
すた SUTA
BY THE WAY, WHERE'S NADE-SHIKO-CHAN?
WE TOLD HER TO WAIT FOR US IN FRONT OF THE GUEST-HOUSE.
AYA-CHAN, LOOK.
AHHH...!
THIS YAM MOCHI ISH SHO GOOD.
むっち MUCCHI (MUNCH)
むっち MUCCHI
YAM MOCHI
ODEN
WARABI MOCHI
SHE'S EATING AGAIN.
SHE GOES WHERE SHE WANTS TOO...

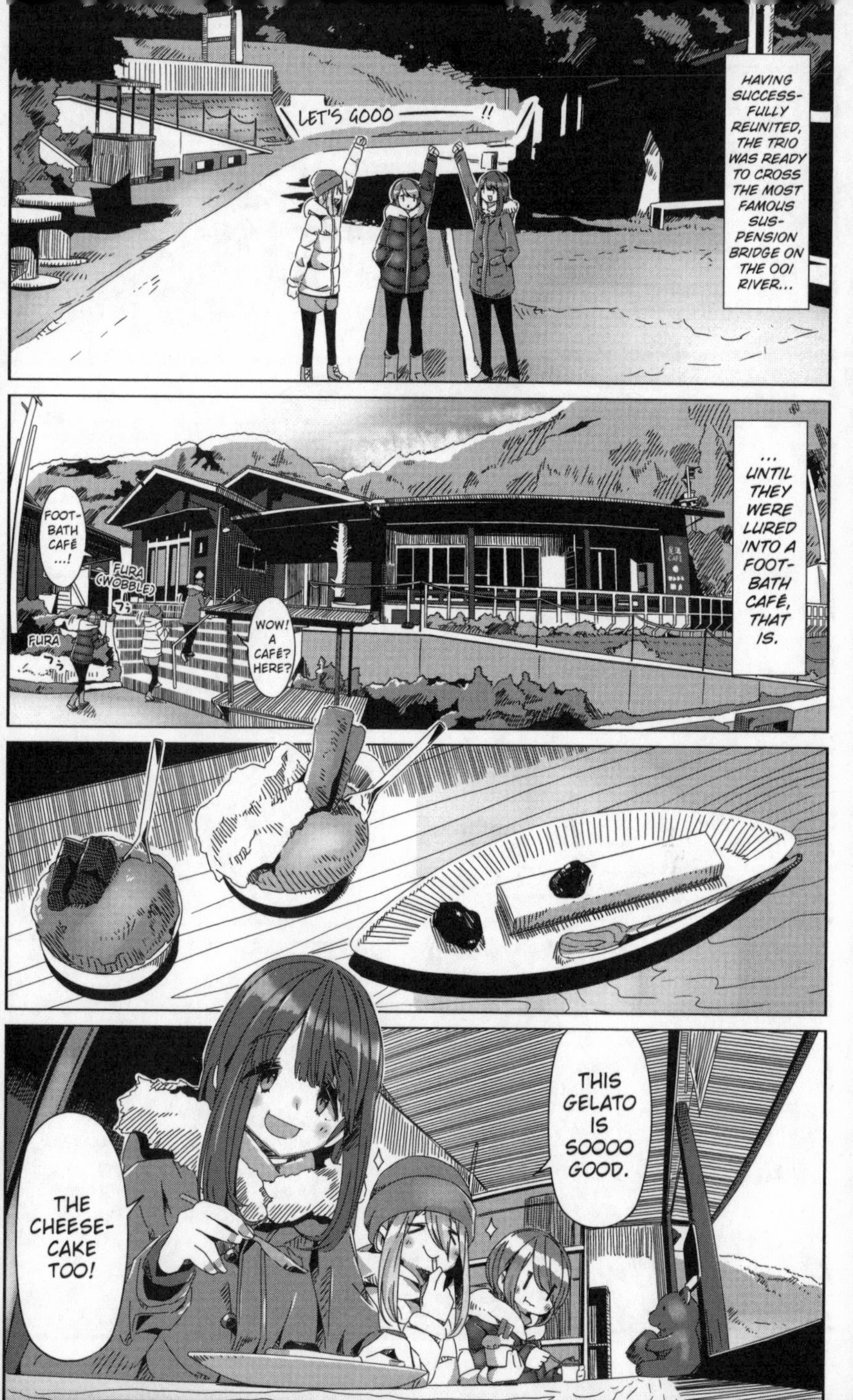
HAVING SUCCESSFULLY REUNITED, THE TRIO WAS READY TO CROSS THE MOST FAMOUS SUSPENSION BRIDGE ON THE OOI RIVER...
LET'S GOOO——!!
...UNTIL THEY WERE LURED INTO A FOOTBATH CAFÉ, THAT IS.
WOW! A CAFÉ? HERE?
FOOTBATH CAFÉ ...!
FURA (WOBBLE)
FURA
THIS GELATO IS SOOOO GOOD.
THE CHEESECAKE TOO!

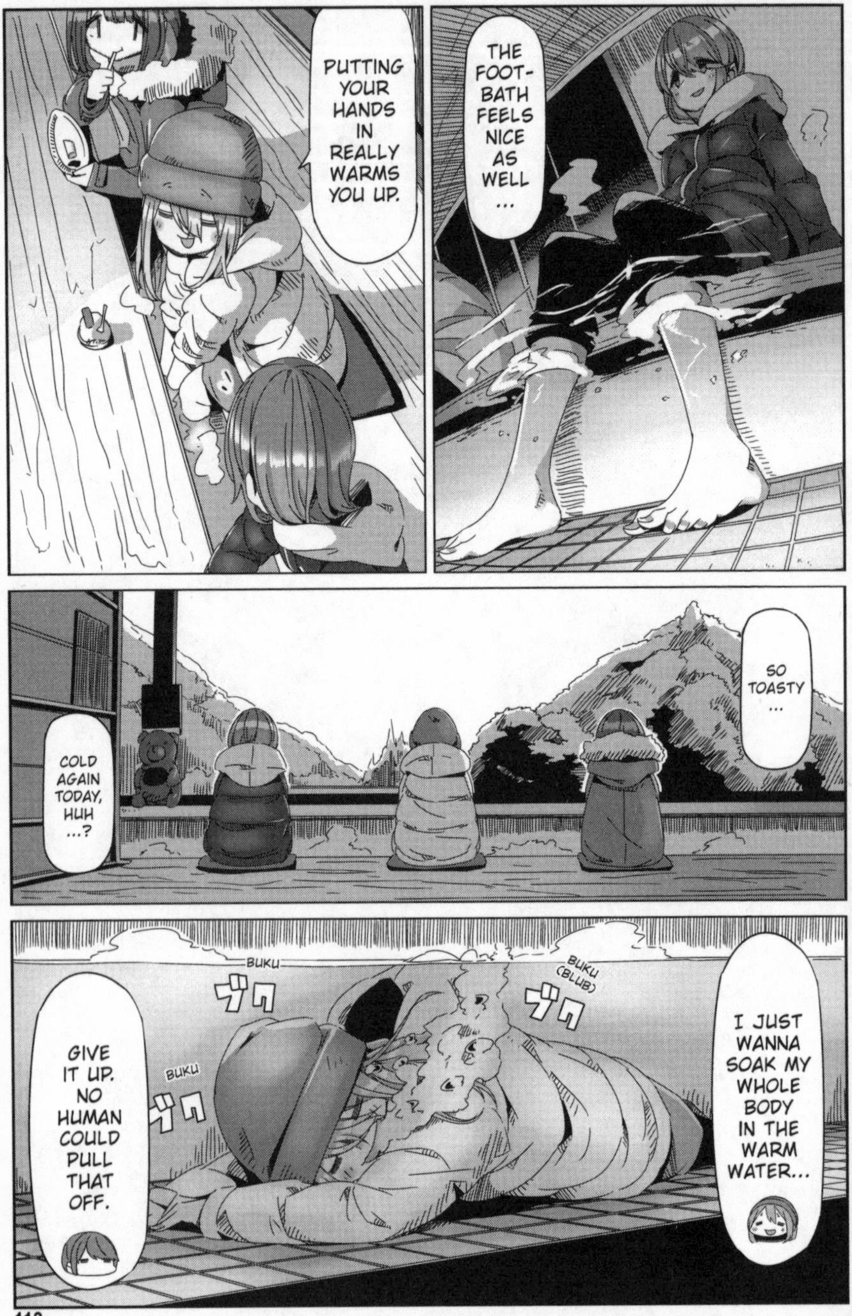
THE FOOT-BATH FEELS NICE AS WELL...
PUTTING YOUR HANDS IN REALLY WARMS YOU UP.
SO TOASTY...
COLD AGAIN TODAY, HUH...?
I JUST WANNA SOAK MY WHOLE BODY IN THE WARM WATER...
BUKU (BLUB)
BUKU
BUKU
GIVE IT UP. NO HUMAN COULD PULL THAT OFF.

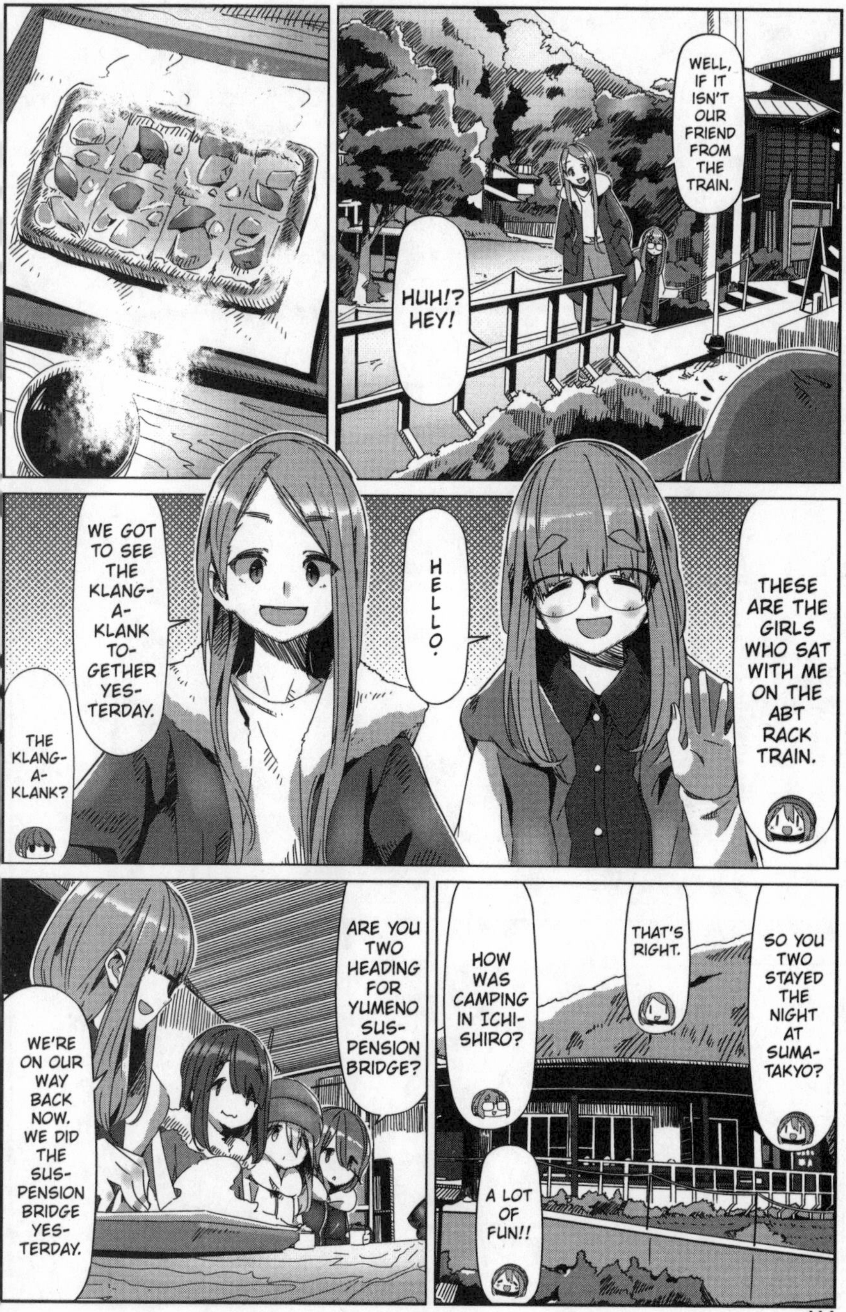

WELL, IF IT ISN'T OUR FRIEND FROM THE TRAIN.
HUH!? HEY!
THESE ARE THE GIRLS WHO SAT WITH ME ON THE ABT RACK TRAIN.
HELLO.
WE GOT TO SEE THE KLANG-A-KLANK TOGETHER YESTERDAY.
THE KLANG-A-KLANK?
SO YOU TWO STAYED THE NIGHT AT SUMATAKYO?
THAT'S RIGHT.
HOW WAS CAMPING IN ICHISHIRO?
A LOT OF FUN!!
ARE YOU TWO HEADING FOR YUMENO SUSPENSION BRIDGE?
WE'RE ON OUR WAY BACK NOW. WE DID THE SUSPENSION BRIDGE YESTERDAY.

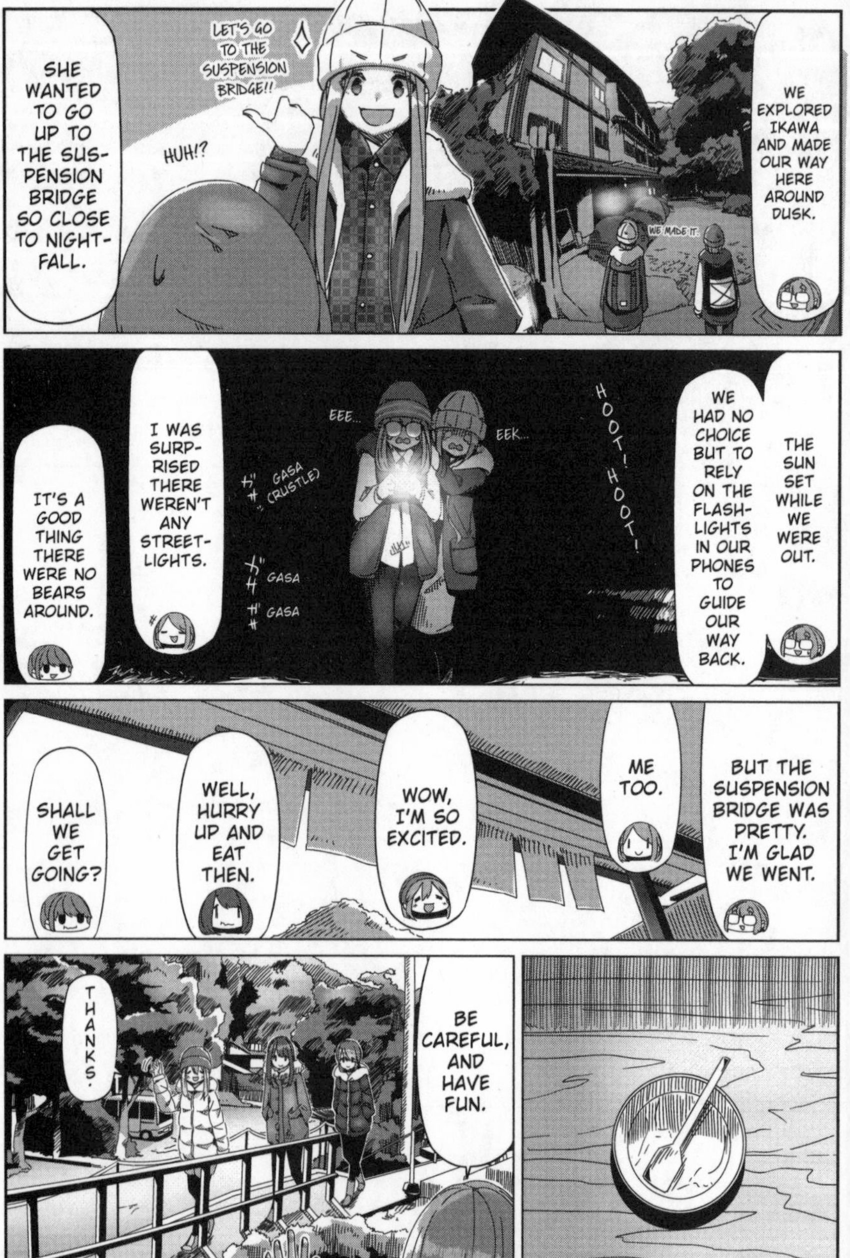
WE EXPLORED IKAWA AND MADE OUR WAY HERE AROUND DUSK.
WE MADE IT.
LET'S GO TO THE SUSPENSION BRIDGE!!
HUH!?
SHE WANTED TO GO UP TO THE SUSPENSION BRIDGE SO CLOSE TO NIGHTFALL.
THE SUN SET WHILE WE WERE OUT.
WE HAD NO CHOICE BUT TO RELY ON THE FLASHLIGHTS IN OUR PHONES TO GUIDE OUR WAY BACK.
HOOT! HOOT!
EEK...
EEE...
GASA (RUSTLE)
GASA
GASA
I WAS SURPRISED THERE WEREN'T ANY STREETLIGHTS.
IT'S A GOOD THING THERE WERE NO BEARS AROUND.
BUT THE SUSPENSION BRIDGE WAS PRETTY. I'M GLAD WE WENT.
ME TOO.
WOW, I'M SO EXCITED.
WELL, HURRY UP AND EAT THEN.
SHALL WE GET GOING?
BE CAREFUL, AND HAVE FUN.
THANKS.

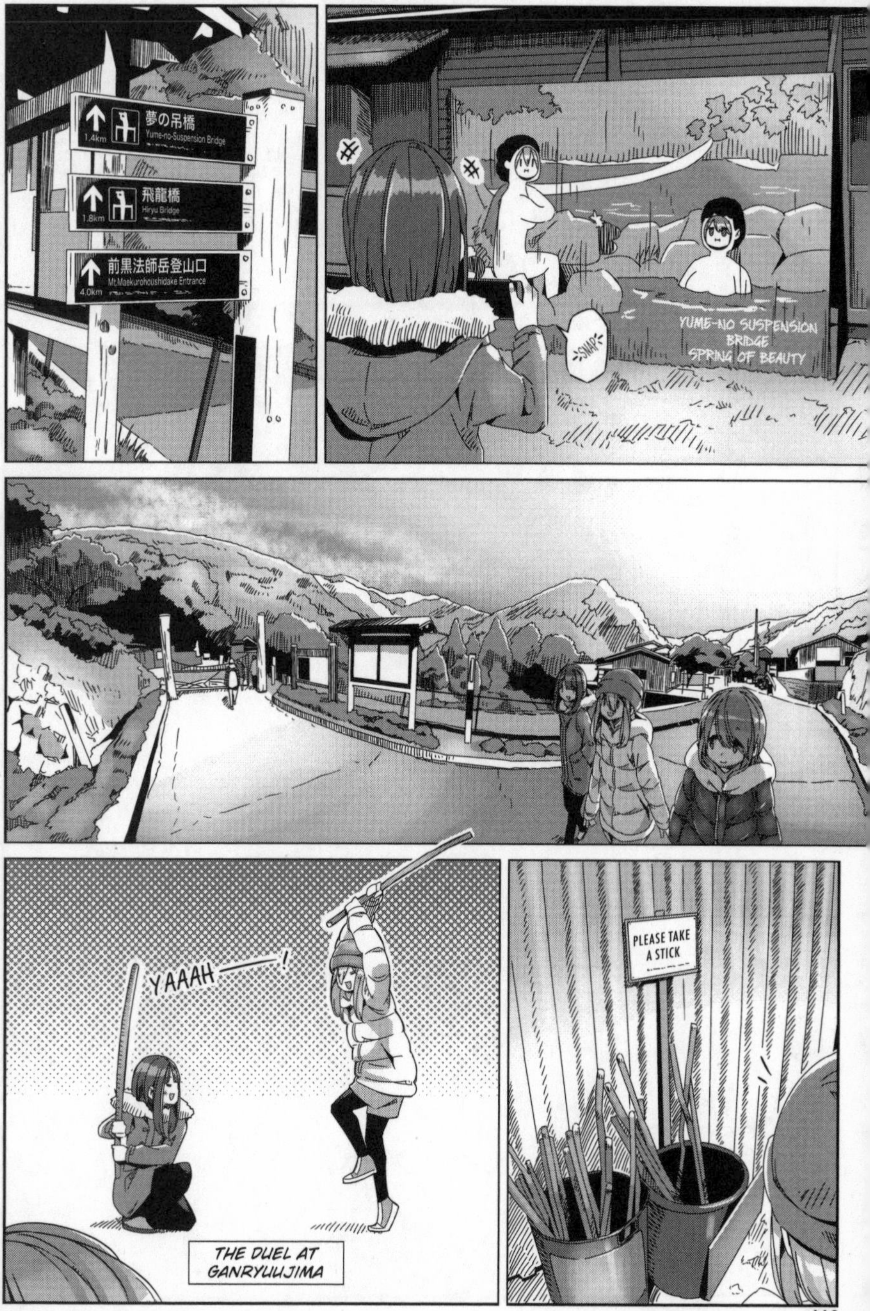
SNAP
YUME-NO SUSPENSION BRIDGE SPRING OF BEAUTY
夢の吊橋
Yume-no-Suspension Bridge
1.4km
飛龍橋
Hiryu Bridge
1.8km
前黒法師岳登山口
Mt.Maekurohoushidake Entrance
4.0km
PLEASE TAKE A STICK
YAAAH——!
THE DUEL AT GANRYUUJIMA

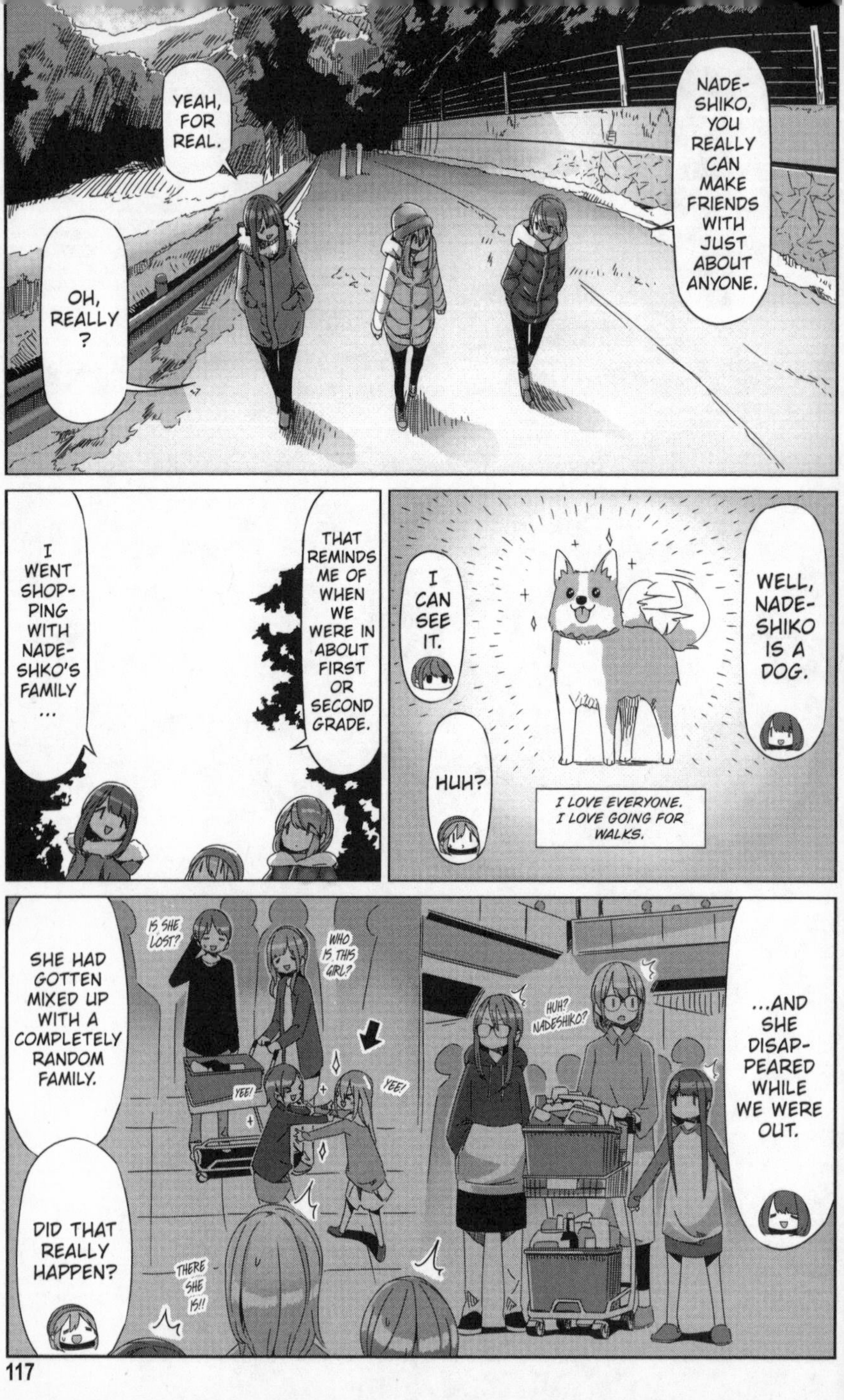
NADESHIKO, YOU REALLY CAN MAKE FRIENDS WITH JUST ABOUT ANYONE.
YEAH, FOR REAL.
OH, REALLY?
WELL, NADESHIKO IS A DOG.
I CAN SEE IT.
HUH?
I LOVE EVERYONE. I LOVE GOING FOR WALKS.
THAT REMINDS ME OF WHEN WE WERE IN ABOUT FIRST OR SECOND GRADE.
I WENT SHOPPING WITH NADESHKO'S FAMILY...
...AND SHE DISAPPEARED WHILE WE WERE OUT.
HUH? NADESHIKO?
WHO IS THIS GIRL?
IS SHE LOST?
SHE HAD GOTTEN MIXED UP WITH A COMPLETELY RANDOM FAMILY.
YEE!
YEE!
THERE SHE IS!!
DID THAT REALLY HAPPEN?

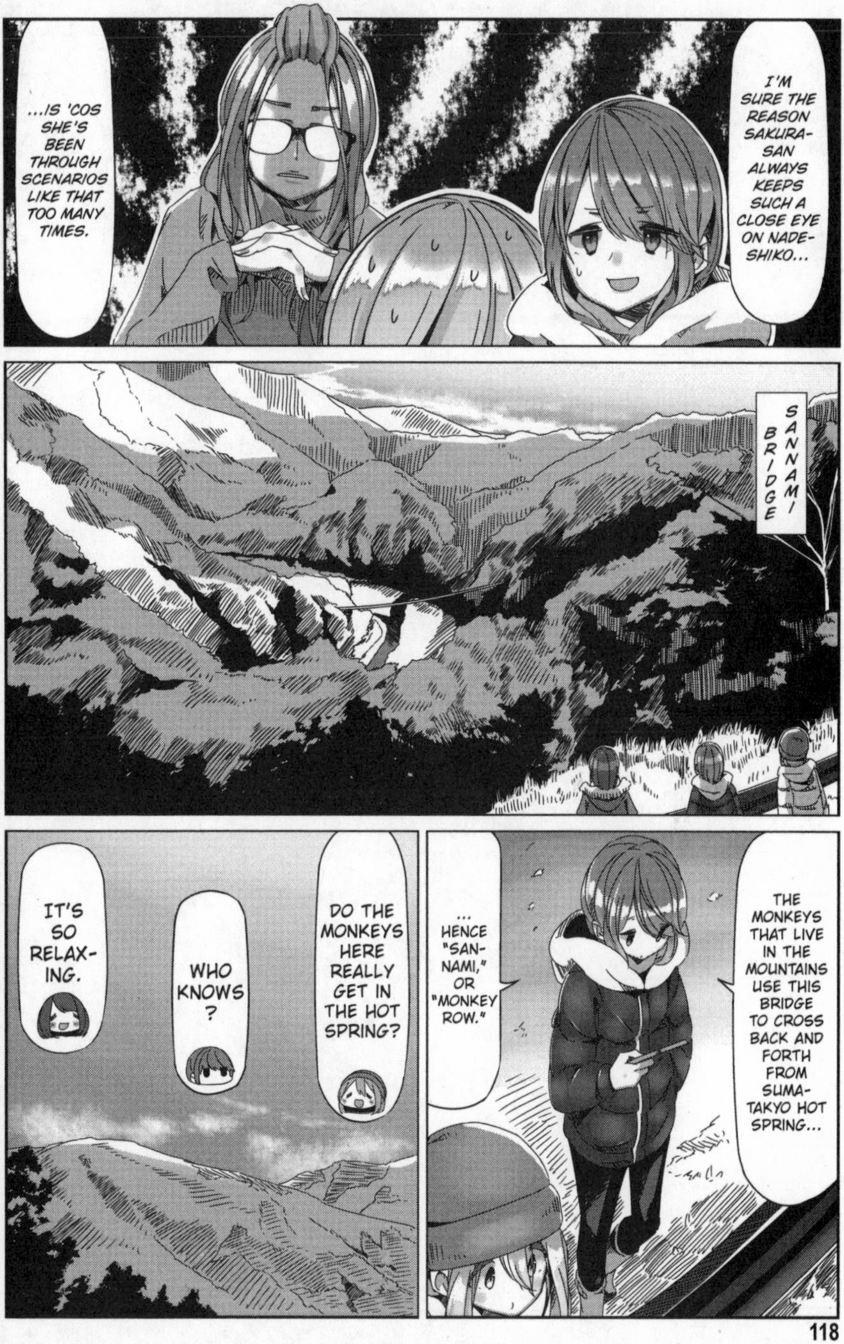
I'M SURE THE REASON SAKURA-SAN ALWAYS KEEPS SUCH A CLOSE EYE ON NADE-SHIKO...
...IS 'COS SHE'S BEEN THROUGH SCENARIOS LIKE THAT TOO MANY TIMES.
SANNAMI BRIDGE
THE MONKEYS THAT LIVE IN THE MOUNTAINS USE THIS BRIDGE TO CROSS BACK AND FORTH FROM SUMA-TAKYO HOT SPRING...
... HENCE "SAN-NAMI," OR "MONKEY ROW."
DO THE MONKEYS HERE REALLY GET IN THE HOT SPRING?
WHO KNOWS?
IT'S SO RELAX-ING.

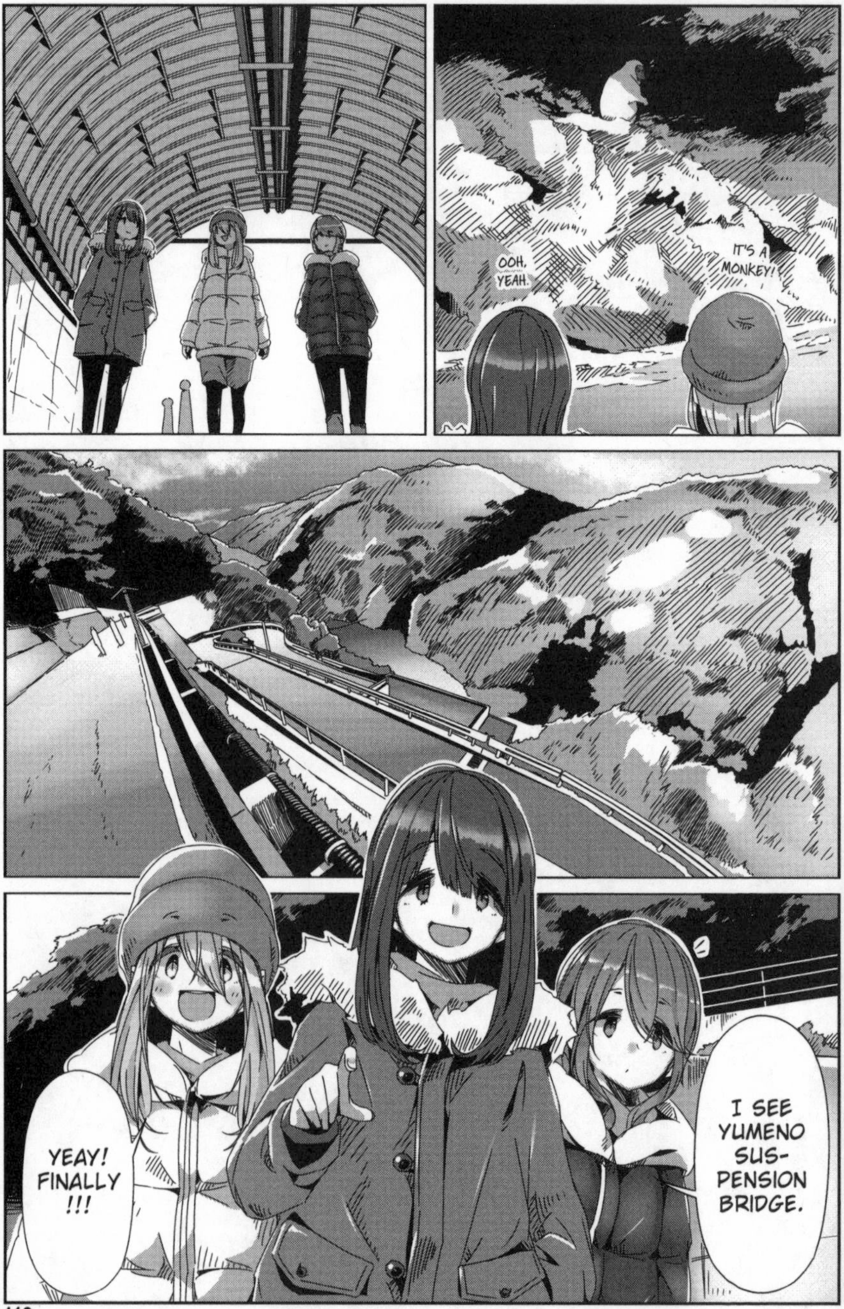
IT'S A MONKEY!
OOH, YEAH.
I SEE YUMENO SUS-PENSION BRIDGE.
YEAY! FINALLY !!!

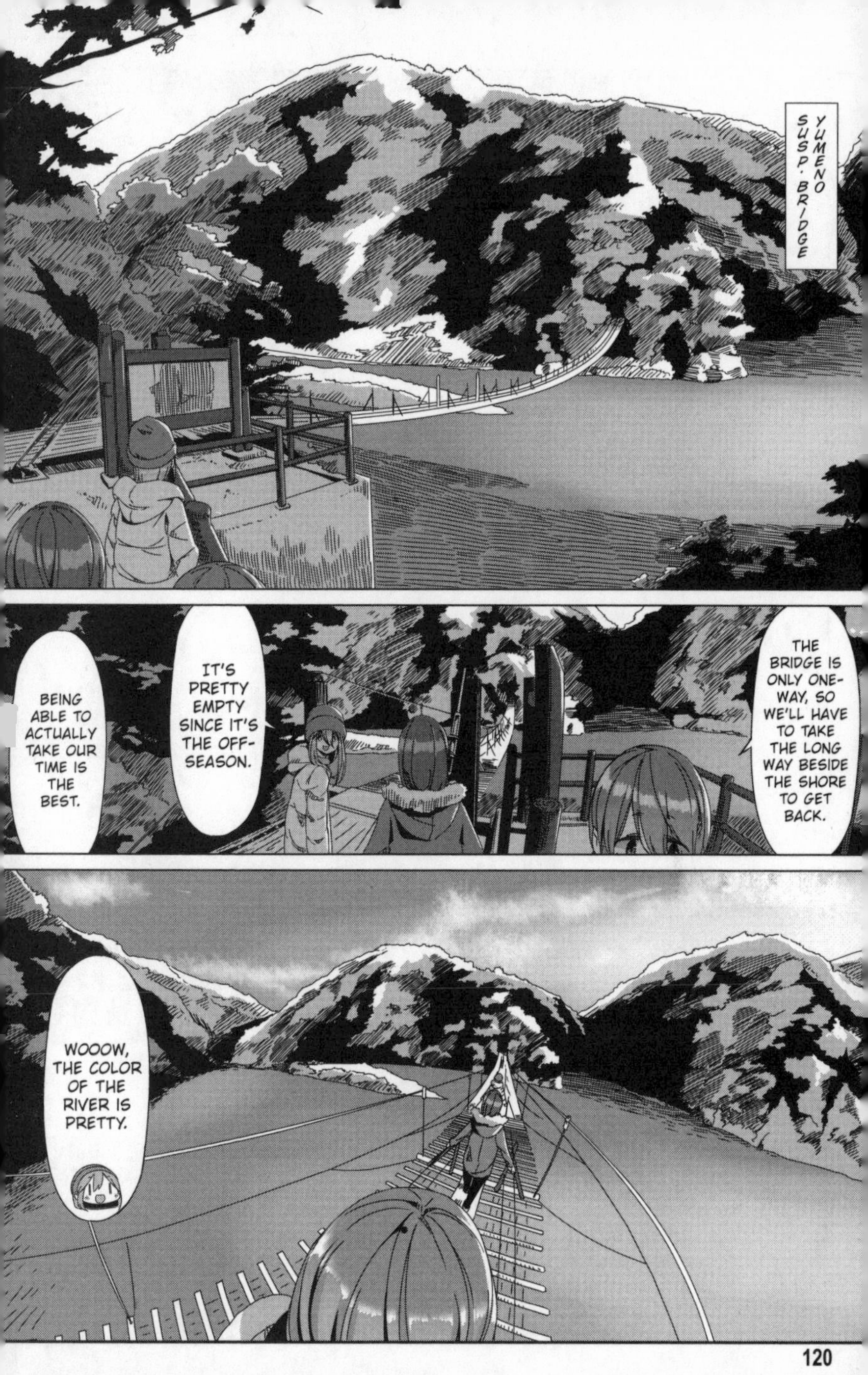
YUMENO SUSP. BRIDGE
THE BRIDGE IS ONLY ONE-WAY, SO WE'LL HAVE TO TAKE THE LONG WAY BESIDE THE SHORE TO GET BACK.
IT'S PRETTY EMPTY SINCE IT'S THE OFF-SEASON.
BEING ABLE TO ACTUALLY TAKE OUR TIME IS THE BEST.
WOOOW, THE COLOR OF THE RIVER IS PRETTY.

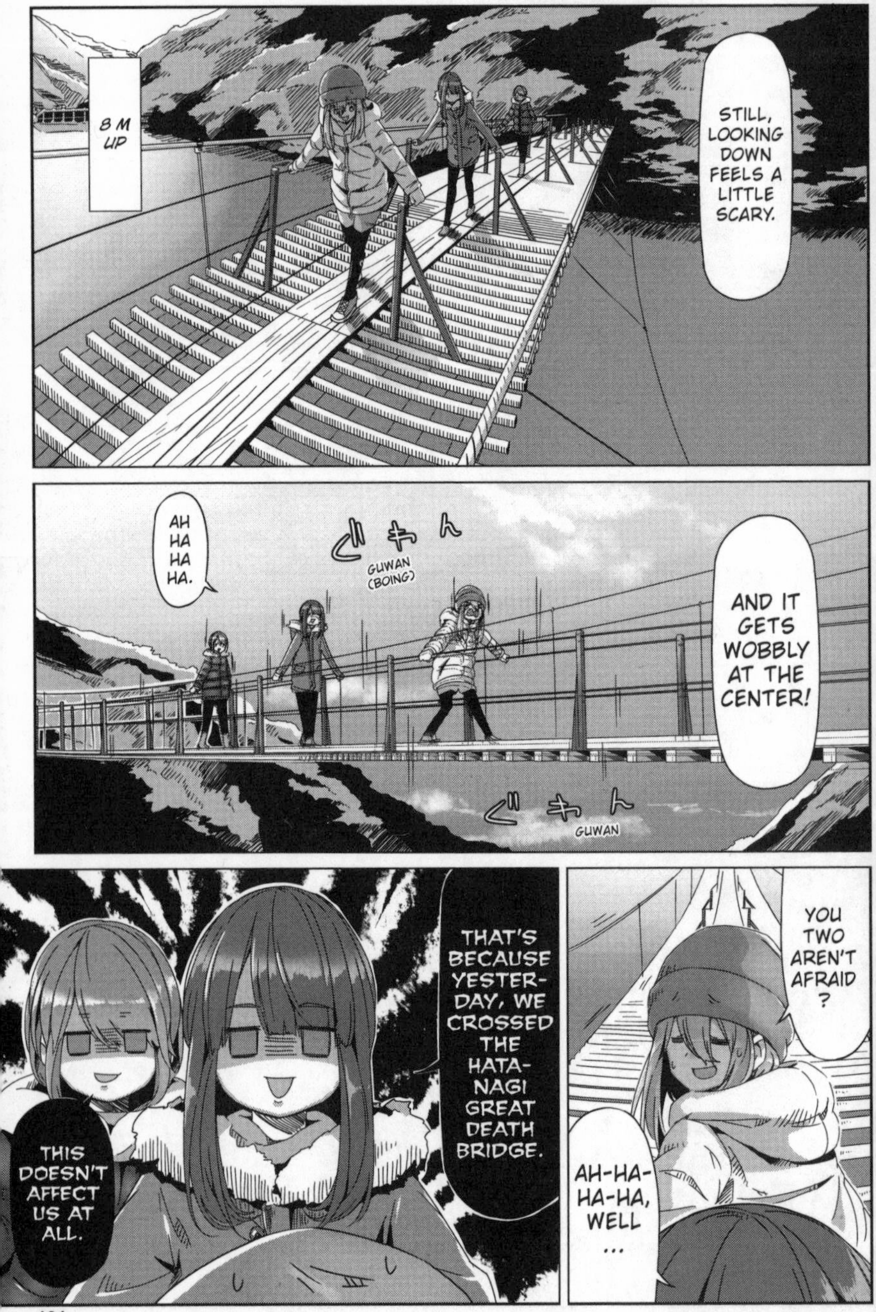
STILL, LOOKING DOWN FEELS A LITTLE SCARY.
8 M UP
AND IT GETS WOBBLY AT THE CENTER!
ぐわん
GUWAN (BOING)
AH HA HA HA HA.
ぐわん
GUWAN
YOU TWO AREN'T AFRAID?
AH-HA-HA-HA, WELL...
THAT'S BECAUSE YESTERDAY, WE CROSSED THE HATA-NAGI GREAT DEATH BRIDGE.
THIS DOESN'T AFFECT US AT ALL.

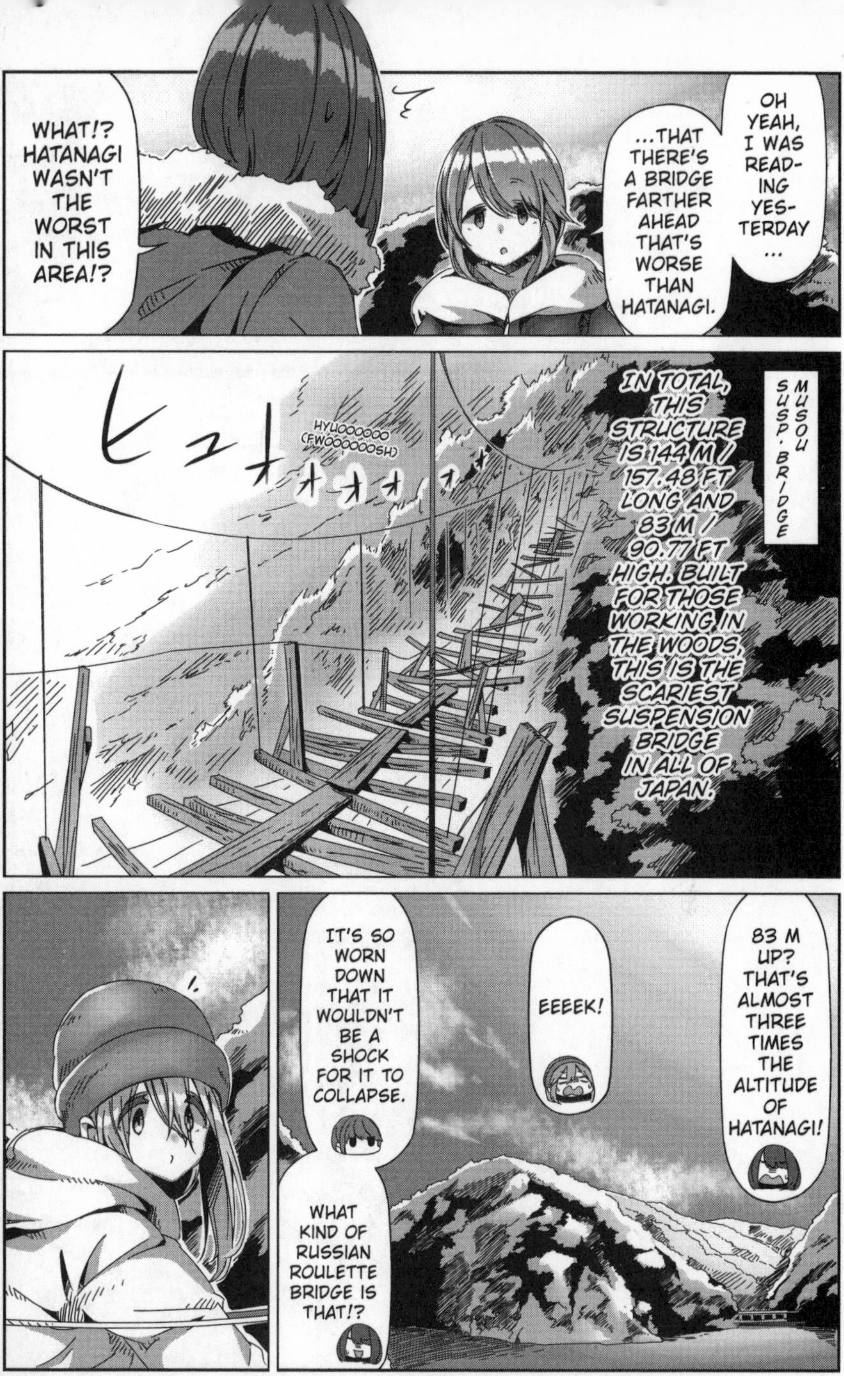
OH YEAH, I WAS READING YESTERDAY...
...THAT THERE'S A BRIDGE FARTHER AHEAD THAT'S WORSE THAN HATANAGI.
WHAT!? HATANAGI WASN'T THE WORST IN THIS AREA!?
MUSOU SUSP. BRIDGE
IN TOTAL, THIS STRUCTURE IS 144 M / 157.48 FT LONG AND 83 M / 90.77 FT HIGH. BUILT FOR THOSE WORKING IN THE WOODS, THIS IS THE SCARIEST SUSPENSION BRIDGE IN ALL OF JAPAN.
HYUOOOOOO (FWOOOOOOSH)
83 M UP? THAT'S ALMOST THREE TIMES THE ALTITUDE OF HATANAGI!
EEEEK!
IT'S SO WORN DOWN THAT IT WOULDN'T BE A SHOCK FOR IT TO COLLAPSE.
WHAT KIND OF RUSSIAN ROULETTE BRIDGE IS THAT!?

CURRENTLY, MUSOU SUSPENSION BRIDGE IS IN ALMOST COMPLETE DISREPAIR, SO IT'S UNCROSSABLE.

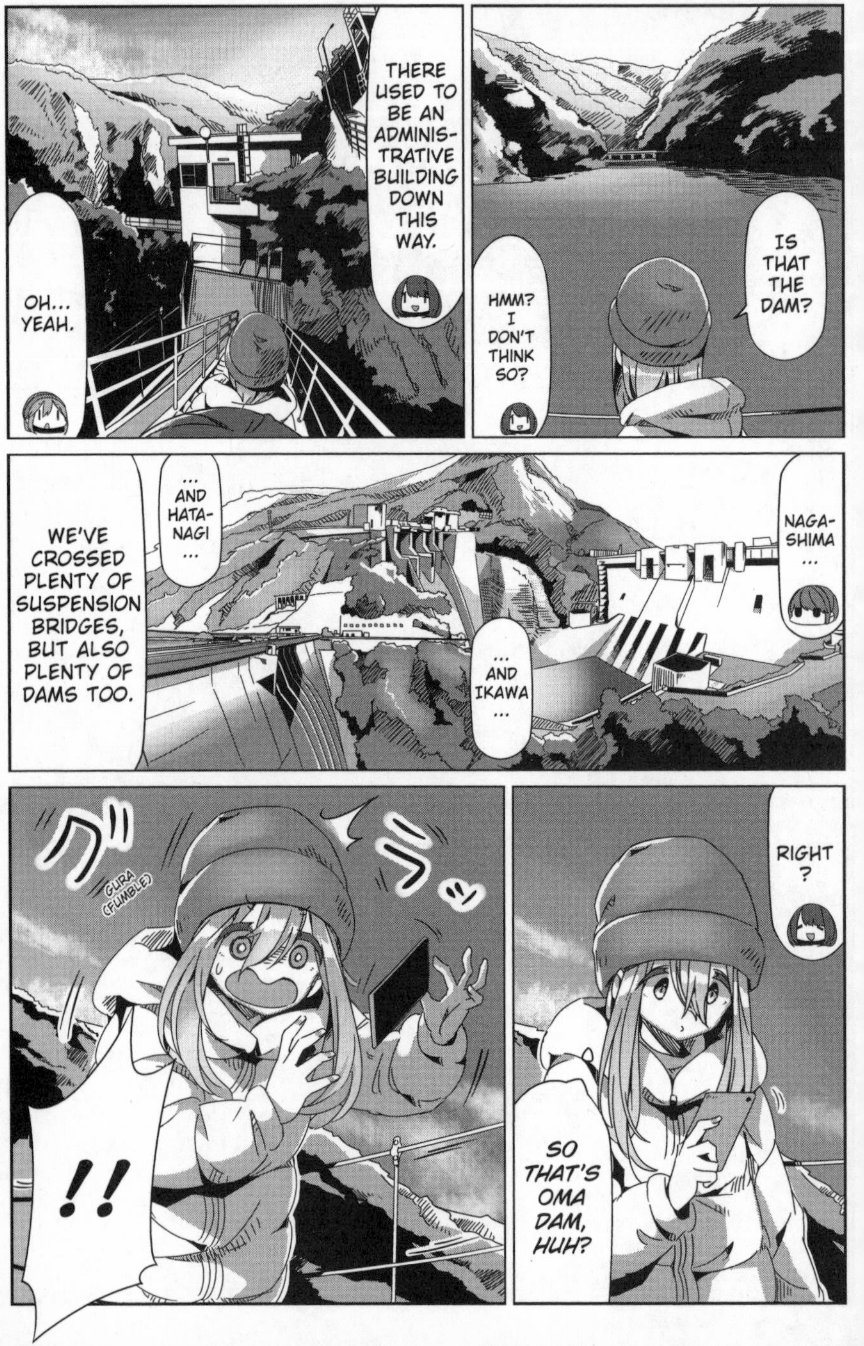
IS THAT THE DAM?
HMM? I DON'T THINK SO?
THERE USED TO BE AN ADMINIS-TRATIVE BUILDING DOWN THIS WAY.
OH... YEAH.
NAGA-SHIMA ...
... AND HATA-NAGI ...
... AND IKAWA ...
WE'VE CROSSED PLENTY OF SUSPENSION BRIDGES, BUT ALSO PLENTY OF DAMS TOO.
RIGHT ?
SO THAT'S OMA DAM, HUH?
グラッ
GURA (FUMBLE)
!!

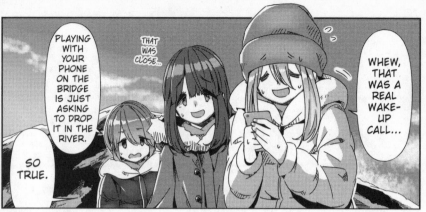

WHEW, THAT WAS A REAL WAKE-UP CALL...
THAT WAS CLOSE...
PLAYING WITH YOUR PHONE ON THE BRIDGE IS JUST ASKING TO DROP IT IN THE RIVER.
SO TRUE.
...THE PHONES OF THOSE TRYING TO TAKE PICTURES FOR SOCIAL MEDIA ...
I BET ...
...ARE SLEEPING AT THE BOTTOM OF THIS RIVER BED.
KOPO (BLUB)
KOPO
WHOA, THAT HAS TO BE TERRIBLE FOR THE AREA.
SNAP

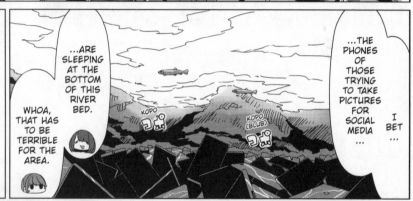

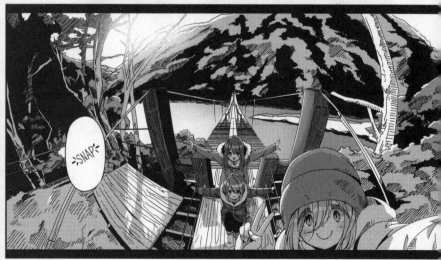

SIGN: TAKE YOUR TIME AND TAKE BREAKS AS NEEDED. THERE ARE 300 STEPS HERE.

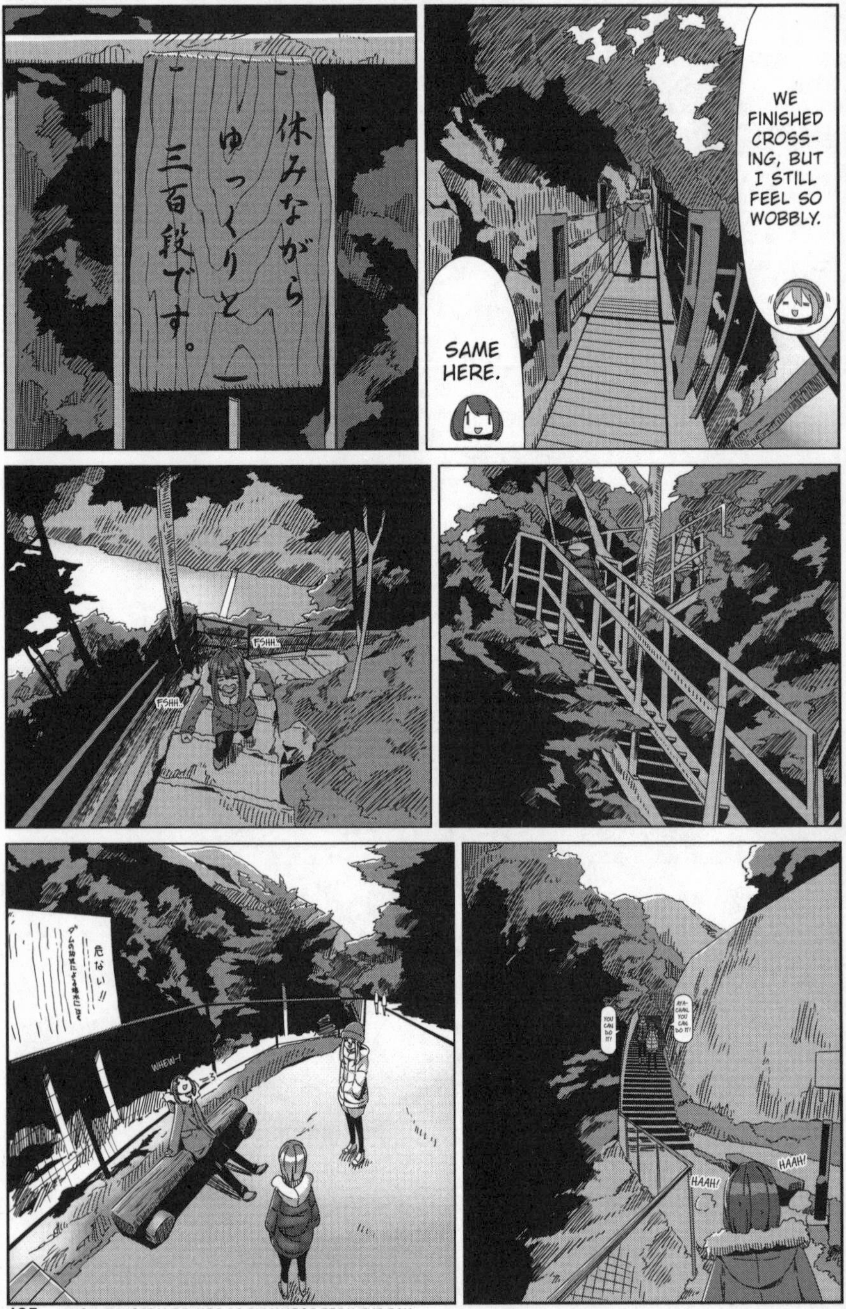
WE FINISHED CROSSING, BUT I STILL FEEL SO WOBBLY.
SAME HERE.
休みながらゆっくりと三百段です。
FSHH..
FSHH..
AYA-CHAN, YOU CAN DO IT!
YOU CAN DO IT!
HAAH!
HAAH!
危ない!!
WHEW~!

SIGN: DANGER!! BEWARE OF DISCHARGE FROM THE DAM.

SIGN: SOBA / MATSUTAKE

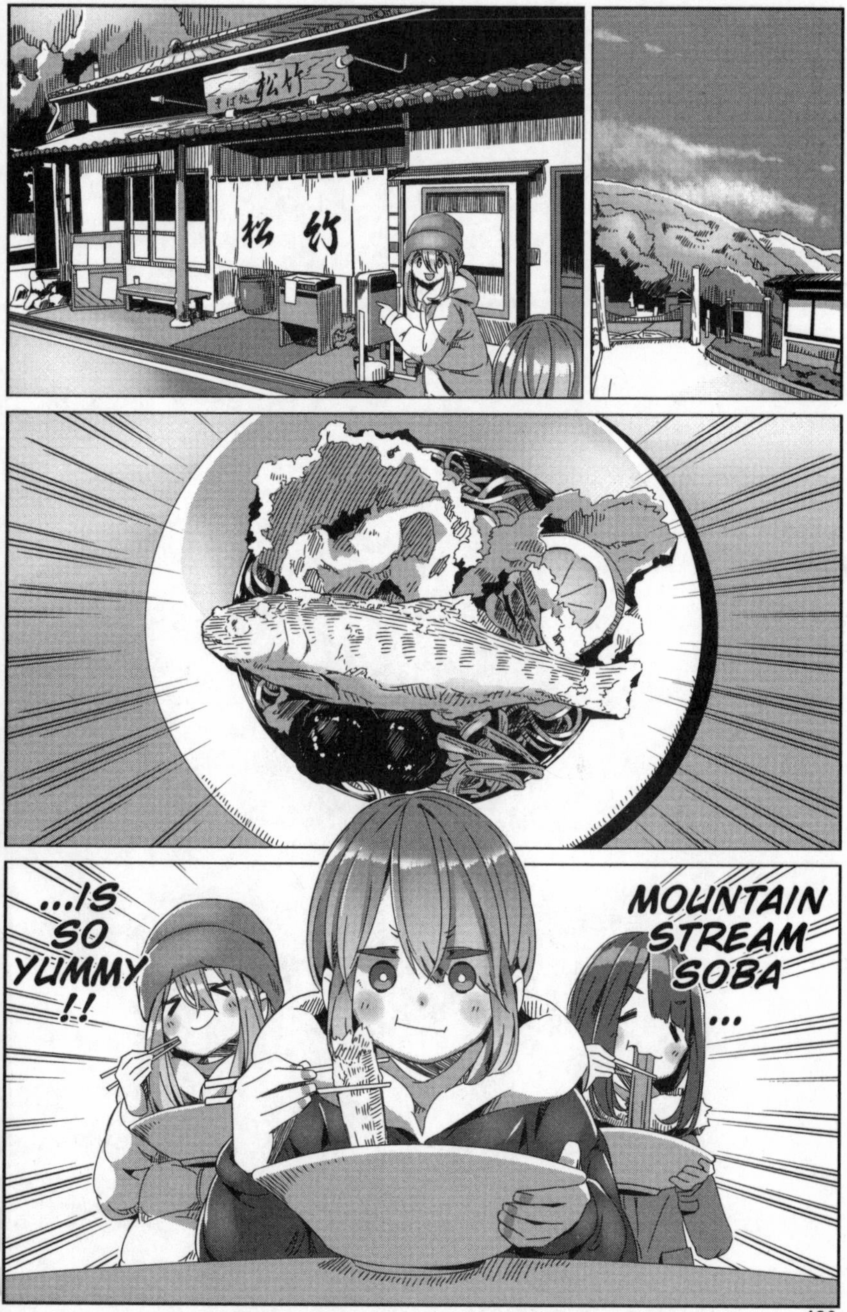
松竹
松竹
MOUNTAIN STREAM SOBA ...
...IS SO YUMMY!!

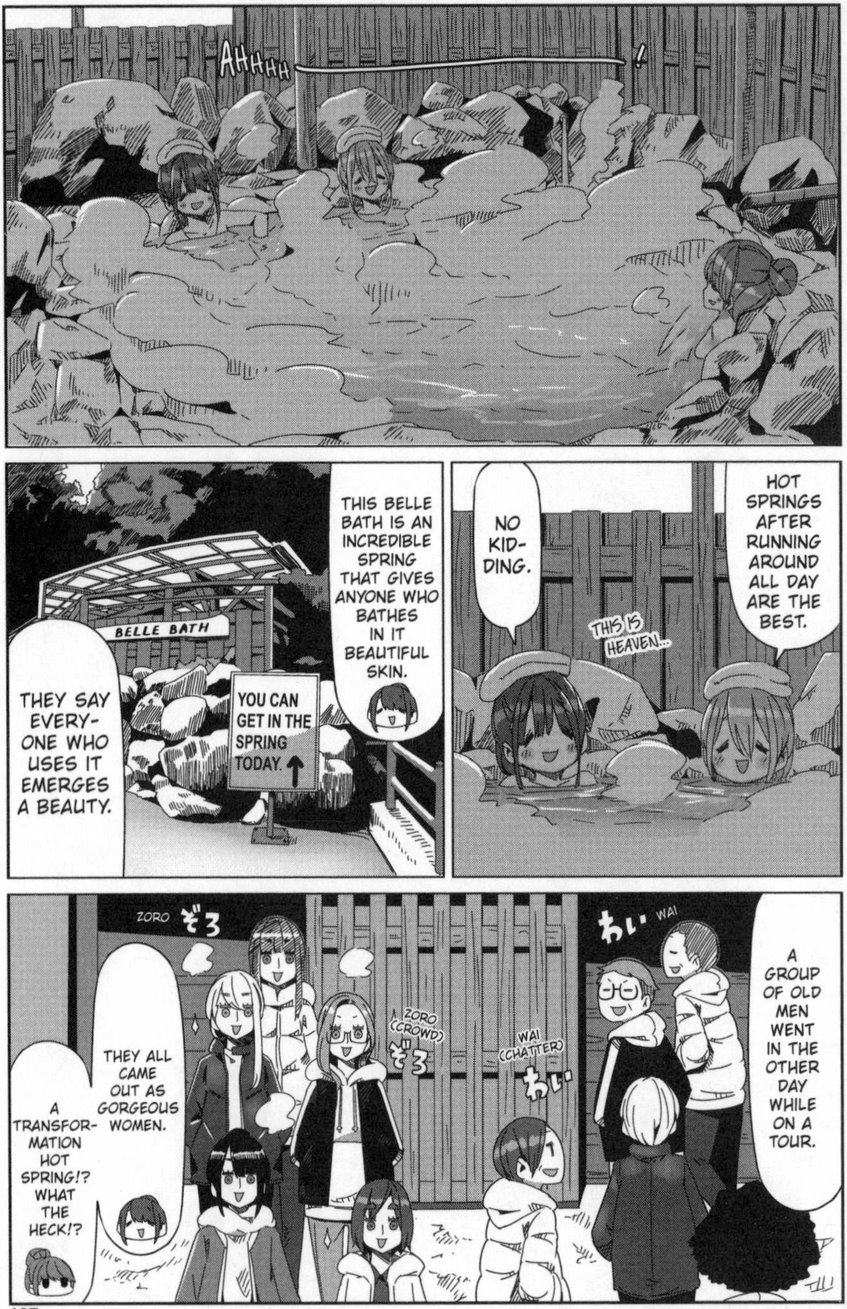

AHHHHH—!
HOT SPRINGS AFTER RUNNING AROUND ALL DAY ARE THE BEST.
NO KID-DING.
THIS IS HEAVEN...
THIS BELLE BATH IS AN INCREDIBLE SPRING THAT GIVES ANYONE WHO BATHES IN IT BEAUTIFUL SKIN.
BELLE BATH
YOU CAN GET IN THE SPRING TODAY.
THEY SAY EVERY-ONE WHO USES IT EMERGES A BEAUTY.
A GROUP OF OLD MEN WENT IN THE OTHER DAY WHILE ON A TOUR.
わい WAI
WAI (CHATTER) わい
ZORO (CROWD) ぞろ
ZORO ぞろ
THEY ALL CAME OUT AS GORGEOUS WOMEN.
A TRANSFOR-MATION HOT SPRING!? WHAT THE HECK!?

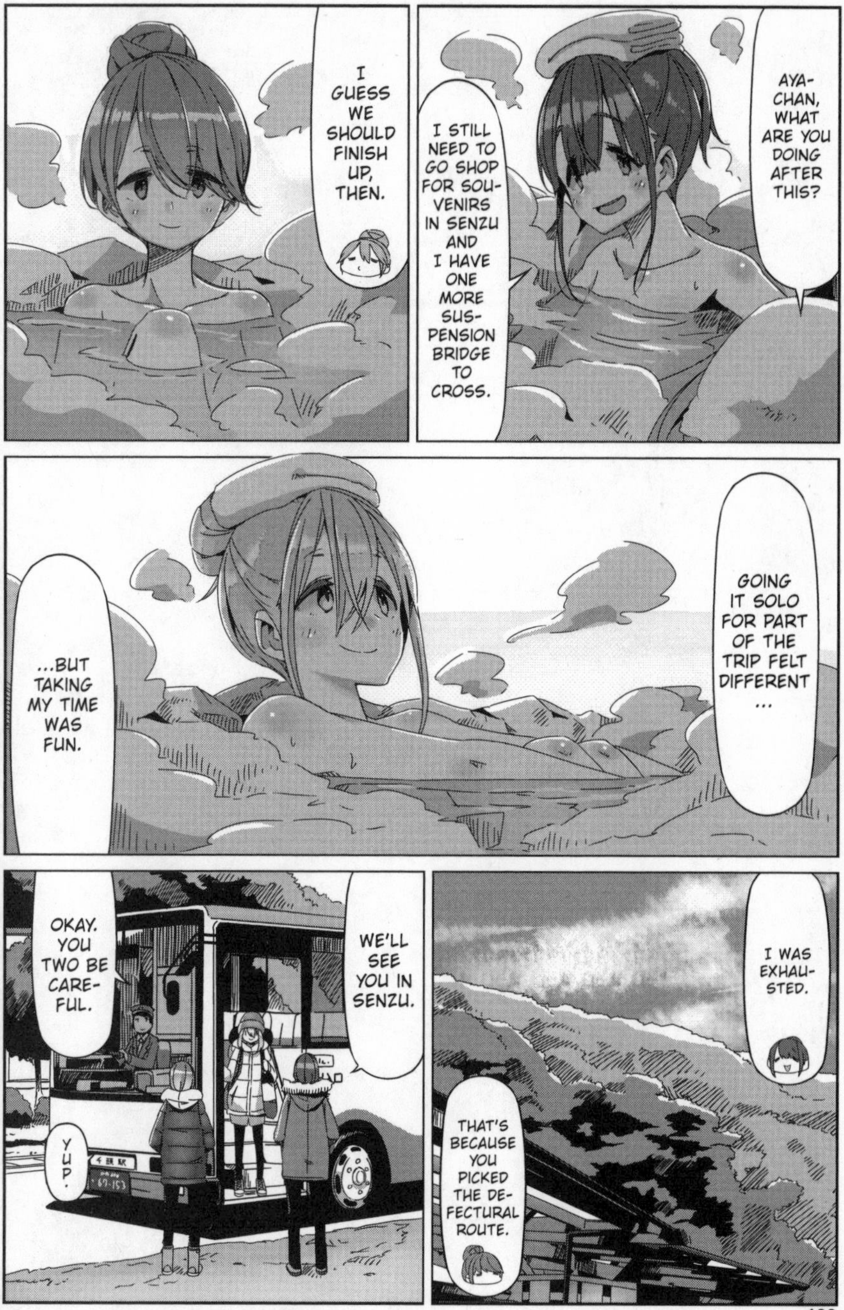
AYA-CHAN, WHAT ARE YOU DOING AFTER THIS?
I STILL NEED TO GO SHOP FOR SOU-VENIRS IN SENZU AND I HAVE ONE MORE SUS-PENSION BRIDGE TO CROSS.
I GUESS WE SHOULD FINISH UP, THEN.
GOING IT SOLO FOR PART OF THE TRIP FELT DIFFERENT...
...BUT TAKING MY TIME WAS FUN.
I WAS EXHAU-STED.
THAT'S BECAUSE YOU PICKED THE DE-FECTURAL ROUTE.
WE'LL SEE YOU IN SENZU.
OKAY. YOU TWO BE CARE-FUL.
YUP.

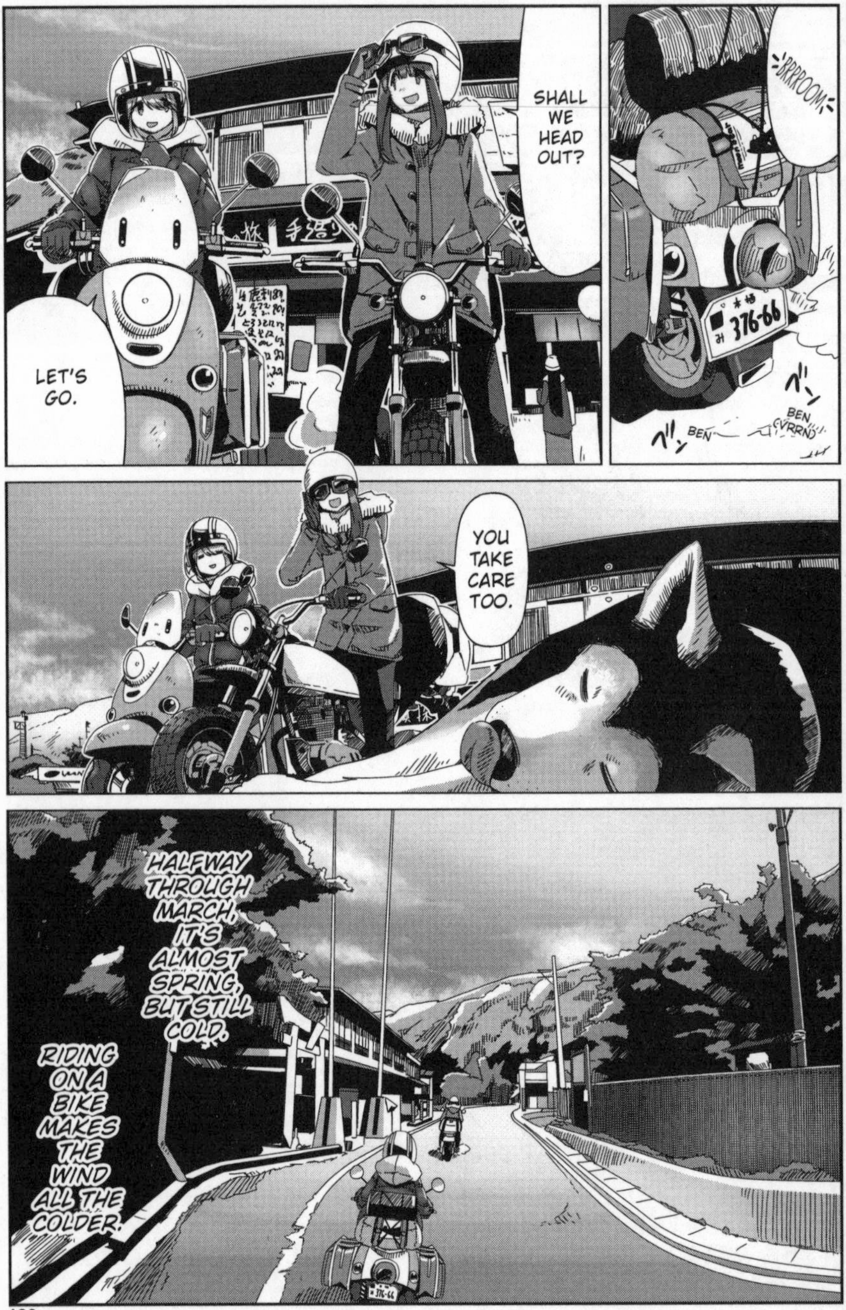
BRRROOM
ベン
BEN
ベン
BEN
VRRRN
SHALL WE HEAD OUT?
LET'S GO.
YOU TAKE CARE TOO.
HALFWAY THROUGH MARCH, IT'S ALMOST SPRING, BUT STILL COLD.
RIDING ON A BIKE MAKES THE WIND ALL THE COLDER.

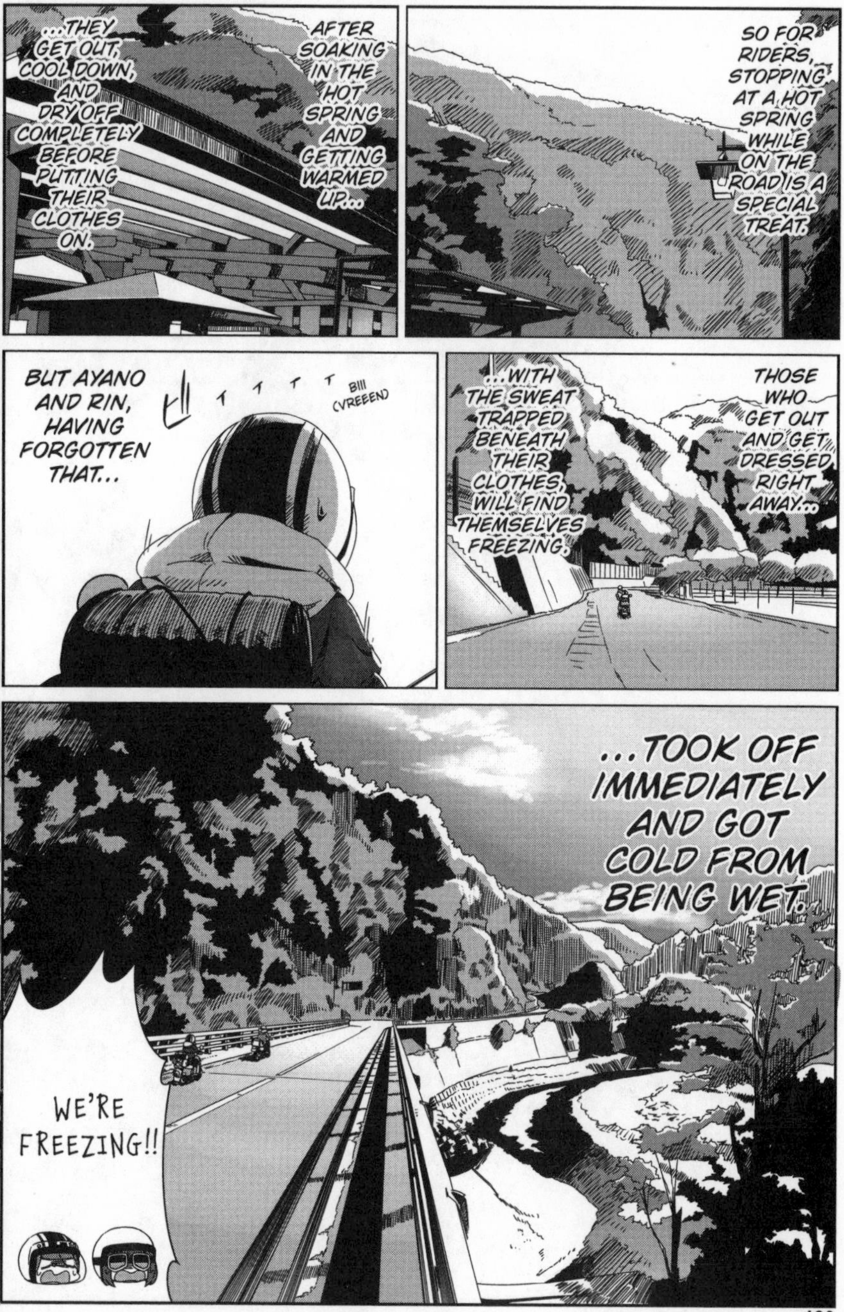
SO FOR RIDERS, STOPPING AT A HOT SPRING WHILE ON THE ROAD IS A SPECIAL TREAT.
AFTER SOAKING IN THE HOT SPRING AND GETTING WARMED UP...
...THEY GET OUT, COOL DOWN, AND DRY OFF COMPLETELY BEFORE PUTTING THEIR CLOTHES ON.
THOSE WHO GET OUT AND GET DRESSED RIGHT AWAY...
...WITH THE SWEAT TRAPPED BENEATH THEIR CLOTHES, WILL FIND THEMSELVES FREEZING.
BIII (VREEEN)
BUT AYANO AND RIN, HAVING FORGOTTEN THAT...
...TOOK OFF IMMEDIATELY AND GOT COLD FROM BEING WET.
WE'RE FREEZING!!

WE FINISHED CROSSING, BUT I STILL FEEL SO WOBBLY.

SAME HERE.

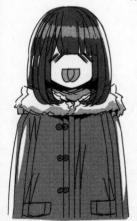
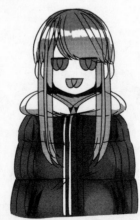
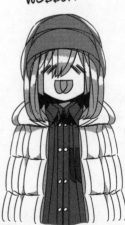

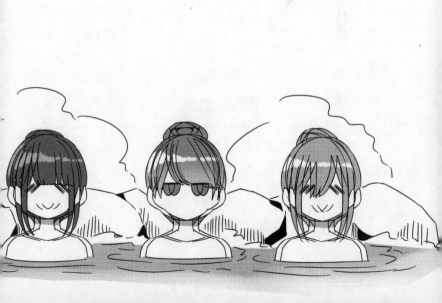

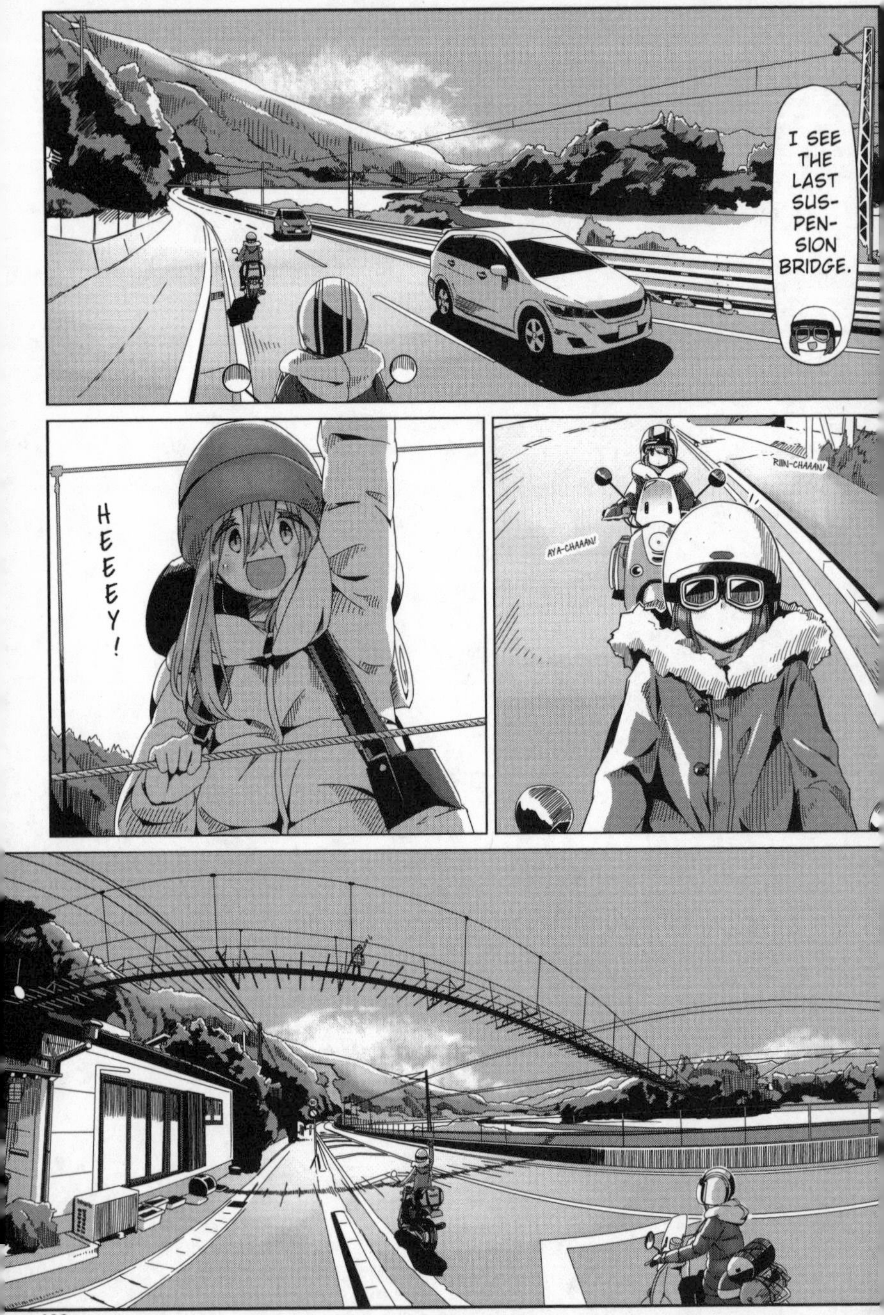
I SEE THE LAST SUSPENSION BRIDGE.
RIIIN-CHAAAN!
AYA-CHAAAN!
HEEEY!

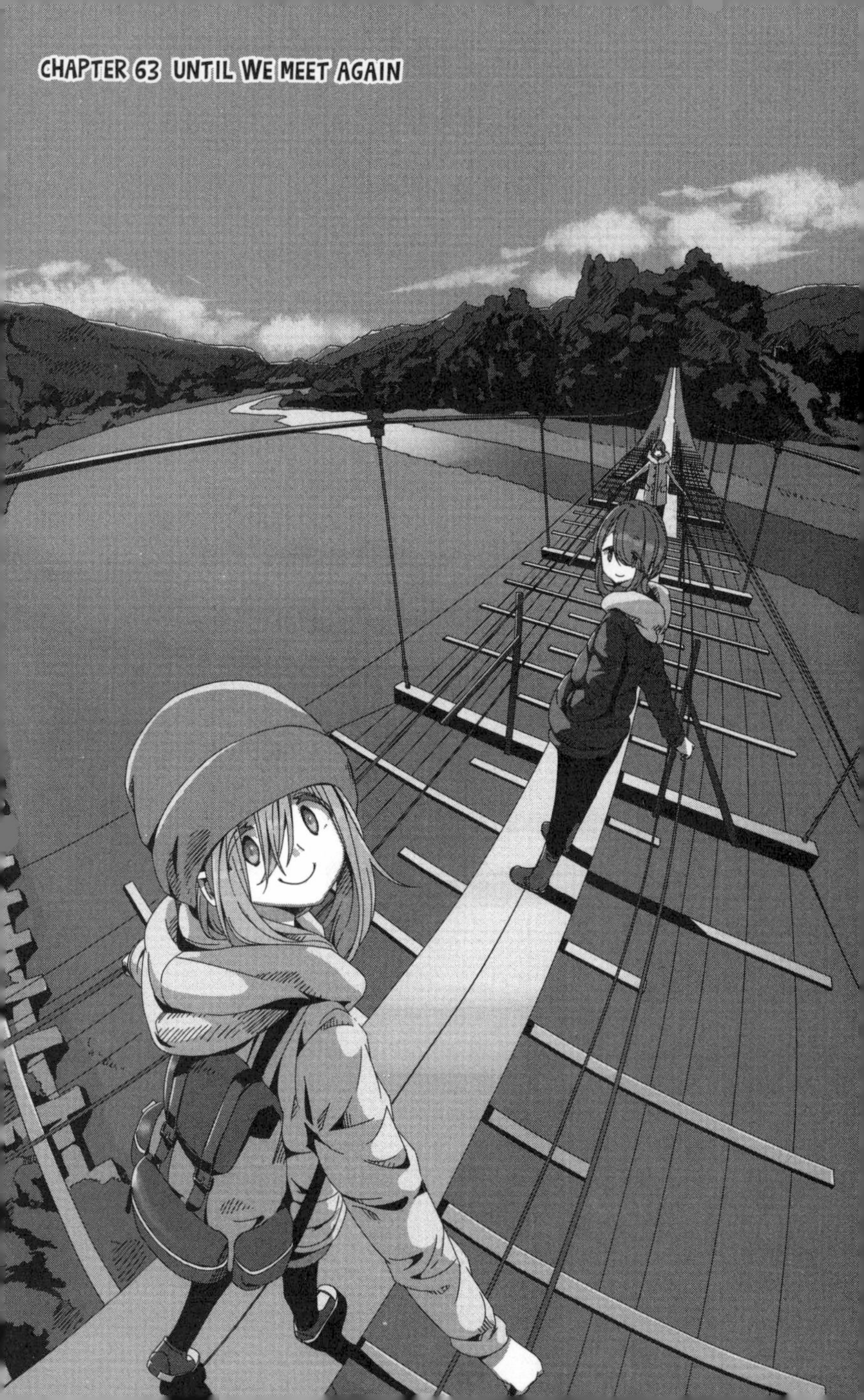
CHAPTER 63 UNTIL WE MEET AGAIN

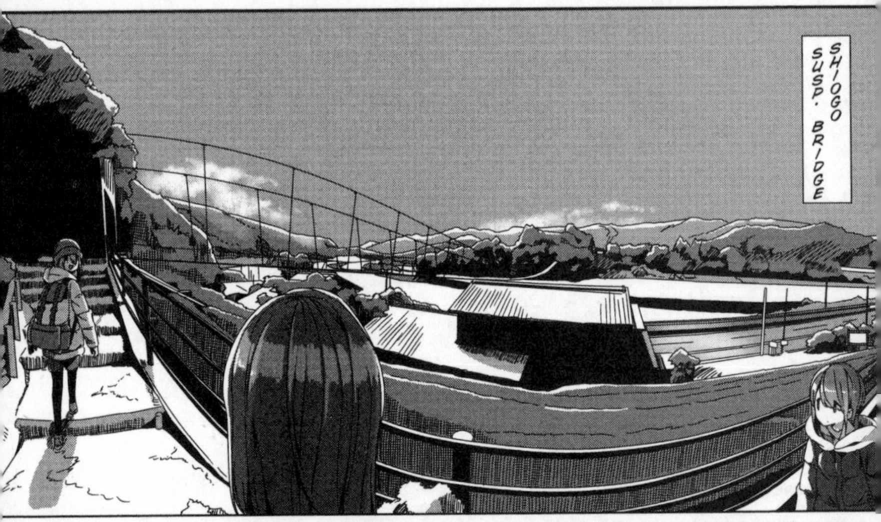
SHIOGO SUSP. BRIDGE
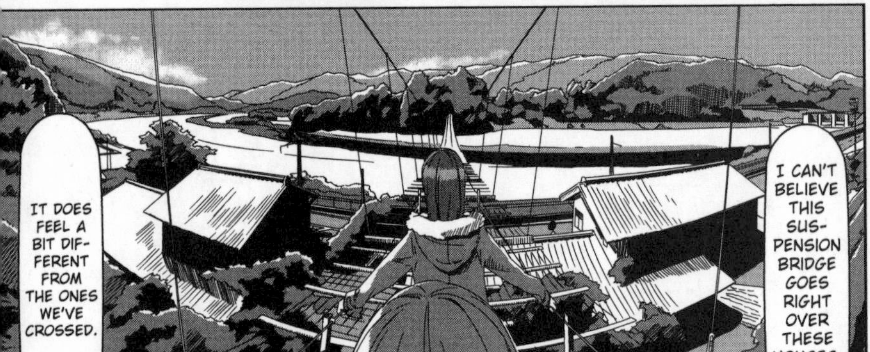
I CAN'T BELIEVE THIS SUS-PENSION BRIDGE GOES RIGHT OVER THESE HOUSES.
IT DOES FEEL A BIT DIF-FERENT FROM THE ONES WE'VE CROSSED.
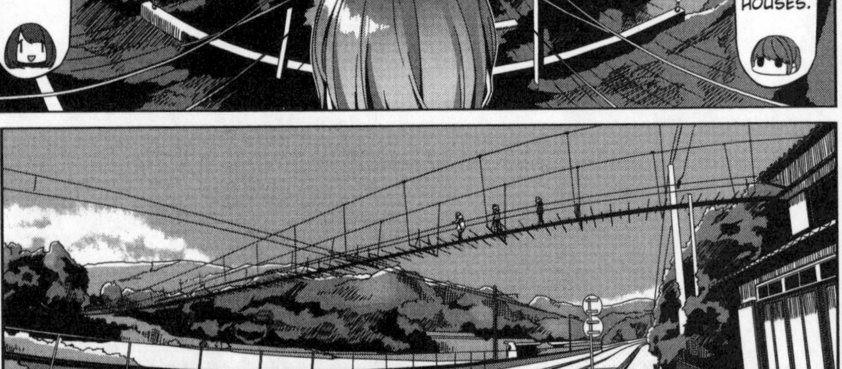

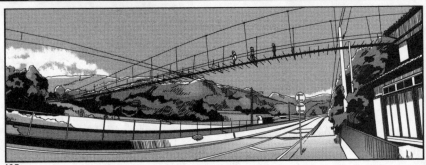

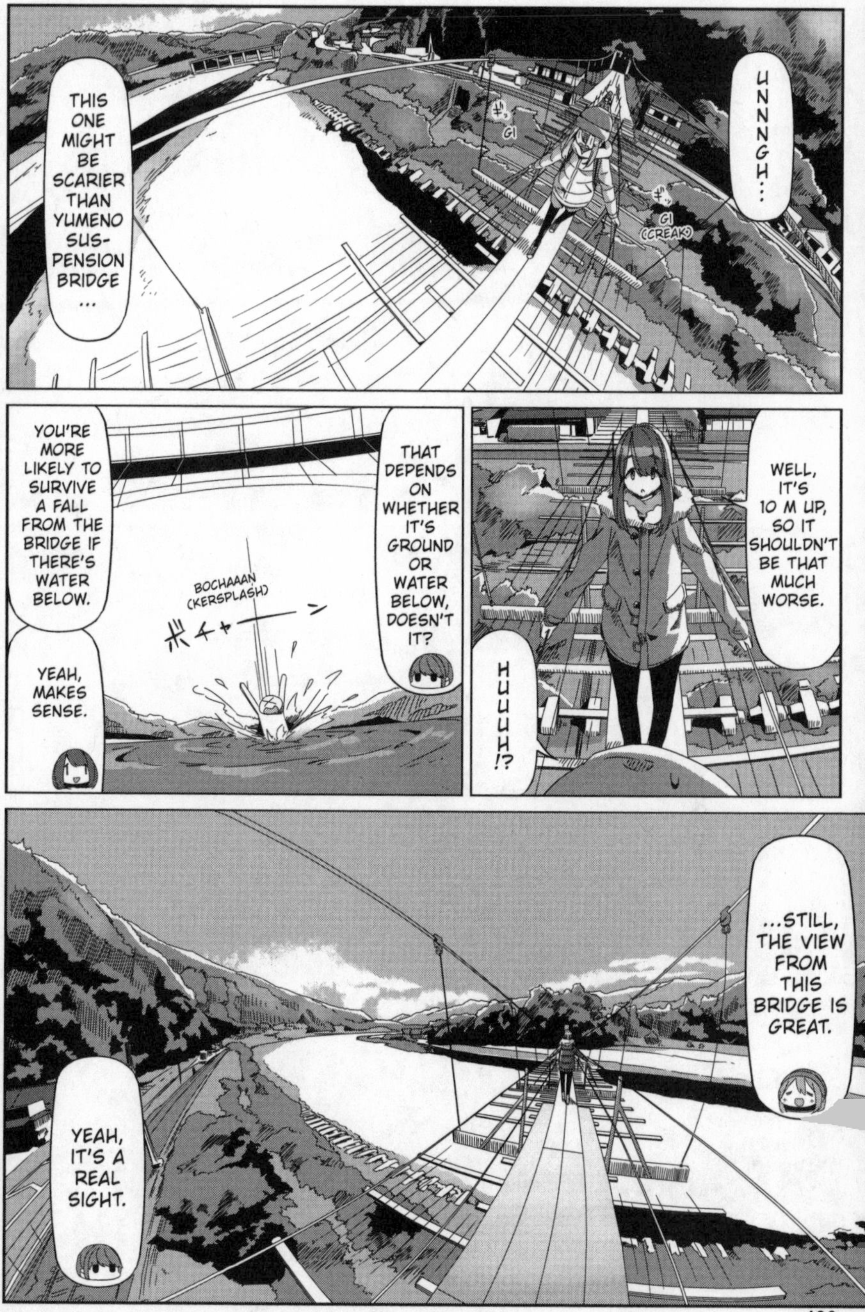
UNNNGH...
GI
GI (CREAK)
THIS ONE MIGHT BE SCARIER THAN YUMENO SUS-PENSION BRIDGE...
WELL, IT'S 10 M UP, SO IT SHOULDN'T BE THAT MUCH WORSE.
HUUUH!?
YOU'RE MORE LIKELY TO SURVIVE A FALL FROM THE BRIDGE IF THERE'S WATER BELOW.
THAT DEPENDS ON WHETHER IT'S GROUND OR WATER BELOW, DOESN'T IT?
BOCHAAAN (KERSPLASH)
ボチャーーン
YEAH, MAKES SENSE.
...STILL, THE VIEW FROM THIS BRIDGE IS GREAT.
YEAH, IT'S A REAL SIGHT.

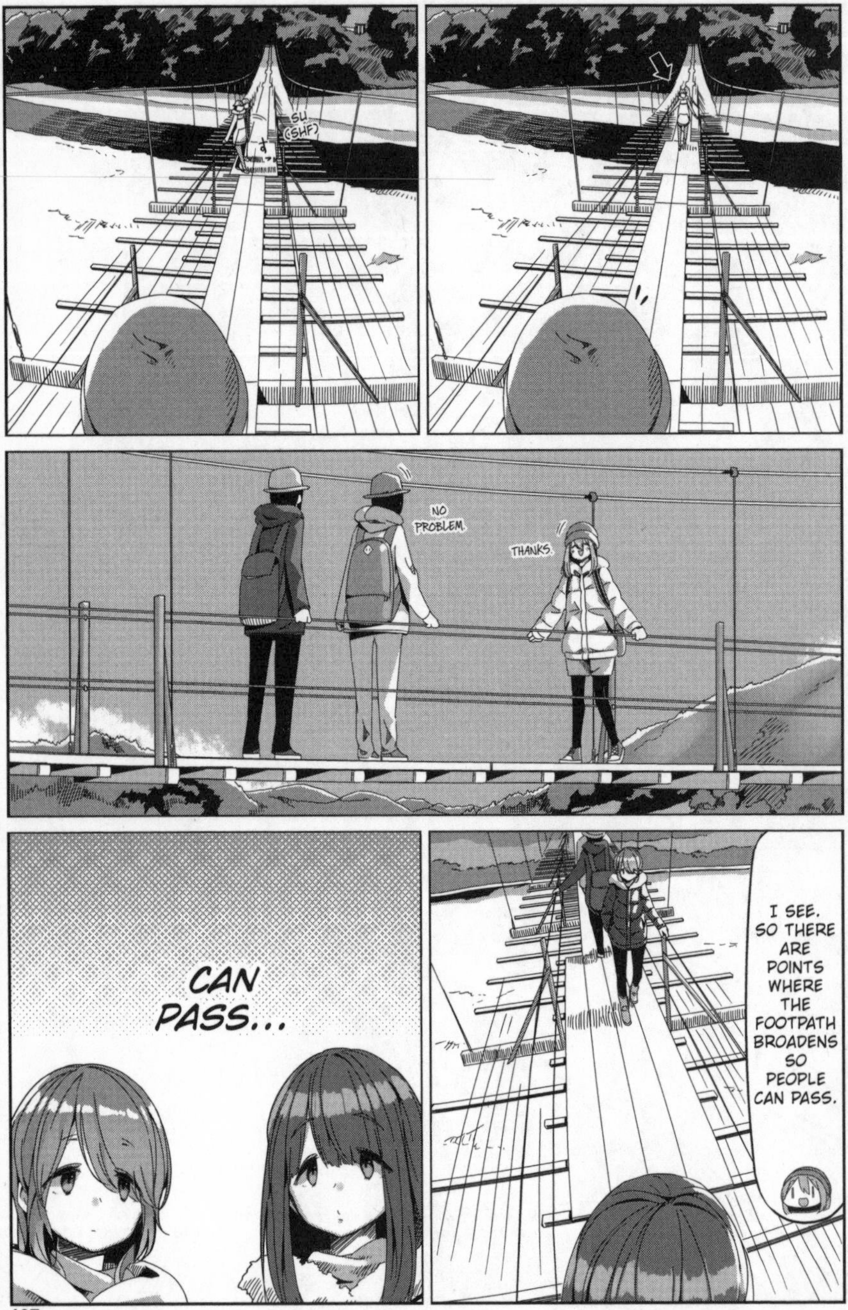
す
SU (SHF)
THANKS.
NO PROBLEM.
I SEE. SO THERE ARE POINTS WHERE THE FOOTPATH BROADENS SO PEOPLE CAN PASS.
CAN PASS...

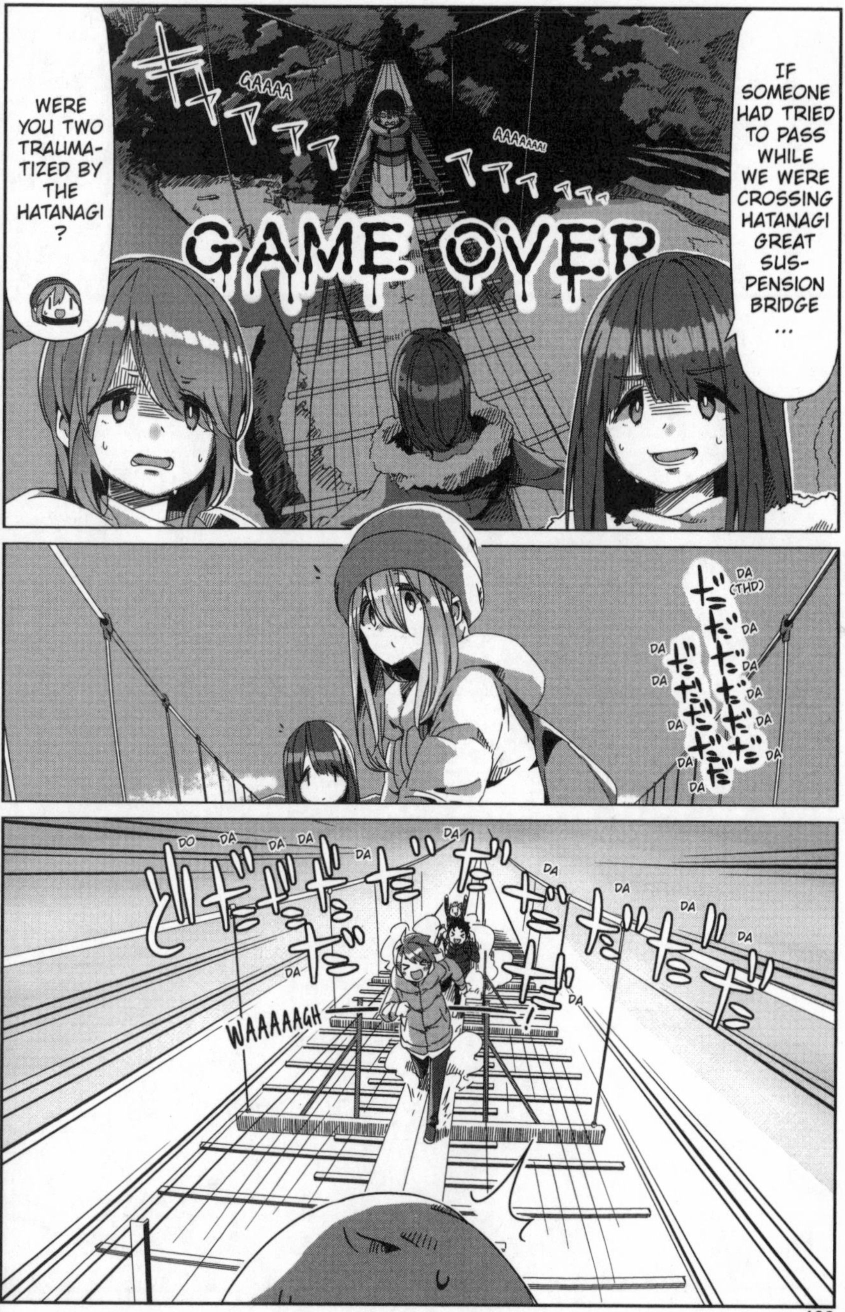
IF SOMEONE HAD TRIED TO PASS WHILE WE WERE CROSSING HATANAGI GREAT SUSPENSION BRIDGE...
GAAAA
AAAAAAA!
GAME OVER
WERE YOU TWO TRAUMATIZED BY THE HATANAGI?
DA (THD) DA DA DA DA DA DA DA DA DA
DO DA DA DA DA DA DA DA DA DA DA
WAAAAAGH

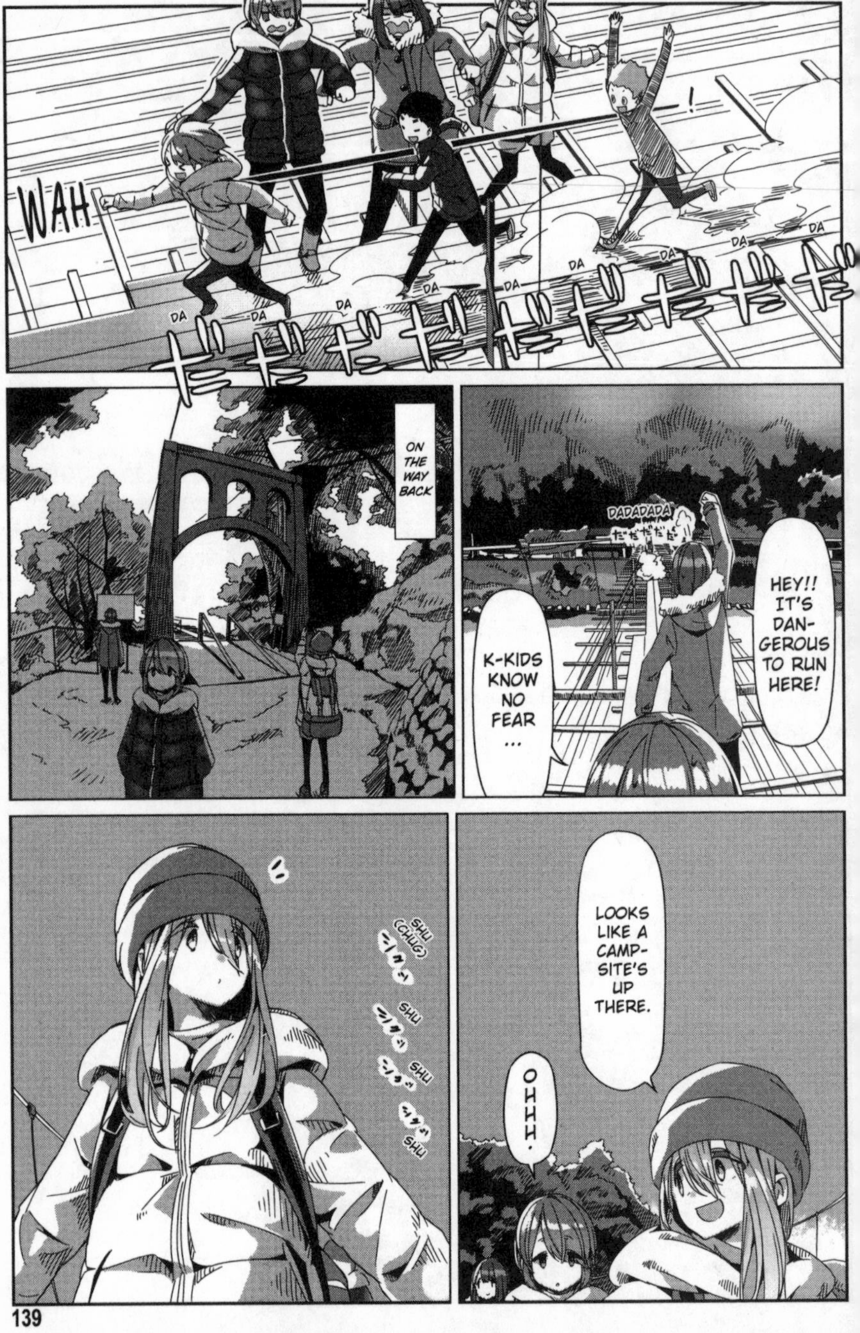
WAH
DA DA DA DA DA DA DA DA DA
HEY!! IT'S DAN-GEROUS TO RUN HERE!
DADADADA
K-KIDS KNOW NO FEAR...
ON THE WAY BACK
LOOKS LIKE A CAMP-SITE'S UP THERE.
OHHH.
SHU (CHUG)
SHU
SHU
SHU

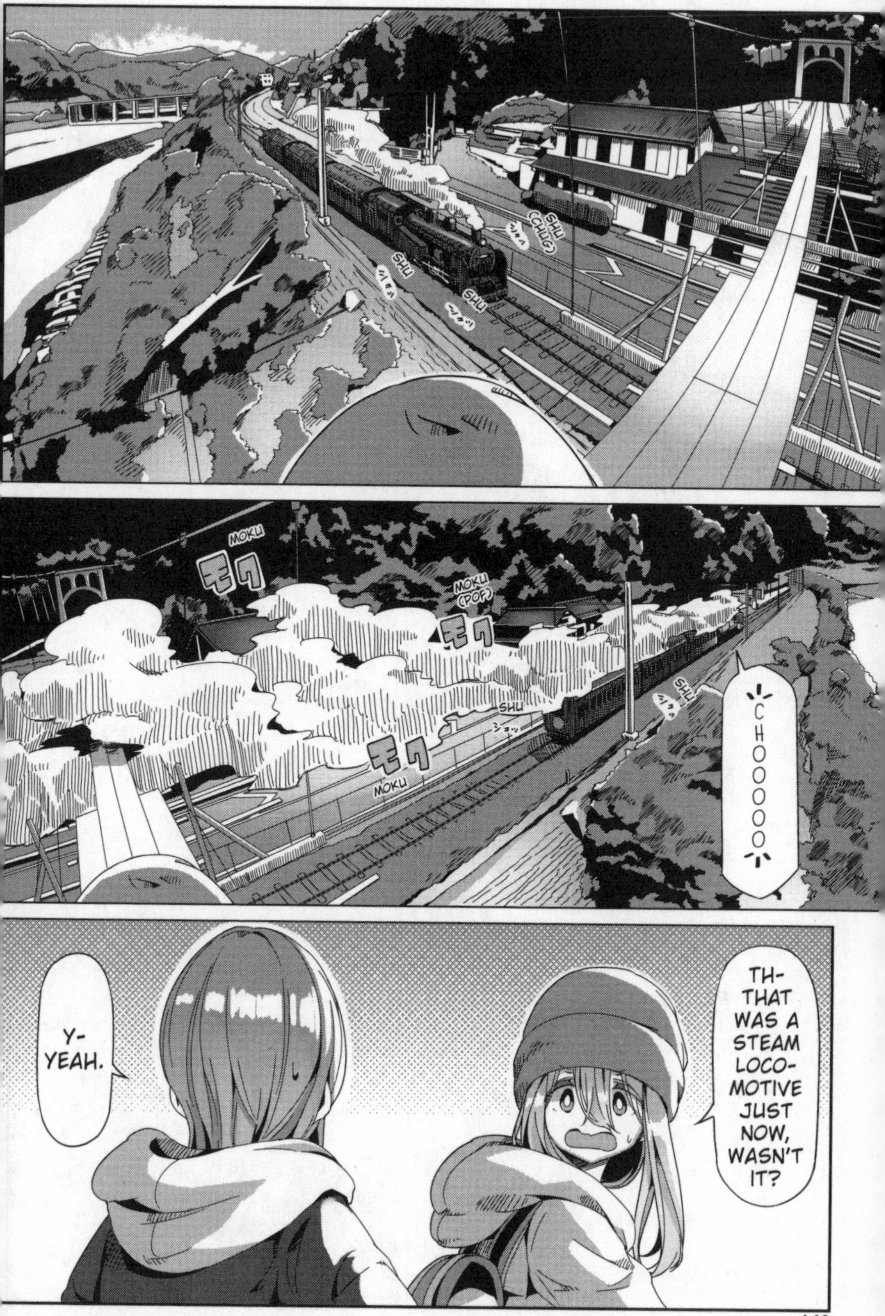
SHU (CHUG)
SHU
SHU
MOKU
MOKU (POF)
SHU
SHU
MOKU
CHOOOOOO
TH-THAT WAS A STEAM LOCO-MOTIVE JUST NOW, WASN'T IT?
Y-YEAH.

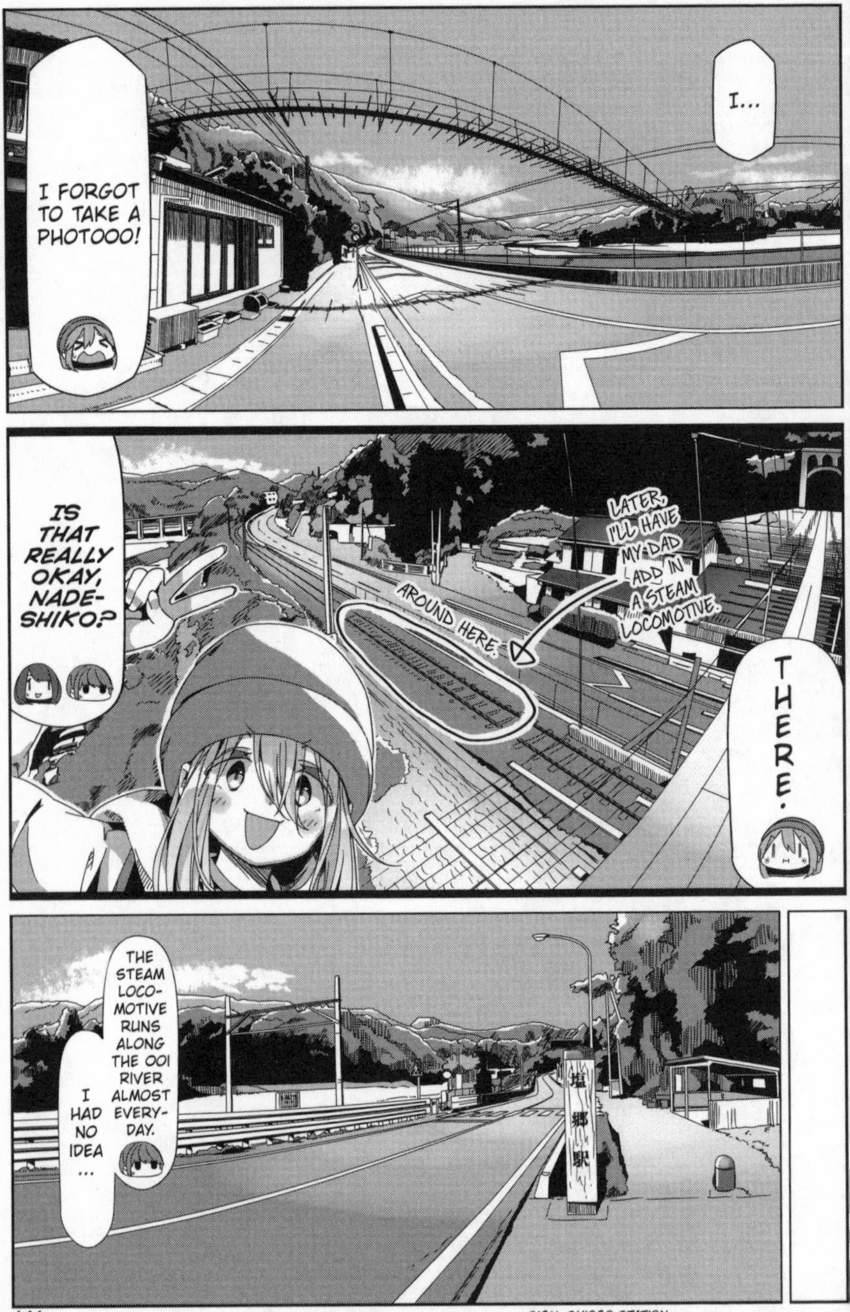
I...
I FORGOT TO TAKE A PHOTOOO!
THERE.
LATER, I'LL HAVE MY DAD ADD IN A STEAM LOCOMOTIVE.
AROUND HERE.
IS THAT REALLY OKAY, NADE-SHIKO?
THE STEAM LOCO-MOTIVE RUNS ALONG THE OOI RIVER ALMOST EVERY-DAY.
I HAD NO IDEA ...
塩郷駅

SIGN: SHIOGO STATION

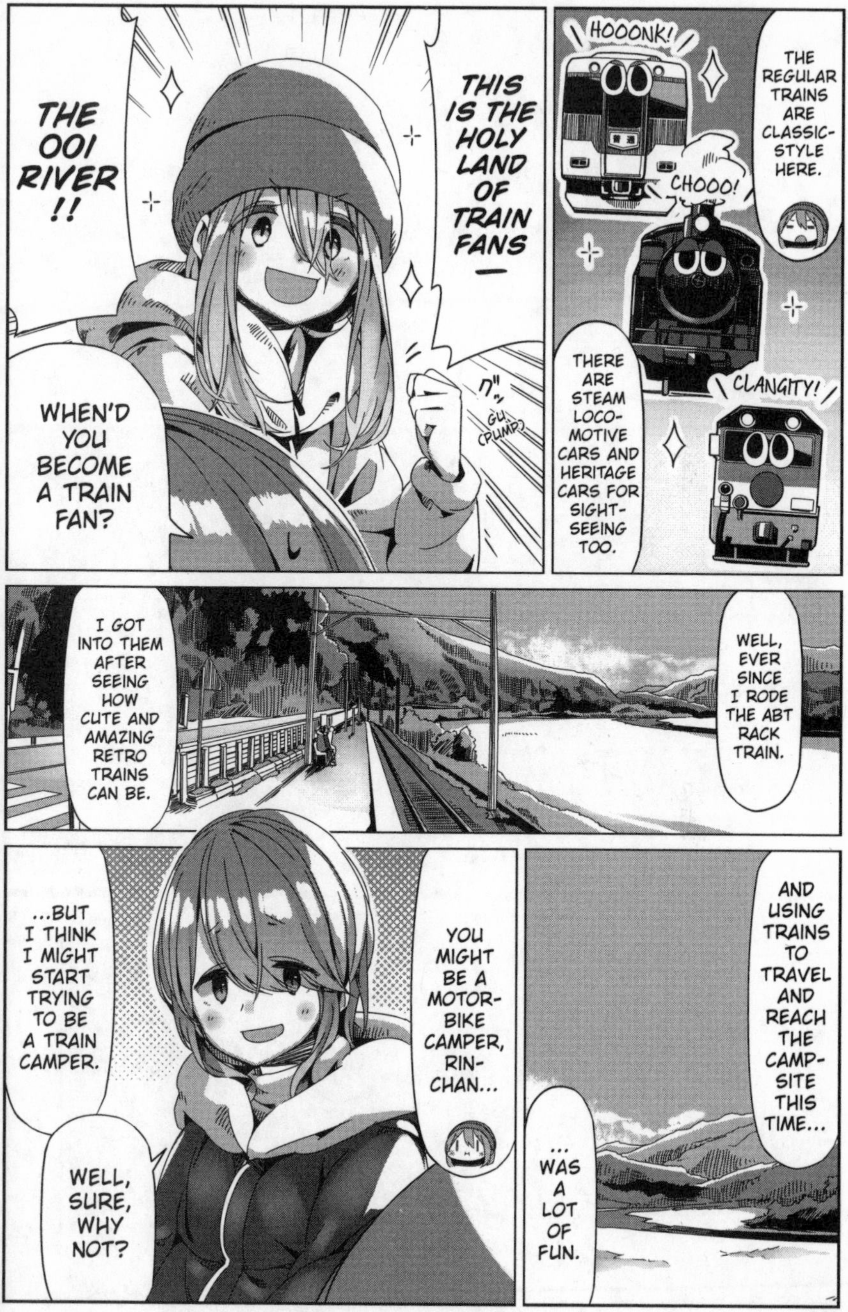
THE REGULAR TRAINS ARE CLASSIC-STYLE HERE.
HOOONK!
CHOOO!
THERE ARE STEAM LOCO-MOTIVE CARS AND HERITAGE CARS FOR SIGHT-SEEING TOO.
CLANGITY!
THIS IS THE HOLY LAND OF TRAIN FANS—
THE OOI RIVER!!
GU (PUMP)
WHEN'D YOU BECOME A TRAIN FAN?
WELL, EVER SINCE I RODE THE ABT RACK TRAIN.
I GOT INTO THEM AFTER SEEING HOW CUTE AND AMAZING RETRO TRAINS CAN BE.
AND USING TRAINS TO TRAVEL AND REACH THE CAMP-SITE THIS TIME...
...WAS A LOT OF FUN.
YOU MIGHT BE A MOTOR-BIKE CAMPER, RIN-CHAN...
...BUT I THINK I MIGHT START TRYING TO BE A TRAIN CAMPER.
WELL, SURE, WHY NOT?

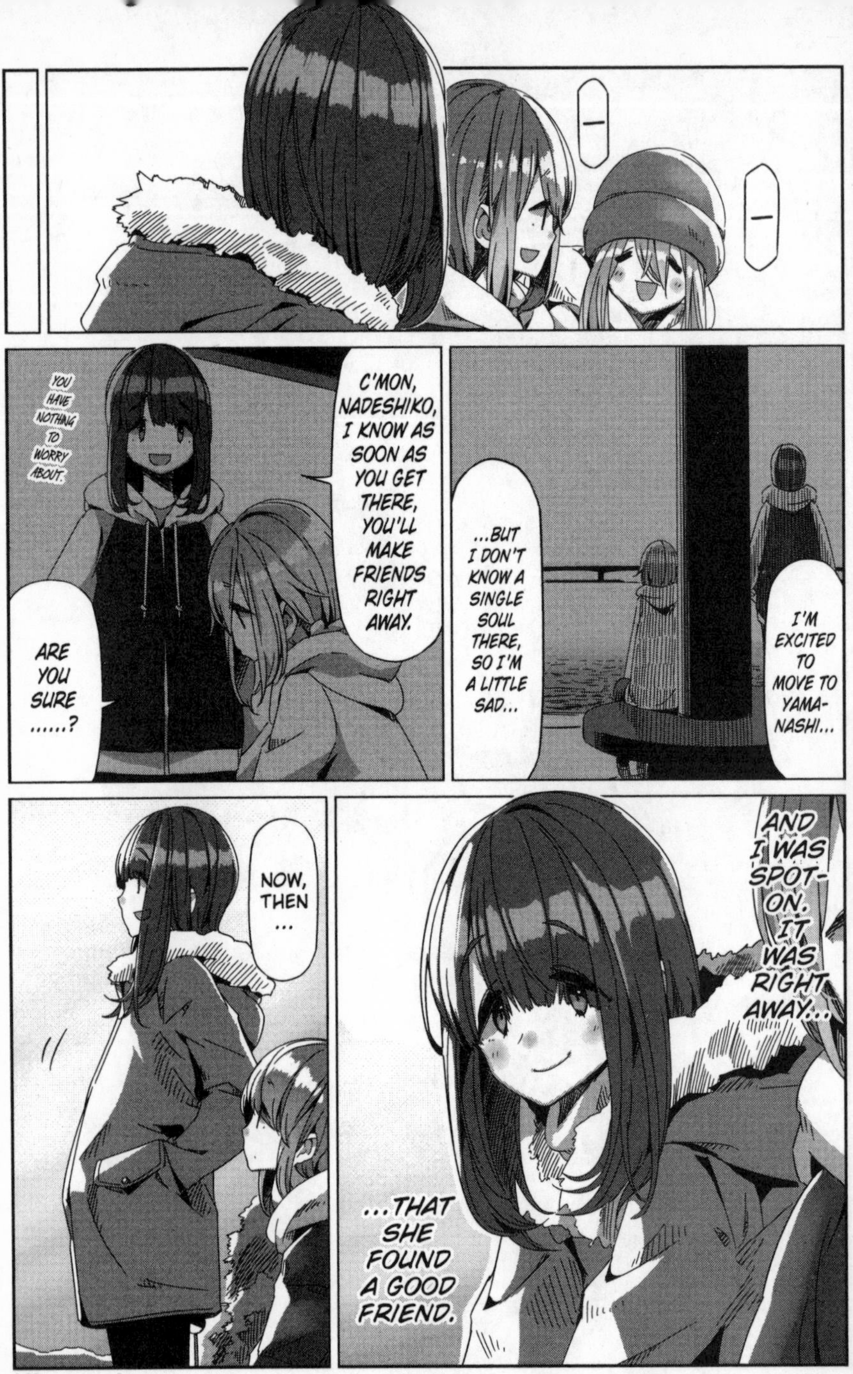
—
—
I'M EXCITED TO MOVE TO YAMANASHI...
...BUT I DON'T KNOW A SINGLE SOUL THERE, SO I'M A LITTLE SAD...
C'MON, NADESHIKO, I KNOW AS SOON AS YOU GET THERE, YOU'LL MAKE FRIENDS RIGHT AWAY.
YOU HAVE NOTHING TO WORRY ABOUT.
ARE YOU SURE ......?
AND I WAS SPOT-ON. IT WAS RIGHT AWAY...
...THAT SHE FOUND A GOOD FRIEND.
NOW, THEN ...

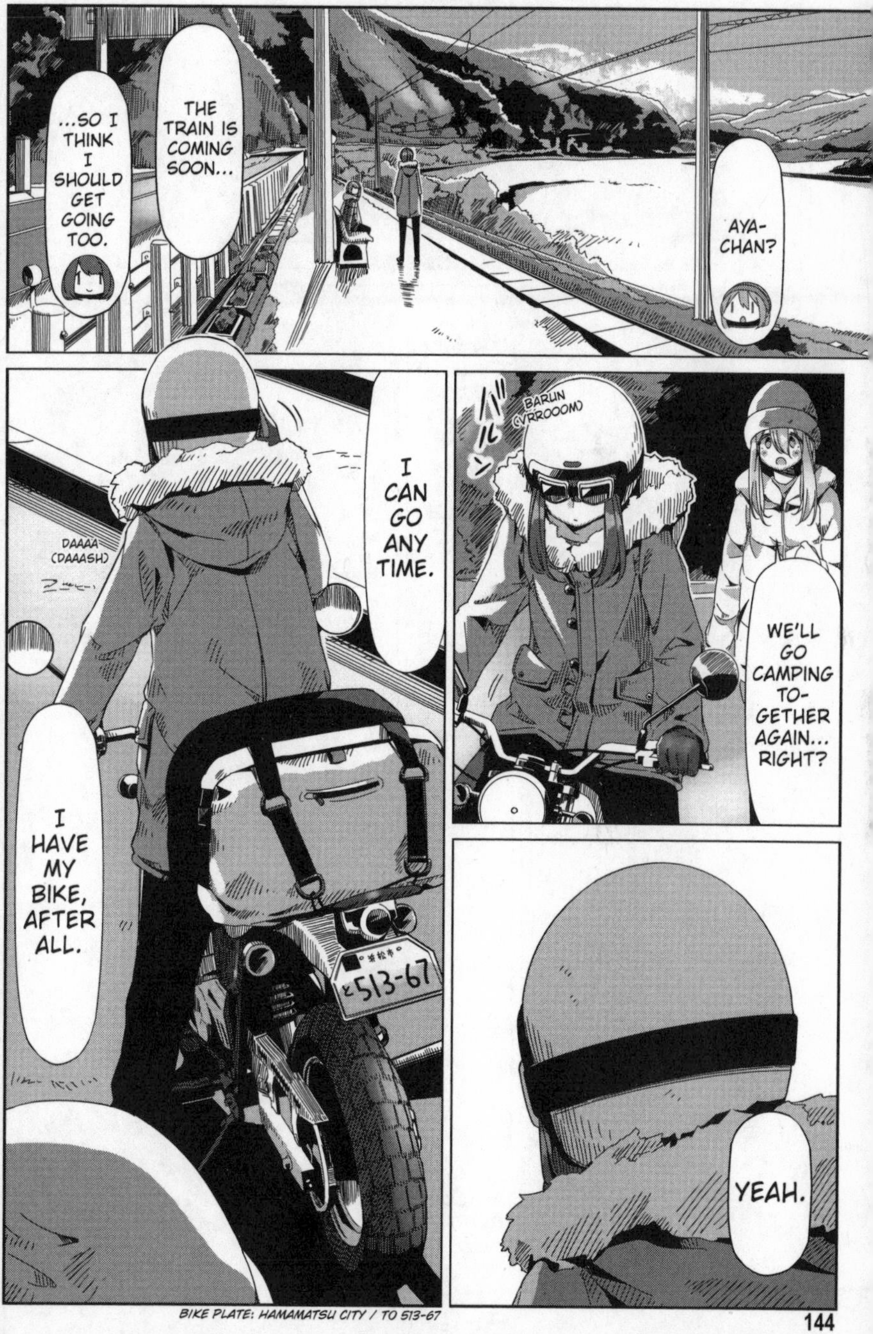
AYA-CHAN?
THE TRAIN IS COMING SOON...
...SO I THINK I SHOULD GET GOING TOO.
BARUN (VRROOOM)
WE'LL GO CAMPING TO-GETHER AGAIN... RIGHT?
YEAH.
I CAN GO ANY TIME.
DAAAA (DAAASH)
I HAVE MY BIKE, AFTER ALL.

BIKE PLATE: HAMAMATSU CITY / TO 513-67

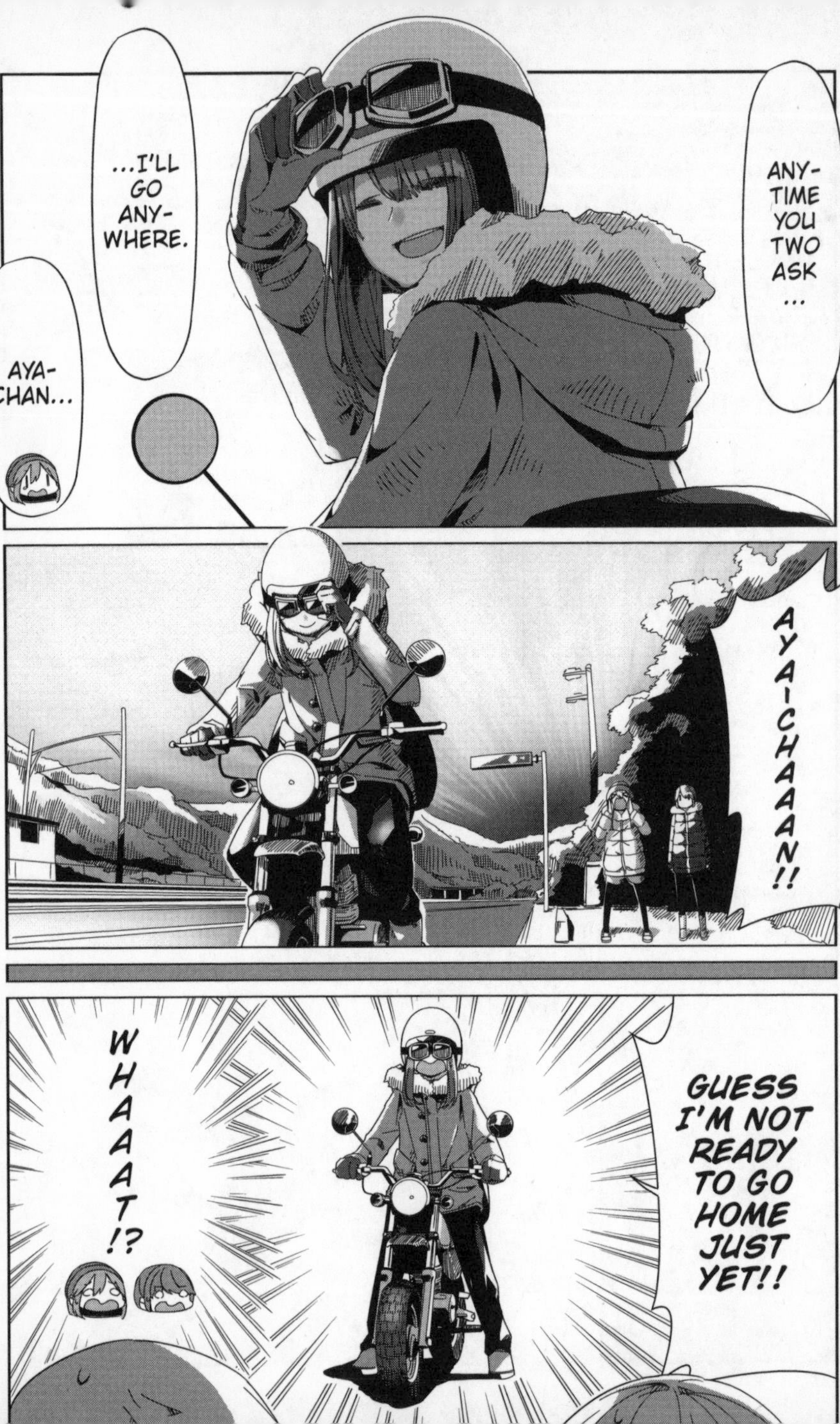
ANY-TIME YOU TWO ASK...
...I'LL GO ANY-WHERE.
AYA-CHAN...
AYA-CHAAAAN!!
GUESS I'M NOT READY TO GO HOME JUST YET!!
WHAAAT!?

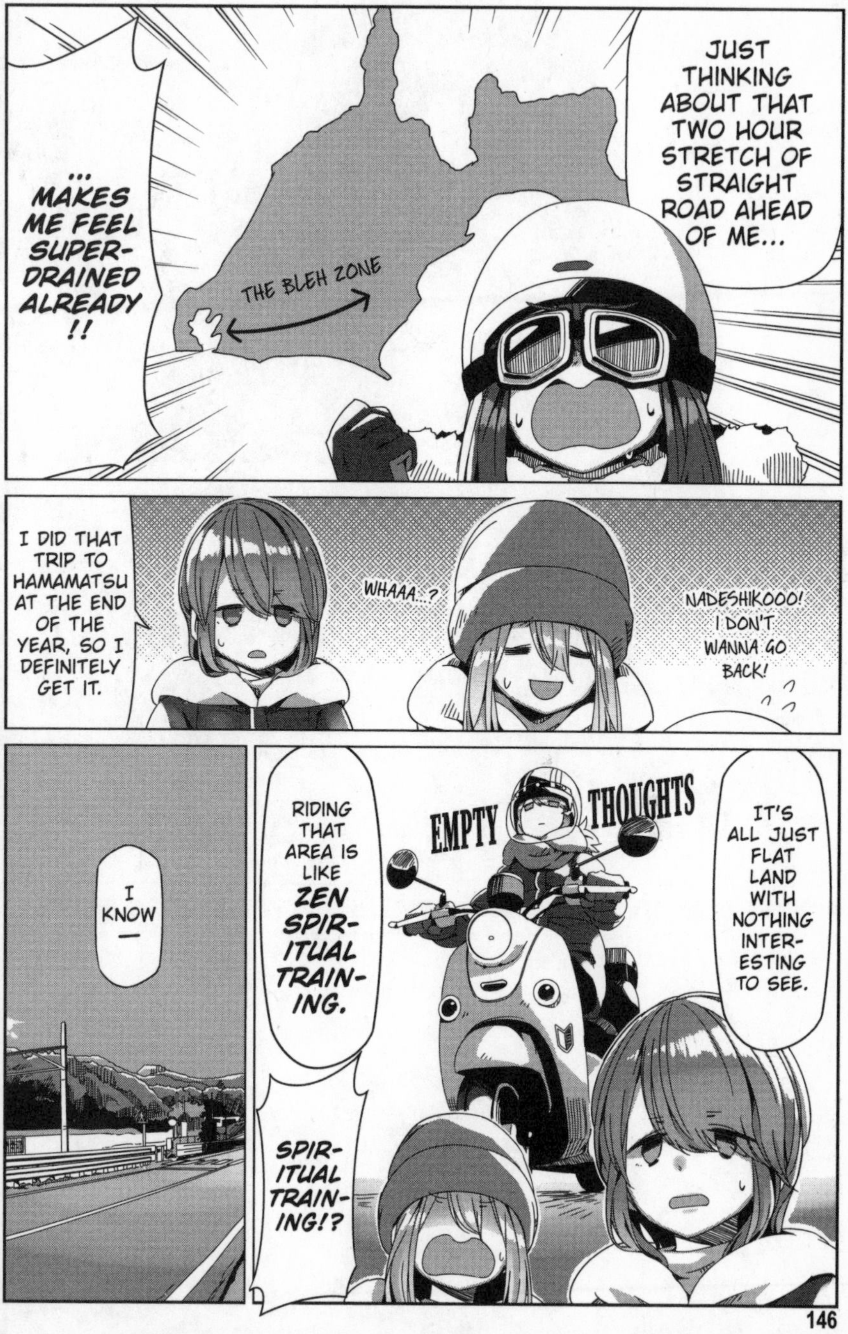
JUST THINKING ABOUT THAT TWO HOUR STRETCH OF STRAIGHT ROAD AHEAD OF ME...
THE BLEH ZONE
...MAKES ME FEEL SUPER-DRAINED ALREADY!!
NADESHIKOOO! I DON'T WANNA GO BACK!
WHAAA...?
I DID THAT TRIP TO HAMAMATSU AT THE END OF THE YEAR, SO I DEFINITELY GET IT.
IT'S ALL JUST FLAT LAND WITH NOTHING INTER-ESTING TO SEE.
EMPTY THOUGHTS
RIDING THAT AREA IS LIKE ZEN SPIR-ITUAL TRAIN-ING.
SPIR-ITUAL TRAIN-ING!?
I KNOW —

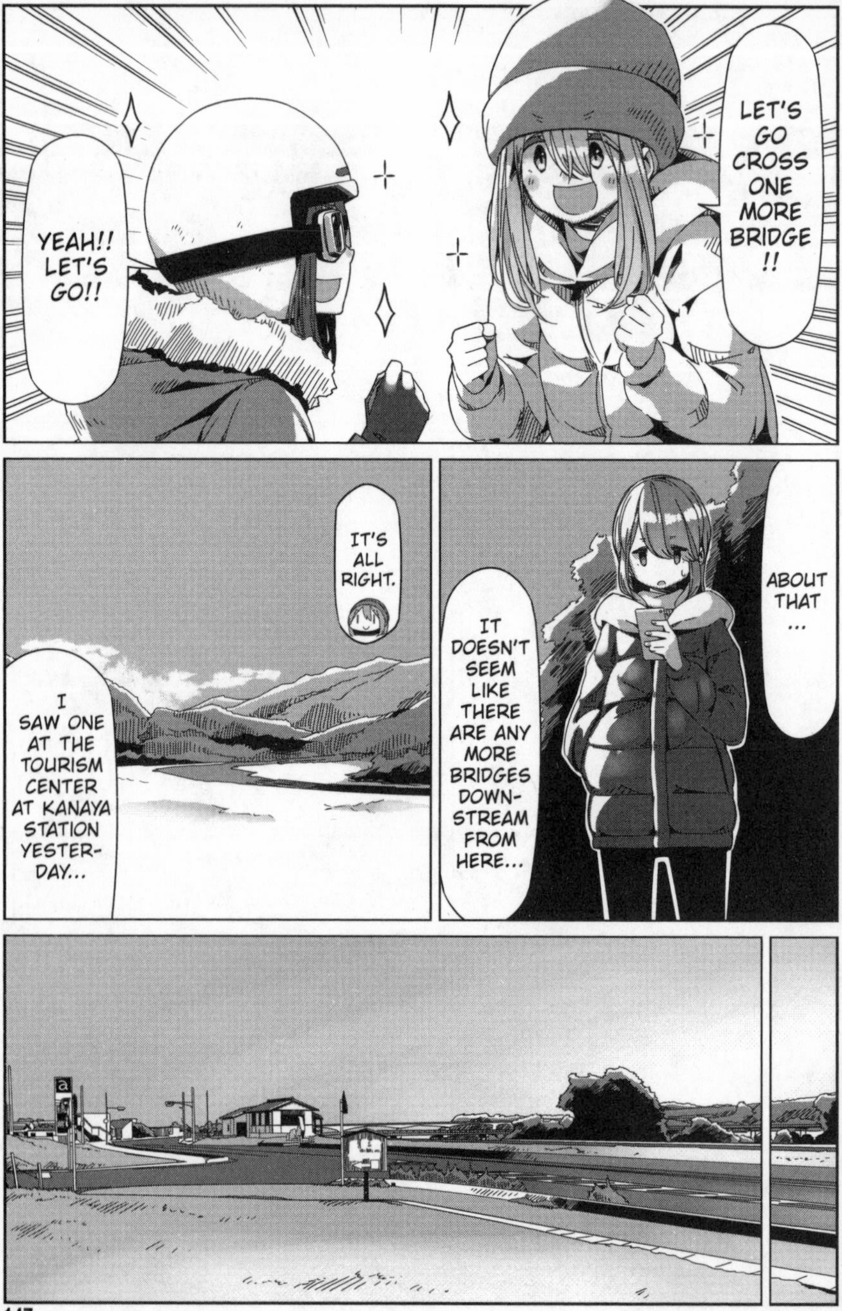
LET'S GO CROSS ONE MORE BRIDGE!!
YEAH!! LET'S GO!!
ABOUT THAT...
IT DOESN'T SEEM LIKE THERE ARE ANY MORE BRIDGES DOWN-STREAM FROM HERE...
IT'S ALL RIGHT.
I SAW ONE AT THE TOURISM CENTER AT KANAYA STATION YESTER-DAY...

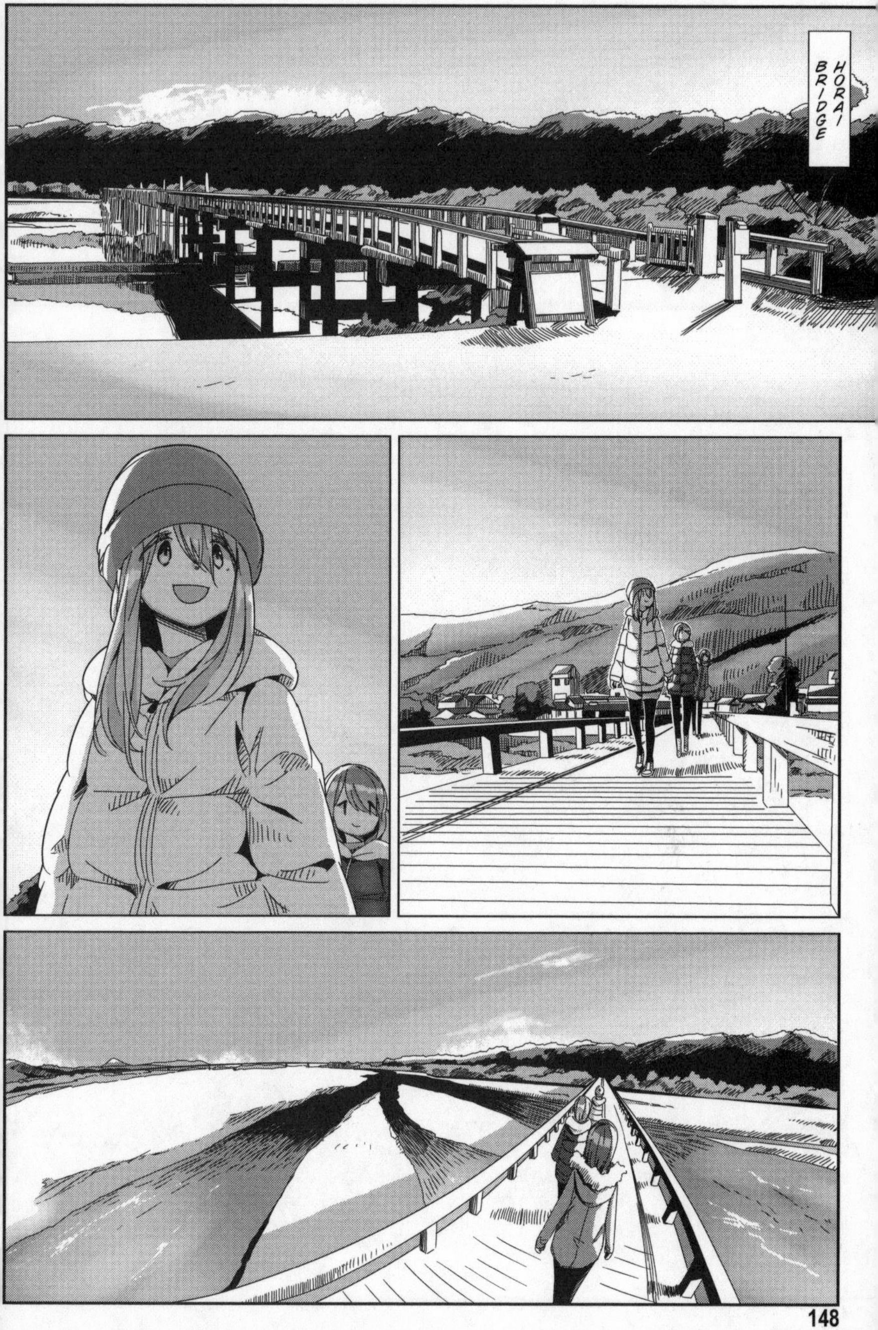
HORAI BRIDGE

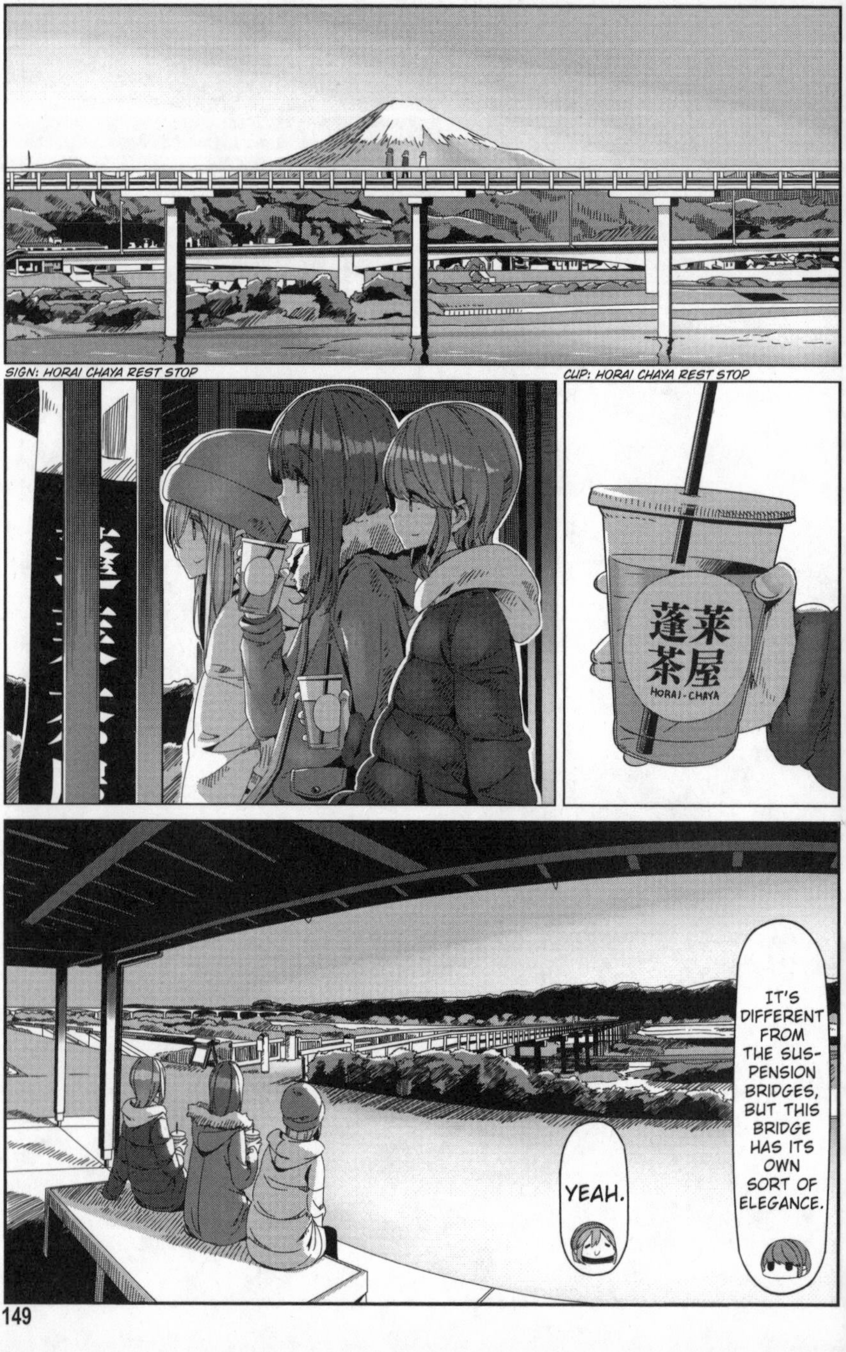
CUP: HORAI CHAYA REST STOP
蓬莱
茶屋
HORAI-CHAYA
SIGN: HORAI CHAYA REST STOP
IT'S DIFFERENT FROM THE SUS-PENSION BRIDGES, BUT THIS BRIDGE HAS ITS OWN SORT OF ELEGANCE.
YEAH.

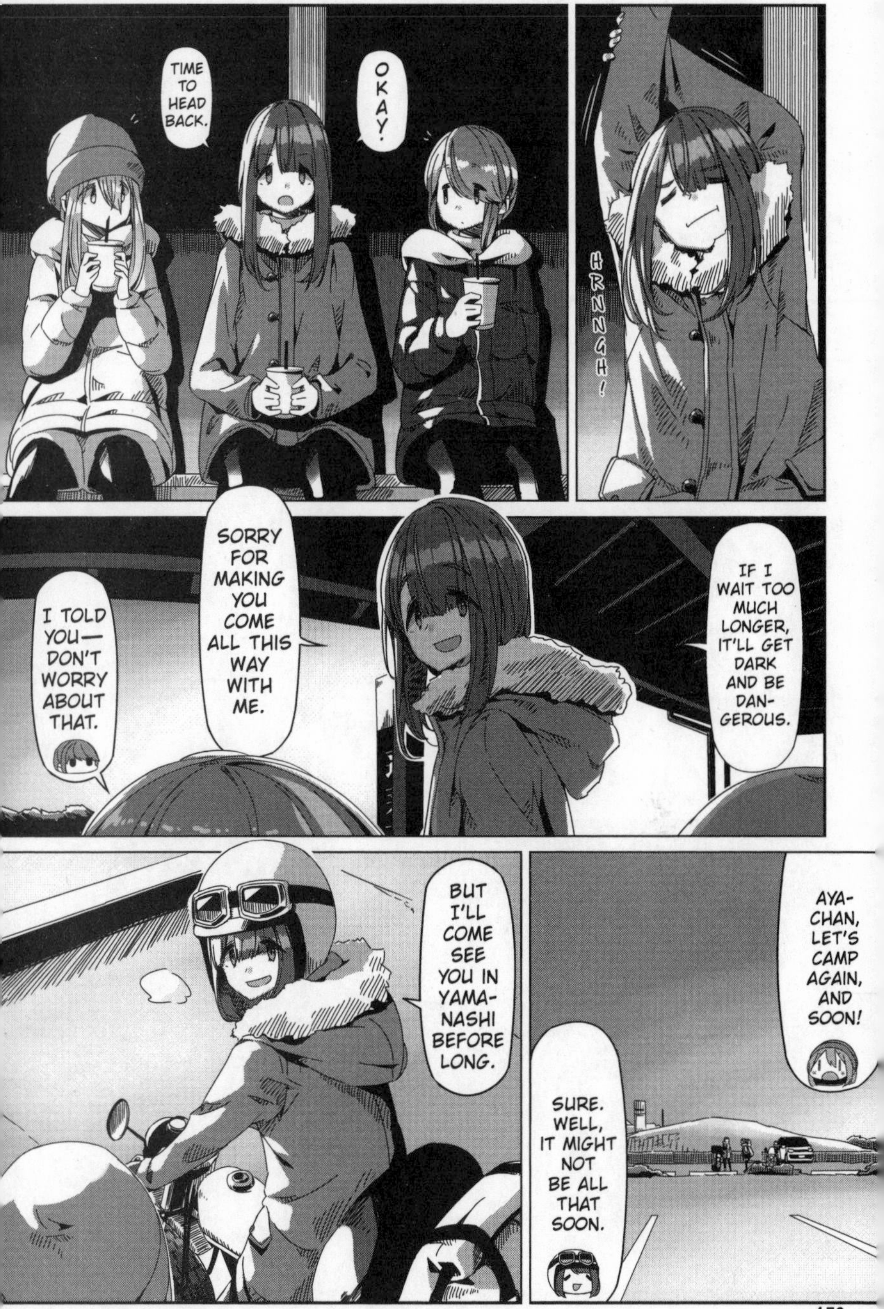
HRNNGH!
TIME TO HEAD BACK.
OKAY.
IF I WAIT TOO MUCH LONGER, IT'LL GET DARK AND BE DANGEROUS.
SORRY FOR MAKING YOU COME ALL THIS WAY WITH ME.
I TOLD YOU—DON'T WORRY ABOUT THAT.
AYA-CHAN, LET'S CAMP AGAIN, AND SOON!
SURE. WELL, IT MIGHT NOT BE ALL THAT SOON.
BUT I'LL COME SEE YOU IN YAMANASHI BEFORE LONG.

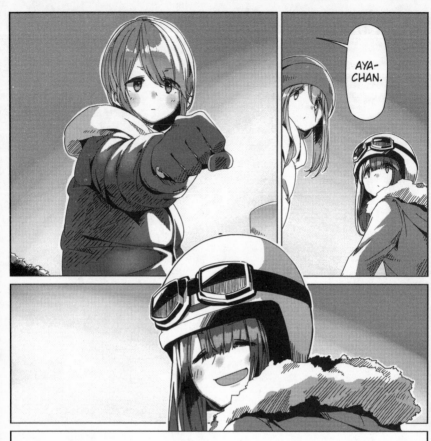

AYA-
CHAN.

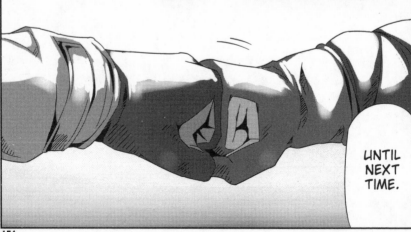

UNTIL
NEXT
TIME.

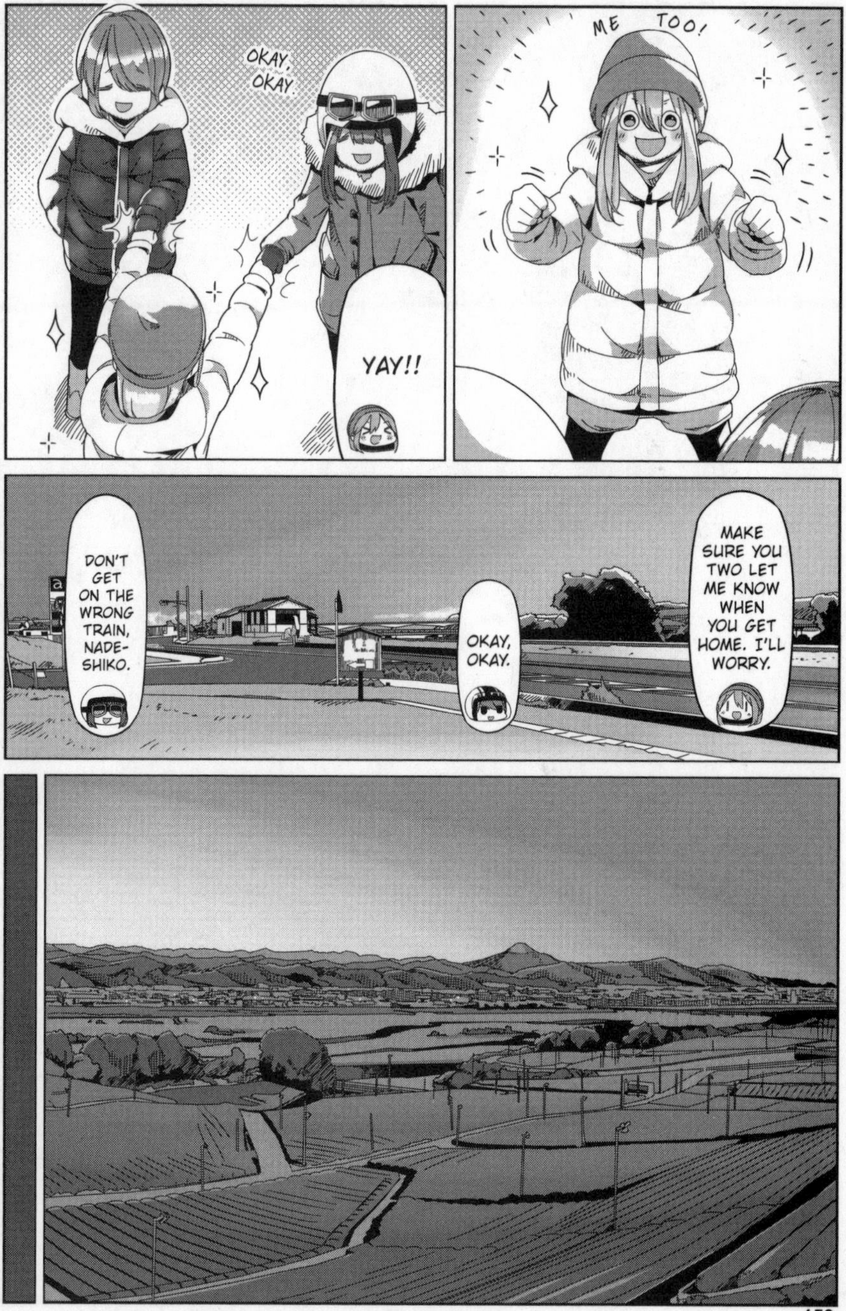
ME TOO!
OKAY, OKAY.
YAY!!
MAKE SURE YOU TWO LET ME KNOW WHEN YOU GET HOME. I'LL WORRY.
OKAY, OKAY.
DON'T GET ON THE WRONG TRAIN, NADE-SHIKO.

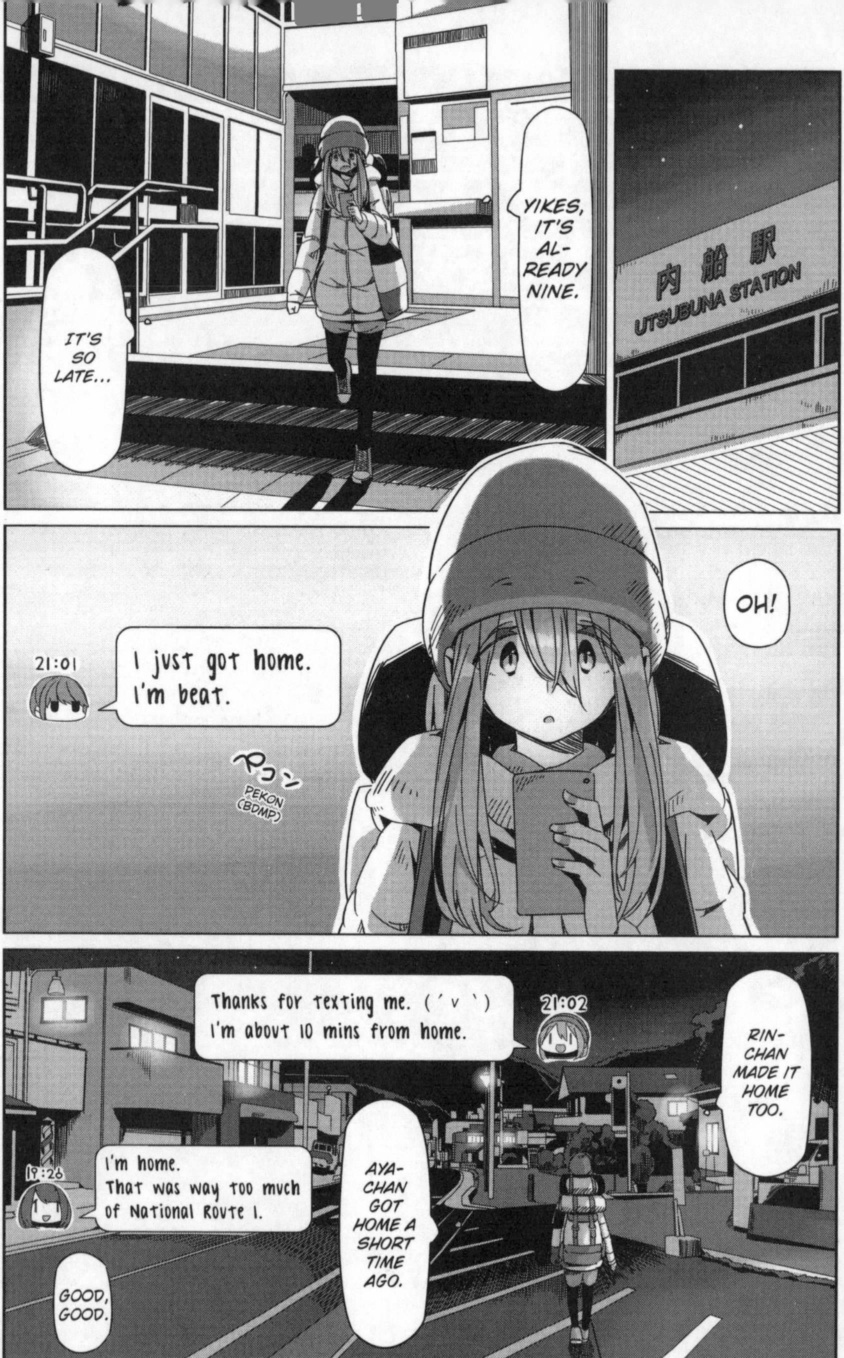

内船駅
UTSUBUNA STATION
YIKES, IT'S AL-READY NINE.
IT'S SO LATE...
OH!
21:01
I just got home. I'm beat.
ペコン
PEKON (BDMP)
RIN-CHAN MADE IT HOME TOO.
21:02
Thanks for texting me. (´ v `)
I'm about 10 mins from home.
AYA-CHAN GOT HOME A SHORT TIME AGO.
19:26
I'm home.
That was way too much of National Route 1.
GOOD, GOOD.

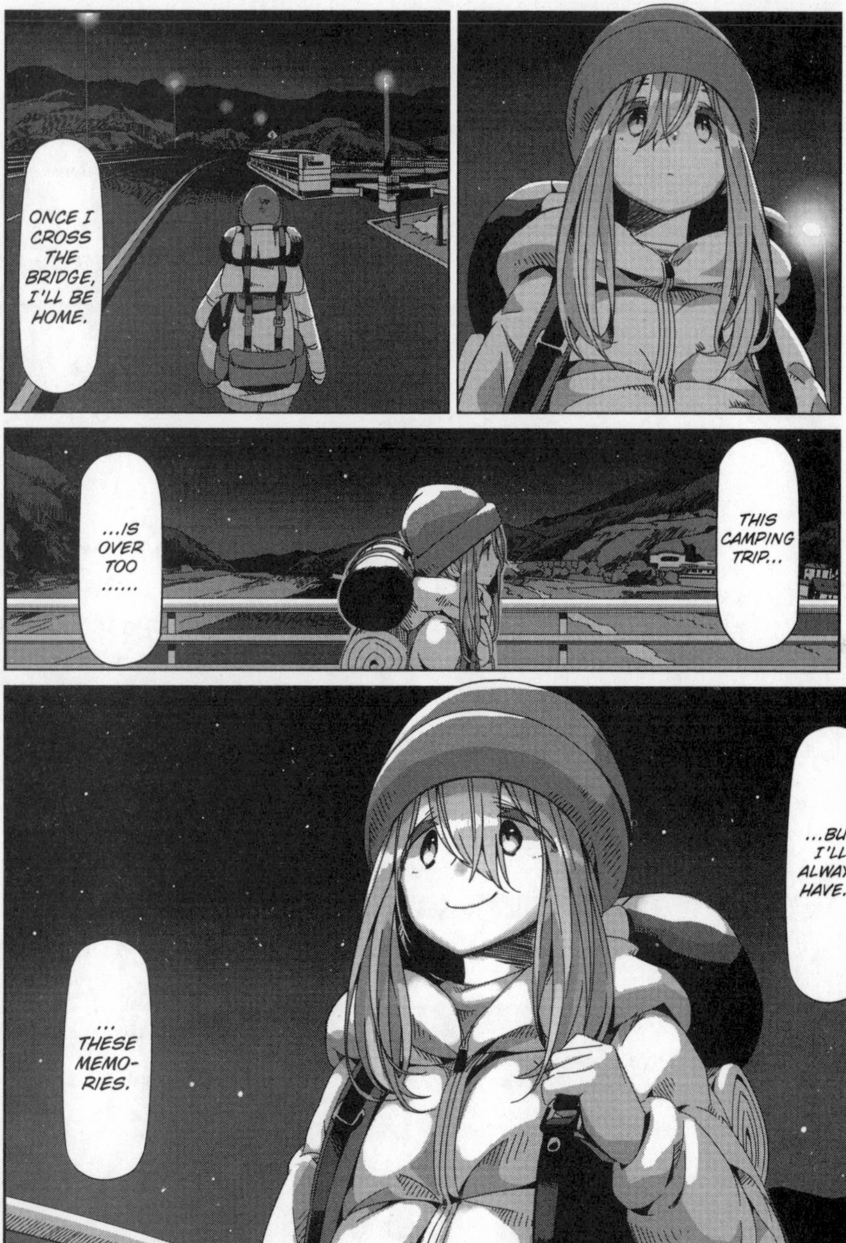
ONCE I CROSS THE BRIDGE, I'LL BE HOME.
THIS CAMPING TRIP...
...IS OVER TOO ......
...BUT I'LL ALWAYS HAVE...
... THESE MEMO-RIES.

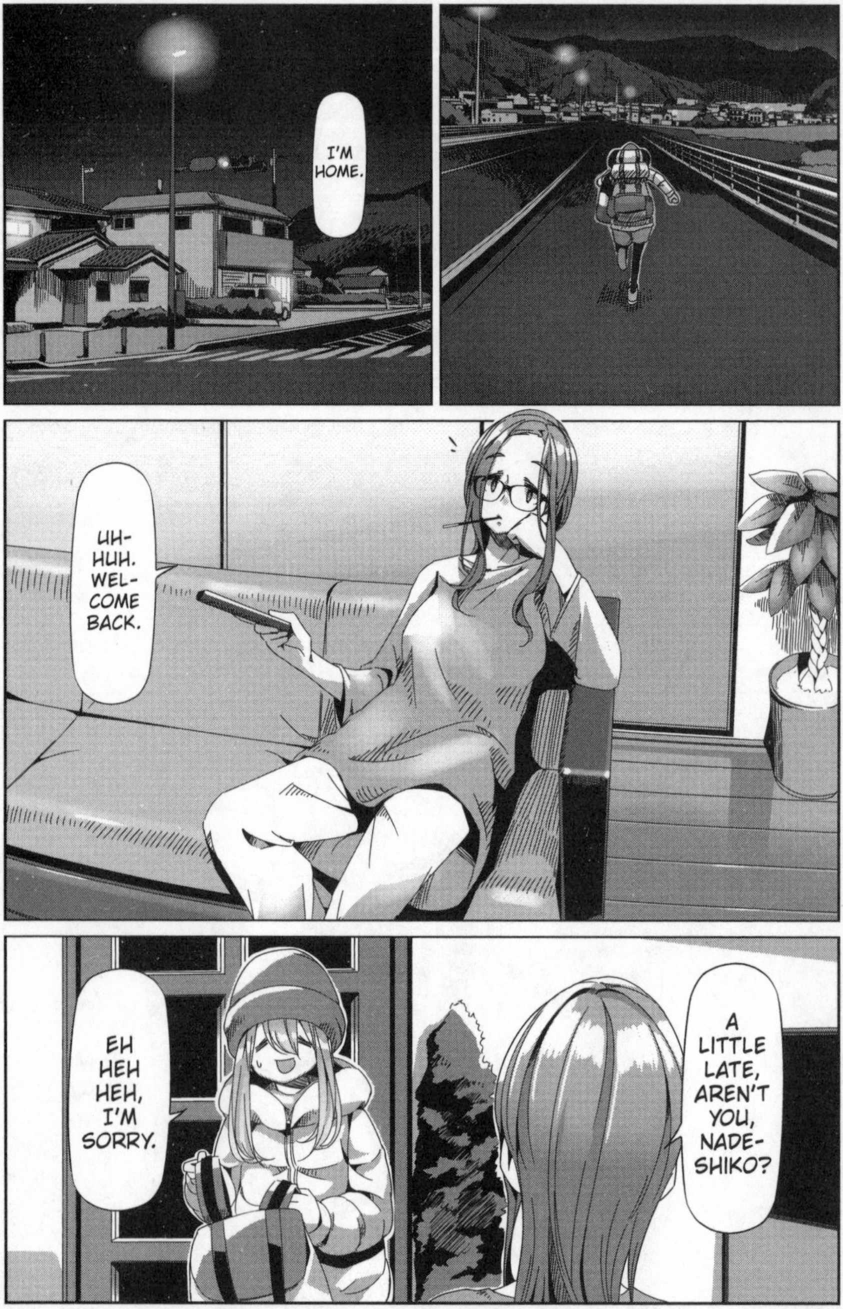
I'M HOME.
UH-HUH. WELCOME BACK.
A LITTLE LATE, AREN'T YOU, NADESHIKO?
EH HEH HEH, I'M SORRY.

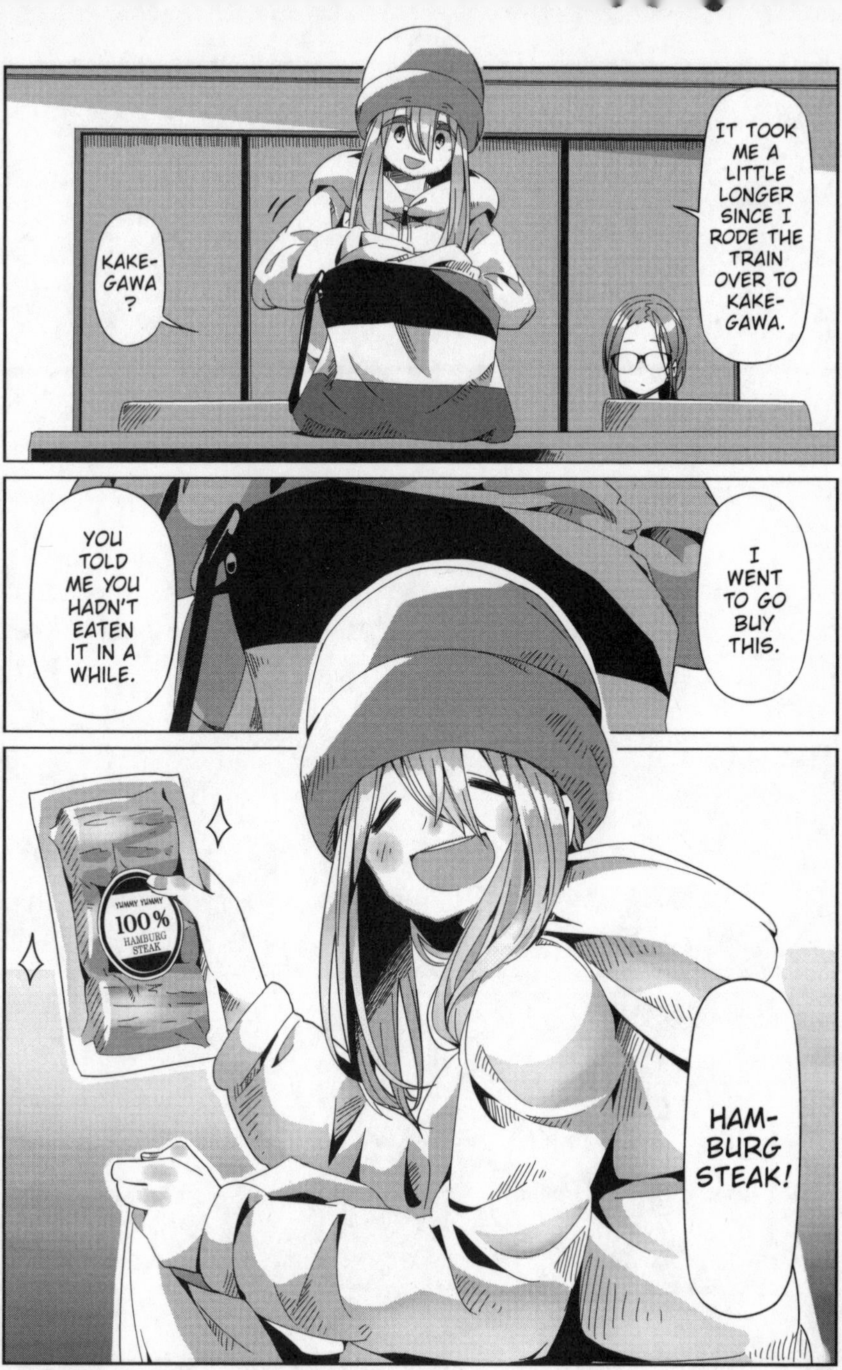
IT TOOK ME A LITTLE LONGER SINCE I RODE THE TRAIN OVER TO KAKE-GAWA.
KAKE-GAWA?
I WENT TO GO BUY THIS.
YOU TOLD ME YOU HADN'T EATEN IT IN A WHILE.
YUMMY YUMMY 100% HAMBURG STEAK
HAM-BURG STEAK!

TRANSLATION NOTES

COMMON HONORIFICS

no honorific: Indicates familiarity or closeness; if used without permission or reason, addressing someone in this manner would constitute an insult.
-san: The Japanese equivalent of Mr./Mrs./Miss. If a situation calls for politeness, this is the fail-safe honorific.
-kun: Used most often when referring to boys, this indicates affection or familiarity. Occasionally used by older men among their peers, but it may also be used by anyone referring to a person of lower standing.
-chan: An affectionate honorific indicating familiarity used mostly in reference to girls; also used in reference to cute persons or animals regardless of gender.
-sensei: A respectful term for teachers, artists, or high-level professionals.

(o)nee: Japanese equivalent to "older sis."
(o)nii: Japanese equivalent to "older bro."

100 yen is approximately 1 USD.
1 centimeter is approximately 0.39 inches. 1 kilometer is approximately 0.621 miles.

Ooi and the "oi" in names such as Okuoi Kojo Station refer to the same river. Spellings can differ depending on how the Japanese word is romanized.

PAGE 5
Delectable: The original Japanese phrase here was "*oishuu gozaimashita*," an elegant way of saying something was delicious. It was popularized by food critic and Iron Chef judge Asako Kishi.

PAGE 8
Diesel Train: Generally, commuter trains are electric-powered in Japan, and so the common word for train in Japanese reflects this: *densha*, or "electric vehicle." The note at the bottom of the page originally pointed out that Nadeshiko's use of *densha* was technically incorrect.

PAGE 27
***Chikuwa* bread**: In addition to Chikuwa's name being a pun on "chihuahua," *chikuwa* is a type of Japanese fishcake shaped like a sausage. *Chikuwa* bread is basically a bun with *chikuwa* in the middle.

PAGE 28
Sunny day to ya!: This is a loose translation of the original Japanese *yanbai desu*, a local greeting in Kawanehon. It roughly means "nice weather."

YOU CAN ORDER THIS HAMBURG STEAK ONLINE TOO.
REALLY!?

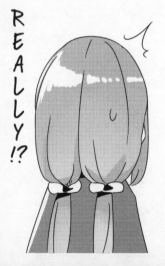

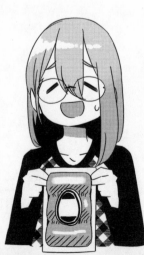

TRANSLATION NOTES (continued)

PAGE 34
Oden: A Japanese stew consisting primarily of fishcakes, vegetables, and other ingredients. In Shizuoka, *oden* is commonly made using a broth with beef stock and dark soy sauce, and ingredients are served on skewers, as shown.

PAGE 45
Grandkid Riders: This is a parody of the *Kamen Rider* franchise of live-action kids' shows, which feature costumed heroes who famously ride motorcycles.

PAGE 53
"It took a dentist four years to build this": Heiichirou Satou was the dentist who built the Ikawa giant Buddha statue.

PAGE 61
Nirayama Reverberatory Furnaces: Four furnaces constructed in Nirayama (now part of Izunokuni) to cast cannons in the mid-1800s.

PAGE 66
Majiuma: A fictional brand name that also sounds like "seriously tasty" in Japanese.

Amazake: A sweet and nonalcoholic fermented rice drink.

PAGE 81
Yakiniku: A Japanese style of grilling meat derived from Korean barbecue.

PAGE 87
Kohishikari: This is a parody of one of the most popular types of Japanese rice crop, *koshihikari*.

PAGE 111
Warabi mochi: A gelatin-like snack made from bracken-root starch and covered in roasted soybean flour.

PAGE 116
The duel at Ganryuujima: This is the duel fought by the famed swordsman and philosopher Musashi Miyamoto against Kojirou Sasaki. It is the most famous of Miyamoto's many bouts.

PAGE 149
Horai Chaya rest stop: This is a reference to Horaibashi Yakunashi Chaya, a rest stop that serves tea, located in Shimada, Shizuoka. *Chaya* literally means "teahouse."

PAGE 161
Kanji: The reason Nadeshiko says every site name wrong is because *kanji* characters can often have multiple pronunciations depending on how they're being used, with names being especially challenging in this regard. The correct readings (from right to left) are Shoujiko (Lake Shouji), Isawaonsen (Isawa Hot Spring), Oshinohakkai (Eight Ponds of Oshino).

PAGE 162
Hiragana and Katakana: Unlike *kanji*, *hiragana* and *katakana* in written Japanese function more like alphabets instead of ideograms, so they're much easier to read.

PAGE 166
Jingisukan: Named after Genghis Khan, it's a mutton dish popular in Hokkaido made using a special skillet.

◁ SIDE STORIES BEGIN ON THE NEXT PAGE ◁

ROOM CAMP

AFTER-SCHOOL 90 THAT FRESH-MADE TASTE

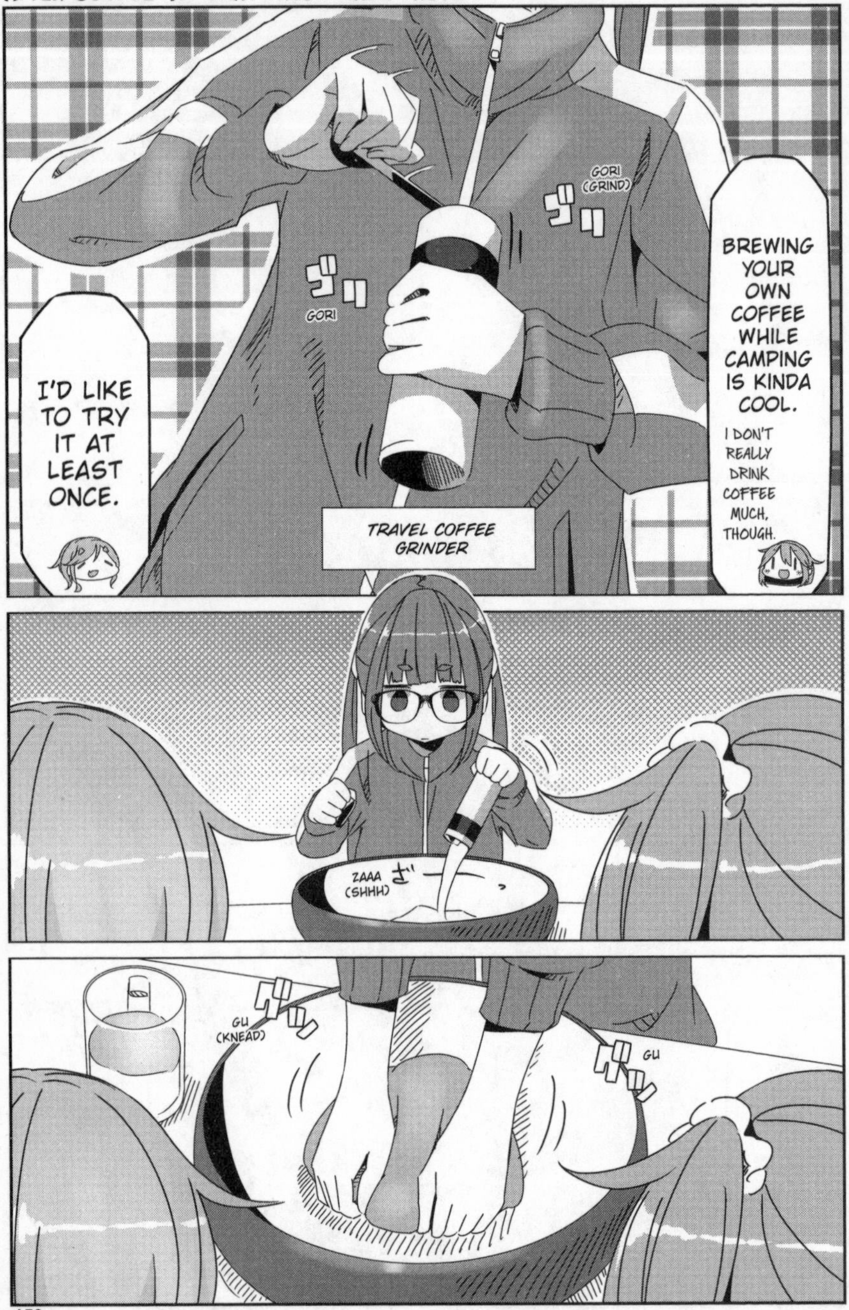
BREWING YOUR OWN COFFEE WHILE CAMPING IS KINDA COOL.
I DON'T REALLY DRINK COFFEE MUCH, THOUGH.
GORI (GRIND)
GORI
TRAVEL COFFEE GRINDER
I'D LIKE TO TRY IT AT LEAST ONCE.
ZAAA (SHHH)
GU
GU (KNEAD)

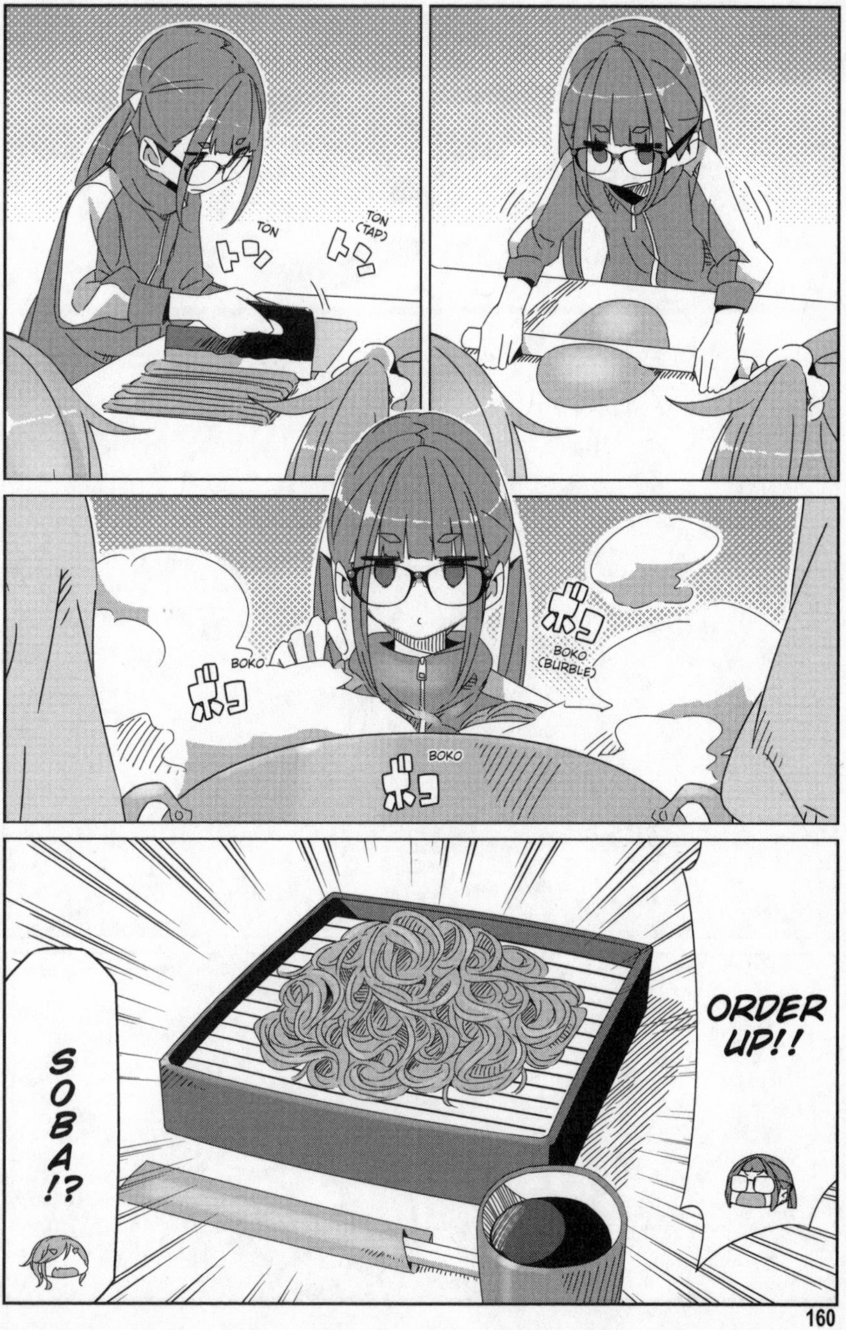
TON
トン
TON (TAP)
トン
BOKO (BURBLE)
ボコ
BOKO
ボコ
BOKO
ボコ
ORDER UP!!
SOBA!?

AFTER-SCHOOL 91 THE REASON FOR USING HIRAGANA

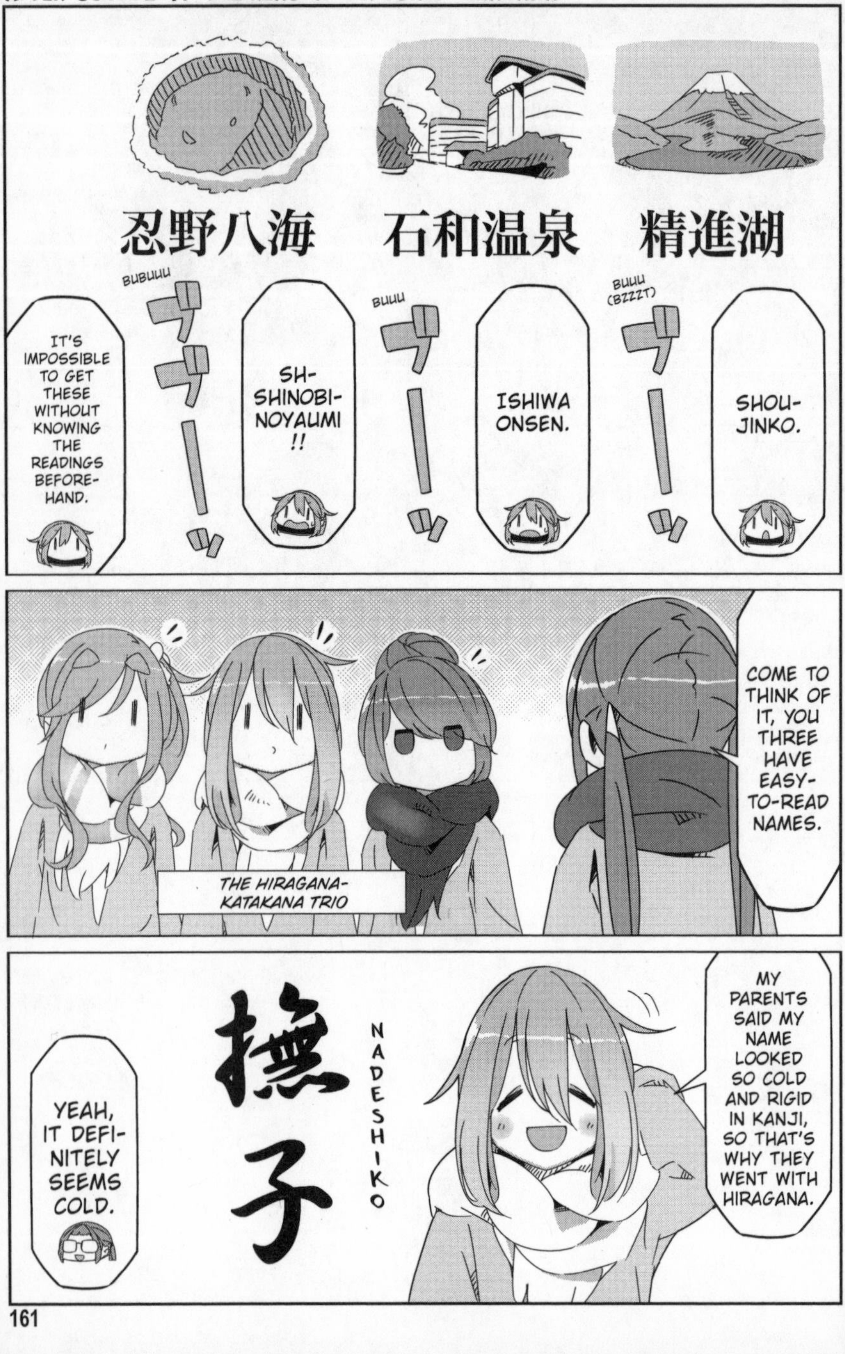
精進湖
石和温泉
忍野八海
SHOU-JINKO.
BUUU (BZZZT)
ISHIWA ONSEN.
BUUU
SH-SHINOBI-NOYAUMI !!
BUBUUU
IT'S IMPOSSIBLE TO GET THESE WITHOUT KNOWING THE READINGS BEFORE-HAND.
COME TO THINK OF IT, YOU THREE HAVE EASY-TO-READ NAMES.
THE HIRAGANA-KATAKANA TRIO
MY PARENTS SAID MY NAME LOOKED SO COLD AND RIGID IN KANJI, SO THAT'S WHY THEY WENT WITH HIRAGANA.
NADESHIKO
撫子
YEAH, IT DEFINITELY SEEMS COLD.

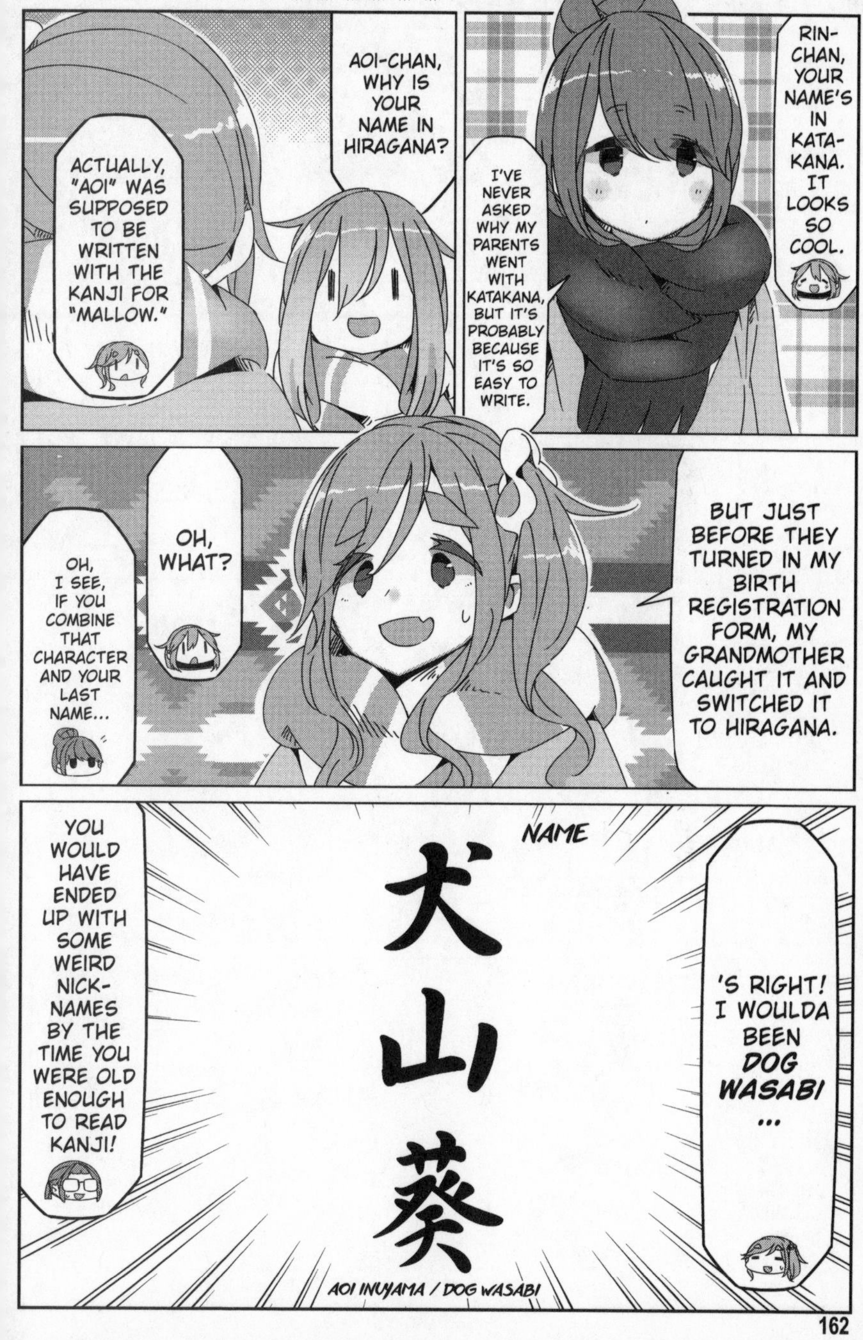
RIN-CHAN, YOUR NAME'S IN KATAKANA. IT LOOKS SO COOL.
I'VE NEVER ASKED WHY MY PARENTS WENT WITH KATAKANA, BUT IT'S PROBABLY BECAUSE IT'S SO EASY TO WRITE.
AOI-CHAN, WHY IS YOUR NAME IN HIRAGANA?
ACTUALLY, "AOI" WAS SUPPOSED TO BE WRITTEN WITH THE KANJI FOR "MALLOW."
BUT JUST BEFORE THEY TURNED IN MY BIRTH REGISTRATION FORM, MY GRANDMOTHER CAUGHT IT AND SWITCHED IT TO HIRAGANA.
OH, WHAT?
OH, I SEE, IF YOU COMBINE THAT CHARACTER AND YOUR LAST NAME...
NAME
犬山葵
AOI INUYAMA / DOG WASABI
'S RIGHT! I WOULDA BEEN *DOG WASABI* ...
YOU WOULD HAVE ENDED UP WITH SOME WEIRD NICK-NAMES BY THE TIME YOU WERE OLD ENOUGH TO READ KANJI!

AFTER-SCHOOL 92 THE RESOLUTION OF THE DEBATE

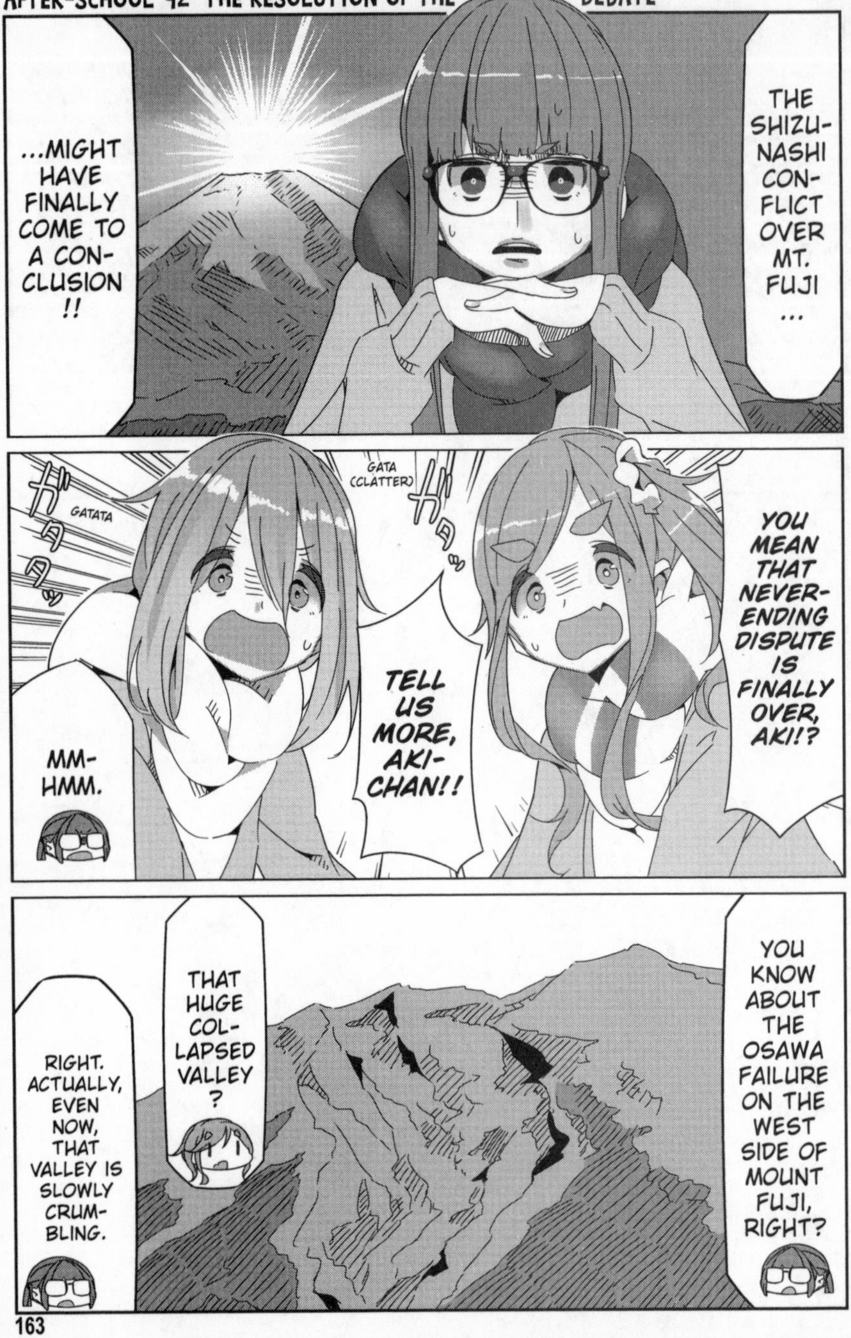
THE SHIZUNASHI CONFLICT OVER MT. FUJI...
...MIGHT HAVE FINALLY COME TO A CONCLUSION!!
YOU MEAN THAT NEVER-ENDING DISPUTE IS FINALLY OVER, AKI!?
GATA (CLATTER)
TELL US MORE, AKI-CHAN!!
GATATA
MM-HMM.
YOU KNOW ABOUT THE OSAWA FAILURE ON THE WEST SIDE OF MOUNT FUJI, RIGHT?
THAT HUGE COLLAPSED VALLEY?
RIGHT. ACTUALLY, EVEN NOW, THAT VALLEY IS SLOWLY CRUMBLING.

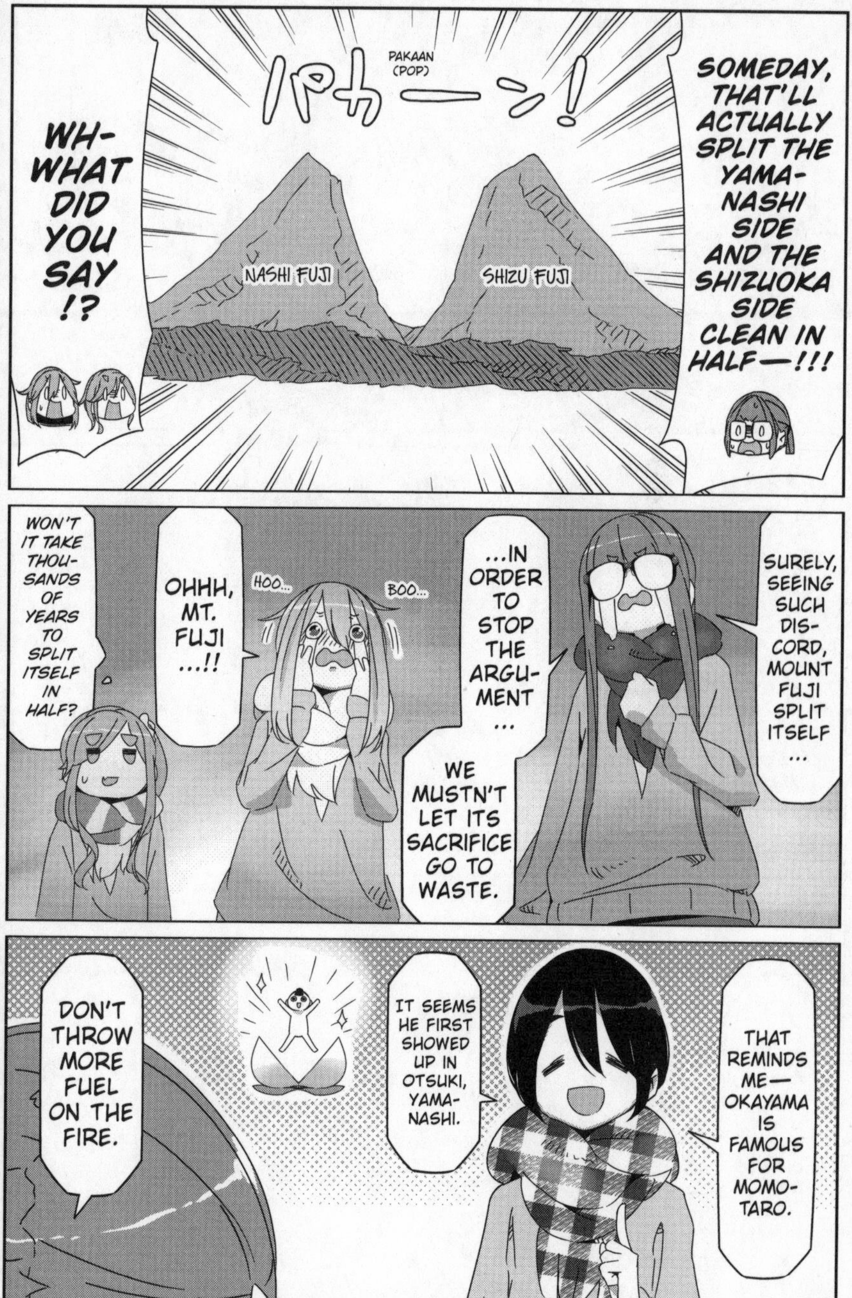
SOMEDAY, THAT'LL ACTUALLY SPLIT THE YAMANASHI SIDE AND THE SHIZUOKA SIDE CLEAN IN HALF—!!!
パカーン!
PAKAAN (POP)
SHIZU FUJI
NASHI FUJI
WH-WHAT DID YOU SAY!?
SURELY, SEEING SUCH DISCORD, MOUNT FUJI SPLIT ITSELF...
...IN ORDER TO STOP THE ARGUMENT...
WE MUSTN'T LET ITS SACRIFICE GO TO WASTE.
BOO...
HOO...
OHHH, MT. FUJI...!!
WON'T IT TAKE THOUSANDS OF YEARS TO SPLIT ITSELF IN HALF?
THAT REMINDS ME—OKAYAMA IS FAMOUS FOR MOMOTARO.
IT SEEMS HE FIRST SHOWED UP IN OTSUKI, YAMANASHI.
DON'T THROW MORE FUEL ON THE FIRE.

AFTER-SCHOOL 93 IF I GO TO HOKKAIDO

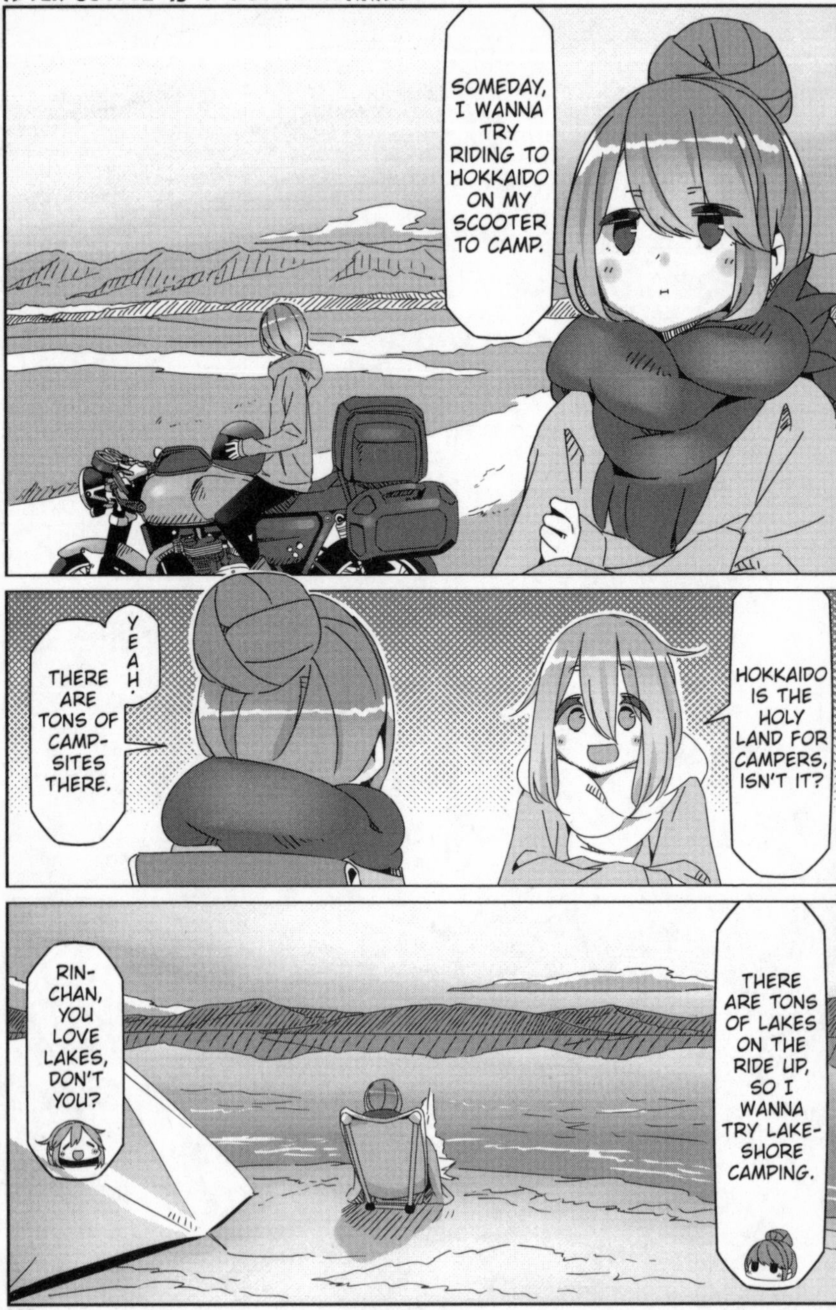
SOMEDAY, I WANNA TRY RIDING TO HOKKAIDO ON MY SCOOTER TO CAMP.
HOKKAIDO IS THE HOLY LAND FOR CAMPERS, ISN'T IT?
YEAH.
THERE ARE TONS OF CAMP-SITES THERE.
THERE ARE TONS OF LAKES ON THE RIDE UP, SO I WANNA TRY LAKE-SHORE CAMPING.
RIN-CHAN, YOU LOVE LAKES, DON'T YOU?

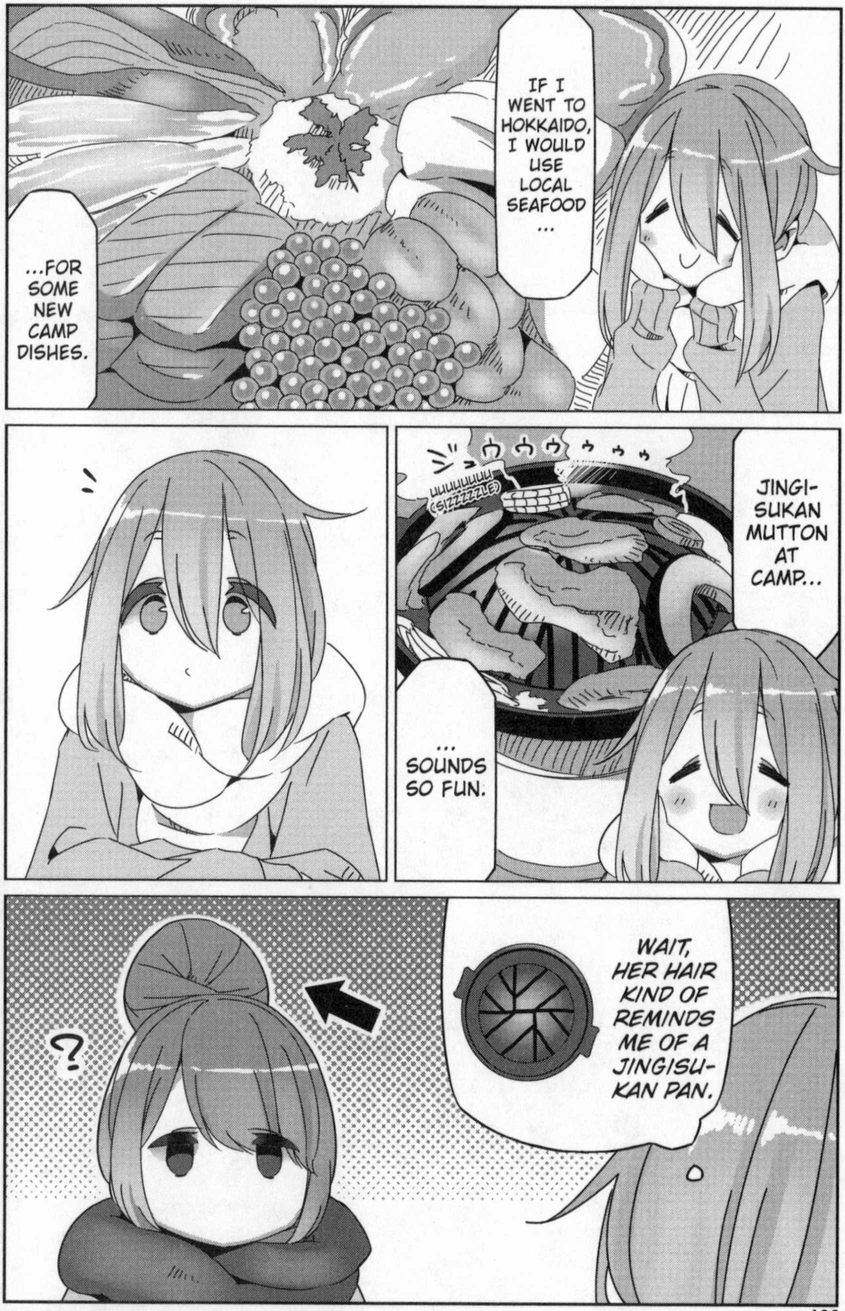
IF I WENT TO HOKKAIDO, I WOULD USE LOCAL SEAFOOD ...
...FOR SOME NEW CAMP DISHES.
JINGI-SUKAN MUTTON AT CAMP...
UUUUUUUU (SIZZZZZZLE)
... SOUNDS SO FUN.
WAIT, HER HAIR KIND OF REMINDS ME OF A JINGISU-KAN PAN.
?

AFTER-SCHOOL 94 A BIGGER IZU

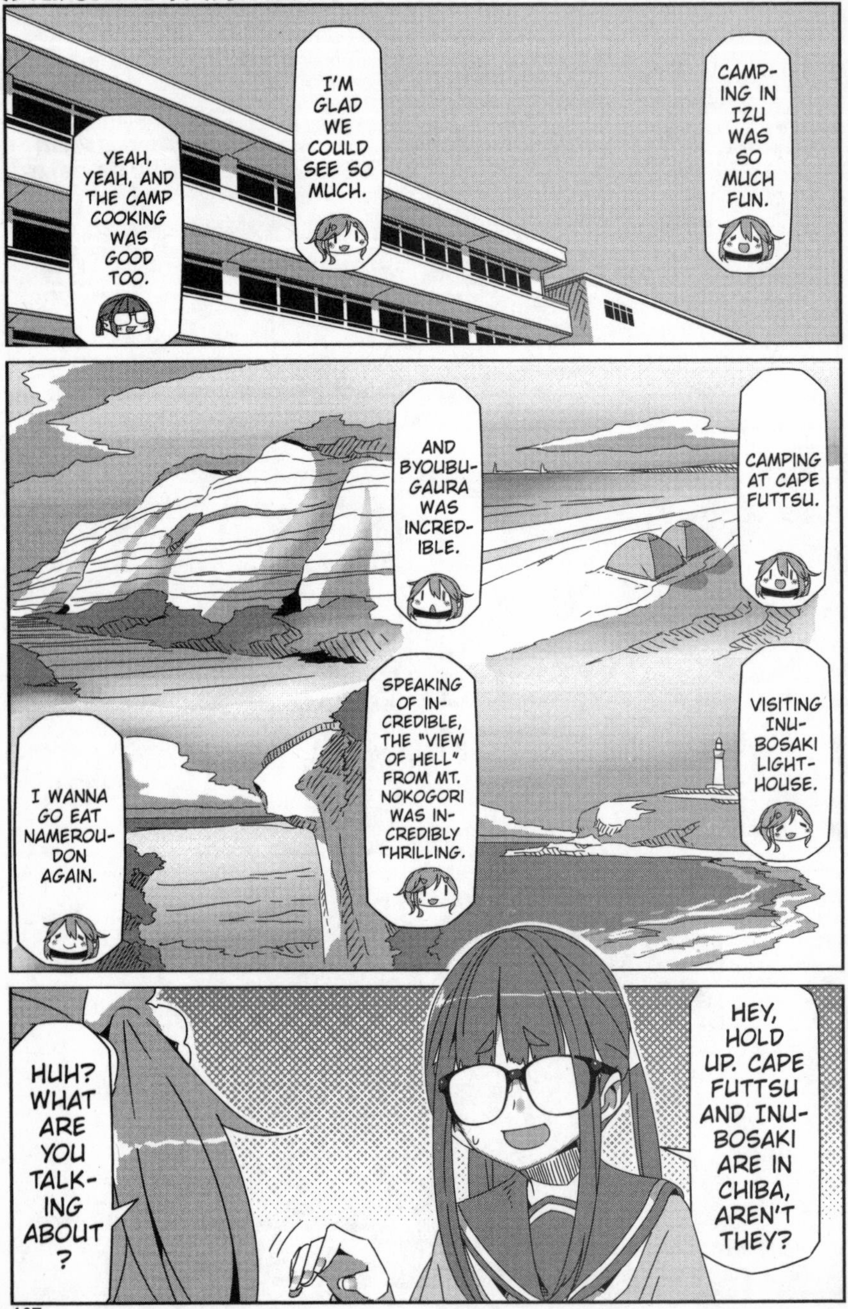
CAMPING IN IZU WAS SO MUCH FUN.
I'M GLAD WE COULD SEE SO MUCH.
YEAH, YEAH, AND THE CAMP COOKING WAS GOOD TOO.
CAMPING AT CAPE FUTTSU.
AND BYOUBUGAURA WAS INCREDIBLE.
VISITING INUBOSAKI LIGHTHOUSE.
SPEAKING OF INCREDIBLE, THE "VIEW OF HELL" FROM MT. NOKOGORI WAS INCREDIBLY THRILLING.
I WANNA GO EAT NAMEROU-DON AGAIN.
HEY, HOLD UP. CAPE FUTTSU AND INUBOSAKI ARE IN CHIBA, AREN'T THEY?
HUH? WHAT ARE YOU TALKING ABOUT?

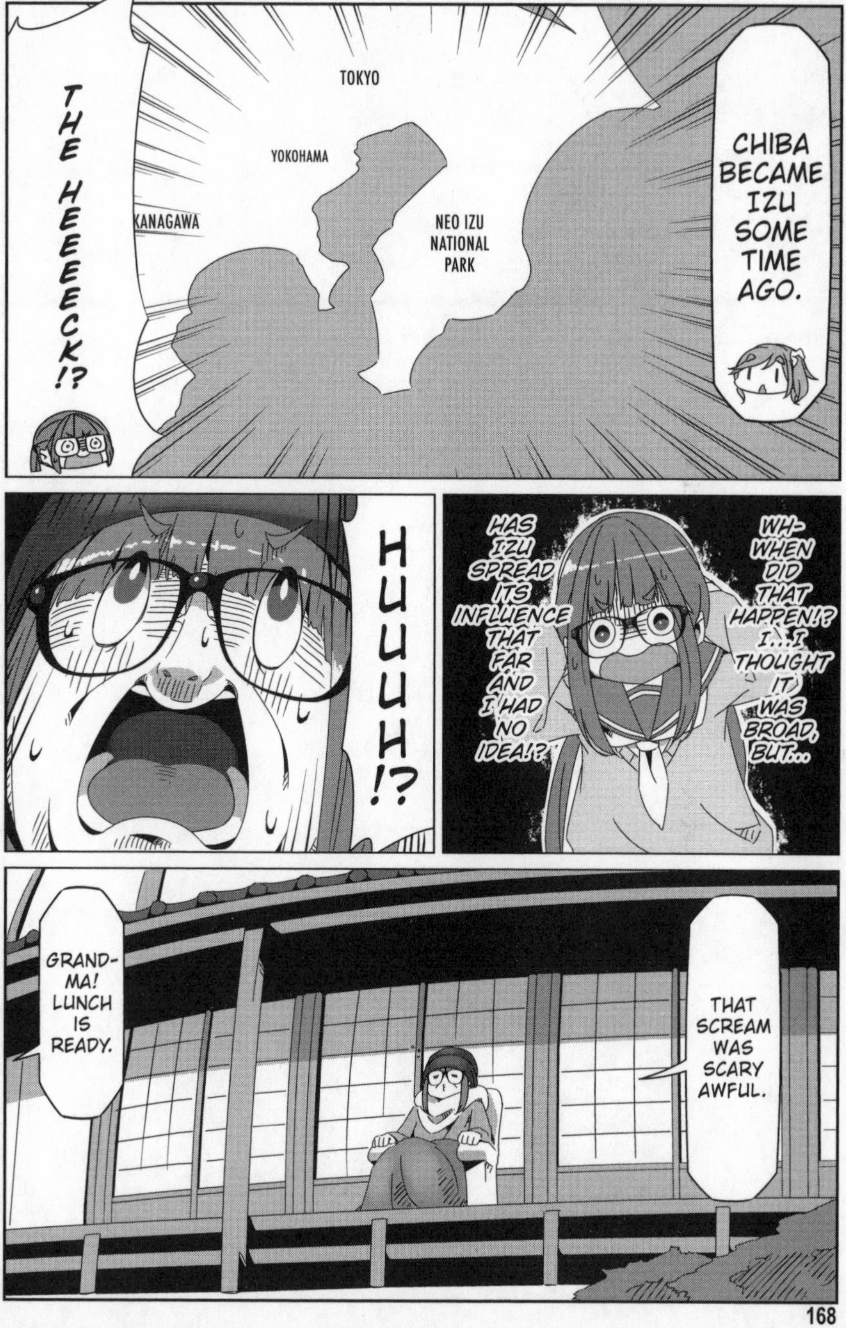
CHIBA BECAME IZU SOME TIME AGO.
TOKYO
YOKOHAMA
NEO IZU NATIONAL PARK
KANAGAWA
THE HEEEECK!?
WH-WHEN DID THAT HAPPEN!? I... I THOUGHT IT WAS BROAD, BUT...
HAS IZU SPREAD ITS INFLUENCE THAT FAR AND I HAD NO IDEA!?
HUUUH!?
THAT SCREAM WAS SCARY AWFUL.
GRAND-MA! LUNCH IS READY.

AFTER-SCHOOL 95 POLE-STYLE BODY PILLOW

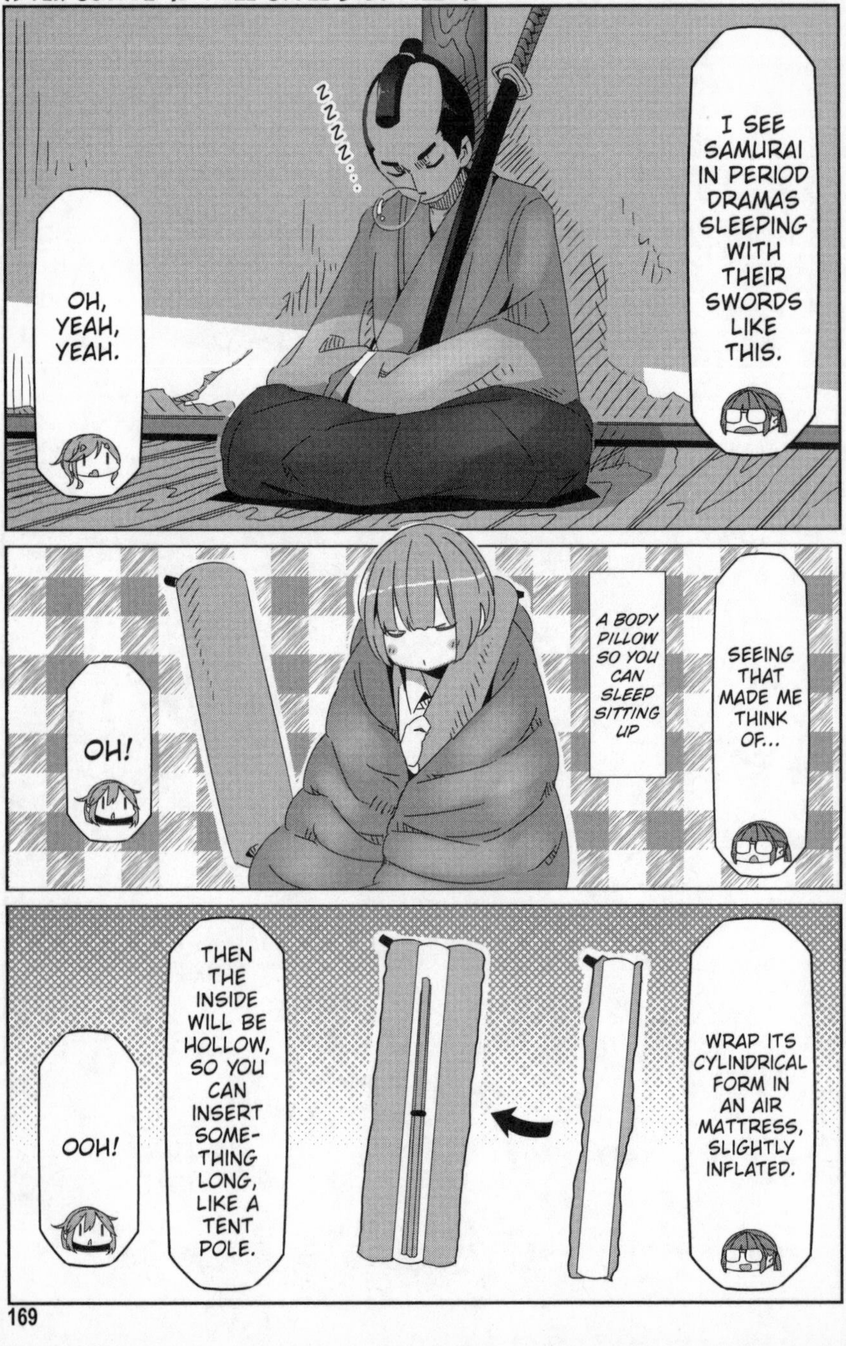
I SEE SAMURAI IN PERIOD DRAMAS SLEEPING WITH THEIR SWORDS LIKE THIS.
ZZZZ...
OH, YEAH, YEAH.
SEEING THAT MADE ME THINK OF...
A BODY PILLOW SO YOU CAN SLEEP SITTING UP
OH!
WRAP ITS CYLINDRICAL FORM IN AN AIR MATTRESS, SLIGHTLY INFLATED.
THEN THE INSIDE WILL BE HOLLOW, SO YOU CAN INSERT SOME-THING LONG, LIKE A TENT POLE.
OOH!

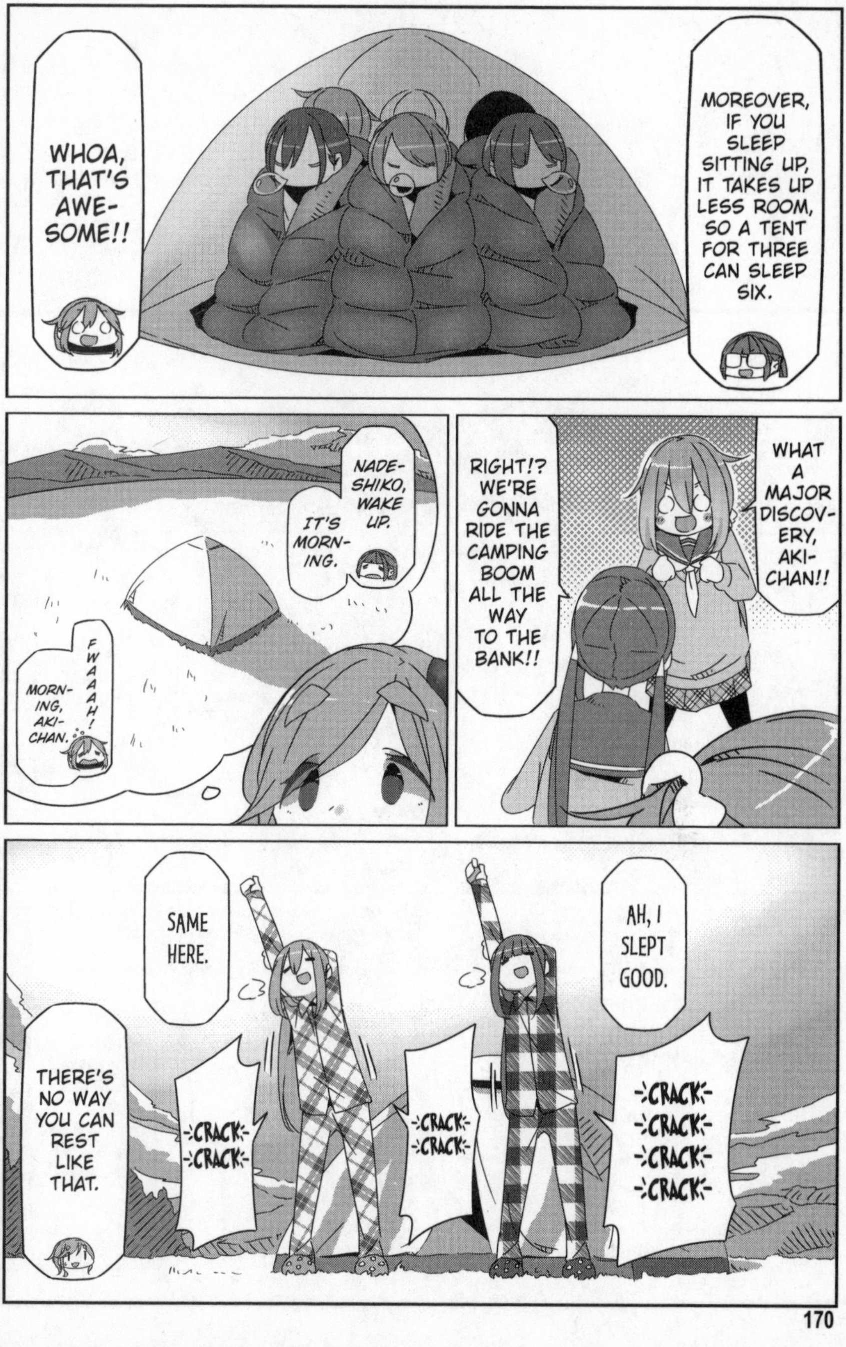
MOREOVER, IF YOU SLEEP SITTING UP, IT TAKES UP LESS ROOM, SO A TENT FOR THREE CAN SLEEP SIX.
WHOA, THAT'S AWE-SOME!!
WHAT A MAJOR DISCOV-ERY, AKI-CHAN!!
RIGHT!? WE'RE GONNA RIDE THE CAMPING BOOM ALL THE WAY TO THE BANK!!
NADE-SHIKO, WAKE UP.
IT'S MORN-ING.
FWAAAAH!
MORN-ING, AKI-CHAN.
AH, I SLEPT GOOD.
SAME HERE.
-CRACK- -CRACK- -CRACK- -CRACK-
-CRACK- -CRACK-
-CRACK- -CRACK-
THERE'S NO WAY YOU CAN REST LIKE THAT.

AFTER-SCHOOL 96 A WAY TO STOP PEOPLE FROM TRIPPING

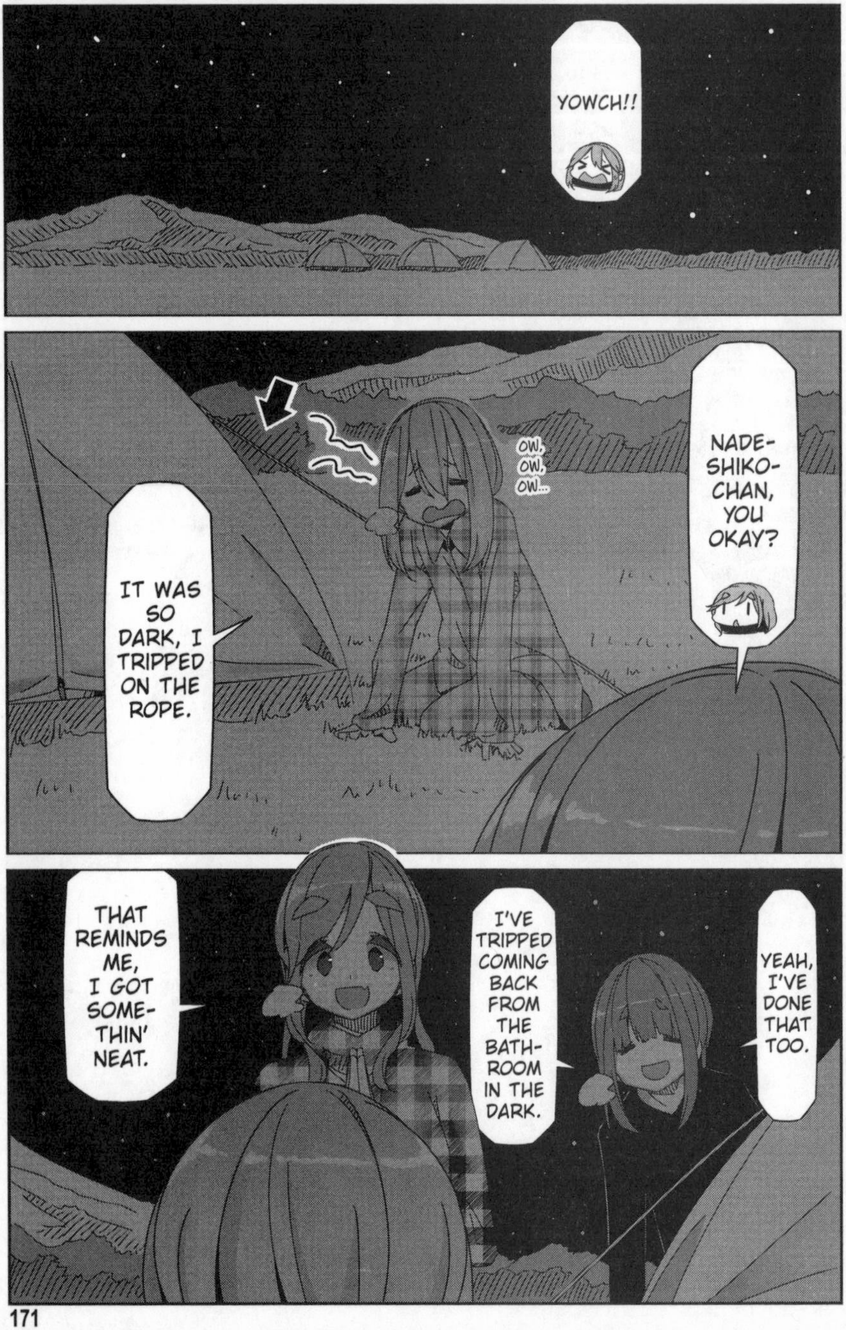
YOWCH!!
NADESHIKO-CHAN, YOU OKAY?
OW, OW, OW...
IT WAS SO DARK, I TRIPPED ON THE ROPE.
YEAH, I'VE DONE THAT TOO.
I'VE TRIPPED COMING BACK FROM THE BATHROOM IN THE DARK.
THAT REMINDS ME, I GOT SOMETHIN' NEAT.

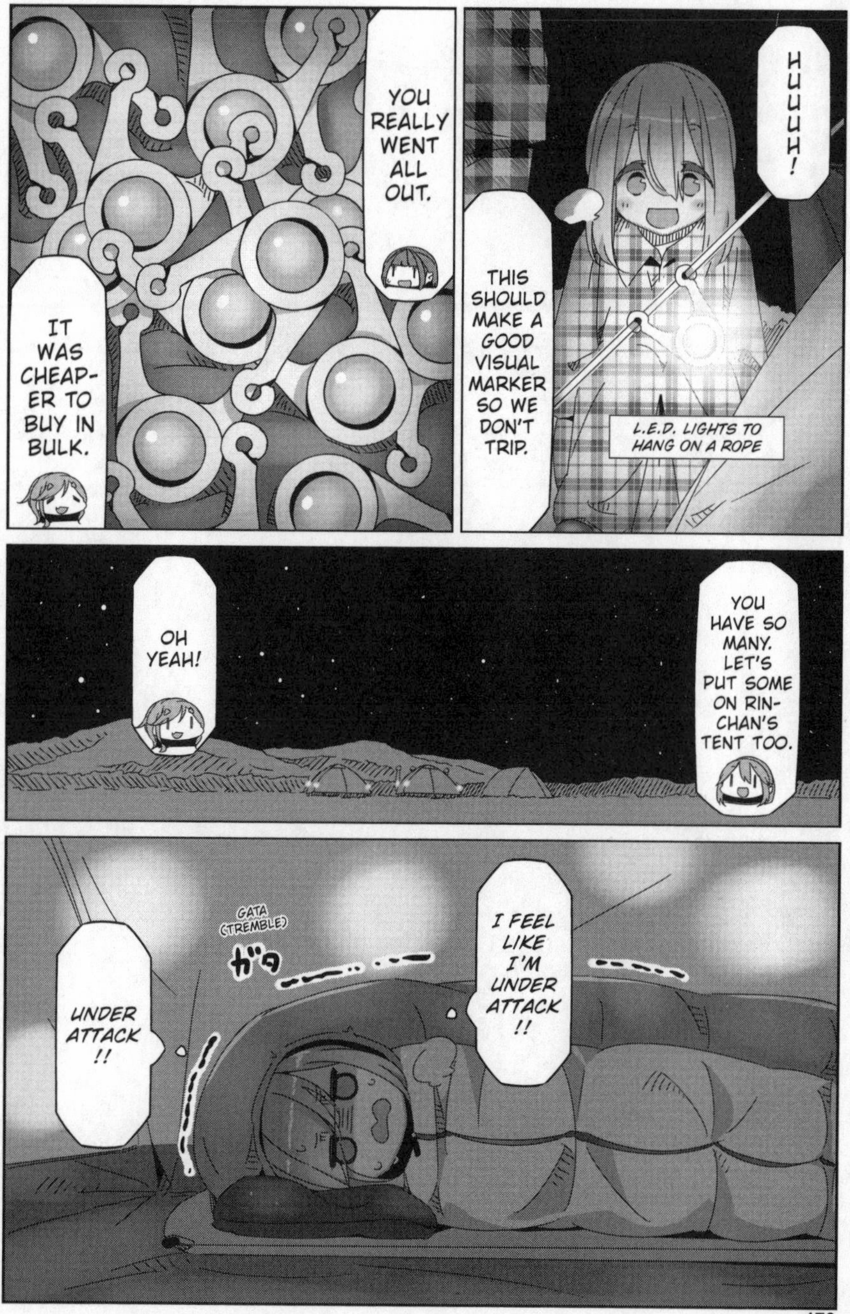
HUUUH!
THIS SHOULD MAKE A GOOD VISUAL MARKER SO WE DON'T TRIP.
L.E.D. LIGHTS TO HANG ON A ROPE
YOU REALLY WENT ALL OUT.
IT WAS CHEAPER-ER TO BUY IN BULK.
YOU HAVE SO MANY. LET'S PUT SOME ON RIN-CHAN'S TENT TOO.
OH YEAH!
I FEEL LIKE I'M UNDER ATTACK!!
GATA (TREMBLE)
UNDER ATTACK!!

AFTER-SCHOOL 97 HOKUTO URBAN LEGENDS

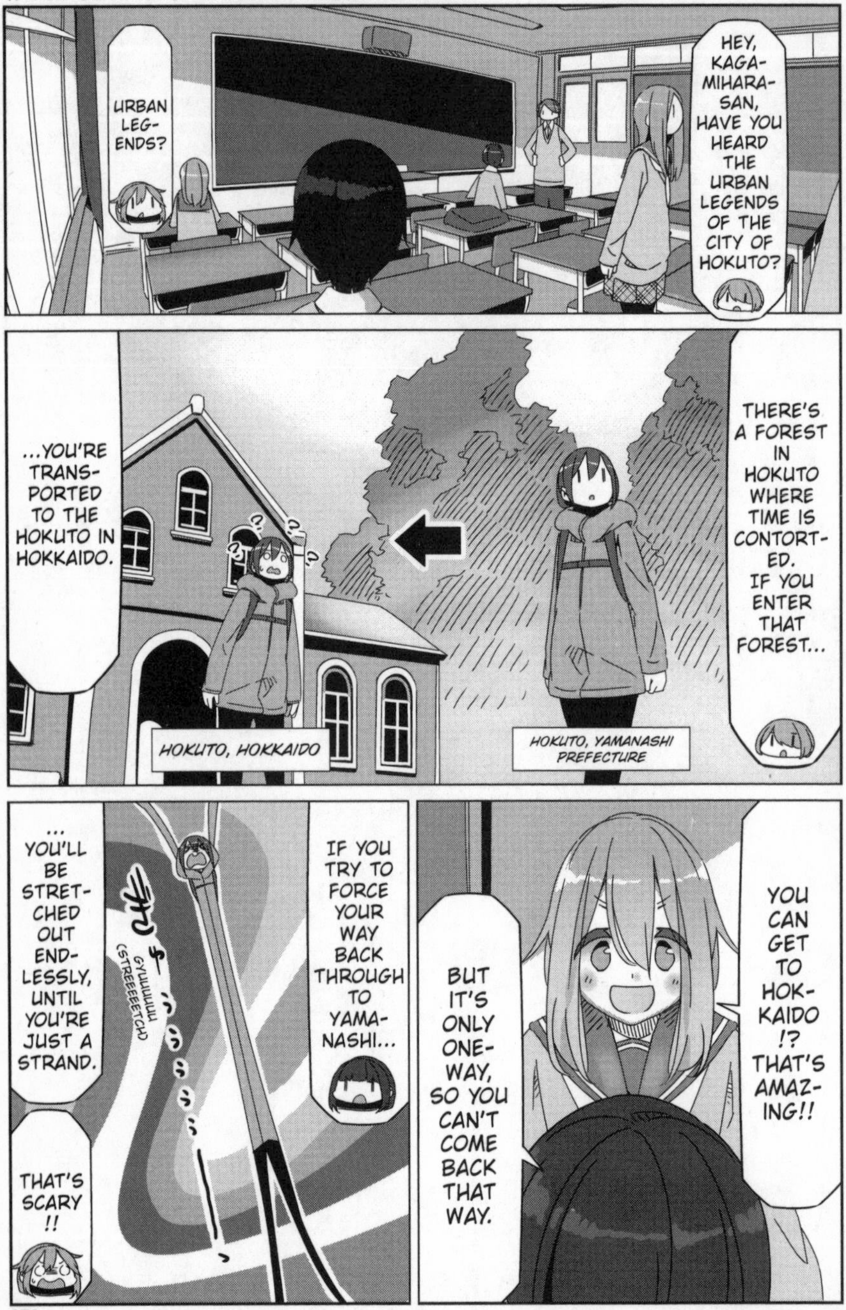
HEY, KAGAMIHARA-SAN, HAVE YOU HEARD THE URBAN LEGENDS OF THE CITY OF HOKUTO?
URBAN LEGENDS?
THERE'S A FOREST IN HOKUTO WHERE TIME IS CONTORTED. IF YOU ENTER THAT FOREST...
...YOU'RE TRANSPORTED TO THE HOKUTO IN HOKKAIDO.
HOKUTO, YAMANASHI PREFECTURE
HOKUTO, HOKKAIDO
YOU CAN GET TO HOKKAIDO!? THAT'S AMAZING!!
BUT IT'S ONLY ONE-WAY, SO YOU CAN'T COME BACK THAT WAY.
IF YOU TRY TO FORCE YOUR WAY BACK THROUGH TO YAMANASHI...
...YOU'LL BE STRETCHED OUT ENDLESSLY, UNTIL YOU'RE JUST A STRAND.
GYUUUUUU (STREEEEEETCH)
THAT'S SCARY!!

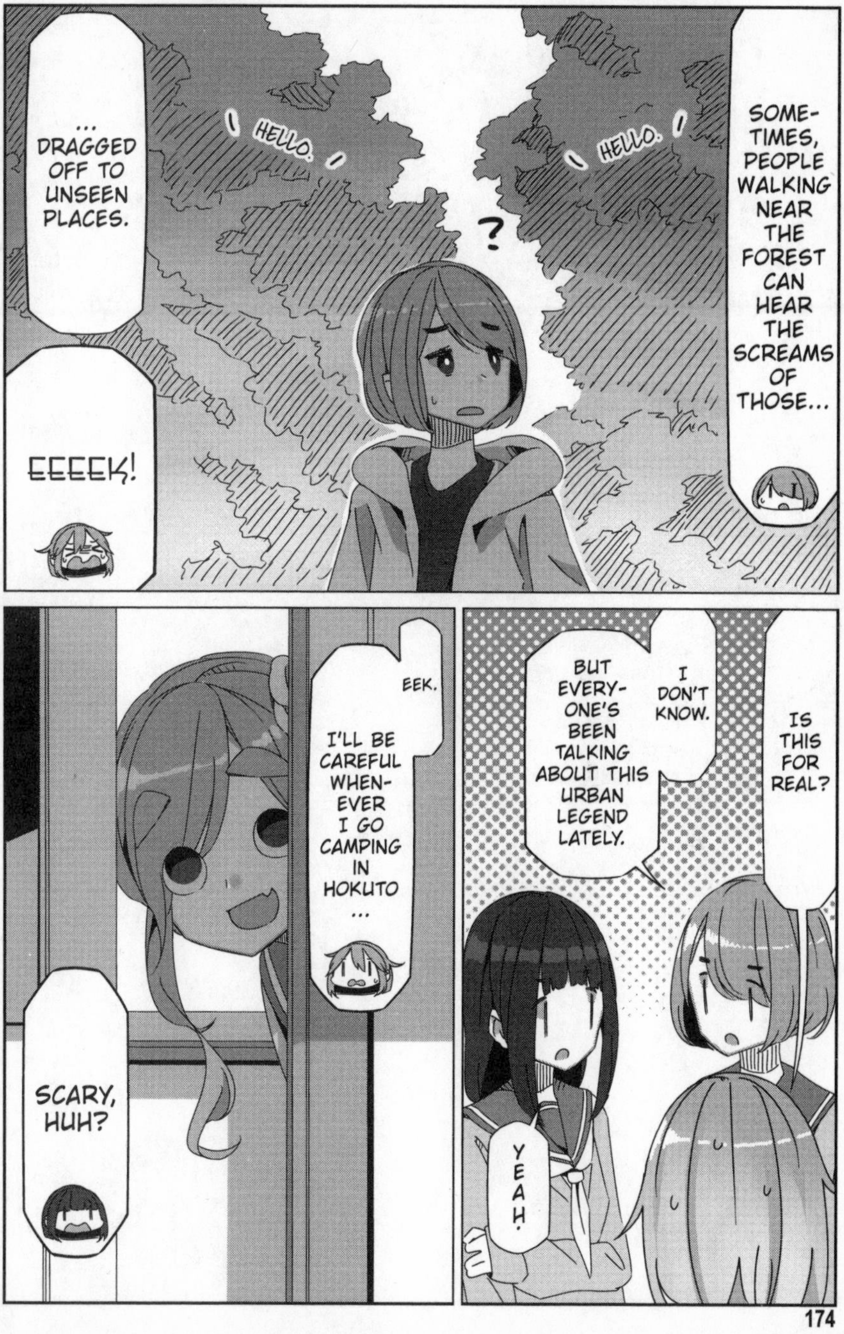
SOME-TIMES, PEOPLE WALKING NEAR THE FOREST CAN HEAR THE SCREAMS OF THOSE...
HELLO.
HELLO.
?
...DRAGGED OFF TO UNSEEN PLACES.
EEEEK!
IS THIS FOR REAL?
I DON'T KNOW.
BUT EVERY-ONE'S BEEN TALKING ABOUT THIS URBAN LEGEND LATELY.
YEAH.
EEK.
I'LL BE CAREFUL WHEN-EVER I GO CAMPING IN HOKUTO...
SCARY, HUH?

AFTER-SCHOOL 98 CAMP SNACK STAPLES

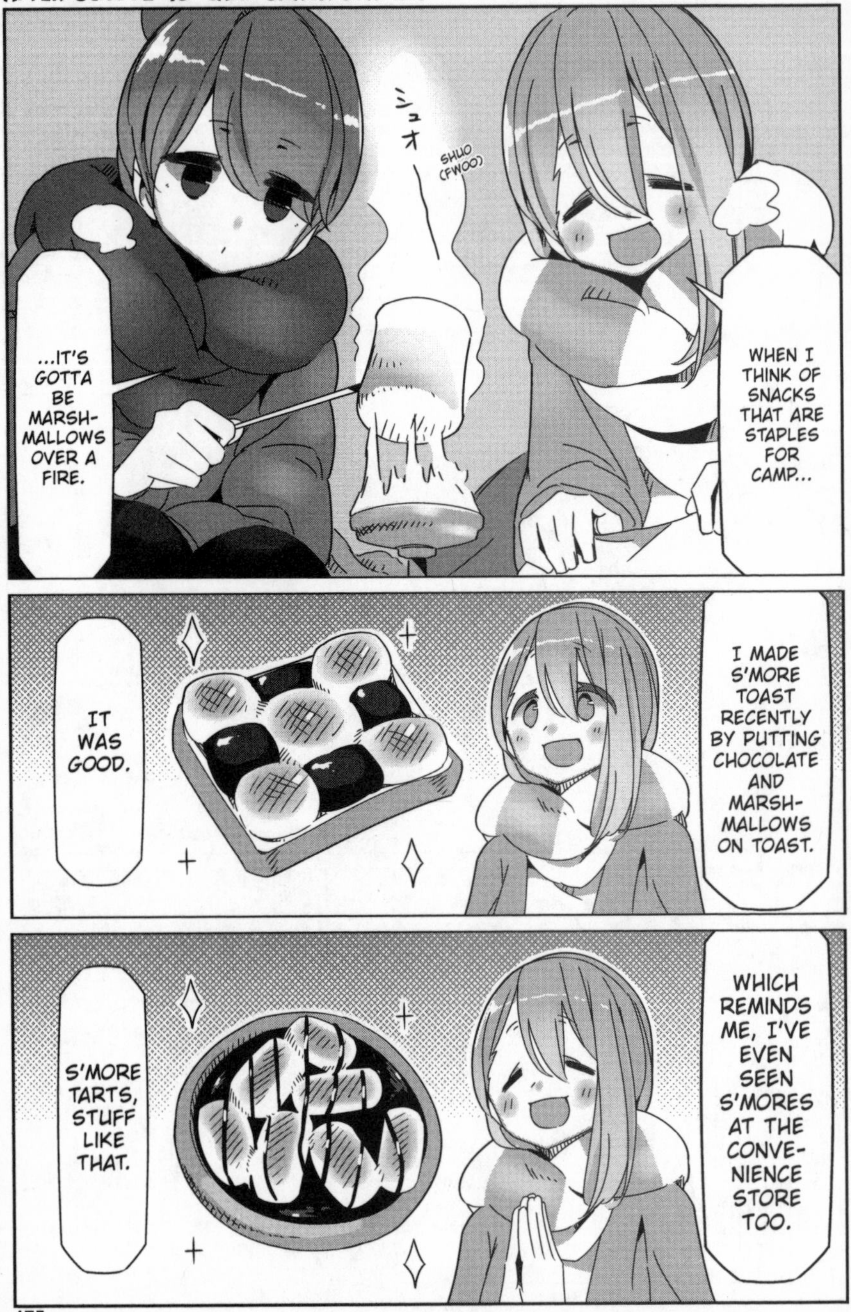

WHEN I THINK OF SNACKS THAT ARE STAPLES FOR CAMP...
シュオ
SHUO (FWOO)
...IT'S GOTTA BE MARSHMALLOWS OVER A FIRE.
I MADE S'MORE TOAST RECENTLY BY PUTTING CHOCOLATE AND MARSHMALLOWS ON TOAST.
IT WAS GOOD.
WHICH REMINDS ME, I'VE EVEN SEEN S'MORES AT THE CONVENIENCE STORE TOO.
S'MORE TARTS, STUFF LIKE THAT.

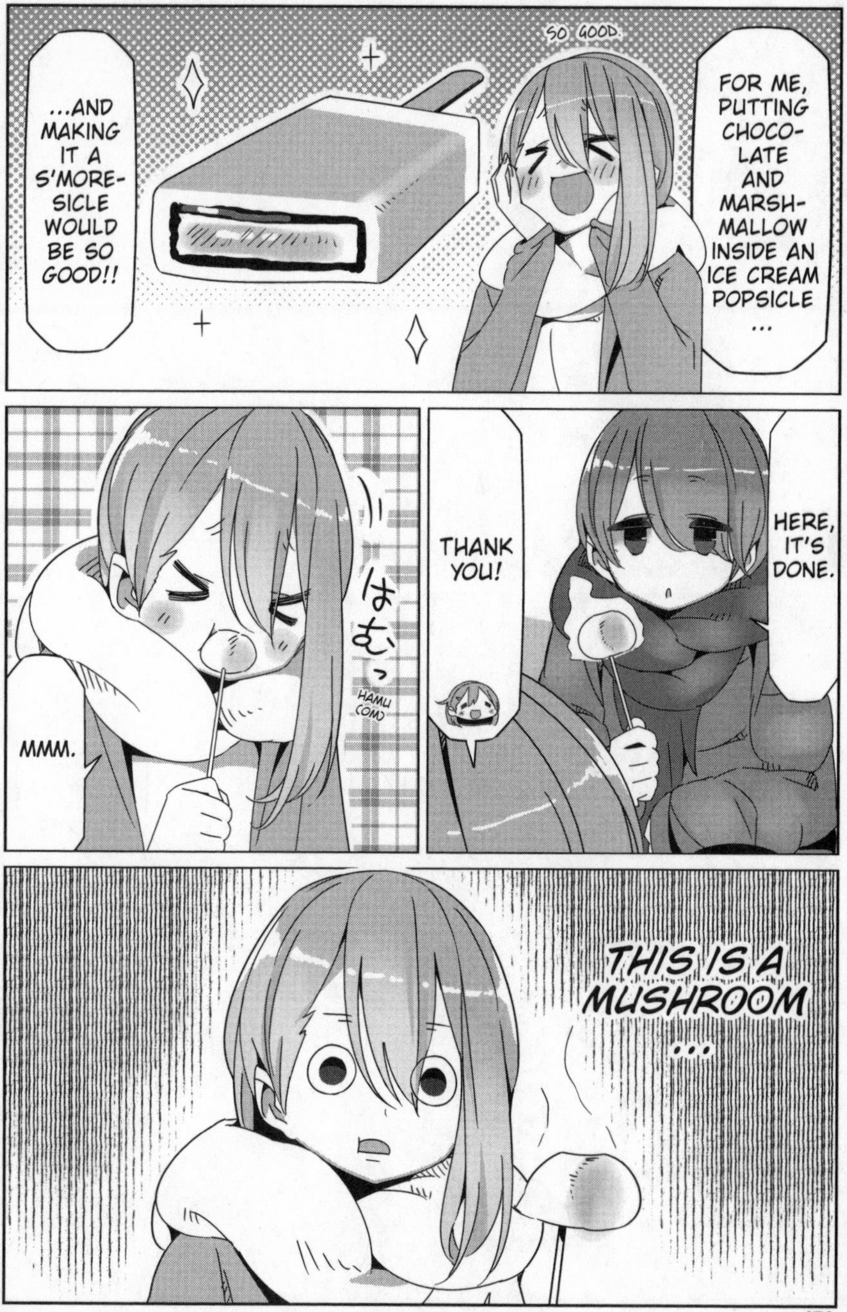
SO GOOD.
FOR ME, PUTTING CHOCO-LATE AND MARSH-MALLOW INSIDE AN ICE CREAM POPSICLE...
...AND MAKING IT A S'MORE-SICLE WOULD BE SO GOOD!!
HERE, IT'S DONE.
THANK YOU!
はむっ
HAMU (OM)
MMM.
THIS IS A MUSHROOM...

HOW DID YOU LIKE VOLUME 11 OF *LAID-BACK CAMP*?
THIS VOLUME CONTAINS THE CONCLUSION OF THE OOI RIVER ARC.

WHEN I WAS COMING UP WITH A STORY, I WAS CAUGHT BETWEEN ICHISHIRO AND HATANAGI. I HAD DECIDED FOR NADESHIKO TO BE FOCUSED ON THE AREA AROUND ICHISHIRO, BUT THE CAMPSITES IN HATANAGI ARE NICE TOO, SO PLEASE VISIT THEM. BEYOND THE HATANAGI GREAT SUSPENSION BRIDGE THAT RIN AND AYANO VISITED IS A NICE GRASS CAMPSITE FOR MOUNTAIN CLIMBERS (THE HATANAGI DEATH ROAD IS A BONUS STAGE).

THIS HAS BEEN AFRO.

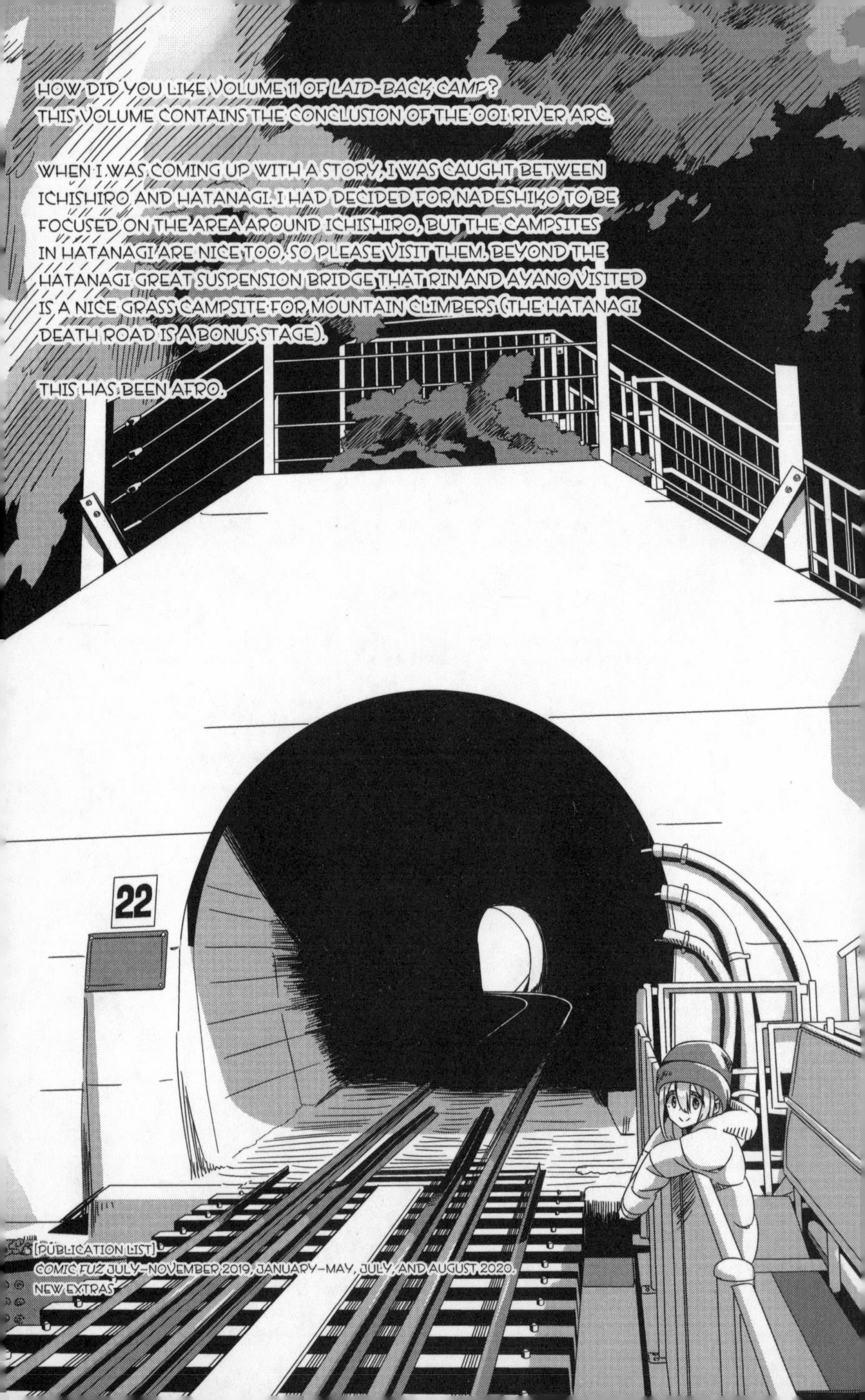
22

[PUBLICATION LIST]
COMIC FUZ JULY–NOVEMBER 2019, JANUARY–MAY, JULY, AND AUGUST 2020.
NEW EXTRAS

LAID BACK CAMP 11

Afro

Translation: **Amber Tamosaitis** ✳ Lettering: **DK**

YURUCAMP Vol. 11
© 2021 afro. All rights reserved. First published in Japan in 2021 by HOUBUNSHA CO., LTD., Tokyo. English translation rights in United States, Canada, and United Kingdom arranged with HOUBUNSHA CO., LTD. through Tuttle-Mori Agency, Inc., Tokyo.

English translation © 2022 by Yen Press, LLC

Yen Press
150 West 30th Street, 19th Floor
New York, NY 10001

Visit us at yenpress.com
facebook.com/yenpress
twitter.com/yenpress
yenpress.tumblr.com
instagram.com/yenpress

First Yen Press Edition: April 2022

Yen Press is an imprint of Yen Press, LLC.
The Yen Press name and logo are trademarks of Yen Press, LLC.

The publisher is not responsible for websites (or their content) that are not owned by the publisher.

Library of Congress Control Number: 2017959206

ISBNs: 978-1-9753-3583-0 (paperback)
        978-1-9753-3584-7 (ebook)

10 9 8 7 6 5 4 3 2 1

WOR

Printed in the United States of America

D1296743